THE QUEEN
AND
THE TOWER

Book 1 of the Nightcraft Quartet

Shannon Page

Published by Outland Entertainment LLC
3119 Gillham Road
Kansas City, MO 64109

Founder/Creative Director: Jeremy D. Mohler
Editor-in-Chief: Alana Joli Abbott
Senior Editor: Gwendolyn Nix

ISBN: 978-1-947659-45-2
Worldwide Rights
Created in the United States of America

Cover Illustration: Matthew Warlick
Cover Design: Jeremy D. Mohler
Interior Layout: Mikael Brodu

Visit **outlandentertainment.com** to see more, or follow us on our Facebook Page **facebook.com/outlandentertainment/**

For Mom,
who taught me how to read:
the greatest gift ever

— CHAPTER ONE —

I put my foot on the shovel, tightened my grip, and dug. Another lump of damp, loamy earth joined the growing pile. Moonlight danced through the trees; a gentle wind rustled the hydrangea bushes at the corner of the yard. Elnor prowled nearby, padding noiselessly on the garden path, hunting moths. Far down the hill, I could hear the squeal of the F-Market streetcar as it made its turn at the Castro, the sound of a party on someone's deck, and the slow wail of an ambulance.

A sudden dart of light as the back door of the coven house opened, then closed. I blinked, letting my eyes adjust.

Niad. Of course. I kept digging. I was starting to get to clay.

Light footsteps pattered down the stairs as she approached. "Oh, Callie, it's you," she said, as though she hadn't seen me come out here an hour ago. "Doing a little midnight gardening?"

"No." I dropped another shovel-load onto the pile and turned back to the hole. Elnor had now come up to its edge and peered down, sniffing. "Research."

I could almost hear Niad's eyebrow raise. "Oh? I must confess, then, to an even more imperfect understanding of molecular biogenetics than I had previously realized."

Stifling a sigh, I leaned on the shovel and looked up at her. She had let her ice-blond hair out of its usual bun; loose waves cascaded down her back, turning to catch the moonlight. My own hair was tightly bound. I didn't want it interfering.

"I'm building something."

"In a hole?"

"No, with the dirt." I looked at the pile. I needed at least twice as much soil as that. It was going to be a long night. "I'm making a piece of equipment."

"With a pile of dirt?"

"Yes."

"Oh well then, carry on," she said, clearly already growing bored. "It's just, some of the sisters were wondering."

"You can let them know everything's fine," I said. "Go to bed, Niad."

"No need—I slept last night." But she turned and went back to the house.

Actually, I was glad it had been Niad; another sister might have offered to help. For the major work we did as a coven, all thirteen of us participated—which was kind of the point of a coven, after all. But, large as this project was, I needed to pour only my own magic into it, or the result would be blurred. The creature would not know who its mistress was.

Nearly an hour later, muscles aching from the exertion, I stood over the mound of dirt, assessing my resources as I thought about the monumental effort that still lay ahead of me. Dinner had been quite a while ago; should I have something more to eat? No, I still felt strong.

I bent down, first just feeling, then shaping the dirt with my bare hands, adding a little water from the hose periodically. Elnor kept her distance as I formed the head first, then the neck and torso, packing the earth tight, reaching underneath to help differentiate the body from the earth beneath it. Then I built legs, complete with stumpy feet, adding a suggestion of toes with my fingernail. And then arms, paying particular attention to the fingers, the opposable thumbs. It would need to be able to use its hands.

Stepping back, I inspected my work. *It needs more of a face than that,* I thought, and crouched over once more to give it some features. Artistic talent was not my strong suit. It didn't matter if the creature was ugly, but you should be able to tell which side was the front.

With that in mind, I fashioned hair out of a handful of desiccated daffodil foliage, tucking the ends into the top of the head and combing it out straight with my fingers. I went back and gave more attention to the articulation of the knees and elbows, then the ankles and wrists, then the fingers. I made sure the neck was thin enough to move, yet strong enough to hold up the large head.

Finally, I stood before my creature again, holding a short stick, considering. After a minute I tossed the stick aside and instead added some mud padding, forming hips and breasts. Witches generally choose to bear daughters, not sons, after all.

A hint of the rising sun tinged the eastern horizon, showing wisps of fog chasing down the hills and hugging the bay. Niad had come out to check on me twice more during the night, pretending to be concerned for my energy, my well-being, my I-don't-even-know-what. "I'll show everyone when it's *done*," I finally told her, my voice tighter than I'd really intended. "And yes, Leonora knows what I'm doing."

I had timed my work to coincide with the dawn, for its positive liminal energy—my creature would be one of light, not darkness. All was now ready. Putting any lingering annoyance at my coven sister out of my mind, along with everything else, I sat cross-legged by the creature's head. Elnor settled on my lap. I let myself ease into the subtle shift of focus that opened one's attention and receptivity to the world around us—far beyond anything we see with our eyes. Elnor channeled and returned that energy, amplifying and honing it. We sat with the energy for a long while. I held the intention in my mind, and my heart, and my belly.

When the eastern glow told me that the sun was near, I reached for the chalice beside me. In it, I had gathered the elements I'd need for this working: lavender, to encourage benevolent energy; chamomile, fig, and rue, for protection; gardenia and rosemary, for courage. I'd mixed these botanicals in a strong elixir of Commanding Oil—from a batch I had made with my own hands, eschewing the coven's supply.

I placed droplets of the mixture on the creature's forehead, then leaned over and dribbled more over her chest, where a heart would be. Then I plucked two black hairs from Elnor's back, laying them at the base of the throat. They vanished into the dark mud.

At last, as the sun broke the horizon, I focused on the figure. I guided all the power within me, and invited all the forces that surrounded me, to bring life to this lump of lowly mud. I had studied and prepared, and I knew I was powerful...but was I actually going to be able to create *life*?

Focus, Callie, I told myself. *This is no time for doubt.* I wove ætheric energy and my own essence, and Elnor's feline power, braiding it all together into something greater than its elements. I felt the power around me build, responding to my entreaty, to the natural energy that flows through all the world, to the desire to grow and transform and *live* that even the most inanimate object holds. I sent my own power back into the building force, redoubling, folding, swirling it into an ever-growing sphere of intensity. The storm of energy shifted color, from a purple-blue that only my witch sight could see, lightening through red and orange and yellow, now visible to anyone, sun-bright and hot against my face.

I had to move quickly now—this was liable to attract attention. The house was warded against human notice, but I needed no more interruptions from my sisters. I began a low chant. Words in a language no one speaks any longer. Not to one another, anyway.

Merenoc gee'a folco Essūlå

I brushed my hands through the creature's desiccated hair, imagining it silky and full of life; then I touched her shoulders, arms, elbows, wrists, imagining them supple, mobile.

Eveen fancont o tenc ollan

I brushed my fingertips against her eyes, sending sight into them; her ears, opening them to the sounds of the world; her throat, bringing her voice.

Lian abree mellendoc uchi

I sprinkled crushed sage over her upper body, then touched every pulse point I could reach from where I sat. The scent mixed with the oils in the misty morning air.

Essūlå, Essūlå, Essūlå!

I chanted the last line again, then put my hands on the creature's forehead, willing life into her. My hands were hot from the gathered power; did I feel an answering heat in my creature?

Essūlå, Essūlå, Essūlå!

I closed my eyes once more, focusing, pouring all I had into the incantation, into this one task. This and this alone. The rest of the world fell away. I breathed mud breath, my blood flowed through dirt veins, my toes were pebbles and my lips were crushed maple leaves in autumn.

Essūlå, Essūlå, Essūlå!

I rocked slowly, leaning into my work. The creature was warm under my hands, and she was warmer, and she…moved!

Keeping my hands in place, I observed the shimmer of triumph that passed through me, and let it go. I was not done; this part was the most precarious of all. I continued the chant, all four lines once more, sending life into all her parts and pieces, exploring every channel, opening all her senses to this world. Binding her to me.

She moved again, shifting under my touch, turning her head slightly, testing her limbs. Still I continued, my eyes remaining closed, endowing her with all I had, all I could give. I felt her eyes flutter open, her new-grown eyelashes sending the tiniest breeze to my hands. I felt the rest of her move, nowhere near my actual touch—our bodies were energetically intertwined, every movement of hers echoed in my own skin and bones.

At last, I knew she was made. I drew my hands away, drew my own energy back into myself. Letting her go was like pulling a splinter from deep in my heart, but also suffused with joy. I was breathing hard, almost gasping for breath—with exhaustion and exultation.

"Calendula Isadora! What is *that*?"

I opened my eyes. Leonora, our coven mother, had paused at the bottom of the porch steps. Her voluminous robes stopped a moment after she did, then swished back around her ample body. Grieka, her familiar, peeked her head out from under one of the layers of skirts. Behind her were three coven sisters: Sirianna, Maela, and (naturally) Niad. I hadn't even heard the door open, I'd been so focused.

"Research," I said, turning to look at my creation. She looked back at me—mud-brown eyes expressionless. But alive! "I told you I needed something safe to use in my experiments."

"You did *not* tell me you were making a golem!" Leonora said, her voice stern as she and her entourage stepped down into the garden.

I got to my feet. "This is—"

"This is a *golem*," Leonora repeated.

"Yes it is! Golem," I said to the creature.

"Yes, Mistress," she said.

Elnor stood by the thing, sniffing at her side, tail up and bushy. The four witches simply stared at it. The sun had now fully risen; sounds of humans at their breakfasts and starting their commutes began to filter up the hill. I grinned and glanced at my coven mother and sisters, ready to enjoy their surprise, admiration, and envy as I explored the creature's capabilities.

"Stand up, please," I said to it.

My golem bent both legs, then both arms, putting her palms flat on the ground beneath her. I could almost see her working out the mechanics of it all. Then she rolled to one side, pushed herself up to one hip, and shambled to her feet.

"Oh, my goodness," Sirianna said, taking a hesitant step forward and staring.

Droplets of mud fell from the golem's back and hair. She was truly hideous—ungainly, crude-featured, way too large. She was *fantastic*. "Yes, Mistress."

"You may call me Callie," I said.

"Yes, Mistress Callie."

I broke into a huge smile. *I did it, I did it!*

"You...this..." Leonora stopped.

I had never seen my coven mother at a loss for words. Not in the twenty-five years I'd been a member of this coven, or the twelve years I'd been educated here before that.

"How...how did you do it, Callie?" Sirianna's long russet hair twisted and cavorted in the morning sunlight, moving like it had a mind of its own. Which, in a manner of speaking, it did.

"She's been out here digging in the mud all night," Niad put in before I could respond. "And we all felt the flood of energy. She probably burned more power doing this than the whole house uses in a week."

"I didn't take any coven energy," I said, feeling defensive. "I used only my own."

Maela frowned. "It's been six hundred years since any witch made a golem. That I know of, at least."

"This is...highly unusual," Leonora finally managed, gazing at the golem, who stared back at her quite impassively. "You know this is not our magic."

"Magic is magic," I said with a frustrated shrug. "Is this a problem?"

Leonora shook her head and looked at me. "I don't know!"

The admission shocked all of us. Sirianna and Maela both turned and gaped at Leonora; Niad shifted uncomfortably. "Um..." I said.

"It is...quite impressive, I'll grant you that," Leonora said. "And so completely out of bounds. When the other covens learn of this..."

"They'll be horrified!" Niad said, seeming half-hopeful, half-frightened.

Sirianna muttered, "I don't know. I think they'll be impressed." She pushed a strand of hair out of her eyes; it immediately pushed forward again.

"Impressed...yes," Maela said, in the soft, vague voice she used when she was receiving a vision. "It is a fork in the road, I see, and not a small one..."

Leonora gave Maela a cautious glance, before turning to me with something more of her usual stern poise. "What are your plans for it?"

"I told you. I want to try some things that aren't safe to use on natural, living creatures, but I need to see how they work in a functioning system."

"That's what humans are for," Niad muttered, just to get a rise out of me. I ignored her.

"So I thought I'd build one of these," I said to Leonora, then turned back to the golem, feeling myself fill with pride once more. "And I did. It worked."

"Your intention is to use it in these particular experiments, then unmake it and return to your Petri dishes?"

"What? Um…" I took a step back, putting a hand up as if Leonora had proposed to tear the creature apart herself. "I…I don't know. I need to see what she can do."

Niad snorted. "'She'? Watch, now Callie will name it."

"And why not?" I asked, then turned back to the golem. Mud and rock, stone and clay…petro… "Golem, I name you Petrana."

"Yes, Mistress Callie."

"Golems are dangerous creatures, Calendula," Leonora said. "This is not a doll for your amusement. Are you not familiar with the lore?"

"Yes, of course," I said. "But that's only if their maker overreaches—tries to do something evil with them. I didn't make Petrana to conquer anyone or grab power. I just want her to be good—I want to help us all."

Niad shook her head. "And who appointed you savior of *us all*?"

"Niadine, that is enough." Leonora turned back to me. "All that refers to human makers. When a witch makes a golem…"

A cold fear began to fill my belly. Was she going to force me to unmake Petrana? To kill her, just when I had brought her to life? "A witch has *more* control over a golem, not less," I said, trying to keep my voice steady. "I read that Goody Blendenbrough's golem saved human children from drowning, even when the townspeople tried to drive the creature away, and Blendenbrough with it."

"That's a story," Niad scoffed.

Leonora watched me another long moment, then gave a brisk nod. "All right," she said. "We will leave it for now. You will keep the creature on the grounds at all times, preferably in the house. Do not let any human see it, ever. You are to use it strictly in your biological research, and unmake it the moment its purpose is served, or when I command you to do so. Is this clear?"

"Yes, Mother," I said. I put a hand on Petrana's now-cool flesh. It still felt like mud, but my hand came away clean.

"You are to see that the creature conducts itself in such a way as to not disturb the work of the rest of the house," Leonora went on. "It should be kept out of the way when not in use."

"Okay, but…maybe she can help out? When I'm not using her?"

"Help out doing what?"

"I don't know." I struggled to think. I really was tired from the night's labors. And hungry. "She's big and strong—she can lift things, do heavy chores?"

"You made a *golem* to help with the *housework*?" Niad snorted.

"Niadine Laurette!" Leonora snapped, then turned back to me. "We shall see. I...will consult with other covens about this." She paused, shaking her head. "Calendula, I just don't know what to do with you."

"Um," I said.

"And I believe it is time for breakfast." Leonora turned on her heel and headed back to the house, my three sisters following.

"Come on, Petrana," I said, and led my golem inside.

My room was small enough already; adding an eight-foot-tall mud-creature did not help. I cleared a space in the corner by the closet and stashed Petrana there before breakfast. I wasn't ready to endure the rest of the house openly freaking out about her just yet. Though Niad was only ninety-three (barely out of her first blush of youth, by witch standards), the older sisters generally rallied behind her more conservative opinions. At forty-five, I was the youngest full coven member, and something of a rebel, or at least a nonconformist. Sirianna usually took my side in any dispute, as did the students; Maela often did as well.

In other words, I pretty much always lost.

It wasn't supposed to be this way. The coven system had been created to take advantage of the centuries of experience accrued by older witches: they would, in theory anyway, pass their wisdom along to younger generations in a loving, family-like setting. Our coven particularly, as a teaching coven, was designed to guide and instruct its students and junior full members into witchkind life. Except...witchkind life was only part of the story—a smaller part all the time, in my opinion. The world outside our little confines was changing rapidly. To a four-hundred-year-old witch, the modern human-dominated world probably looked like a passing fad, easily ignored. A youngster like me saw things differently.

Or maybe it was because I was a scientist. As I saw it, witchkind in general, and my coven particularly, was in danger of irrelevancy at the very least if we did not adapt. Yes, magic was important, and we were powerful; but history had already shown that humans' sheer numbers could help them win the day.

Not that I thought we should be trying to *defeat* humans—not at all! I liked humans, some of them very much. I wasn't Niad, after all. I just felt that witchkind's separatist, us-versus-them stance wasn't doing either species any good. We could learn from them, and we could teach them things.

Well, we could, *if* we had been permitted to reveal our nature to them. But that was strictly prohibited by the Convocation of Elders. Many of whom remembered firsthand that nasty little business in Salem.

Maybe Niad was right to ally with the older crowd. She certainly enjoyed the benefits of our elders' favor: she was Leonora's second-in-command, with the biggest bedroom, the lightest teaching load, and a generous discretionary allowance. But I knew there was more to life than household perks.

Anyway, it wasn't in my nature to be teacher's pet.

After a tense breakfast and a lengthy nap, I sent a message through the æther to my best friend Logan: *Hey, I need to get out of the house. You free?*

Sure, she sent back a few minutes later. *Come by the stand, I'm just finishing up with a client.*

I quickly French-braided my hair, tied it off, and slipped out of the house and onto one of the major ley lines leading down to the bay. I emerged behind an unoccupied building on North Point. After glancing around to make sure I hadn't been seen, I walked the few blocks to the Embarcadero and the entrance to Pier 39, enjoying the fresh smell of salt water.

Logan spotted me and smiled, waving me over to her fabric-draped table. I took the red velvet-cushioned guest chair across from her.

She scooped up her tarot cards and set them aside. Her blond hair, bangs and all, was pulled back and tucked into the snood she wore while working; the effect only highlighted her bright, piercing blue eyes. She leaned forward and gazed at me, taking the measure of my aura and energy. "You made the golem last night."

I nodded. "Does it show?"

Now she grinned again. "Not exactly. I can see a huge energy drain, but mostly, you told me you were going to."

"Ah."

"So, did it work?"

"Yes!" I told her all about it, pulling a small zone of inattention around us as a human approached looking for a tarot reading. Confused, the human shook his head, stared a moment, and wandered off toward the other tourist attractions of the pier.

Logan shook her head admiringly when I finished. "I can't wait to see her."

"She's not much to look at," I admitted. But I was still bursting with pride. At least here was someone who appreciated what I'd done.

"Callie, you are too modest." She leaned forward once more with an earnest gaze. "The fact that you created her at all!"

"Tell that to my sisters," I muttered.

My best friend gave me a sympathetic smile. "Yeah."

"Sometimes I think I should just live alone. *You* don't have to put up with this crap."

"So why don't you?"

I shook my head. "Because I'm in a coven, silly."

"Is there a rule that you have to live there?"

"Sure there is—" I started, but then thought about it. "Actually, I don't know if there's a *rule* per se, but...well, everyone does."

"Except for witches who aren't in covens," she indicated herself, "and ones who take a leave of absence to form a union," she waved in the general direction of my parents' Pacific Heights home, "and retired witches who haven't moved Beyond. Oh, and every single warlock, of course. But other than that, you're totally right: everyone lives in covens."

I snickered. "Fine, point taken. But..."

"But what? You even own a house."

"It's rented out."

She just gazed at me.

"Um..." I continued. "I guess my renters did just give notice, didn't they?"

"Yes, I believe you mentioned that." She picked up her cards and began shuffling them idly, trying to hide a small smile. Under the table, I could feel her familiar, a big orange tom named Willson, rubbing against my ankle. I reached down to scratch him behind the ears.

Could I move out? *Should* I move out? Oh, Leonora would absolutely freak.

"I'll even help you move," Logan went on.

"Let me think about it," I said. "I've never actually lived alone, you know? I went straight from my parents' house to the coven."

"I know. And I don't mean to push." She held her tarot deck, letting the cards fall from one hand to the other. "But you've felt stifled there for a while—and it's only been getting worse. I know you need more lab space." Now she gave me a wicked grin. "And then there's Raymond."

"Indeed." I grinned back at her as I thought more. My house was still here in the city; I could get back to the coven house in a heartbeat if I needed to. And more privacy...yeah, that would be *really* good. Then I sighed. "I don't want to just run away from my problems, though. I should really try and work things out there. They're my chosen family, after all."

Logan rolled her eyes. "Niad never chose you, and you didn't choose her." Before I could protest, she went on. "But yes: take your time, there's no deadline here. I just want you to be happy."

I smiled at my best friend. With such a warm heart and a generous spirit, she would have been welcome in any number of covens. The fact that she had chosen to go her own way when she came of age at twenty had felt tragic and baffling to me at the time, but as the years went on, I had to admit that her life suited her. She was shy and intro-verted, craving her alone time. Her apartment was small, cheerful, peaceful. She had Willson, and work she enjoyed, and a best friend.

Would I enjoy alone time myself? Or would I just get lonely?

I thought about Niad's haughty sniping about Petrana, about Sirianna's aghast face, the students' discomfort, Leonora's stern disapproval. There was real fear underneath all those reactions.

Wasn't I already quite alone, even in a crowded coven house?

— CHAPTER TWO —

nd so it came to pass that, not three weeks later, I found myself packing my belongings.

More specifically, my lovely assistant, the creature of mud and stones, was. Or at least that was the theory.

"You can put more than one thing in each box," I said to Petrana, stifling a weary sigh. "Fill them all the way to the top, please."

"Yes, Mistress Callie," she said in her toneless voice. She bent over, taking a sweater out of one box and carefully placing it in the one next to it. Then she straightened up, shuffled over to a third box, bent laboriously down and reached inside for its sweater, and began to repeat the process.

Blessed Mother, this would take all day. How hard would it be to just send it all through the æther? "They don't need to be organized, Petrana; just put everything in the dresser into as few boxes as possible. I'll set what I want from the closet on the bed for you to pack after that." I turned away—it was easier not to watch—and started sorting through my jeans and T-shirts. I pushed aside most of the gowns, dresses, and long robes. There wouldn't be much call for witchkind formalwear at my new house.

Maela had come by for a concerned chat, and Niad had already popped in to bother me three times, each excuse more transparent than the last. Now I heard footsteps outside my door again. *What is it now?* was on the tip of my tongue as I peered through the solid wood, preparing some choice words for her. But this time it was young Gracie, shadowed by two other students, Mina and Kat.

I opened the door. "Come in," I said, smiling at the girls and patting a bit of vacant space on my bed.

After glancing uncomfortably at my golem, the younger witchlets sat down—there wasn't enough room for everyone to stand up anyway. Gracie gave me an uncertain smile and hovered near the edge of the dresser, paying unusual attention to my perfume bottles as Petrana continued to pack.

"What's up?" I asked.

Gracie shrugged. "Oh nothing, we just…you know, wanted to see how it was going?"

"Fine. I think I'm close." I glanced around the room. "I'm not taking everything; I'll be back here too often to need a lot of it over there."

"You will?" Gracie's heart-shaped face filled with relief.

I reached over and ruffled her dark hair, which curled around my hand before falling into some semblance of order. "Of course I will. You'll hardly know I'm gone."

"So why do you have to move out?" Her voice was plaintive, though I could see she was working to keep it from climbing to a whine.

I gave her a gentle smile. "I don't *have* to, Gracie, I want to. There's not nearly enough room for my work here, and my golem and I are getting in everyone's way." Which was a mild way of putting it.

"Can we visit you there?" Mina piped up from the bed.

"Of course you can! Whenever you like—as long as Leonora says it's okay."

Gracie shifted from foot to foot. "Isn't it dangerous to live alone?"

Mina gave me an uncertain glance. "We heard solitary witches don't live as long."

"Sometimes they don't, but that's probably because they drain their essences by working all their magic alone. I won't be doing that." *Just some of it.* I peered at Mina. "Who's filling your head with such stories?"

She shrugged. "We learned in Human Studies that lone witches get hunted down by humans, and burned."

"Or drowned," said Kat.

Human Studies! I might have known. Had Niad sent these girls to me just now, or had she been working on them for weeks? "Mina, nothing like that has happened in over three hundred years. Niad shouldn't be scaring you like that."

Gracie chimed in. "She says that Leonora remembers such times, and so do Honor and Ruth. She says that humans are unpredictable and can shift on a moment's notice, and that we always, always have to be on our guard against them." She frowned at me. "You aren't going to live in a house with humans, are you?"

"Blessed Mother, no. I'll be living alone, just me and Elnor, and Petrana. And probably only for a few years." Never mind who I might or might not let visit me there—not their business. I shook my head.

"It's perfectly safe, as are humans. You know that as well as I do. Don't you all have human friends at home?"

"Well." Gracie leaned over to pet Elnor, not meeting my eye. "Sure."

"Do they seem like monsters to you?"

"No," she muttered.

"That's because they aren't." I reached for the last few sweaters in my bottom drawer and handed them to Petrana, who seemed finally to have gotten the complicated logistics worked out, though this was still taking forever.

Mina and Kat got the hint, and hopped down from my bed.

"Do you need any help?" Kat asked.

"Sure, girls, thank you." There were a few boxes of books stacked by the door; I pointed to them. "Those could go downstairs, if you can lift them."

The younger girls each hefted a box. I noticed Kat using a little power to help her bear the weight, and suppressed an urge to caution her. Being overprotective was no way to teach a witch how to manage her resources.

Gracie hung back as the other girls left.

"Okay, what is it really?" I asked, as soon as they were out of earshot.

"I just wish..." She gave me a helpless look. "You're our favorite teacher."

"I'll still be your teacher." I smiled at her. "You don't think you're getting out of biology classes, do you? And I'll be back for all the regular rituals, and lots of dinners. You're not losing anything."

"But we are." She fiddled with the perfume bottles again. "You're just...just better than..." She didn't finish the sentence. "You understand us. You're more *like* us. You know?"

"It's important for you to be able to relate to all witches, Gracie—not just the ones closest to your age. Maybe that will become easier if I'm not here for you to run to all the time."

"It won't." Her voice was suddenly fierce. "*Nothing* will be easier. I don't fit in here; I don't understand anything, why I have to be stuck here all week. Weekends off aren't enough; I miss my parents, I never even *see* my human friends any more, and now *you're* leaving."

"You are here to learn who you are, and how to wield your power," I told her. "Nobody fits in anywhere when they're fifteen, I promise you. Me particularly." *And I still don't*, I thought, not that that would be helpful to point out at the moment. "In five years, you can do anything you like."

"Five *years*!?" Now she was whining. "That's *forever*!" Her dark eyes filled with tears.

"Okay, Gracie, that's enough," I said. "You're more mature than this."

"I am *not*! I thought *you'd* understand!" She turned and fled the room.

Elnor bumped her head against my leg as the door slammed. I scratched her ears and let her soft purr comfort me a moment as I resisted the urge to chase after Gracie. Finally, with a sigh, I returned my attention to Petrana, who had finished the dresser but seemed thoroughly confused by the few dresses I'd draped across the bed.

Golems may be biddable, but they are not at all smart.

Forty-five years old, and I had never lived alone a day in my life. I wasn't frightened, not at all; it just felt…weird. Different.

I went ahead with Elnor first, a little early, traveling up the ley line and emerging on the front porch. I stood there a moment, glancing up and down the quiet street, before using the key to let us in.

The house felt somehow emptier than ever, even when it had been between tenants before. Empty and…expectant? What do houses know? Was it aware that I was its owner? Did it know I was a witch— did it truly "know" anything at all? There is magic in every molecule of matter and every iota of space, and this was a very old house. Well, by San Francisco standards, anyway.

A knock on the door interrupted my musings. I went to let Logan in. The movers, with a truck full of my clothes, books, chemicals, cauldrons, flasks, and herbs, plus a large sealed wardrobe box containing Petrana, would be along in an hour or so. Being human, they would have to negotiate actual mundane physical space, with traffic and everything.

"Oh my goodness, this *is* gorgeous," Logan said, as she stepped in and looked around the grand entryway. "I hope you were charging your renters a fortune."

"Enough," I said, smiling. My father had bought me the house as an investment when I'd joined the coven twenty-five years ago. I'd cashed the rent checks, invested the proceeds, and given the whole business very little thought over the years.

Elnor gave Logan a look, obviously wondering where Willson was. "You go explore," I told her. "This is our home now." My familiar began sniffing corners in the front parlor. She had been here before, but now the house required far deeper scrutiny. Who knew what threats it might hold?

Logan tugged on the pocket doors separating the front and second parlors, finally pulling them closed. "These could use a little oil," she said.

"I'll probably leave them open most of the time. I like the space of the two rooms together." I grinned, sending my senses around the house. Three stories, so many rooms, all *mine*! Mine alone. It did feel good.

I showed Logan around the first floor, our footsteps echoing in the empty rooms. Despite its decades of human tenants, it remained lovely: a very classic San Francisco Victorian, not completely brutalized by "modernization".

"This dining room is amazing," she said, running a hand across the built-in sideboard. "I love the leaded glass on this piece. And that chandelier!"

"I'm kind of amazed it's still here," I said.

She smiled. "This room has 'elegant dinner party' written all over it."

"Ha!" I snorted. "Did you hit your head on something? Remember this is me you're talking about."

In the kitchen, Logan laughed when I peered at the stove as though I'd never seen one before. "I'll show you how to use it," she said.

I grumbled something about "can't teach an old witch new tricks."

Back in the front hall, we were about to head up to the second floor when I noticed a small door underneath the staircase. Opening it, I peered into the dim depths of a musty closet. Elnor brushed past me at once, disappearing inside. I almost followed, but she'd want to claim the space first, especially if its energetic boundaries were soft.

"Willson can't stay out of closets either," Logan said with a smile.

"Cats," I agreed.

This grand old house had seen a lot of lives in its hundred and twenty years. It had been remodeled over and over, carved into flats, then later recombined into one house again. It remained full of stray, random walls, mismatched windows, and what seemed like far too many doors. I wasn't sure I'd ever even entered all these rooms.

"Oh, wait, I almost forgot: housewarming present!" Logan reached into her purse and pulled out a small lace-trimmed bag, tied with a red ribbon.

"What is it?" I sniffed it. "Mmm, lavender."

"And mugwort." She smiled. "To protect the house."

"Thank you!" Her gift reminded me: I'd prepared a batch of modified Mistress of the House potion myself. I pulled my own bag—a Ziploc—out of my jeans pocket, then sprinkled a little of both powders in the corners of the entry hall. "We should do the downstairs rooms before we go up."

"Want help?"

I thought a moment. "No, I ought to do it myself."

"Right." Logan waited in the front hall as I went through the first floor once more, sprinkling every corner. "All right, ready," I said.

We climbed the stairs and walked through the second floor. I did the corners here as we went.

"These windows let in so much good light," Logan said.

"Yeah, as long as those trees don't get any taller." I made a mental note to update the spell suppressing their growth. "This will be my bedroom," I told her, pushing open the door to a smallish but very charming room near the back of the house, with a window seat and a good closet, and a tiny half-bath leading directly off it.

"Nice."

"And then that front room will be a sort of study. The other bedrooms can be guest rooms, I think."

"Does Petrana get a bedroom?"

"I don't know," I said with a frown. "I thought I'd just keep her in the lab. But you're right—it would be good to have a place to stash her, even though she doesn't sleep, or even lie down." My golem had been just standing in my coven house bedroom when I wasn't using her in experiments. It would be nice to sleep without her looming presence. "She can have this one, next to mine, I guess."

"Where are you going to work?" Logan asked. "Is there a third floor?"

"There sure is! It's the best part."

We climbed a narrower staircase, emerging into a finished attic, almost as high-ceilinged as the lower floors.

"Wow!" Logan said, looking around. "This is huge."

"Voila—the lab." Most of the space was one large room, with only a few smaller cubbies and closets along the back wall. "Bench along there"—I pointed to the wall opposite the staircase—"and equipment over there. Storage in those cabinets."

"I'm envious. I so want this room."

I smiled at her. "You don't do science."

"I don't care—I just want to work in this space! It's great."

"Come hang out with me whenever you like, bring your work."

She nodded, still walking through the space. "I just might. Thanks." She opened one of the closets and looked in, then closed it and leaned against the door. "So, how's the coven taking all this?"

"Ha!" I looked in a second closet, then leaned against the wall next to her. "Pretty much how you'd expect. Niad never misses a chance to be bitchy; most of the older sisters are quieter about it. Leonora doesn't like it, but ultimately she okayed it. I know she wanted the golem out of the house."

"She's letting you keep it, though?" Logan asked.

"For now. She's still talking to the other covens about it. She says she's worried about the effect of foreign magic on our workings."

Logan wrinkled her nose. "There are endless flavors of magic. Coven magic isn't the only viable kind."

"I know!" I agreed. "She's just hidebound, she hates change."

"Most older witches do."

I nodded. "But mostly I think she's just humoring me. I'm sure she thinks I'll come to my senses, unmake the golem, and move back into the coven house before six months go by."

Logan shrugged. "Maybe you will."

"Maybe." I gazed around the room. "Hard to imagine, though," I added with a grin. What had seemed so unthinkable a few weeks ago now filled me with excitement.

"There is much to be said for living alone."

"The students are having some trouble with it," I admitted. "Particularly Gracie."

"Hmm, yes, I imagine she would." Logan gave me a gentle smile. "She's at a tough age."

"Yeah. I wish I could make things easier for her, but...only time can do that." I pushed off the wall and walked over to the front windows, looking down at the street. "The movers should be getting here soon."

We walked back down the creaking staircase. I looked around the second floor for my familiar. "Elnor! Here, kitty kitty." My voice echoed; I saw no cat.

"She's probably still in the closet downstairs," Logan said.

But she wasn't there either. I walked down the long hall toward the back of the house, peering into every room, finally finding her in the kitchen, glaring out the back window. "There you are."

She glanced over at me, then returned her attention to the backyard. Her energy was unsettled, spiky.

What was she seeing? I shifted my gaze, opening my sight to the full range of energetic information there. At first I saw only a confusing jumble of minor forces—purples and oranges and a dull red laced with blue, all wrapped around each other—human energies, plus those of their pets. This was why we kept our witch-sight shuttered most of the time. Then I noticed a small rosette of golden light right where Elnor was staring.

"It's just a squirrel, silly," I said. "Seriously, haven't you heard about the cat who cried wolf?"

Elnor ignored me, still staring at the terrifying threat from outside.

"I'll hate to see what you do when you meet your first neighbor cat," I muttered, as the doorbell rang. Logan opened the door to the movers; I headed down the hall to tell them where to put everything.

All the boxes that had crowded my tiny room in the coven house would have fit in one corner of the front parlor here. Distributed among the three floors, you could hardly tell I'd moved in. There was a *lot* of furniture shopping in my future. Fortunately, Logan had already volunteered to help with that. We'd made a date for next week before she left.

After I unpacked Petrana, she stood in the front parlor, staring blankly ahead. I should have been used to her by now, but even I had to admit she was rather uncanny. Alive-but-not. "Go clean the kitchen," I told her. "You should find supplies in the pantry. Don't forget the cabinets. Or the floors."

She dutifully shuffled off. I peered through the walls a moment, watching her find what she needed. The broom looked like a toy in her massive hands.

I collected Elnor and climbed back to the third floor to carve my pentacle: the focus and center of all the magic I would work here. In the big open room, she jumped down out of my arms and began once again inspecting every corner, sniffing closely at the baseboards, sneezing when she got some Mistress of the House in her nose. I sat down in the absolute center of the floor, cross-legged, and waited for her to finish. When I could tell she had found nothing dangerous or threatening and had turned her attention to the mice in the walls, I called her to come sit on my lap. She did, then nudged me, looking for an ear-scritching. I obliged. There is nothing to be gained from rushing a cat.

We sat a few minutes, letting our energy settle, getting used to the new space. I'd spent so little time here; it had been an investment, not a home. Not *my* home. Slowly, I began to focus my power, bringing my awareness from the edges of the property, to the house, to this room—narrowing and honing as usual. After a minute, Elnor turned her yellow eyes up to me, giving her assent to our work, joining her magic to mine. I concentrated further and slowed my breathing. My familiar followed my focus closely, letting me channel power through her. She amplified and modulated my magic as I formed the space at the edge of my fingertips into something like a scalpel, strong enough to cut wood. We gathered potent energy until I was ready to draw. Then I leaned forward, tracing the image in my mind across the floor with one finger. The pentacle slowly formed beneath it, carved a quarter-inch deep.

A fancy witch—or a wealthy coven—might have spent the resources to add a dark wood inlay into the grooves, but this didn't need to be pretty. It just needed to work.

Twenty minutes later, it was done. I was out of breath, and suddenly very hungry. Elnor got to her feet stiffly, sneezed again, and stretched luxuriantly before making her way back to the baseboards. I lay back on the hard floor, letting my energy recover. Rest first, then food.

The pentacle must have been carved correctly; I felt better within a few minutes, if still starving. I sat up and dug through my jeans pocket for my cell phone, and dialed Raymond.

"Hey you," he answered.

"Hey sweetie," I said. "Whatcha doing?"

"Waiting for my girl to invite me over to her new place."

I chuckled. "There's no place to sit and nothing to eat. But I'll give you a tour if you take me out to dinner first."

"How 'bout I bring Chinese? I know how to sit on a floor."

"God, that sounds good. Bring lots." I thought about the empty kitchen, that vast unfamiliar stove. Had I even plugged in the fridge? "Especially the General's chicken—two orders, if you're going to hog it all like you did last time."

"Will do! Text me the address?"

"Yep."

I hung up, sent the text, then shoved the phone back into my pocket, reminding myself I'd need to find the power cord and charge it up soon. Complicated, fussy little devices. Witchkind don't use them, of course; we can communicate easily through the æther.

The trouble is, that only works witchkind-to-witchkind. Witchkind-to-human requires their clunky technology.

And Raymond, the man I had been quietly dating for nearly a year now…was human.

— CHAPTER THREE —

I shut Petrana in "her" room, closed the stairway door leading to the third floor, and poked through a few boxes on the first floor, finally coming up with cushions, a blanket, and a small lamp with an amber mica shade. A box of books served as a table. Raymond could coax music out of his cell phone (who said humans had no magic?). I looked around, satisfied. Finally! My first intimate *dîner pour deux*, in my very own home.

In fact, the first time Raymond had been able to visit me at all. Oh yes, getting my own place was a very good idea.

I was at the door before he rang the bell. "Come in!"

He stepped in, looking around with a smile. "Great pad!" Then he pulled me into one of his strong arms for a kiss. The other arm was clutching a paper bag emitting a very enticing aroma.

My stomach growled, but the kiss was pretty enticing too. Our embrace might have gone further, if it hadn't been rudely interrupted by an angry feline sound at my feet.

"Oh, Elnor, really," I said to her, pulling away from Raymond. "Don't be like that, you can see he's no danger."

"So, this is your cat!" Raymond bent down. "We meet at last, little kitty." He reached out a tentative hand. Elnor hissed, then sniffed at him, tail and back fur standing straight up. She glanced up at me, puzzlement on her feline face.

Yes, that's right, he's not a warlock, I thought. "It's okay," I said to her. "This is Raymond. He's been invited. Raymond, this is Elnor."

She gave me another quick look, then lowered her tail an inch or so. Raymond kept his hand out—offering, but not reaching. "Here, kitty," he crooned in a gentle voice. Elnor took a step forward, still sniffing. Finally, she allowed him to scratch her ears, while still holding her posture very alert.

Raymond smiled up at me. "Cats usually like me," he said. "She must be kinda shy."

"Yeah," I said, not elaborating.

Her dignity attended to, Elnor withdrew, still watching us both.

"So, show me around?"

"Dinner first, then tour," I said, leading him into the front parlor. "I'm starved."

We sat on the cushions and ate from little white cartons with disposable bamboo chopsticks. And I enjoyed it so much more than I had any number of elegant banquets at the coven house.

Which had at least as much to do with the company as the food, delicious as it was. I smiled as I watched Raymond wolf down moo shoo pork and the General's chicken. His brilliant tattoos looked gorgeous in the lamp light, swirly and red-gold; dragons and lizards and snakes twining around one another down his muscular arms— almost alive. His reddish-blond hair was pulled back in a neat ponytail. I looked forward to liberating it soon.

"So, you finally did it!" he said. "Moved out of that commune and got a place of your own! I love it."

I smiled weakly. Though I hadn't ever been overtly dishonest with him, Raymond did not know much about the rest of my life, for obvious reasons. When we first got together, I'd told him I lived in an intentional community that valued its privacy—which he had somehow translated into "commune," with a side helping of "we're polyamorous." Which served the purpose well enough, though it was kind of amusing, how he so very carefully did not pry into my home life. He probably imagined some sort of co-op filled with wacky characters who practiced weird rituals. Instead, it was just a house full of ancient crones who cast spells under the light of the moon and...

Oh, never mind.

"Yeah," I said, and quickly changed the topic: "How was work?"

"Eh—same ole same ole. That reno we're doing in the Mission got hung up waiting for another permit, so Dad got us started on a bathroom remodel in Upper Haight. You should come see, it's awesome."

"Maybe I will," I said, shoveling more chow mein into my mouth. "I could use some bathroom ideas."

Witchkind was not forbidden to have relations with humans; it happened all the time. We just knew better than to take such liaisons the least bit seriously. Any formal union with a human partner—legal contract, financial agreements, potential children—was, of course, impossible. And Raymond was nearly twenty years younger than me, though he had no clue about that. Humans, with their shorter life spans, mature more quickly than witchkind, so we were effectively the same age anyway. But when I'd met him, I never imagined he would be more than a one-night stand. Or two nights. A week at the most.

He was the bass player in a very good local rock band...and sexy beyond belief. Rough and rugged, yet sweet. I had caught their set at a bar one night, then stuck around and bought him a drink. I'd even told him I was a witch, because who would believe it was actually true? "Oh, cool, so's my sister," he'd said, explaining that she was a Wiccan, and a midwife; that both she and his mother had a touch of "the sight," as he called it. I hadn't bothered to correct his misconceptions. "You'd love Christine, you guys should get together!"

Dude, I'd thought. *You're doing this whole 'pick up a girl in a bar' thing wrong—enough about your sister already!* "Sure," I'd said, then changed the subject to something more likely to steer us into bed.

When I had finally gotten him to take me home, it was so delightful that I went back for seconds a few nights later. And then again the following week. After that...well, he had grown on me. He was kind and sensitive, honest as the day was long, and more interested in me than in himself. In other words, nothing like any warlock I had ever dated. Our conversations were long and always surprising—how many construction workers read modern philosophy books? His interest in music was wide-ranging and passionate; he had quirky but informed opinions about everything. He teased me about being an imperialist, because I owned a pet. (Never mind that the truth was almost exactly the opposite of that—at least in Elnor's mind.) Yet his manner was always mild, humble even; he seemed to have no idea how intelligent he was.

And the bed sports...oh, Blessed Mother, we were good together. Now that I'd moved out of the coven house, I would be able to see him so much more freely.

"Finished?" I asked him, as he put down his carton.

"Taking a breather," he said, grinning at me. "I don't know where you put all that." He reached out and poked me in the belly. "You got a secret compartment?"

"Vile creature!" I chortled, twisting away from him. "That tickles!"

"I'll show you some tickling."

Then we put those cushions to good use.

Early the next morning, I sat at the foot of the futon in my bedroom, watching Raymond sleep. It continued to be a marvel to me, how much sleep humans needed. Seven or eight hours, every single night! How did they get anything done?

He hadn't been like this on the rare occasions when I'd managed to escape the coven house for an overnight stay in his apartment. Sure, he'd always complained good-naturedly that I was keeping him from his sleep. Apparently he'd actually meant it.

After a minute, I got up, dropped my robe on the floor and pulled some clothes on, and slipped out of the room, closing the door quietly behind me. I tugged my hair into a loose knot as Elnor followed me up to the third floor, where I spent a few hours unpacking boxes and starting to get the lab set up.

My research focused on improving witchkind reproduction. Fertility is a real challenge for us. My mother's line was unusually prolific, though it didn't begin to approach human fecundity; at forty-five, I still had no siblings. If we weren't so long-lived, our kind might have died out long ago.

I didn't just want to test things in Petrana; I'd also been hoping she would serve as a proof of concept for my research in the creation of microscopic homunculi. These "tiny helpers" should, in theory, be able to travel through a witch's system, encouraging the release of eggs and guiding a warlock's sperm to them. Unfortunately, our immune system was so powerful, I hadn't managed to keep any homunculi alive for more than a few minutes before they were absorbed and destroyed. If I couldn't get some traction on this soon, I would make an appointment to consult my mentor, Dr. Gregorio Andromedus.

This morning, after unpacking most of the equipment and putting supplies in cabinets, I did get a small experiment started, though I left Petrana shut in her room for now. Once the experiment was underway, I pulled out my Mabel's Glass for a look. The Glass was a small, spelled device that looked like an elongated pair of opera glasses. Like most witchkind lab equipment, it was designed to filter out the influence of our own individual magic, so that there would be at least some chance of obtaining objective results.

Holding the Glass close to my face, I peered into the crucible. Alas, the little creatures sprang to life, twitched around for less than a minute, then expired. Again. What was I missing here?

A noise from downstairs brought my attention back to my surroundings. I glanced up; soft, foggy morning light came through the windows. I covered the crucible with a containment spell, locked the third-floor door behind me, and headed down. Raymond was in the kitchen, clutching the espresso pot he'd brought over, trying to figure out how to get the stove to light.

"Morning," I said, going over to give him a kiss.

"Coffee," he mumbled, then straightened his arms out in front of him and staggered across the floor. "Caawwwww...feeeeeee..."

"You dweeb," I giggled. "You're the least convincing zombie I've ever seen." I looked at the stove. Right, I should probably fix that pilot light. Turning to block my hands from his view, I sent a flick of magic at the burner. "There you go."

"How did you do that?" He set the espresso pot on the stove, positioning the handle away from the flame.

I shrugged. "Just takes the right touch."

"If you were a normal, coffee-drinking human being, you'd understand the importance of not having to deal with complicated machinery before said coffee."

I smiled. "Good thing I'm a normal tea-drinking being, then."

Once he'd gotten himself sufficiently caffeinated, he opened the fridge, then turned back to me with a frown. "Where's your food? Is this thing even plugged in?"

"I moved in *yesterday*, dude," I pointed out. "We can go out."

"Aw, no, I wanted to cook you breakfast. First breakfast, new house. I'll run down to the BiMart and get eggs and stuff."

"No need!" But I was smiling, touched.

Raymond grinned back at me. "Just sit tight, milady. Drink your sad and sorry excuse for a morning beverage. I'll be back in a flash."

He was as good as his word; soon the kitchen was filled with the cheery sounds and enticing aroma of bacon sizzling and omelettes browning nicely at the edges. I could see that Elnor was struggling hard with conflicting imperatives: continue to treat this human man as a bizarre, foreign threat; or angle for a piece of bacon. She finally just gave up and sat at his feet. "Oops," Raymond said, nudging a scrap of bacon out of the pan and onto the floor. Elnor pounced on it, pretty much swallowed it whole, then gazed lovingly up at him.

"Traitor," I said from the table.

"I told you cats usually like me."

"Well, sure, when you bribe them like that."

He brought two plates of beautifully arranged food to the table, setting mine before me with a flourish. We dug in.

"So, what's on for today?" he asked after a minute.

I chewed and swallowed. "Boxes, boxes, boxes. Plus maybe some furniture shopping."

"Need help?"

"Don't you need to work?"

He shrugged. "I could take a day off. Or even half a day, come home in the afternoon. Dad's working on bids right now; Craig can handle the Haight bathroom without me for a few hours."

I thought about it. And then about the fact that, though we had been dating almost a year, this was the longest stretch of time we'd ever spent together. It hadn't even occurred to me that he'd want to stick around even longer. And what did he mean by "come home"? Surely he didn't think...? "No, I'm good," I said. "You go on to work. Maybe I'll need help with heavier stuff on the weekend."

He gazed at me a moment, then turned back to his plate. "Okay." After another bite, he said, "So...this is it till the weekend?" His tone was carefully casual.

"You can come over tonight," I blurted out, because I felt bad. "But..." I stopped, stymied. I wouldn't be able to do half of what I needed to if he was hanging around. With all the tension at the coven house these last few weeks, I'd hardly thought about what life outside would really look like, day to day. "I, um, don't know what my schedule will be, exactly."

He looked back up at me, somehow seeming both hopeful and hurt. "You got an extra key? I'll let myself in."

"No, just the one," I said. "Give me a call when you get off work. I'll probably be here."

Raymond was an intuitive, perceptive man. He heard what I wasn't saying. "Sure." He took a last bite of eggs, then pushed his plate back and got up. "I should get to work, then."

I got up too, pulling him into an embrace. He stood stiffly against me for a moment, then relaxed. "Hey. Thanks for breakfast...and dinner last night...and dessert," I said.

He brushed a gentle kiss against my ear, then cupped my ass and gave it a squeeze. "My pleasure, babe. Any time."

"See you tonight."

"Yep."

— CHAPTER FOUR —

Rose's was the unofficial hangout for younger witchkind—anyone under a hundred or so. From the outside it looked like a crappy dive bar, and not one of the cool hipstery kind, either. Just a place that time forgot.

Inside, well, it didn't look a whole lot spiffier. At least, not in the front room. Scuffed old floors, ripped vinyl seats in dark booths, and a pervasive smell of spilled beer and...worse things. The back room, however, was another story. It was furnished with deep couches, oriental carpets, and adorable little marble-topped tables scattered here and there. Dim red lighting gave it a Paris-in-the-twenties atmosphere; heady incense burned in one corner.

This part of the building was off limits to humans. Even the wait staff was all witchkind.

The place was hopping when Logan and I got there Friday night. We barely managed to squeeze onto the corner of a couch and order two Smoldering Dragonflies.

As we toasted, I raised my voice and said, "Happy birthday!"

Logan blushed and shook her head, but she was smiling, her blue eyes bright. Her hair was loose; it moved softly around her face, reflecting the atmosphere of relaxed magic around us. My own braid twitched gently against my back. I'd probably liberate it before the night was through, but for now, it was nice to not have to think about it.

"Hey, happy birthday!" said a witch from the next table. "How many years?"

"Forty-three," Logan said proudly.

"Just a baby!" The witch and her companions laughed good-naturedly and toasted her.

"How's the love nest?" Logan asked, as we turned back to each other.

I rolled my eyes. "Oh, just fantastic."

"What's wrong?"

I sighed. "Raymond's been there almost every night, for over a week now. It's... You know."

She peered at me. "No, I don't know. What?"

"Moving is a lot of work. I'm really busy, and tired, and stuff. I'm sure it'll all settle out in time." Logan gave me a patient expression; after a minute, I went on. "It's like he thinks he gets to *live* with me or something."

"But wasn't spending more time with him part of the appeal of moving out?"

"Well, yeah." I shrugged. "Except now I feel crowded."

"So just tell him you need more space, more time to settle in."

"He keeps offering to *help*." I sipped my drink, struggling with how to put it, exactly. "I never really realized how *much* there is that we can't share. It was so much easier to keep my life partitioned when we just had little scraps of time together. Now it's all awkward. It feels like I'm lying to him."

Logan frowned, and picked up her own drink. "Well, you are, aren't you?"

I sighed again. "I'm not lying. I'm just not telling him everything."

She gave me a look.

"After the very first night, he asked for a house key," I said. "It's weird not to give him one, but—well, I can't."

"I see." Her expression turned sympathetic. "No, you can't really have him rummaging through your herbs and cauldrons and spell books, can you?"

"I could probably explain most of it away," I said. "His sister is Wiccan; he wouldn't have to know that what I do is real."

"Has he seen your golem?"

"Blessed Mother, no."

Logan snickered.

"But that's just it," I went on. "She's no use to me shut away, but he can't, *cannot* see her. He's already wondering why I keep certain rooms locked—not to mention the key-to-the-house thing. So far, I've put him off with excuses about the mess, and wanting to get stuff organized, and all that; but that's no good long term. I don't know what to do."

"Seems like you've got two choices," Logan said, leaning forward. "Let him in further, or push him away entirely."

"What does 'let him in further' mean, if I can't tell him I'm a witch?"

"That is the crux of the problem, isn't it?"

I took a deep drink, enjoying the sweet burn. "Why did I ever think it was a good idea to date a human?!"

"Because warlocks are self-absorbed assholes?" She glanced around the room, where witches outnumbered warlocks nearly five to one—just as they did in our general population. For some reason, warlocks thought this made them special. "Because you never expected to actually fall in love with a human?"

"I don't know. I don't want to think about it any more. I can't wait to go furniture shopping on Wednesday. What time should we start?"

"Way to deflect," she said with a grin. "I am entirely fooled, and have forgotten completely what we were talking about."

I laughed. "If it weren't your birthday…"

"I know," she said. "We'll get together after breakfast, start at Grand Central Antiques and go from there."

A soft amber glow around the doorframe indicated that someone had requested entrance; we glanced over to see who it was. A flicker of patterned red lights indicated a party of four.

The door opened and in walked Niad, wearing something impossibly tight and black and chic, her ice-blond head held high, a confident smile on her flawless face. On her arm was the most gorgeous warlock I'd ever seen. He was hugely powerful, too; the energy practically radiated off him. "Oh, my goodness," Logan said with a low gasp. "Who in the world is that?"

"I have no blessed idea," I breathed.

"Wow." With Niad and the stranger were two youngish warlocks from the East Bay set. Logan continued to stare, then shook her head and turned back to me with a saucy grin. "Blessed Mother, the universe finally decides to give me the birthday present I so clearly deserve!"

"Huh?"

"She never keeps a lover for more than a week. When she dumps him, he's mine, all mine!"

"Even though warlocks are self-absorbed assholes?"

Logan gave a happy sigh. "I don't have to *listen* to him; it'll be more than enough just to *look* at him."

I laughed, watching the little group make its rounds, all three warlocks preening like good barnyard roosters. Niad seemed at least as proud as them, having pretty much doubled the male population of the room. After a few minutes of greetings and introductions at other tables, her eyes lit on me and Logan in our corner. She sashayed over, tugging her escort.

"Calendula! Such a delight to see you. You've been quite the stranger at home, I thought I'd have to wait till Tuesday for the pleasure." She leaned down for an air-kiss.

I complied, barely rising from my seat. "Niadine Laurette, elder sister of my coven. It gives me unutterable joy to see you, for the second day in a row." Beside me, I could feel Logan quivering with suppressed laughter.

Niad turned to the warlock on her arm, lavishing the full radiance of her smile upon him. Up close, he was even more gorgeous. His teeth were very white in contrast with his lovely Mediterranean-tawny skin. His hair was long and dark, loose and shining as it hung down his back, barely moving in the magical air. His eyes were bright green, very light. And his cheekbones...oh. Oh my. "I have the very great honor," Niad said, "of introducing Jeremiah Andromedus. Jeremiah, this is Calendula Isadora, baby sister of my coven."

I gaped at them both. "Andromedus?" *But that would mean...*

Jeremiah took my hand, raised it briefly to his lips, then lowered it with a smile. I felt the thrum of his power through his skin. It made me want to both drop the hand, and never let it go. "Yes. Gregorio Andromedus is my father."

"I had no idea he had a son," I blurted out. Warlocks were famously reserved about their personal lives. Yet Gregorio was not just my mentor; he was also my father's oldest friend, going back hundreds of years. I'd known him all my life. No one ever thought to mention a *son*?

The warlock glanced at Logan. I remembered my manners, as Niad was surely not going to introduce her. "This is Logandina Fleur," I said. "Also known as the birthday girl."

"Charmed!" He took her hand and kissed it; I could see her eyes widen as she sensed his strong magic.

"Call me Logan," she said, blushing very prettily.

"And you must all call me Jeremy," he said.

Niad gave his arm another tug. "Well, we just wanted to say hello—"

"Ah, this is ideal!" Jeremy said, claiming a suddenly vacated table beside ours. Niad frowned, but sat down, careful to show quite a bit of slender thigh as she crossed her legs. Jeremy introduced the other two warlocks: Marcus and Paolo. I stifled my amusement at this perfect stranger introducing us to guys we'd known all our lives. They pushed the two tables together and called out for snifters of Bulgarian frog brandy.

Logan shot me a quick, panicked look. She might talk a big game with me, but she was truly very shy.

I leaned forward, prepared to take the conversational lead. But Jeremy jumped in, saying, "My father has spoken of you several times since I arrived, Calendula Isadora. I am delighted to get the chance to meet you."

"Please, call me Callie," I said. "How kind of your father. Where are you visiting from?"

Niad raised her eyebrows, clearly delighted to be in possession of more information than me. "The Old Country," she said.

Their drinks arrived. Jeremy picked up his glass of brandy and swirled it, watching as the green lines dissipated into the amber liquid and sent up a little curl of smoke. He sniffed, took a sip, and then finally turned back to Logan and me with a lazy, self-assured smile. "I am not visiting, though. I live here now."

While that could be good news for Logan and her designs on the guy—if she was at all serious about that—I understood so much from that smile. He was a gorgeous, powerful warlock from a prominent, ancient family, and he darn well knew it. He clearly assumed he had the pick of any witch in the room—and in the city beyond. How kind of him, deigning to bestow some of his precious attention on little old us.

"Oh wow!" I said, putting on my best raised-by-humans air. "Don't you just love it here? I sure do! But I've never been to the Old Country! Do they have indoor plumbing there?" I grinned at him and took a sip of my Smoldering Dragonfly.

Niad gaped at me, clearly convinced I'd lost my mind; then she exchanged an eye-roll with Paolo and Marcus. To my surprise, though, Jeremy laughed—an easy, comfortable laugh. "Yes, it is... interesting here. And rather baffling as well."

I dropped the act, now intrigued. "Baffling?"

"So many humans—and you live right among them!" His smirk was gone; he seemed genuinely perplexed. "I don't know how you all do it. I suppose you get used to it?"

Marcus leaned over to whisper something to Paolo and Niad. She snickered and whispered back.

I shrugged. "I don't know, I've always lived here. It seems normal to me." I honed my vision, trying to get a sense of how old he was. His energetic signature was so bright, indicating enormous power; but when I "looked" more closely, I could see that he was probably not even one hundred. Yet I knew Gregorio had lived here longer than that... "What brings you here? And why now?"

"Not your *indoor plumbing*," he said with a teasing smile. "The Old Country is not the backwater it used to be."

Okay, don't answer, Mr. International Man of Mystery, I thought. I felt Logan by my side following the conversation raptly. Hopefully, soon she would be emboldened to say something. "I would love to visit there," I said. "Are there really no humans at all?"

"Oh, there are a few here and there. But one can go days at a time without running into any."

"Wow." Niad and the other two warlocks' whisper-fest continued. Ignoring them, I asked Jeremy, "When did you move there?"

"I didn't—I was born there. My father was doing a research rotation at the university and met my mother. But she died, when I was quite young."

Logan leaned forward, a look of gentle distress on her face. "Oh, I am so sorry! That must have been so hard for you."

Jeremy shrugged. "I was barely three," he said, a bit too casually. "I really don't remember her; in fact, I do not know him well either. When his rotation ended, my father returned here. I was raised by dear friends of his—a diplomatic family."

"He didn't bring you with him?" Logan asked.

"I believe he felt my upbringing there would be more advantageous." He smiled, now looking almost shy. "No disrespect intended toward this lovely city, but he was likely right. My foster parents provided not just a phenomenal education, but every other advantage I could have asked for."

"You didn't...miss your father?" Logan sounded as if her heart was about to break. I knew why, but it was not my story to tell.

"Oh, he visited, from time to time." Jeremy shrugged again with a casual smile that was very nearly convincing. "There is cost as well as privilege in having such an accomplished father."

Well, *that* resonated with me. I shifted uncomfortably, beginning to suspect I had misread that earlier smirk. This warlock was actually seeming like a nice guy.

"But my foster parents were very kind," he went on. "They let me have the run of our small town and the surrounding countryside; I spent far more time exploring caverns and trying to tame mountain goats than I did missing my birth parents."

"Even so." Logan shook her head. "What a difficult thing."

Jeremy gave her a kind smile, and she blushed again, clearly thinking she'd overstepped. In the awkward pause which followed, Marcus leaned in, gave me a smoldering look, and asked, "How's your sex research going, Callie?"

I hadn't run into Marcus in a while. Brown-haired, trendy little goatee, nicely dressed, a bit shy of sixty. Not bad looking, I supposed, but what a loser.

"It's going great, Marcus. Currently, I'm working on developing alternative eicosanoids and cytokines to address the regular inflammatory response resulting from prostaglandins produced during oogenesis." While he chewed on that, I turned back to Jeremy and Logan.

"Gracious," Jeremy said. "I knew you and my father did similar work, but I confess I understand very little about it. That sounds astonishingly complex."

"Oh, I can explain it far more simply than that," I said with a quiet smile. "And the truth is, it's not going all that well. I'm about to see if I can arrange a consultation with your father."

"I am sure he would be delighted to assist."

Niad leaned in more closely to Jeremy, flashing rather a lot of cleavage for such a skinny witch. "So, we should be heading to Spandau soon. Our reservations…"

"Logan's work is fascinating too," I cut in. "She's making a study of human belief systems and their potential for magical interface."

"I am not!" she protested. "I just read their tarot cards."

I shrugged. "You see? And modest, too."

Marcus and Niad both grimaced at her mention of the cards, and Paolo stifled a snort, but Jeremy gave a happy laugh. "Tarot cards! Now there's something I'd like to hear more about. Another drink for the birthday girl!" he called out.

Logan blushed even deeper. "Oh, gosh, no."

"You don't want another drink?" he asked.

"*I* do," Paolo said, turning around to look for the waitress, as Marcus said to Niad, "I love Spandau. I'll go with you."

Niad glared daggers at Jeremy, who did not seem to notice. He listened intently to Logan as she struggled to explain to him why he did not care about her life's work. I sat back, enjoying the show.

After a minute, Niad rose on Marcus's arm. "I will catch you later, darling," she said to Jeremy.

He sprang to his feet. "You truly don't mind if I stay? I would be delighted to try that restaurant another time, but…"

She flashed him a perfect smile. "Of course not. Do enjoy yourself."

Jeremy kissed her hand, released it, and sat back down with us as she left with Marcus. "She has been very kind to me, showing me around and introducing me to everyone, but I confess, the pace is rather wearing me out." He frowned. "I hope I have not offended her."

"I expect she will recover," I said dryly.

He watched me carefully, then gave a small smile. "Good." Then he turned back to Logan. "But it's fascinating—it sounds like working with humans is actually *increasing* your potency. In the Old Country, tools such as tarot would never even be considered. To our loss, I suspect. Interlacing your divinations with human energy—I do want to hear more about that. I'm very interested in interwoven power and nontraditional juxtapositions."

Wow. Gregorio Andromedus's son. I shifted in my chair, looking around the crowded room. Where were those drinks, anyway? The cocktail waitress was having a hard time keeping up, even with magic to assist her in carrying all the extra glasses. "Glenna seems awfully busy," I said. "I'll just go to the bar."

When I got back almost ten minutes later, Logan and Jeremy were still deep in conversation. Paolo had turned his chair around and was flirting with an adjacent table of witches. I set his Bulgarian frog brandy down beside him; he gave me an absent nod.

"Balszt, more or less," Jeremy said as I sat back down at our table, referring to the Old Country's capital. "Actually, a small village about an hour outside the city; you would not have heard of it."

"My parents came from a small village near Balszt," Logan said, her voice filled with wonder.

"Really?"

"What was your town's name?"

"Dolènja."

Logan frowned. "No, that's not my parents' village. It started with a Z."

"Zchellenin?"

"Right! That's it."

"It's not far from Dolènja; I wonder if we have mutual friends." Jeremy glanced at me. "Callie! It seems we have an Old Country connection!"

I nodded, wondering if Logan had told him yet.

She gave me a small, helpless look, then said to Jeremy, "I...doubt we have any friends in common, actually. My parents went back there many years ago, and...vanished."

"Oh, I am so sorry. What happened?"

Logan bit her lip. "I don't know." She took a sip of her drink, seeming to not even taste it. "They came here when I was born—to get away from the troubles. For a long time I had no idea about any of that. We are very sheltered here, you know."

Jeremy nodded, frowning.

Logan went on, "Then, when I was in coven school, my parents got an urgent plea for help from a very good friend there. They tried to keep it from me, but a child knows. Even if they don't know exactly, they know." She sighed. "They agonized about it, but felt they had to help him. So they went, telling me they were taking a short vacation. They left me with the coven school. I...haven't seen them since."

"That is awful." Jeremy looked deeply moved. "You were how old?"

"Almost sixteen." She took another absent sip. "Our coven school mother had some highly placed friends there. They searched extensively, but found nothing."

"They are not in the Beyond?"

"No. So they must..." She trailed off. They had not passed over, but could not be found on this plane. "A fate worse than death" is a cliché among humankind; for us, it was something in which the Iron Rose specialized.

"Oh, Logan. How dreadful for you."

Logan turned abruptly to me. "Callie, look what I've done to our party. You *must* teach me how to make small talk."

"You must *not*," Jeremy said. "This conversation is far more engaging than the inane chit-chat we are usually surrounded with. You speak of things that are *real*—your magical work, your parents. Unlike..." But he was too polite to finish the sentence, even with Niad already gone.

Logan shook her head, but she was also blushing. "Um, thank you."

"And I hope you do not think I make light of your tragedy," Jeremy said.

"Oh, gosh, no," Logan protested. "You are being very kind." She gazed down at the table a moment, then looked up. "It's just so frustrating, to be so separate from the Old Country. Even after all this, I know almost nothing about it."

Jeremy looked somber, almost angry. "I know that, and I must say, I do not entirely agree with the reasons our Elders give for keeping witchkind so fragmented like this."

"Well, it's supposed to keep us safe," I said, remembering what I'd learned in coven school.

"And yet it does no such thing."

"What is it like there, really?" Logan asked. "Are the troubles still so...pervasive?"

Jeremy sat forward. "Well, no—and yes. Day-to-day life goes on much like it does here, though with a more, I don't know, rural European flavor perhaps. But the threat of the Iron Rose is never far from anyone's mind."

She shivered. "I feared as much."

"Just a few months ago, there was an ugly exchange in the town of Frezt. A potter was found dead in his shop—cause unknown. In retaliation, four masked and shielded individuals broke into the home of the deputy mayor and brutally murdered him, along with his wife and daughter. Only their young son escaped, hiding in a closet. The attackers must not have known there was a second child."

"Oh." Logan's face was paler than ever. "How awful."

"Will there be retaliation for the retaliation?" I asked, disturbed as well. He may have disagreed with the Elders' reasons for keeping us separate, but nothing like that happened in San Francisco. At least, not to witchkind.

"Sadly, that is all too likely. As is the way of such things. In fact—"

Paolo's conversation at the next table erupted into laughter, and Shella, one of the witches there, leaned over to share the joke with us.

We laughed politely, but the somber mood was broken—which was probably for the best. Logan was right: this was hardly birthday-party conversation. The room was growing more crowded all the time, and soon the two vacant chairs at our table were claimed. I'm certain the witches were just looking for a place to sit, and not angling to meet the exciting new warlock, not at all. In any event, he continued to have eyes only for Logan.

She was an introvert at heart, though. Near midnight I could see, even without looking magically, that she was spent.

"Doing all right?" I whispered to her.

"Super great," she whispered back, her face pale but wreathed with smiles. "But I should have left hours ago." She gave a small, regretful sigh. "What a guy. I wish I had more energy. I'd love to get to know him better."

"He's not going anywhere—he's just moved here. You'll see him again." *And he's clearly interested*, I thought. "Want me to help extract you?"

She was probably fine to take the ley lines, but there was no sense in her burning even more energy. I saw her into a taxi, then stood savoring the cold night air, trying to decide whether to go home myself. This had been a fun distraction, but on the quiet sidewalk, thoughts of the rest of my life rushed back. What should I do about Raymond? I didn't want to push him away. But I could *not* tell him I was a witch—a real witch. How could I let him in further, but keep him out of everything that made me who I was?

Why did I have to fall in love with him? Why did things have to be so complicated?

Was it love?

Of course it was. The thought of letting him go sent a stab of pain to my heart.

But...

What was the matter with me, anyway?

The bar door opened, letting a burst of noise out. Then Jeremy stood beside me.

"Having a smoke?" he joked.

I laughed politely. "No, just wondering if I should hit the hay. It's been a tough week."

"Oh?" He raised an eyebrow. "I am sorry to hear that. Anything I can do to help?"

No, not you. "I...no, just work stuff, life stuff. It'll all work out, I'm sure." I glanced up at him. "I know Logan would love to see you again," I blurted. *Oh, very smooth,* I thought with a cringe. "I mean, it looked like you and she had a lot to talk about."

"I greatly enjoyed our conversation. She is a remarkable witch. One doesn't meet many true independents."

Interesting—so they had talked about her covenless status? I must have missed that when I was getting drinks. "Yes. I'm living in my own house at the moment, but Logan's lived alone forever. Since coven school." I shook my head. "She's amazing."

"She does seem a strong soul." He paused, gazing down the street. A distant cat rummaged through a garbage can. "So, have you made up your mind?"

"About what?"

"Are you running off, or may I buy you another drink?"

I laughed. "Oh, why not? One more won't hurt."

I stayed for three more. Or possibly six.

It takes a lot to get a witch tipsy, but I managed. When I finally staggered back onto the sidewalk, squinting into the sunrise, I could barely manage to find a ley line, and almost let an early-rising human see me vanish.

"Ahh," I sighed a minute later, as the clean unwarded air of my house settled around me. The coven house, bristling with its magical defenses, always felt so...confining. Like a corset, strung tight. The quiet, calm openness here was—

A piercing cry shattered the solitude. I clamped my hands over my ears and turned to face Elnor. "Blessed Mother, must you always do that?"

She gazed at me with unforgiving yellow eyes, their message clear: DINNER TIME AND BREAKFAST TIME BOTH, NEGLIGENT WITCH!

I headed to the kitchen. It would be far more costly not to. Little black-and-white tyrant. Why hadn't I taught Petrana to feed her? Some mistaken notion about my bond with the miserable feline, I supposed.

"Some witches dispense with familiars altogether, you know," I told her, opening a can of tuna. "They just go it alone. Like warlocks."

Elnor ignored me, paying full attention to her meal. She knew a lie when she heard one.

"Well, they should, anyway," I muttered.

— CHAPTER FIVE —

After sleeping a few hours, I worked most of the afternoon in the lab, having barely more success than I'd had earlier. I could *not* figure out how to keep the little creatures alive. I'd seemed to make progress once I tried bending the æther around the Petri dishes just a bit to shield them from stray magic in the air. But that hadn't lasted—the æther slipped back to normal as soon as I let go of it. Now the creatures seemed to be petering out even faster than before.

That would be no solution anyway; I wasn't going to sit around holding my experiment together forever.

"Well, crap," I said, pushing my hair out of my eyes yet again. I'd braided it as usual, but I was exerting so much power, it kept busting loose and crawling all over the place.

From her corner by the window, Elnor glanced up at me. Beside her, Petrana also gazed back at me impassively, looking as much like a machine as ever. I stifled a sigh of disappointment. Yes, I knew what a golem was; surely it had been unrealistic of me to imagine I'd created a being with any intelligence.

"Come here, kitty," I called to my familiar. Elnor rose, stretched, and came to stand at my feet. "No, jump up." I patted the lab bench.

She gave me a quizzical look—I didn't usually let her up among the potions and reagents—but did as I bid.

"Sniff this," I said, pointing at the latest Petri dish. "See if there's anything alive there, if I'm missing anything." Maybe it was there, but just too subtle for me to detect.

She bent down and smelled the dish thoroughly, whiskers twitching. After a minute, she looked back up at me.

I began petting her, opening my awareness to hers, letting my energy meld with her feline senses. She arched into my hand, welcoming the communion. From her, I gathered impressions... confusion at first about what I wanted, mingled with willingness to help her mistress; displeasure at the strong scent of the reagent; a fleeting thought about her food bowl downstairs, and was that a mouse in the wall?; followed at last by the distinct sense that the Petri dish contained no life whatsoever, and why was I having her sniff it?

With a sigh, I gave her a final scritch around the ears and set her back onto the floor. "Thanks, kitten."

She went to investigate the wall, found nothing, and returned to her patch of sunlight.

I began again, mixing a fresh batch of potion, adding two drops of pneumative, then reaching for my supply of tanglefoot hellebore leaves. "Oh, damn." Empty. I set the beaker down and frowned at it.

"Do you need me to run an errand, Mistress Callie?"

The voice startled me badly, making me almost knock the beaker over as I spun around and stared at my golem. "Did you…how…?" Did Petrana just *take initiative*? She looked back at me, blank as ever. "How did you know I needed something?"

"Your beaker is empty. I can fetch the materials you need, if you give me instructions."

I continued to stare at her. Okay, that was tempting, even encouraging. But weird, and unprecedented. Was she growing, becoming… something more? Just minutes after I had wished her to?

Coincidence, surely.

In any event, I probably should utilize her for troublesome errands. But not this one, not yet. She should be started on much simpler tasks first. "No, thank you, Petrana. You remain here."

"Yes, Mistress Callie."

Shaking my head, I grabbed a satchel and slipped out and onto a ley line.

Once in ley space, I sent my senses around until I found the line I wanted, and flowed onto it. It took me to the far end of Golden Gate Park, beyond the Polo Field, out near the ocean. Here there were fewer tourists and picnickers; the cold and fog discouraged them.

I walked along a narrow path, between some ancient cypress trees. After a few minutes, I made sure that no human saw me as I left the path, walking straight toward a seemingly impenetrable thicket of brambles. The vines parted as I approached, opening the way, though barely.

After another minute or so, a rusted iron gate came into view. It looked locked, but again, I knew better. I did not slow, raising my hand to it as I drew closer. It opened at my touch, swinging open with a gentle protest of its creaking hinges. I wondered whether the gate would even open for Petrana, a witch's creature, as it opened for a witch.

Most witchkind houses, even ones without a botanical focus, kept magical gardens. I would be doing some planting myself in the backyard, when I got more settled. Yet this garden was something else. The herbs and strange night-fruits that grew here were too dangerous for anyone's private yard. I did not like coming here, but I went when I had to, as all witches did.

It tended itself. Even if anyone had been willing to take on such a task, the garden itself would not permit it.

I stepped inside the garden just as the sun set. The air grew more chill around me as the cold magic growing here reasserted itself. I shivered, wishing I'd worn a sweater, but didn't dare use my own magic to warm my blood. Not in here.

Four kinds of hellebore were planted by the back fence, on the right-hand side. Snaking vines of windrush grew just inside the front gate, seeming almost to call to me. I didn't touch them, didn't even turn my head. I walked straight down the right-hand lane, keeping to the path. Small, crowded plots threatened to inundate the worn stones with their dark, exotic herbs and trailing, winding, reaching vines. Ivy clung to the outer walls of the garden, choking out every outside plant that might think to enter. The foggy sky grew ever darker.

At the far back corner, I bent, trying to find the hellebore among the thicket. A black-flowering hibiscus grew low to the ground, turning its huge flowers downward. I reached out, pushing aside its black petals, trying to avoid the thorns of a Venezuelan dragonvine, and almost put one right through my finger when I startled at the sound of a low growl behind me.

I leapt up and wheeled around, but it was merely an old witch, with a hunched back and a basket over one arm. From Jasmine's coven, I thought, though I couldn't remember her name. She grabbed a handful of herbs, sniffed it, and dumped it into her basket, then cleared her throat with an ugly growl.

"Relax, I ain't gonna bite you," she grumbled, reaching for another sprig of bloodfire. "Young witches shouldn't come to dark places if they're gonna be so blessed spooky."

"Sorry, Auntie," I said, blushing.

"You're not picking that, are you?" she said, indicating the hibiscus.

"This?" I took a step away from the plant. "No, I'm just trying to find the hellebore."

"It moved." She pointed to a small, triangle-shaped bed a few rows into the garden. "Last month."

"Oh." I knew better than to ask why—she wouldn't know any more than I would. I walked over and plucked some of the nasty, potent plant, and put it in my bag. "Thanks."

She gave that snuffle-growl again and bared tobacco-stained teeth. Was that supposed to be a smile? "My pleasure. Any time." Friendly though her words may have been, I got the strong impression that she was waiting for me to leave.

Fine with me. I shivered again, heading toward the front gate. I did not look back at her, nor did I glance over at the windrush as I grabbed a handful of it on my way by, stuffing it into my satchel as I hightailed it out of there.

The communal garden always creeped me out something fierce. That, plus my earlier drain of energy in the lab, made me realize I couldn't just dive back into my work. I needed a little break—time just being out in the fresh air. And I definitely needed food. I decided to drop the herbs at home and go get a restorative meal out somewhere. With my new ingredients and a full belly, I ought to be able to get in a good night's work.

I walked back out through the park and grabbed the ley line I'd taken to come here, branching off to a smaller line directly to my house. I was just about to pop out on the front porch and shove the satchel into the front hall when I realized the porch wasn't empty.

"Crap!" I drew back in ley space and focused. "Raymond!" Blessed Mother, that was close. I withdrew further, pausing to catch my breath before I found a private place down the block to emerge. Then I walked up the street toward my house, struggling to appear casual and relaxed.

"Hey, hon," he said, getting to his feet when he saw me.

"Hi, darling." I walked up the steps and kissed him. "What are you doing here?"

He laughed, but it sounded a bit forced. "Um, Saturday night? Dinner?"

"Did I forget a date?" I shifted on my feet, trying to hold the satchel as far from him as possible without looking like I was doing so. The windrush probably wouldn't hurt him, but no sense taking chances.

"Well, no, not a date exactly, but," he shrugged, giving me an adorable-innocent look, "you were busy last night, so I thought…"

"Don't you have band practice?"

"We're doing it Sunday instead. Peter got a solo gig tonight at the Heartfire." He caught sight of the satchel. "Is that groceries?"

"No!" I said, a bit too loud. I turned farther away from him and dug for a house key in my jeans pocket. Of course, there wasn't one there; I'd simply dematerialized and gone through ley space when I'd left. "Um, shoot."

"No key?"

"I...I left the back door open, wait right here!" I dashed down the steps before he could offer to come with me, momentarily spacing on the fact that nearly every house in San Francisco—mine included— abuts its neighbor, without room for even a squirrel to travel in between them. *Crap!* I thought again. He *really* needed to not drop by without warning.

I rushed to the end of the block and around the corner, thinking fast. Had he ever been in my tiny backyard? I didn't think so. Okay, this might work. I slipped into ley space, through the æther, and into the house. I dropped the satchel in the lab and opened the front door a minute later. "Come on in!" I said with a smile.

Raymond glanced to either side of the house, then back at me, looking puzzled. "How did you...?"

"Alleyway! There's an alleyway behind the house! I'll show you some time. But for now, I bought some beer—your favorite!" I grabbed his hand and dragged him into the house.

Several beers and one tumble in bed later, he said, "So, what are we doing for dinner? You want me to pick up some more Chinese?"

I'd been hungry before; I was starving now. But...I could almost hear the fresh herbs calling to me from the floor above. But, I really needed to eat. But, damn it, I really needed to work. But hungry. But...

After I stared at him without responding long enough, the wheels of my brain spinning without traction, he grinned. "All right, gotcha—I know a low-blood-sugar gal when I see one. Back in a jiffy." He rose from the bed and pulled on his faded Levi's. I admired the view. Yes, okay, he was right. Chinese food. Good.

True to his word, he was back in half an hour. I could almost smell the food through the æther as I set paper plates on a little card table in the kitchen.

I scarfed down my usual five or nine helpings, then sat back, happily rubbing my satisfied belly. "Oh, honey, thank you. That was awesome."

He smiled back at me. "So...what now? Wanna go catch a movie or something?"

"Um...you don't think it's kind of late?"

"Is it?" He glanced at his wrist, though I'd never known him to wear a watch. "It's not even nine, I don't think." Then he gave me a wolfish grin. "You wanna just go back to bed?"

I sighed. "Raymond, hon, I...there's a lot I still need to do around here. I haven't got my third-floor work space set up really at all..."

"You want help?"

"No, I really need things set up a specific way. It's easier just to do it myself."

He gazed back at me. "Well, *I* could go to bed, and keep it warm for you..."

"Oh, gosh, I'll likely be up real late." *Maybe even till tomorrow.* "I'm sure you'd be more comfortable at your own place."

"Right." He nodded. "Got it."

I reached out to touch his arm. "I'm sorry, hon, I just...this is a huge change for me, moving out of the...other house...like this. I do love you. But...I need to really get settled into my own place here. Alone."

"Sure. I understand. No problem." He pushed absently at his paper plate and stood up. "Well, I'll get goin', then."

"Want to get together early next week maybe?"

He shrugged, not meeting my eye. "Yeah, sure. Call me."

Monday morning, I left the city, taking a major ley line under the bay to Berkeley. I materialized across the street from the university campus, in the back room of a crowded junk store the Elders maintain as a discreet portal.

"Greetings," I said to old Hubert, sitting behind his battered wooden desk. He was a minor power, despite his age. It was kind of the Elders to find a job for him.

"Mmph," he replied, not lifting his eyes from his book, a bubbling glass of demonbrew by his side. I raised an eyebrow as I went past him. I like a glass of elderflower wine or Witches' Mead as much as anyone, but this seemed...out of place. Wasn't he supposed to be guarding the portal?

Well, Dr. Gregorio Andromedus had probably alerted him to expect me.

I picked my way out of the store, stepping over piles of mismatched china and tarnished family silver and trading cards and steel model cars. Emerging onto the sidewalk, I found myself in a flood of students. Young, chattering, human.

I love their energy, I thought as I waded through the crowd and crossed the street. So fresh, so eager. So uninhibited. So...free.

Once on campus, it was a short walk to the laboratory, which wasn't officially part of the university at all; they had no idea it was there. Dr. Andromedus had built it over eighty years ago in magically altered space nestled in the rafters of the main library building. From this secret perch, he could pursue his own research interests all day, while keeping a close eye on the latest doings of human scientists on the distinguished campus, without any risk of being noticed by them in return. And he was a sucker for books. His own house, which I'd visited a few times over the years, was crammed with books, many from the Old Country.

I climbed the stairs to the top floor of the library, then slipped down a darkened hallway to the lab door—disguised as a broom closet. After glancing around to make sure no humans were watching, I murmured an opening spell, then whispered "*Essūlå*." The door swung open.

Inside, I closed the door, then began to recast its inattention spell.

"Do not bother about that, Calendula," Gregorio said behind me, lifting his right hand and sending a flick of magic toward the door. "It is easier this way."

"Good morning, Dr. Andromedus." I turned to face the eminent warlock. He looked distinguished as ever: neat lab coat over a pale shirt and dark trousers; black hair with a touch of grey at the temples. He'd pass for fifty, maybe sixty, if not for his eyes. It's hard to mask the gravity of eight hundred years. "It's no trouble for me to do it."

He smiled. "Perhaps I am a particularly fussy old man who likes his spells done just so. Come—you brought some samples?"

I followed him to a lab bench, looking around the place. I hadn't been here in two or three years; he'd made some changes. Or maybe just cluttered it up a bit. Or a lot. Didn't there used to be windows? The benches—long wooden tables lined up against the walls—were piled high with crucibles and jars, which in turn were propped precariously against stacks of books and cartons of loose papers. A bright green salamander scurried across the table Gregorio indicated as I went to set my bag on it, just missing being squished. I almost didn't see the other researcher working in the far back corner, a youngish warlock with mussed brown hair, bent over an Oleandascope; I only noticed him when he glanced up at me.

"Yes," I said to Gregorio, bringing out a handful of vials. "I have my last three runs here, one from each day. I tried—"

"Hold a moment, please," he said, taking the vials. "Let me look them over first; then tell me your thoughts. I do not want to start down the wrong trail."

"Sure." I looked around for a place to sit, or lean, finally settling for a wooden stool in the corner. It had only about a foot of papers piled on it, and a few small stones; I added them to a stack on the corner of the nearest bench.

Dr. Andromedus had opened my vials and set them in a test tube rack on the bench before him. He stood back, gazing at them, arms folded across his chest, not moving. I could sense his deep, ancient magic probing them, though I couldn't see what spell or divination he was working. His shields were strong, and probably unconscious—centuries of habit. Not wanting to be rude, I did not pry.

"Hmm," he said, after a few minutes, turning to me. "Now, what seems to be the problem?"

I told him about the fragile little organisms; about bending the æther, and all the other things I'd tried. "I don't know what I'm doing wrong."

He thought a moment longer. "With your permission, I would like to place them in the Zosimos cabinet." He indicated a floor-to-ceiling glass-fronted cabinet next to the bench. Swirling, indistinct colors shone from within. "It can see around corners better than I can."

"Of course," I said, getting down from my stool to take a closer look at the device. My father had a smaller one he sometimes worked with, but I didn't have one. "Is this your own design?"

"Yes," he said with a small smile. "I find, as with the door mechanics, that building my own instruments causes better resonance in all my work."

Well, that I could understand. I could already tell that, once I got this little issue worked out, my work was going to be stronger, less subject to the distracting influences of my coven sisters. Of course, collaborative magic had its own strengths—something witches understood far better than warlocks. The trick was to figure out which job called for which approach.

Gregorio capped the vials and opened the cabinet door. Inside, many small shelves lined the back wall. There were mirrors along the sides, and little folded and bent bits of copper wire sticking out from everywhere. Whatever had been making the swirls of multicolored light had vanished. I smelled lavender, and ozone, and something I couldn't identify at all.

"Here, hold these a moment." Gregorio handed me my vials, then leaned in and began moving the copper wires around, fashioning three loops in the middle of the open part of the cabinet. "All right."

I handed them back, and he perched them in the loops, tightening one for a steadier fit. Then he closed the door and placed his hands on the glass, palms flat.

The lights started up again, this time in hues of green and blue, with an occasional flash of purple.

Gregorio stood back. "Ten minutes or so should do it. May I offer you a beverage?"

"Yes, thank you." I glanced around the cluttered lab. "What do you have?"

"Anything you like."

"Pennyroyal tea?"

"Of course." He waved his hand, and two steaming mugs appeared on the bench. "And I have another chair somewhere…hmm…"

We were soon seated on two folding chairs underneath a nearly obscured window, a small round metal table between us. Across the lab, the Zosimos cabinet made quiet clunking and hissing sounds; the young researcher left his Oleandascope and began tweezing tiny fibers of preserved red Spanish moss out of a jar into a line of Petri dishes. I sipped my tea. "It's delicious, thank you."

"My pleasure." The ancient warlock set his mug down. "I understand you have recently succeeded in creating a very stable golem. An impressive achievement."

"Oh, well, yes. That did work nicely," I said, feeling proud all over again. "Though I haven't really had the chance to make much use of her yet. With the move and all."

"What *are* your plans for its use?"

"I wanted an analogue system to test homunculi in—if I ever succeed in keeping any alive long enough," I said.

"Animals will not do?" He frowned. "It seems to me that a golem's internal workings, while impressive, would hardly equal the complexity of a witch's."

"Well," I said, shifting in my chair, "I was mostly just thinking about toxicity and the like. I won't be able to test for efficacy on her, no."

Still looking puzzled, Gregorio paused a moment, sipping his tea. Then he said, "A golem is a rare and complicated working, heavily laden with lore, both human and witchkind. I have never known anyone so young as you to succeed with one. I was surprised your coven sanctioned it."

"Um." I stared at my tea a moment. The young warlock across the room had stopped his work; was he listening? Or absorbed in what he was doing? I could only see the back of his head, not his face. "Leonora...well, um, she was actually surprised too. After I created it."

"I see." He gazed at me, his grey eyes keen and piercing. "You could think of no simpler mechanism to test for toxicity? Why a golem, Calendula?"

"Well, I..." I started, scrambling to put together something about her being useful around the house. Then I admitted, "I guess I wanted to see if I could do it."

He raised an eyebrow, but allowed a small smile.

"I mean, I always wanted to create something—something big, important," I went on. "Something that's mine. Does that make sense?"

Dr. Andromedus continued to peer at me. "Indeed it does," he finally allowed. Another sip. "Well, you certainly attracted everyone's attention." He started to say something more before abruptly turning to address the young warlock researcher. "Dr. Winterheart, could I trouble you to fetch me a case of beetlewax from the storage room?"

"Of course, Dr. Andromedus," the warlock said at once, as he leapt to his feet and made his way across the lab. "Anything else while I'm there?"

"No, that will be all."

Dr. Winterheart had to turn almost sideways to squeeze past us in the cramped lab; his arm brushed my shoulder as he went by. After the door closed behind him and Gregorio had reset the spell, I looked at my mentor, curious.

"My son greatly enjoyed meeting you last week, Calendula."

"And I enjoyed meeting him." *Though not as much as Logan did*, I thought. "Charming guy. But I never knew you had a son."

"I am afraid that I did not manage to play much of a role in his upbringing." Gregorio's voice was touched with regret.

"He told us…a bit about his life."

"Yes. I lost his mother quite unexpectedly when Jeremiah was very young. It was…a challenging time for me, to say the least." He gave a small sigh, gazing down at his mug. "It seemed to me at the time that an intact family, not touched by grief, would be a far better environment in which to raise a child. I hope I was not mistaken in this." Now he looked up at me. "I fear he is something of a stranger to me."

I thought about what Jeremy had told us. "I think he thinks very highly of his foster parents and his upbringing, and is excited to get to know you now."

Gregorio smiled. "You are a caring and sensitive witch, Calendula. And very patient, to listen to the maunderings of an old warlock. You are also, despite any minor and temporary disagreement with your coven, well-connected; a good person for Jeremiah to know. I hope you will continue to enjoy being generous with your time and friendship."

"Well, sure. But Niad is keeping him pretty busy at the moment."

"I am grateful for Niadine's attention, of course. But I would be particularly glad that he should spend time in *your* company." He gave me a significant look, then returned his gaze to his tea.

What? Are you setting me up with your son? Do you just want to get me away from dating humans, or…? "How did Jeremy's mother die?" I blurted, scrambling for any way to get away from this subject. And it *was* truly weird that my parents had never mentioned any of this—a partner, any children. Gregorio and my father were so close. At least, that's what I'd always thought.

"A mysterious illness. It came from nowhere, striking her down almost without warning, draining her essence. And her spirit…" He shook his head. "I was not myself for a time, after that. Powerful though we may be, we cannot control everything."

"No," I agreed. "What about her spirit?"

"Lost," he said, immediately adding, "Well! Shall we see what the cabinet has to say? This should be enough time."

"How does the Zosimos cabinet work?" I asked, feeling almost forcibly nudged back to the business at hand. *Where could her spirit be if not the Beyond?* I wondered. Was it like what happened to Logan's parents? Yet Gregorio so clearly did not want to talk about it further. "I don't use much large equipment in my own research."

He looked at me with surprise. "Lucas hasn't shown you?"

"No. My father...well, you know how busy he is." The excuse sounded even more feeble than usual. Forty-five years old, and I was *still* wishing my daddy had more time for me.

Gregorio's eyes softened. Sympathy? Concern? "It is rather simple, actually. It works in conjunction with the pneumative to strip away the complexities of the environment and focus the particular question."

Pneumative was an invention of Gregorio's: a sort of über-potion, now widely used in almost all witchkind biological research. It acted as an inert accelerant to other potions, amplifying what they did without bringing contaminant energies of its own. "But how does it do that?"

He smiled. "In this case, the cabinet itself screens out any magical influence from our immediate surroundings—ourselves particularly included." His eyes glimmered as he added, "I did not send Dr. Winterheart away merely so that we could discuss personal matters."

"Ah."

"Once the distractions are cleared, the spells bound to the copper wires delve into your potion in the vials, analyzing the remains of the homunculi. That should give us a much better idea of what exactly is causing them to fail, and at what point in your experiment." He glanced over at the machine. "Let us go have a look."

I followed him to the machine and waited as he again put his palms against the doors. The sounds coming from within had softened to an occasional burble, and the colored lights had nearly ceased flickering. Gregorio nodded, muttered to himself, and opened the doors. A small gust of steam entered the lab room, then dissipated.

He brought the vials to the bench and stood looking at them, sending his magical senses to probe them once again. I did as well, but could not see any difference in their aspect from earlier.

After a minute, he looked up at me, frowning. "That is odd. I see a notable residue of your life essence here. Which pneumative are you using?"

"The twenty-strength, from Magitech. Why?"

"Ah," he said with a nod. "They use an outdated formula."

"I thought they were the standard supplier—that's what everyone uses."

"They were, until last year. I have improved the potency of several of the key ingredients, and removed an impurity in another, but Magitech..." He gave an indulgent smile, shaking his head. "I fear they are more interested in their bottom line than in actually serving their customers. They have insisted that their formula is perfectly good. You should try Stellar Karmaceuticals. They are a little pricier, but certainly worth it. And they keep up with my tinkerings. They should have an even newer formulation within the next few weeks."

"I had no idea."

"It is irresponsible, really. I suppose a Magitech representative visited you? Bearing gifts, even?"

I nodded, thinking about the pert young witch who visited the coven house on a quarterly basis, order sheets at the ready. Yes, now that he mentioned it, she did always seem to arrive with fresh-baked brownies, free samples of pennywort extract, or clever little mood rings (containing actual moods) for the students. She was very popular. I chuckled, chagrined. "Stellar Karmaceuticals, you say? I'll look them up."

"Yes, you will want to do that." He went to a low cabinet by the door and opened it, riffling around within. A small jar fell to the floor and rolled under a lab bench. "Ah. In the meantime, take this, to get you started." He brought out a small, soft-sided purple pouch, bulging with liquid—like a bota bag, but without a drinking spout. "There should be more than enough here until you can place an order."

"Wow, thank you, Dr. Andromedus." Magitech's pneumative wasn't cheap; if this stuff was even more expensive, he'd just handed me a few thousand dollars' worth, as casually as if it were a cup of tea.

He shrugged. "I have plenty more."

"Can I pay you for this?"

"Of course not." Then he grinned. "Consider it a small token of my appreciation, for your efforts in welcoming my son to our city."

I shook my head, smiling. "Well, thank you." But really, Jeremy was perfectly charming. Not to mention easy on the eyes. Why was I being bribed into spending time with him?

Not that Logan would object if we sought out his company.

I wonder if she wants to co-host a dinner party at my house? I thought. *Just a few close friends...some fun people...and San Francisco's newest warlock.*

— CHAPTER SIX —

"S ure," Logan said when I asked her about a dinner party. "But not without a dining table. Have you found one I don't know about?"

"You are as wise as you are helpful."

On Wednesday, we made our planned run through the antique stores, then hit a few kitchen shops before returning to my place with Indian takeout. "I do need to start cooking sooner or later," I said, grabbing another piece of garlic naan from the clutter of cartons on my new-to-me kitchen table (a smaller version of the grand one which now graced my dining room).

"That'll be easier now that you have pots, and more than one pan."

I spooned a bite of bhindi masala onto the naan and glanced over at the full shopping bags lined up in front of the pantry and all over the countertops. "It's not something I have any practice with." My job at the coven had been—still was—teacher, with a side of research; Organza and Peony were our main cooks, with Sirianna and some of the older students assisting.

"You'll be great. It's just like spells, only with bigger batches, and cheaper equipment." Logan grinned at me. "And less poison."

"Poison!" I put a hand to my chest in mock-indignation. "Well I never!"

"Of course not." She watched me chew as she dug into her own meal. "Anyone who likes to eat as much as you do should be a natural at cooking."

When our bellies were full to bursting, I leaned back. "More tea?"

"I couldn't. Should we plan this dinner party?"

"Ugh, I can't even think about food at the moment. Let's work on who to invite."

"Starting with Jeremy?"

"I should say—he's the guest of honor!" I peered at her. "Why, Logan, are you blushing?"

"He invited me to lunch."

"And you're just telling me this *now*?" I leaned forward, pushing my curry-stained plate out of the way. "So what happened? Tell me everything!"

She laughed. "Nothing to tell yet—we're meeting Monday."

"That's fantastic!" I sighed. "Just don't ask me for any useful advice about relationships."

"Oh, Callie. It's still not going well with Raymond?"

"Yes. No. I don't know. I just...I guess I had some fantasy that he'd be able to read my mind and figure out when I want to see him and not see him." I gave a small chuckle. "Or maybe I never really thought this part through."

"Why don't you just tell him what you want? Can't you agree on some kind of schedule?"

"If I knew what I wanted, I would! We're already seeing each other way more than we used to be able to. But no matter how much I give him, he wants more!"

At the kitchen window, Elnor glanced up at my tone before returning to gaze out into the backyard.

"Right." Logan gave me a sympathetic smile. "I guess you still haven't given him a key."

"I can't." I shrugged helplessly. "But I'm so busy. You know how spells go—they're done when they're done, you can't really predict the timing. Dr. Andromedus gave me some new pneumative last week, and I'm already seeing good results with it. So I've been spending more time on experiments." I sighed again. "Last night, I called Raymond when I was done for the evening. It was only ten o'clock, but he said he just wanted to crash."

"So..." She frowned. "You just said he keeps wanting too much time, didn't you? He gave you some space."

"But I didn't want space *then*," I said, feeling whiny and ridiculous. "Now I think maybe he's sulking or something."

"Sulking? That's not normal for him."

"Nothing is normal these days."

"Nothing was 'normal' before, either. You stole time when you could get it."

"Yeah. And it worked fine—there was never enough time together, so it was all precious. But now I don't know what to do. Part of me feels like I should call him again, tell him we need to talk; the other part doesn't want to give in to emotional blackmail, if he is sulking. Like it's his turn to call me, since he turned me down last night."

"Hmm."

"I know, I know—that's petty, I shouldn't be thinking that way."

"Think whatever way you need to," she said, her voice kind. "This is *your* process. Do it however works for you. He can figure out *his* process without your help."

I sighed. "I just want…"

"What *do* you want?" she asked, when I didn't go on.

"I want things to be like they used to be. I want him to walk in here, pick me up in his strong arms, rumple my hair, kiss me from head to toe, and then carry me off to the bedroom."

"Right now?"

I laughed. "Maybe after you leave."

"So you just want a physical relationship with him?"

I shook my head. "No. I mean, that's fantastic, but I also love how he can make me laugh. I miss going out to hear his band, and having him tell me all about some new book he just read. But his body is the first thing that leaps to mind when you ask me what I want." I smiled at her. "You know I'm very physically focused—not just sex, but the things the body knows, before the brain ever gets it. Anyway, physically is how our relationship started. That's all it was ever supposed to be."

"Of course." She frowned, thinking. "It's funny you should be so intuitive at some levels and not at all at others."

"What do you mean?"

"I know how you feel about this, but… Let's read your cards again."

"Oh, jeez, no. Really?" I glanced around the cluttered kitchen—shopping bags everywhere, dirty dishes piled up. "We've got too much to do here; no time for that."

Logan gave me a soft smile. "You still don't want to tell your best friend that her life's work is bullshit."

"I've never said it's bullshit!" I protested, too quickly. "It's just…not the path I took."

"I know, you're a scientist. But don't scientists try all sorts of different approaches to get at the right answer?"

"Sure, but that's different."

"Different how? Do you never go with a gut feeling in your lab?"

"Well, maybe. Sometimes," I admitted.

"So let me do your cards. What can it hurt?"

"What can it help?"

Logan looked at me appraisingly. "I think right now you're in a time of great transition, and you're stuck. Remember what you told me Maela said, about a fork in the road. Tarot can help you figure out what you *really* want, deep down, and point you toward a way to do it."

"It's not therapy, hon."

She laughed. "Look, you're way more intuitive than you give yourself credit for. If you just relax, and bring your witchly intuition and bodily wisdom to the cards, you might be surprised." She reached for her purse. "Come on, it's been forever since we've done a reading. Humor me. You don't have to do anything with it."

I knew she was just trying to help. And, as she said, I didn't have to act on it. "All right."

She handed me the deck. "Shuffle, a bunch of times."

"Yeah, I know." The stiff, oversized cards were as awkward as ever in my hands.

"And think about your questions, but not in any focused sense. Just let your uncertainties and thoughts roam around in your mind."

That was easy. *What should I do about Raymond?* I tried not to bring any magical focus to it, but just think the words. Feel the emotions.

"Okay, that's good," Logan said after a minute, taking the cards back. She began laying them out on the table before us, in her own modification of the traditional Celtic Cross pattern. The Page of Wands and the Four of Cups shared the central, Significator position; she set the Hermit just below them, as the Crossing. She then laid the King of Cups, the Three of Cups, the Fool, and the Three of Wands around the central cards, in the positions of my near and distant past, and near and distant future. The spread finished with three cards along the right: the Eight of Cups, the Four of Swords, and, at the top, the Tower. She took a small, sharp breath as she laid out that last one.

"That's the final outcome, right?" I asked, pointing to the Tower's dramatic imagery of death and destruction, chaos and lightning.

"Yeah," she said, frowning at the cards. "An interesting reading."

"You always say that. What's it mean this time?"

She gave an absentminded chuckle. "You have to let me study it for longer than ten seconds, Callie."

I tried not to fidget as she gazed at them. Finally, she looked up at me. "Actually, I see a lot of relevant themes here." She pointed to the Page of Wands. "He stands for new beginnings, being ready to grow. Finding your strength and independence. Like, oh I don't know, moving out of a coven house into your own home."

"Well, that's encouraging," I said.

She set her hand gently on the Four of Cups. "And this one is matters of the heart. A warning not to take love for granted."

It was just a guy sitting under a tree. "Oh."

"Right." She gave me a sympathetic look. "The reading has a couple of threes, and it's heavy on Cups, the suit of relationships."

"What do threes mean?"

"They have to do with unifying, and with forces bigger than yourself. They're about transition—the kind there's no turning back from. Inevitability. Clearly, your question is about more than just you and Raymond." She pointed to the Fool, in the position of the recent past. "Another new beginning—the ultimate fresh start."

I grinned at her. "Ah, I see—the mysterious wild cards have revealed the astonishing news that I've moved out of the coven house, estranging my sisters, and am confused about my love life. I can see why you think this magic is so freakishly useful. Whatever would I have done without it?"

"Oh, hush," she said, smiling. "We're not done. I also see the power of community, the joy of working together." She pointed to the Three of Cups. "Which resonates for me, with what I know about you. You need others—you don't love solitude, not like I do. I think you won't live alone long." She grazed her hand over the Eight of Cups, at the bottom of the final stack of three. "This one is about emotional stagnation, and recognizing when it's time to move on. More transition."

I looked back at the earlier cards. "So I'm not supposed to take his love for granted, but I'm supposed to be more independent, but live in community, but..."

"Those aren't necessarily contradictions. You can love someone deeply, be a very strong individual, and have a powerful community all at once. In fact, that's a pretty good combination, if it's in balance." She gazed up at me. "And we both know that none of these areas are integrated in your life. You love a human man, but the witchkind world will never accept him as anything more than a temporary plaything for you—no one has ever even met him. You can't let him into the deepest parts of your life, or even let him know they exist—the things that make you who you are. You chose to join a strong coven with a powerful leader, yet I would argue that Leonora has infantilized you—not just you, but all your sisters. The only way you see to break out of this is to defy her—and I don't think you're wrong to do so. I just don't think it's the end of the story. The independence part is now; the community and connection, and perhaps even the deep, integrated love, come later. You can't be a good partner *or* a good community member without being a strong, secure individual."

"Huh." This was all feeling surprisingly insightful, even coming from my best friend. "So what about this?" I pointed to the Tower.

"Well, that is big stuff," she admitted with an uncomfortable smile. "Catastrophic change, sometimes scary, but often for the better. It's about breaking through old, stultified structures and replacing them with something bold and new. With a ton of energy expended in the process, and sometimes people get hurt, but it's always about progress. Ultimately." She looked up at me. I could see tension in her eyes.

"Ultimately when?"

She gave a wan smile. "Such a scientist. If it were measurable, there would be tarot labs."

"Point taken." I studied her face. "Am I going to get hurt?"

"Possibly. I mean, you're hurting already, right?"

"Yeah."

"It may not be more than that. It may be something else entirely. But I really do believe that this is a good outcome. It's huge—it's scary—but it's good. More than that, it's necessary." She patted my hand. "Trust me."

"I do." I looked back over the cards, the whole reading. All these little stories...all about me. "So what have we learned here?" I asked. "I mean, the part about change and fresh starts—that's all clear. But the relationship stuff is a total jumble. I still don't know what's going to happen."

"Well, we weren't so much trying to read the future as to sort out what you want right now. I think we've learned that you're rather conflicted in that arena."

I laughed. "I could have told you that. I think I *did* tell you that."

"Yes. But the cards seem quite clear on the fact that you're doing the right thing by establishing some independence, despite the pushback from your coven. Obviously you do love Raymond, and you do have a real connection with him. And your future points toward a life in the company of others—which goes with what I know of you. But I wonder if taking up with a human man in the first place was, I don't know, some sort of avoidance on your part?"

"What do you mean?"

"Well, where was it supposed to go?" she asked. "It's an intrinsically temporary situation—yet it's the closest you've ever come to being in love, by a long shot. You've dated a lot of warlocks, but you always kick them to the curb the moment they're not perfect. Did you somehow let yourself open up to Raymond precisely *because* it was never going to turn into anything serious? It's interesting that now, with all this opportunity to see him, you're suddenly 'too busy' all the time."

"Huh. Maybe." I thought about it further. "What does love mean?"

"I don't know. You tell me."

"I mean, nothing is permanent. It's not like any of our unions are lifelong anyway. No one wants that. That's why we put end dates into our contracts."

"But you can't even have a union with him. Or children. And humans *do* marry for life—at least, they try to, they think they do. Have you ever told Raymond that was off the table?"

"Well, no. But he hasn't asked…"

"Of course not. Why would he?"

I sighed. "I guess I have been kind of unfair to him."

"It's the way it's done, when we dally with humans."

"Until suddenly it's not a dalliance."

"Exactly."

"So should I call him?"

Logan looked me in the eye. "Yes."

"Why do you say that?" I glanced over the cards again.

"Because you obviously want to. Call him, tell him whatever you need to, be as honest as you can stand to be. Then see what happens. You're not going to move forward on anything else till you get this dealt with, one way or another."

"But I—okay."

"And in a few weeks, we can do another reading, see if anything has shifted." She gathered up the cards, stacked them neatly and put them in their little box. "Meanwhile, you should have plenty to think about here."

"Yeah." I looked at all the full shopping bags. "Like a dinner party."

So I did call him. And he was sulking, a little, but it was obvious that he was also waiting for me to call. He softened at my apology, and we made a date, and we went out, and he spent the night afterwards. And it was lovely, as long as I focused on being with him in the moment, and not talking about anything important in my life. And I got fidgety the next morning, wishing he would go on ahead and leave already, so I could get back to my research. Which I couldn't tell him anything about.

Just like before.

And then my research didn't progress either, and I could *not* figure out why, and I felt frustrated and stymied. Just like before.

"I built a freaking *golem*," I snarled to nobody in particular, or maybe Elnor. "Why can't I make eukaryotes work?"

Elnor stretched, yawned, and glanced at the patch of sun that had abandoned her during her afternoon nap under the lab's back windows. She got up and rectified the situation, moving closer to where Petrana stood motionless. Unused. She hadn't spoken on her own initiative again since offering to go to the magical garden. Which was good, as that had kind of freaked me out a little.

Did she know that? Was that why she'd kept silent?

Was she observing me, learning me? Was I okay with that?

What had I made her for, really?

I could run my own errands, sweep my own floors, or conjure spells to do so. Or hire a maid, for that matter. A golem should be…monumental. *For* something. Something big.

I mean, the fact that I had created her at all was monumental. But now I was stuck fiddling with molecules again, going nowhere. If I wasn't going to use her, I really ought to unmake her.

But I couldn't.

"Come on, Petrana," I said, flicking a quick containment spell over the lab bench. "Let's go talk to Dad."

"Yes, Mistress Callie," she said.

"And not on the ley lines," I decided. "Out in the real world. The walk will do us good."

"Yes, Mistress Callie."

I stood before her, looking her over carefully. Why had I made her so tall? I could magically disguise her rough, muddy skin, tangled weed-hair and expressionless face, but there weren't many eight-foot-tall women walking around out there. Men either, for that matter. The best I could do without remaking her entirely was a mobile zone of inattention. People would see her, but their attention would deflect off before thoughts of *Huh, what a bizarrely tall woman* would register.

At least, I hoped so.

Ten minutes later, the spells cast, Petrana and I walked out the front door of my house. The zone of inattention worked on her shuffling gait, as well; it was hard even for me to watch her amble along.

It was a blustery, chilly February day, San Francisco's false spring still a few weeks away. I shivered in my wool coat, but Petrana of course did not feel the weather.

Nor did she feel curiosity, or a sense of adventure, or, well, anything. She was not nervous about being detected by humans. Inside, outside—it was all the same to her.

Suddenly that made me rather sad. My biggest creation, and so... inert.

"This way," I directed her, turning right when we got to Divisadero. She complied.

We walked past the ever-changing restaurants and cafés and the never-changing bodegas and laundromats, and then the apartment buildings, and then houses, as the street began to climb toward Pacific Heights. Crowds of people passed us. Nobody gave us a second glance.

If I had wanted to prove something about the power of my magic, I had easily done so.

But that wasn't the problem. I knew I was powerful. So what?

The hill steepened further as we approached my parents' fine home. I began thinking about how long it had been since I'd seen either of my folks. They had both responded separately to my dinner party invitation for next week. While the coven was officially my "family," nobody expected a witch to cut her ties to her mother and father, or siblings, if she had any.

I should really see my birth parents more often. What Logan wouldn't give to be able to even know what had happened to hers, and here I was, all but ignoring mine. I'd asked Gregorio Andromedus for help, but not my own father? Yes, he wasn't quite as eminent a scientist as Gregorio, but he had centuries more experience than I did. He'd probably see through my problem at a glance. My dad was a marvelous warlock. A bit reserved, sure; but I knew he loved me. I'd followed him into science in the first place. And now I never thought to include him in my life?

By the time I was climbing the worn brick steps to the lovely three-story house I'd grown up in, Petrana stumping along just behind me, I felt sentimental tears forming in the corners of my eyes. It would be so good to—

My hand brushed against the repulsion spell as I reached for the doorknob. "Huh?" Stung more emotionally than physically, I drew my hand back and tried to peer into the house, but the spell blocked that too. *Dad, Mom?* I sent through the æther, searching for them. *Are you home?*

It was a minute before I had an answer, from Mom. *Oh, hello, darling; no, we're out. Did you need something?*

I just wanted to talk to Dad about some science stuff. When will you be home?

Another silence. They must be pretty far away. *We're looking forward to your dinner party.* Her "voice" grew a little patchy. *I will tell your father you said…* Then the connection faded, and she was gone.

"Well, rats," I said. I turned to Petrana, who just stared back at me impassively. Why hadn't I called ahead? But they were usually home. Weren't they? When *was* the last time I'd been here, anyway?

Feeling worse by the minute, I stomped down the steps and up the garden path back to the street. My golem followed me.

Why did I have to be so alone in the world? Did I truly have so few connections to others? My own parents could leave town on some huge faraway trip and I wouldn't even *know* about it? Yes, I had Logan in my life; she was a treasure, and I did see her often enough. But other than that? I had a boyfriend I couldn't share anything with, a coven I was estranged from, and—well, that was about it. A familiar. A personality-less golem. Some students. Was this the best I could show for forty-five years of life?

I trudged down the sidewalk, falling deeper into angry frustration. Why did it even matter? What was I even trying to prove, with my stupid genetics research? It had seemed so big and important once upon a time—helping witchkind conceive—but now it seemed pointless. Most witches never left their covens; they didn't want to have children. There were so few warlocks anyway. Did anyone but me think this was a problem?

I wanted to accomplish something *real*. Something with consequences. Something that would do good for all of witchkind—and not just witchkind, but for humans as well. Why did we have to be so—

Calendula Isadora! Leonora's voice snapped through my brain; I about fell over from shock. *What in the world are you doing?*

I—what? I glanced behind me and saw at once. My spells of deflection and disguise, while not too onerous, did require at least a little bit of attention. Petrana was now perfectly visible in her actual form. In the street, a car slowed down, the humans inside staring at both of us. *Crap!* I flicked my hands at Petrana, refreshing her disguise. The car drove on. My heart pounded.

I believe I told you that creature was not to be taken outside! Leonora thundered.

I stopped myself short from snapping back at her, because it would come out as something like "You're not the boss of me," when, in fact, she was. I took a deep breath, doublechecked the spells, and sent, *I am so sorry. I was bringing her to work with my father, but he wasn't home. It won't happen again.*

See that it does not, she said, and closed the channel.

My golem and I returned home without further incident. Unless you count my growing despair. Had I really accomplished anything by moving out? I hadn't even felt Leonora's monitoring of me. It was no kind of independence, if my coven mother could peer at me at any time, night or day, across the city, and bawl me out like I was a three-year-old. I'd left a stifling coven house and its strictures, only to be expected to lock myself up in my own house? Never being able to make a true connection with Raymond or anyone else?

If we were so powerful, why were *we* the ones hiding all the time?

Didn't we used to rule the world? What had happened to witchkind?

— CHAPTER SEVEN —

T he house was transformed. Candles flickered from the sideboard, casting a soft glow over the dining room table. Crystal wine glasses sparkled, a burgundy tablecloth draped to the floor, and in the dim light, you couldn't tell that the chairs didn't match perfectly.

My original idea had been for a fun, informal party, introducing Jeremy to some of the younger set: Sirianna and maybe Maela from the coven, a few of the gang from Rose's, Logan of course, maybe even one or two of the older students. Cocktails, a buffet, games afterward.

But after I'd told Logan about my frustrations, about Leonora's still-tight leash around my neck, she'd gently suggested a strategy of appeasement. And the more I thought about it, I realized she was right. Hosting a more traditional, formal dinner party, using my first official social event as a venue to honor my elders, rather than continuing to chafe against them, made a good deal of sense. Jeremy would have plenty of time to meet folks. If I followed some of witch-kind's smaller rules and expectations for a while, I might find myself with more space to challenge the larger ones.

That was the theory, anyway.

I stood studying the table, rearranging place cards, then moving them back again. "What do you want me to do with the casserole?" Logan called from the kitchen.

"Hang on, I'll be right there."

I switched Leonora's and my mother's place cards again. I had put my father at the foot of the table, with myself (as hostess) at the head. The highest-honored lady should be at his right hand, and no one ranks higher than one's mother. But Leonora was also my mother, legally. Further, she was far older than Mom; my birth mother was not even a hundred.

Tradition also dictated separating couples. I left Mom's card in the center-right spot of the table, between Gregorio (at my right) and the gentleman he had offered to bring to round out the gender balance. I'd have rather had another witch—or even just kept the party at seven—but that wouldn't be traditional. If I was going to do this, I ought to do it right.

That left Logan at my left hand, and Jeremy next to her. That, at least, was simple: they were not officially a couple, so I could seat them together, but their lunch had gone very well. I could hardly get her to stop burbling about it and focus on the dinner.

Who knew seating eight people could be so complicated! The older generation made it look effortless. Then again, they'd been raised in an age when people entertained like this all the time. Perhaps when the last of them chose to move Beyond, witchkind could finally let go of these old protocols.

Logan appeared in the doorway, face flushed, wiping her hands on an apron. "I took it out. You want to come look at it?"

"Yes, thanks." I followed her to the kitchen. "It smells wonderful."

"The table looks great too."

We grinned at each other. "I think we're actually going to pull this off," I said.

I paused as I saw Petrana at the sink, washing pots and pans. "You're not letting her do the china, are you?" I asked Logan.

"No, just the unbreakables. But you should let her try. It's the only way she'll learn."

"Yeah, I know. Not tonight, though."

"Of course not." Logan watched the golem a minute. "She's progressing well, I think. I didn't have to explain anything to her about the dishes."

"Yeah. No one will ever mistake her for an independent intelligence, though."

"But that wasn't ever the point of her."

"True." I looked at the casserole on the stove. "That looks great," I told Logan. "How's the lamb?"

"It's all ready to go in. You only want to cook it for twenty minutes, so wait till everyone's arrived."

"Right." She'd told me all this already. I'd probably make her tell me again.

"Which is in half an hour," Logan said. "All right if I go change now?"

"Oh! Sure. Sorry."

"No problem," she said with a smile.

Logan left for the second floor. I glanced down at my own outfit. Since she'd been doing most of the cooking, I was still clean. Except for a spot on my sleeve, almost invisible against the midnight blue velvet of the dress. Sauce? Oil? I had no idea. I pointed at it, sending the stain scattering into microscopic particles and dissipating into the air. I patted my hair, but it was still behaving. It liked being in a French twist.

Okay. I was ready as I was going to get.

I went back in to stare at the table again, then opened a bottle of Margaux, leaving it to breathe on the sideboard. Elderflower wine chilled in the fridge. I didn't have any Witches' Mead—that took days to brew, and I only wanted to try so many new things at once—but I did have various bottles of aged Bulgarian frog brandy, including my father's favorite.

Yes. Ready.

Logan came back downstairs after a few minutes, looking spectacular in a floor-length ginger silk gown with black embroidered daisies at the hem and neckline. Her hair was held gently back in two feathered, bejeweled combs just behind her bangs; her blond tresses flowed out, mingling with the longest feathers. Logan's familiar, Willson, followed at her heels. Elnor was right behind him, tagging along like a kitten.

"Gorgeous!" I said, as Logan spun, letting the skirt flare out.

"I never get to wear this." She smiled. "Thanks for throwing such a fancy party. It's going to be great."

"I hope so."

"Have a glass of wine, it'll relax you."

"How come you're so calm?" I asked her. "You're supposed to be the shy one."

"It's not my party. I can go hide in the kitchen any time it gets to be too much."

"You can *not*!" I said. "You think an empty spot at a table for eight won't be noticed?"

"Kidding, kidding!" She laughed and patted my arm. "Seriously, here, drink some wine." She reached for the Margaux.

"No, not that one—I'm saving it for the rack of lamb. I'll just get a glass of elderflower."

Ten minutes later I sensed the essences of both my parents, and was already at the door to welcome them in when the bell chimed.

"It looks lovely, my dear!" Mother exclaimed after stepping over the threshold. She gave me a light kiss on the cheek, handing her coat to Petrana with barely a glance.

"You look great, Mom," I said. She brought no familiar—she had never replaced Promise when the calico had passed on a few years ago—but she was wearing her finest gown: a Dior from her trousseau in the early sixties, slender and apple-green, with a matching short jacket of ruffled organza. Dad's forest green suit complemented her dress without calling undue attention. I smiled to myself. I could almost hear their ritual conversation as they'd dressed, debating the venue, the participants, the formality (or not) of the occasion. It was sweet that they'd done it for me.

Mother stepped from the entry hall into the front parlor and looked around. "You've done so much—where did you get the rug? And the sofa! You told me you didn't have one."

"I didn't, then. Logan's taken me shopping at all the best places." I leaned up to kiss my dad, then turned to my best friend, waiting in the front hall behind me. "She's a home decorating genius."

"It looks very nice," my father allowed.

Petrana hung their coats in the deep under-stair closet, then stood stolidly by, waiting for the next guests. Logan fetched cocktails for my parents as Elnor registered her token objection to the presence of a male in her domain. I petted her fur back down. "Three more warlocks are coming this evening, and they are invited, so just chill, you." Her tail lashed back and forth a few times, but she purred. "You don't do this for Willson," I added.

We sat down, and I was about to ask my parents about their trip when I felt Leonora materialize on the front steps. She held back a moment, perhaps taking the measure of things inside, before ringing the doorbell.

"Greetings, Mother Leonora, and welcome," I said, drawing the door open. "Please, come in."

My coven mother was dressed in a plain, heavy overrobe of a purple so dark it was almost black. I could see enough of the clothing beneath her robe to realize that she must have dug all the way back to the Elizabethan part of her closet, where she kept favorite items from when she had come of age. The woven, beaded snood cradling her salt-and-pepper hair was also a clue. Leonora's familiar, Grieka, twined about her ankles, nearly unseen amid the many layers of petticoats and skirts.

"Thank you, Calendula Isadora." She stepped over the threshold, looking around with an appraising eye, and saw Logan. "Greetings, Logandina Fleur," she said to the covenless witch. There was perfect correctness in her tone, if no warmth.

"Leonora Scanza," Logan replied, with a short, practiced curtsey.

I helped my coven mother out of the overrobe and handed it to Petrana. Leonora's dress underneath was gorgeous—and ancient indeed. The tight-bodiced gown was puce, heavily embroidered with golden thread, small emeralds, and jet buttons. Though she had kept the lace ruff to a frugal minimum, perhaps in a nod to comfort, I could see that the sleeves were sumo-wrestler thick. The full, bell-shaped kirtle skirt pushed against the robes, cascading to the floor in a weighty fall of larger jet amulets and semi-precious gemstones. The back was less heavily decorated than the front, but I still saw a splash of garnets and tourmalines amid the jet beads.

Well. She had certainly taken my "formal dinner party" invitation seriously. I didn't know whether to be flattered or terrified.

"What can I get you to drink?" I asked.

I sensed her scan my kitchen quickly before returning her attention to me. "Elderflower wine would be fine, thank you."

Logan hurried off to get her a glass as I escorted Leonora into the front parlor. "Lucas Grandion, Belladonna Isis," she greeted my parents, less coolly than she had Logan.

"Oh, hi Leonora," my mother said with a big smile. "What an amazing dress!" Mom was technically still a member of the coven led by Isadora, a botanical worker, though she'd taken a leave of absence decades ago to sign the contract with my father, then extended her leave when they renewed their contract. Coven life, and its attendant courtesies, were a distant memory for her, though Leonora merely nodded at Mom's lack of formality.

Father rose and gave Leonora a short bow. Grieka glared at him before joining the other cats sniffing around under the coffee table, all of whom were clearly wondering why there weren't any appetizers set out.

Even my largest chair would not contain my substantial coven mother in such a battery of garments. She chose a padded, armless stool I'd picked up at a neighborhood estate sale and sat carefully, arranging her skirts in a fetching arc around her.

"So, this is the house," Leonora observed, looking through the open pocket doors into the second parlor. "It seems to be well constructed, though I detect some unfamiliar energies."

"It has only ever been inhabited by humans," my father said. "Until now."

"Is that so?" she asked, glancing at me, adding "Thank you" as Logan brought her wine.

"So far as I have been given to understand," Father answered. "Why?"

"Its energetic boundaries feel a little softer than normal." She peered toward the entryway.

"Elnor is particularly fond of that closet," I put in.

Dad smiled. "Well, the house is quite old, for San Francisco. Well-built structures atop strong ley lines can mature and take on...not life, of course, but a better harmony with their surroundings and occupants. As you are of course aware, Leonora."

She nodded. "Was that the reason you chose it?"

"Yes, plus, the price was good. It felt solid and stable—still does—and this is a decent enough neighborhood. Of course, it was purchased as an investment, not a home."

I moved to the front window, monitoring the energy fields around my house for the arrival of more guests as I parsed the conversation so far. What was Leonora digging for? Was Father criticizing me? Their words were all very polite, very mild. I made myself go sit down and sip my drink.

I felt nothing before the doorbell rang—my next guest, I presumed, though fully shielded. Springing up to answer the door, I almost tripped over the party of cats who were now in the middle of the floor. "You guys! Go find some other room to play in." Elnor glanced up at me, and ignored my command.

I opened the door to find Jeremy there. He handed me a small faceted bottle filled with amber-colored liquid, closed with a jeweled stopper. "I know you said not to bring anything, but this is just a small housewarming gift. Put it away to enjoy later."

"Thank you! What is it?"

"Frajella ice wine, from the Old Country."

"Wow. That's...amazing!" He remained on the porch, smiling, until I realized that his gift had thrown me off the ritual of greeting. "Come in, please—welcome to my home."

He stepped over the threshold and paused, surprised. "No wards?"

"No," I said. "They're really not necessary here."

"I'm not sure I've ever been to a witchkind dwelling without them," he remarked. "Even in San Francisco." He shrugged out of his long wool coat—gorgeous, if a bit too warm for this climate. Petrana stepped forward to take it; Jeremy started to hand it to her absently, then gave a little jerk of further surprise. "What...oh, um," he faltered, still clutching his coat.

"This is Petrana," I said.

"Yes! Your golem, of course. Father told me about it." He relinquished the coat, somewhat reluctantly. "You...named it?"

"Well, yes," I said, feeling a little silly. "She doesn't have a whole lot of personality, but it would feel weird to treat her like a machine."

He opened his mouth and closed it again. From the front parlor, I could hear my mother laugh at something.

"Come in," I said, leading Jeremy into the room. Logan blushed and smiled at him; he went to sit next to her.

"Can I get you a frog brandy?" I asked.

"Yes, thank you."

I was just returning from the kitchen with it (and musing that buying a sideboard for this room too would be a good idea) when I sensed Gregorio's arrival, along with a second, less familiar presence. I handed Jeremy his glass as the doorbell rang again.

"Greetings, Calendula Isadora," Gregorio said as I opened the door. "I am afraid Dr. Winterheart is indisposed, so I took the liberty of substituting another of my assistants. You remember Dr. Sebastian Fallon?"

"Yes, of course, nice to see you again." How many young warlocks did Gregorio have in his stable? How were there even room for them in his lab? I shook Dr. Fallon's slightly damp hand. He was wearing an awfully nice suit, almost as nice as Gregorio's own. It set off his dark hair and eyes quite elegantly. "Please, do come in."

Both men nodded and stepped inside. "Thanks for including me!" Dr. Fallon burbled, as if I'd had anything to do with it. He grinned as he looked around the entryway, ignoring the grumbling hostility of the familiars. Warlocks must be used to such things. "Nice house!"

"Thanks," I said with a smile. "And please, call me Callie."

Logan stood at the parlor door. "Bulgarian frog brandies? Or something else?"

"A brandy would be delightful," Gregorio said, and Dr. Fallon nodded agreement.

Neither man was wearing an overcoat, so Petrana stood by, even more awkwardly than usual. Logan had wanted me to have her serve drinks, but I wasn't ready for that. "That's all for now," I said to her. "Please wait in the kitchen until I need you next."

"Yes, Mistress Callie." She walked off down the long hallway, her stride looking maybe a little more natural than before.

Gregorio watched her with undisguised approval, then turned to me. "Truly remarkable, that."

I shrugged, though I couldn't entirely hide my delight at his compliment. I ushered the warlocks into the front parlor; a moment later, Logan returned with their drinks. Dr. Fallon took the chair I had been sitting in, so I sat on the couch between my birth parents. "So!" I said, smiling around at everyone. "Thank you all so much for coming."

"It is an honor to be invited," Gregorio said smoothly.

"Indeed," my mother said, patting my knee. "My little girl is growing up at last!" She smiled brightly. "I mean, of course you are a responsible woman of the world, and a member of the city's best coven, and all."

I kept a smile pasted on my face as I glanced around the room, trying not to cringe noticeably. Everyone—Leonora, most importantly—seemed to be taking the remark in the spirit it was intended. "Thank you, Mother," I said.

Logan caught my eye from across the room, giving me a smile of gentle reassurance as she sipped her drink. Gregorio's expression was unreadable; Jeremy looked—amused?

"This is an awesome house," Dr. Fallon said. "And can I just say, I find it very refreshing, the idea of witches living alone."

I looked at him, my eyes widening. What was *this* about?

"'Refreshing' is one way to regard it, I suppose," Leonora said, her voice dangerously mild. "May *I* just say, there is nothing quite like the focused power of thirteen witches living and working together, day after day, in an unbroken chain of graceful industry."

No one else seemed to catch her undertone—well, no one reacted to it, anyway. Perhaps I was being oversensitive. Or perhaps I knew Leonora better than the rest of them did. My father nodded and smiled. Gregorio said, "It is true, though, the rate of change in the world today is unprecedented."

"But that's how we learn and grow, isn't it, Dr. Andromedus?" Dr. Fallon asked.

"Of course." Gregorio turned to my mother. "Which reminds me, Belladonna Isis: Lucas mentioned the other day that you have received a new contact from the Beyond, without benefit of a full Circle. That is quite extraordinary."

"Oh, it was nothing so spectacular." She gazed back at him with her cool brown eyes. Her earlier burble of excitement was now just a polite smile. "One of my ancestresses sent me a dream, that's all."

"A dream?" Gregorio raised an eyebrow: a perfect, practiced motion. "And you are sure that...?"

"Yes. She described a means of botanical divination I had never even heard of. When I awoke, I performed it three times, and it holds true."

"Ah." Gregorio went on looking at my mother as though they were the only two people in the room. "I have not heard of such a thing in quite an age," he said at last. "I am impressed."

"I did find it interesting myself, yes." My mother's smile was starting to seem a bit fixed. "Though I am not sure what it means." She turned to my father with a softer look on her face. "Lucas, you don't need to brag about me. I've no need to impress anyone."

"I'm just proud of you, my dear." My father shrugged. "Why shouldn't everyone know how your work is going?"

"I am always interested to hear such things," Gregorio said. "It is a crucial part of what keeps us a viable community." He set his empty glass down on the table beside his chair.

"Can I get you another?" I was already on my feet even as I asked the question.

"Yes, thank you."

Back in the kitchen, I took a few deep, calming breaths. Why in the world had I thought throwing all these people together would work? My silly mother. And this Dr. Fallon—a complete wild card. I just had to get through the evening, somehow.

I refilled the drink, then remembered the rack of lamb, prepped and ready to go. It looked amazing: Logan had chopped a bucketload of garlic and rosemary and I don't even know what other spices, creating a paste that encrusted the meat. Tiny red potatoes, steamed to tenderness, sat around the roast, garnished with parsley. She was a marvelous cook. Maybe good food would distract everyone. Maybe we could just all talk about nothing for the entire evening.

I put the meat into the preheated oven, set a small timing spell, and glanced around the kitchen, checking to see what else I'd forgotten. The casserole still sat at the back of the stove. I tasted a bit of it, from the corner. Delicious. Would it need reheating?

Petrana stood against the back wall, impassive as ever. "You can sit down if you like," I told her.

"Do you want me to sit, Mistress Callie?"

"I...honestly have no idea," I told her. "I mean, if *you* want to, then yes." Was she even capable of wanting? "I can't decide if you're a person or not."

"I am a golem."

"Yeah." I stared at her. "*Do* you have feelings?"

"If you want me to have feelings, Mistress Callie."

"How does that even *work*?" Before she could answer, I went on. "I'm sorry, Petrana, I shouldn't be asking you to explain yourself to me." *What is the matter with me? Focus.* "I don't care if you sit or stand."

Without a direct order, she simply stood there. I made myself turn away from her, picking up Gregorio's drink. Then I realized I should have checked on everyone else's. I opened a line of energetic awareness to the front parlor and looked through. Mother could use a refresher, as could Logan. My glass appeared to be empty as well. Actually, within a few minutes, everyone would be ready for another.

But was there time? Twenty minutes was going fast. There would be wine with the meal.

Logan appeared in the kitchen doorway. "Everything all right?"

"Yes—should we get folks to the table?"

She sniffed the air, looking at the stove. Willson strolled up behind her, also sniffing. "The meat needs to rest after it comes out, and it's still got at least ten more minutes in there. So, not yet." Then she studied me. "I didn't think *you'd* hide in the kitchen. Come back, relax. Everything's fine."

"No it's not!" I hissed. "What was I thinking! They're all just humoring me!"

"And what if they are?" she asked, her voice kind. "They're here because they love you. This is your family, and your oldest friends."

"And your new boyfriend, and some dweeby warlock I hardly know!"

She shrugged. "So?"

"So...yes, okay, I suppose he's harmless. If he can just manage to keep his mouth shut."

"It's a *dinner party*, Callie. One evening. Food and drink and conversation. Nothing to be afraid of, nothing bad is going to happen. Okay?"

I sighed. "Okay. Yes." Then I smiled at her. "Sorry."

She gave me a quick hug. "No problem. Now, let's go enjoy ourselves."

"Right. Can you take this in to Dr. Andromedus?" I handed her the glass of brandy, grabbed the bottle of elderflower wine, and followed her back out.

I finally relaxed a little once we were seated around the dining table. Here, the rules seemed clearer, and there was something for everyone to do: eat, sip wine, and compliment everything. Plus, the formal seating chart meant that I had Logan right next to me. Her calm presence was a continued comfort. After a few minutes, the table broke up into several smaller conversations. Dr. Fallon, at the far end, began telling my mother a story. She leaned in, looking fascinated. My father also listened, with an air of polite, professional detachment.

"Father," Jeremy said to Gregorio at our end of the table, "you never mentioned that Logan here has a connection to the Old Country. I was wondering if we could help her find out what might have transpired with her parents."

"Her parents?" Gregorio dabbed at the corner of his mouth with his napkin.

"Augustus Schriff and Lorenna Rosemary. Did you know them?"

"Yes, of course I did," Gregorio said, giving Logan a gentle smile as he set his napkin down. "Though I fear I cannot help Logandina any more than I already have," he went on, to Jeremy. "All the San Francisco Elders, as well as the major covens, devoted a great deal of attention to this matter when Augustus and Lorenna disappeared. Unfortunately, the trail went completely cold after they left Zchellenin. I cannot imagine the passage of so many years has made information any *easier* to obtain."

"All the same, I thought I might look into it when I travel back to the Old Country next month," Jeremy said. "It would be no trouble for me to ask around."

"Your itinerary is already quite full," Gregorio said. "I am not certain you will have room to add another large endeavor…particularly one which has already been so thoroughly explored by so many others before you."

Jeremy and Logan exchanged a brief, warm glance before he looked back to his father. "All the same, I'd love to see what I can find out—when I can make the time, of course. Assuming you have no objections?"

"Of course not. I would be greatly interested to learn anything you may discover on the matter. The incident still disturbs me." Gregorio turned again to Logan, his eyes kind. "As I know it does you quite a bit more, my dear."

Logan blushed and glanced down at her plate as her shyness took over momentarily. Then she cleared her throat. "It's...baffling, honestly. I feel as though we ought to be able to know everything. To be able to find them."

"Not if those aligned against us are equally powerful."

"Oh?" I asked.

Jeremy turned to me. "There are...factions... In the Old Country, at least. It's complicated." He glanced across the table at his father, as if asking permission to bring such unpleasant topics to the dinner table.

Leonora leaned forward and interjected, "We provide a thorough education regarding the Old Country here, young man. Its history and its politics. I should have thought Calendula would recall discussion of these matters from her own training."

I felt my face redden with chagrin—I might have known she'd be listening to our conversation from her end of the table. Of course I'd studied the Iron Rose and the troubles, though it had been decades since my school days. But beyond what Jeremy had mentioned at Logan's birthday gathering, I knew very few recent details; there was not a lot of correspondence between the Old Country and here. "Right," I managed.

Logan patted my knee under the table as Jeremy answered smoothly. "You must forgive me, Leonora Scanza. My understanding of the world outside the Old Country is grievously incomplete. I meant no insult to San Francisco's educational system or to your esteemed coven in particular."

"Hm," she allowed.

"I would be pleased to learn more, in fact," he went on. "I have a great interest in everything about the wider world—it is why I have come here. Education is the foundation of so much." He gave her a humble smile, his bright eyes warm and glowing. "Though of course, a coven mother of your stature would surely have little time to school a newcomer like me."

I stifled a smile at this. Old Country manners were certainly, well, thicker than ours here.

Leonora did not appear to share my opinion. She smiled more naturally. "I would be pleased to assist in the continuance of your education. Send me a note next week, and we shall find a convenient time."

At the corner of my awareness, I thought I heard my cell phone ringing. Up on the second floor, in my bedroom... I sent my senses out, seeking the only one who would be calling me.

Oh no.

At my right hand, Gregorio seemed to sense my alarm, and mistook its cause. "Allow me," he said, refilling my glass of Margaux.

"Thank you..." I murmured, helpless as the doorbell rang.

Conversation stopped as the entire table looked at me.

"I...excuse me," I said, pushing my chair back.

I almost ran into Petrana in the hallway, coming to take the latest guest's coat, as instructed. "No! Back to the kitchen!" I hissed at her.

"Yes, Mistress Callie."

Reaching the front hall, I cracked the door, standing to block the narrow opening. "Raymond," I said. "It's not a good—"

"I know," he said. He was disheveled, breathing a bit heavily. I could see beads of sweat on his forehead. He clutched his phone. "It's *never* a good time. You said you wanted to see me, and then broke our date. I haven't seen you in a week. You don't answer your phone. You don't talk to me, you don't have time for me..."

"I will—I promise," I said. "Tomorrow. Just—busy—can we do this tomorrow?"

"If you're breaking up with me, just do it now!" He took a step forward. I could smell beer on his breath. A *lot* of beer. "Who you got in there?" He blinked, then seemed to actually see me. "Fancy dress."

"I'm having some...family...over for dinner. Raymond, you *have* to go."

"I'm not good enough to meet your family?" He took another step forward. Now his foot was on the threshold. Being human, of course, he did not even know about ritual permission to enter. He could just bluster in here...

I took a step back, startled at the thought; he followed me right in. "Been dating a year, and I've never even *heard* about any family of yours!" he said, his voice rising.

"Raymond, get *out* of here!" Panicked, I glanced back—there were footsteps in the hallway behind me—oh no, there was my mother, with Jeremy right behind her.

"Darling?" my mother asked, one sculpted eyebrow raised, the skirt of her Dior gown falling perfectly around her slender ankles.

"Um, this is, um, Raymond," I stammered, still somehow trying to salvage the situation. "Raymond, this is my mother, Belladonna Isis, and...Jeremiah Andromedus."

Raymond glared at me, then at the two of them. His mouth hung open. Maybe it was the names, or the beer; maybe it was just because my mother didn't look a day older than I did.

"Calendula?" Jeremy asked, his accent smooth and cultured. "Do you need any assistance?"

"Assistance!" Raymond snarled as he reanimated and stepped toward Jeremy.

My hands moved almost of their own volition as I cast a spell of fog on Raymond's mind. With a small sigh, he crumpled to the floor, his eyes open but blank.

"Oh Blessed Mother," I moaned. "I'm so—"

"Is this...the human?" Mom asked, unnecessarily.

"Yes." I turned to Jeremy. "I'm so sorry! I..."

Jeremy glanced down at Raymond. I followed his gaze; my boyfriend was a sorry sight indeed. Tattered jeans, rough leather jacket, tangled hair. He needed a shave. And a bath. Jeremy cleared his throat and said, "I take it this is not merely a matter of putting him out on the street and erasing his mind?"

"No! I, er, no." If I'd thought I was blushing earlier, that was nothing to what was happening now. "I've been...he's...I'm seeing him."

"Seeing?"

I heard the scrape of chairs on the dining room's hardwood floor. Logan and Gregorio had followed us to the front hall, the old warlock laying a protective hand on her arm. My father, Dr. Fallon, and Leonora now crowded in behind them.

"Oh dear," my father said wearily.

"Is he injured?" Dr. Fallon asked, leaning down to examine Raymond.

"Er—no, just fogged," I said.

Leonora loomed behind him now. "Calendula? What is the meaning of this?"

"Mother Leonora, I can explain."

"It's the human," my birth mother told her. "The one she has been—"

"*That* is not the part I am confused about," Leonora interrupted. "I did not expect she would invite him to our gathering."

"I didn't!" I squeaked. "He just...turned up."

"I see," Leonora said, gazing at Raymond in obvious disdain.

"We need to get him onto the couch!" I said, desperate for—I didn't even know what. Distraction. For this not to be happening.

But it was.

Gregorio pointed at Raymond, sending the power necessary to move my human boyfriend into the next room and onto the couch in one smooth motion. He did it without even looking winded. "There you are, Calendula," he said, with an indulgent smile.

I rushed into the front parlor, resisting the urge to wring my hands. The rest of the guests followed me. Elnor was already there, sniffing at Raymond suspiciously. She rubbed against my calves, sending feline comfort to her mistress.

It wasn't nearly enough.

Raymond was technically awake, though perceiving—and, hopefully, remembering—nothing. His breathing had softened; his glazed-over eyes pointed in the general direction of the ceiling.

"Now perhaps you see why such relationships are unwise," Leonora said, adjusting the skirts of her magnificent costume. "Humans do not belong in our world, nor we in theirs; eventually, one comes to realize this."

"Callie, we've talked about this," my birth mother put in, gently.

Gregorio gave a benevolent chuckle. "Nevertheless, every new generation feels the need to test boundaries, to learn for themselves. Did you never dally in such experiments, Leonora Scanza?"

She sniffed. "Surely I did not go so far as to give humans free access to any dwelling of mine."

"I haven't given him free access," I said, turning to face her, my voice rising. "He doesn't even have a key."

"He not only knows where it is, he appears to be entirely comfortable dropping by," Leonora said, sternly. "I agreed to your move here so that you might conduct your *research* more easily."

"That's not fair!" I almost shouted. "I barely see him—that's what he's mad about."

My father cleared his throat and gave my mother a knowing glance. She patted my arm.

I struggled to fight down a surge of anger. How dare they lecture me like I was a child? "Leonora, you don't own me—none of you do. This is my home, which I *do* own. I fulfill all my responsibilities to the coven, to witchkind, and to the world at large. Nobody, and I mean *nobody*, has the right to tell me who I should or shouldn't associate with—here or anywhere else."

My guests gazed back at me, stunned at my outburst. Leonora looked livid, my father embarrassed; my mother simply looked sad. At the back of the group, I could see Dr. Fallon nodding, very subtly.

So much for a lovely evening. I might as well finish. "Yes, I am dating this man. This *human*. And he's clearly drunk, and angry at me because I've had very little time for him lately—not that that is anyone's business but his and mine either." I took another breath. "I'm sorry this happened during our dinner party, and I'm particularly sorry that Logan's delicious meal is now sitting cold on the table."

"Oh, I…" Logan murmured. "Gosh, don't worry about that." She put her hand on the back of a chair, leaning into it, looking a little ill. Oh, how she hated conflict.

"Should we…be leaving him in the fog this long?" Dr. Fallon asked, tentatively. "It can damage his mind."

"No—of course not," I said. Did even he think I was an idiot? It had been what, two minutes?

"Just turn him out," Leonora said. "He will learn not to impose like this if you are firm with him. As you should have been from the start."

Oh, Raymond, why did you have to do this! "I am not going to turn him out," I said to her, gritting my teeth. "He's not a dog."

Dr. Fallon bent down, laying Raymond's limp arm across his chest. "Humans are fascinating—their internal processes so much like ours, yet so fundamentally different. He is quite intoxicated, isn't he."

"He just needs to sleep it off," I said. I put my hand on Raymond's forehead, then opened my energetic awareness to the rhythm of his heartbeat, breathing, and jumbled, frozen thoughts. I eased the fog away while inserting *sleep* messages in its place, sending him down deep before letting go of any magical influence on him.

His eyes closed. A soft snore escaped his nose.

I removed my hand and stood back up. Dr. Fallon touched Raymond's forehead, then chest, and nodded. "Yes, that will be all right, I think."

Logan had her hand on her stomach; she looked distinctly uncomfortable. Her familiar, Willson, was hovering close to her. Elnor went and sniffed at him, then looked at me.

"Dear, are you all right?" my mother asked Logan. "You look pale."

"I…I'm feeling a little overwhelmed," she said. "I think I need to sit down for a few minutes." She sank into the chair she was holding onto and closed her eyes. What was wrong? This was more than an aversion to conflict. I went to put a hand on her forehead, opening my senses once again. Her essence was oddly low, and I sensed a turbulence in her stomach. Willson sat near her feet, Elnor and Grieka right by him.

"There *has* been a great deal of unfortunate excitement," Leonora said, pointedly.

"Indeed," Gregorio put in, looking sober. "Dr. Fallon, perhaps you could take a look at Logandina as well?"

"Oh! Yes." He jumped up from Raymond and went to Logan's chair. "Have you been ill recently?" he asked her.

"No," Logan murmured.

"Too much excitement?" I asked.

"I don't know. I just need a minute. I'm sure I'll be fine." She gave us all a wan smile, then closed her eyes again. "I'm so sorry."

"Don't apologize!" I stood back as Dr. Fallon continued to examine her. "Do you want anything? Tea?"

"Nothing. Just rest. Thank you."

Dr. Fallon glanced up at me, then at Gregorio, with a worried frown.

"Let me have a look," the elder warlock said. He took Logan's hand in his, reading her pulse and all the energetic information behind it. After a minute, he said, "No, there is no recent illness here. I detect something sudden. And…" He paused, looking perplexed. "It seems externally sourced."

"Externally sourced?" I asked.

"An infectious agent, a grave injury—something of that sort." Gregorio frowned.

"Well, she obviously hasn't been injured," I said. "Food poisoning maybe?"

"I am trying to determine the cause." Gregorio's tone was short; his eyes were focused somewhere else even as he held onto her hand. I waited, tense. Beside me, I could feel both my mother and Leonora opening channels as well, though they were looking outward.

"I cannot detect any origin—it seems to simply appear," Gregorio said, a minute later. "This is outside my area of expertise. A healer should be called at once." He let go of her hand and stood up, his focus shifting away again for a moment. "Manka is available. I've sent a message."

On the couch, Raymond let out another snore. Willson leapt up onto Logan's chair, settling next to her as she slumped down further. Was she falling asleep, or passing out? Her hand draped to the floor; her pretty gown was being crushed underneath her. Her hair lay limp, inert, bangs flat against her damp forehead.

"Logan!" I said, more alarmed by the moment. I grabbed her hand again. Her skin was clammy. Her breathing was almost undetectable.

"I find nothing of danger in the immediate area," Leonora put in, closing her channel. "Fortunate that she happened to be in company when it happened, at least." Beside her, my mother nodded, frowning.

I bristled at the implication. *Yes, Leonora,* I thought, *please tell us more about the perils of living alone.*

Willson began yowling, jumping down to pace the floor around his mistress's feet. His distress was infectious; the other familiars starting meowing as well.

"Dr. Andromedus," Dr. Fallon said, his voice tense. "She seems to be actively leaching essence—it's lower every minute. What *is* this?"

Gregorio shook his head. "I cannot say. Her system is under assault, seemingly from nowhere."

"Assault? *Why?*" I felt like one of the cats, pacing around and yowling ineffectually. "Where is her essence going?"

"That is what I am attempting to find out," Dr. Andromedus said, leaning in closer. "I can slow the drain, but until we discover what is causing this…" He waved his hands and muttered a string of words, laying a complicated spell over her. She gave a soft sigh, and seemed to breathe more easily. "I have seen something like this once before, but not for many decades," the warlock added, almost under his breath. "I thought…"

My panicked mind tried to make sense of this. Then I remembered. "Your…consort?" Jeremy's mother.

For a moment, Gregorio's face became an open book, showing unimaginable pain. "It could be," he said in a near-whisper. Then he almost visibly pulled himself together and addressed the room. "Logandina is safe for the moment. When Manka gets here, she should be able to provide more insight. Meanwhile, let us move her to a more appropriate venue than this chair." He glanced, with some distaste, at Raymond, still snoring on the sofa.

I felt helpless, desperate. "Um…beds, upstairs…"

"No need." Gregorio flicked his fingers, pulling a daybed through the æther and setting it in the second parlor.

"You two, lift her—gently," Leonora commanded, pointing to Jeremy and Dr. Fallon. They picked up the unconscious Logan manually and laid her on the daybed. I pulled a small chair over and sat in it, taking Logan's hand.

"Should I give her some of my essence?" I asked.

"Perhaps," Gregorio said. "Let us wait and see what Manka prescribes, though. There is no immediate danger now."

The rest of the party milled around in the second parlor, waiting for the healer. She would come on the ley line, of course, but it would still take a few minutes.

My birth mother said, "Would anyone like some tea?"

I nodded. "Thank you."

Mom went off to the kitchen, returning a minute later with cups for everyone. I took one sip of mine and set it down. At least Willson had stopped yowling. Now he lay curled at Logan's feet, purring insistently. I reached for Logan's forehead again, brushing aside lank bangs. Was her essence lower than a minute ago? I couldn't tell. I took my hand away. Tried to sip my tea.

Leonora carried her cup into the front parlor, taking her former seat there. Most of the others drifted toward the front room as well, pointedly ignoring Raymond.

After basically forever, I felt Manka's presence approaching the house, and hurried over to bid her enter.

Manka wore simple, dark, traditional robes, short-sleeved to allow for freedom of movement. Her long salt-and-pepper hair was pulled back into a ponytail fastened by a red cord; the cord's long tails wove around the ponytail, holding it firm. She carried a black leather bag, within which I could hear bottles and jars clinking.

"Thank you, Calendula Isadora," she said, stepping over the threshold. "The patient—?"

"In here."

In the second parlor, Manka bent to examine Logan, touching her at all the energetic nexuses. After a minute, she pulled three bottles out of her bag, pouring a bit of powder from each of them into the palm of her hand. She spat into her palm, rubbed the powders into a paste, and placed bits of the paste on Logan's wrists, temples, and the base of her throat. Then she leaned in again, holding perfectly still for several minutes.

She straightened up and addressed us all. "It is an essence-draining illness, though one I have not encountered before," she said, her mouth a grim line. "I cannot identify the origin, or even its point of entry into her system."

"Neither could Dr. Andromedus or Dr. Fallon," I said. "What *is* it?"

She looked around at all of us. "This just happened?"

"Yes," Gregorio said, "and quite suddenly. We were all enjoying a quiet dinner party, which was, er, briefly interrupted." His eyes darted toward the front parlor. "Logandina Fleur took ill immediately thereafter."

"Surely the human could have had nothing to do with that," my father put in.

"Of course not," Leonora said.

Manka shook her head. "And the rest of you feel fine?"

"Yes," I said, to nods of agreement all around.

"I would like to examine any remains of the meal," Manka said. "You are certain she did not eat or drink anything that no one else did?"

"I don't think so," I said. "It's all still in there." I waved toward the dining room.

She nodded and began to pull out a number of vials, then suddenly stopped. "Wait—there is an unaccounted-for presence." She looked at me sharply. "I sense your essence...in some way partitioned."

"What? Oh—Petrana." At Manka's quizzical look, I said, "My golem."

The healer blinked at me. Had she not heard? She would be the only one in the city, if so. "I will need to examine the creature as well."

"Of course. Do you want me to get her now?"

"Not yet. I am not finished with the patient. Is the golem capable of working magic?"

"Um, only a bit. Little things...nothing like this." I felt desperate. "Can you *heal* Logan?"

"In theory, any magical injury can be made whole," Manka said, in the weary but gentle tone of one who has given unpleasant news many times over her long life. "If I knew the exact nature of the infectious agent, I could simply untie its knot, as it were. Unfortunately, that may take some time. I shall need to take some blood and saliva from the patient, in addition to samples of whatever she consumed."

"But, this is crazy!" I protested. "Diseases don't just...*attack* like this!"

My father gave me a sad smile as Gregorio said, "Calendula, it appears that one has. As I mentioned, I have in fact seen something similar to this before, though a long time ago. I will work with Manka to determine the cause."

I sat back down in the little chair and took Logan's limp hand. "I just don't understand."

My father came and put a gentle hand on my shoulder.

"Take heart," Gregorio said. "We will solve this mystery."

— CHAPTER EIGHT —

I hugged my parents goodbye and closed the front door behind them. Gregorio and Manka had already left with the samples. Now only Leonora, Dr. Fallon, and Jeremy remained. The green-eyed warlock sat by Logan's bedside, holding her hand in his. If only she'd been conscious to know it.

"You might have asked Belladonna to stay," Leonora said in a quiet voice. Her whole disapproving demeanor had softened in the last few minutes. Logan's crisis seemed to have shifted something in her. At least for now. "She clearly wishes to help you."

"I…" I shrugged. "I know. But her help… I know she means well, but I think she still sees me as a witchlet of sixteen."

Leonora smiled. "I understand." She reached down and petted Grieka absently. "Given Logandina's life focus, however, she might well respond to Belladonna's more intuitively-based care."

"Wild magic," I murmured. Yes, my mother and my best friend did have that in common. Perhaps I should invite Mom back. Tomorrow. "I just need it to be a little…quieter around here right now."

"I understand that as well." Leonora got to her feet. "And I will leave you to whatever peace you may manage to find." She eyed Raymond, still in his spelled sleep on the couch. Logan's illness had certainly put *that* issue into perspective.

"Good night, Mother," I said.

She picked up her cat. "I will see myself out."

"Do you mind if I stay a little longer?" Jeremy asked softly, after my coven mother had gone. "I think her essence may be strengthening a little, though it's hard to tell."

"Really?" I glanced at Dr. Fallon, who had just examined her again a moment ago.

"It might be," the young warlock said. "If so, it's subtle. At the very least, Dr. Andromedus's spell seems to be holding—her essence is no longer draining away."

I put my hand on Logan's forehead to see for myself. It was as they said: not worsening. "Stay as long as you like," I told Jeremy. "I know she'd be thrilled to have your company if she were awake."

He smiled at me and turned his gaze back to her.

"Would you like some help cleaning up?" Dr. Fallon asked.

Oh, Blessed Mother, the half-eaten dinner was still all over the table. We'd never even gotten to dessert. "My golem—" I started, then changed my mind. It was hard to imagine a warlock willing to wash dishes, but... "Yes, I would, thank you."

He followed me into the dining room. "I'd just like to say..." He hesitated. "In spite of everything that's happened, and at the risk of sounding completely insensitive, it really has been such a pleasure to get to know you better, Callie."

"Well, thank you, Dr. Fallon."

"Please, call me Sebastian."

"Sure." I smiled back at him.

Together, we carried all the dishes to the kitchen, put the extra food away, and began washing up, all by hand. I wasn't sure I could focus on doing it magically. And there was something soothing about hot water and soap, the rhythm of the movements. Making things clean, one by one.

"Actually..." Sebastian said as he dried the dishes, stacking them on the kitchen table for me to put away later, "I've been hoping all evening for a chance to talk with you more privately."

Oh for crying out loud, what was this? "More privately"? This was just *not* the time. "What is your area of research, Sebastian?" I blurted out, reaching for the first safe subject that came to mind.

"I plan to be a healer, actually," he said.

"Really?" I turned to look at him, surprised.

"Yes. My work with Dr. Andromedus is just a general internship, getting a basic biological education before focusing on patient care."

"Isn't that a bit...unusual for a warlock?"

He gave me a shy smile as he took another plate out of the drainer. "I suppose. But I've always felt drawn to it. I tried a few other things, but they didn't work out. Finally, I just decided to go for it."

I thought about how Manka had interacted with him—or hadn't, rather. She'd come in, examined Logan, spoken to me, and Leonora, and Gregorio...and left. I hadn't even noticed. Was she avoiding him deliberately? Did she even know? "Are you getting much pushback?"

"Some," he admitted. "But times are changing, don't you think? I mean, just look at your party tonight. Traditional in form, yes; but there's nothing traditional about a dinner being given by an unaffiliated witch and a witch who's not living in her coven—much less one who's openly dating a human."

"Yeah." *And what's your point?* I added silently. He'd as much as said this earlier.

"And you invited two prominent Elders, the city's most important coven leader, a botanical worker, and a medical intern. What a varied group! All together, hanging out, as equals."

"Well, I'm related to half of those people," I pointed out, smiling. "And don't forget that the human is drunk and spelled, sleeping on my couch."

He gave a rueful grin in return. "Well. There is that." Then he grew more serious. "But that still makes my point, doesn't it? Not that long ago, someone like Leonora would just have thrown him onto the street, no discussion, wouldn't she? Probably blanked his mind permanently in the process. Coven mothers *did* have what amounted to ownership of the witches in their houses, didn't they?"

"I don't know," I said, thinking about it. "No, not quite like that. Or at least that hasn't been the case for a long while. When we blood-swear to a coven, we agree to a lot of general things about honor and respect and—well, not blind obedience, but we do agree to honor the coven mother's leadership." I ran a platter under the hot water and soaped it up. "There aren't such ironclad rules, though." I smiled at him. "It is assumed, I guess, that a good witch will spend her un-unioned life in a coven house… Like people might assume warlocks wouldn't choose to become healers. Is that what you're getting at?"

"It's nothing my parents ever imagined I'd be doing, put it that way."

"I'll bet not. How are they taking it?"

"It's not the only thing I've surprised them with," he said, giving me a teasing smile. "My dating life is probably even more complicated than yours."

"Oh?" I turned from the sink to look at him, and dried my hands. This was proving to be a more interesting conversation by the minute.

"They haven't given up on finding me a nice witch to form a union with," he said. "My mother never tires of explaining to me that as long as we had a child or two, I would be free to spend the rest of my time with…*whatever fellows I like.*" He gave the last phrase such an ironic lilt that I could almost hear his mother's voice, though I had never met her.

"Oh!" I gave a short laugh. "You really aren't too wedded to tradition then, are you?"

"No." We shared a smile as he dried off one last platter. "Not witchkind tradition, anyway. Humans are well ahead of us in this one."

"Yes." I thought a moment. Though witchkind society strongly held to notions of bedroom privacy, formal unions were explicitly contracted between one warlock and one witch, as such arrangements were chiefly intended for procreation. I didn't know, or know of, any openly gay witches or warlocks. "Does Gregorio know?"

"Who can tell what someone like Dr. Andromedus knows?" he said casually. "But I have never discussed it with him. My parents know, of course, and I have no idea who else they may have told." He shrugged. "There are a few others. It's not a dire secret, but...it's nothing I tend to advertise. I'm sure you understand."

I nodded. Everything I'd thought about this man was turning upside down. And here I'd been wondering if he was working up to asking me out.

"That's why I've wanted this chance to talk," he said. "It's so rare to meet someone—anyone, really—who's...testing any of the unexamined assumptions that define our lives."

"I suppose," I said slowly. He wasn't wrong; Logan had been living this way for decades, but beyond me, she largely kept to herself. "I just...needed more space for my research. And I was finding coven life increasingly stifling. I'm nearly a half-century old; I felt it was time for a bit more freedom. Not just for dating whoever I want to, though that is certainly a big part of it."

"Exactly," he said with a smile.

"I always thought it was witches who were locked into tradition, while you guys were totally free." I picked up a stack of dishes and started putting them in the cupboard. "I guess it's all more complicated than I realized."

Now that I thought about it, most of the warlocks I knew were either scientist-scholars, managed money, or pursued some form of politics, like Jeremy. They rarely seemed to go into anything so mundane as lower level education, or gardening, or the decorative arts...or healing.

I wondered how many warlocks felt as constrained as I did, how many were privately struggling with the same kinds of questions.

Clearly not all of them. I recalled Jeremy's companions at Rose's on the night of Logan's birthday—their sneering dismissal of an unaffiliated witch, one who worked with *tarot*. We all had a ways to go, it seemed.

But talking to each other like this—this was a good start, I thought.

"There we are," Sebastian said, handing me the big platter. I placed it on a high shelf in the cabinet. "I'll go check on the patient one last time, and then leave you to that peace you wanted."

"You can stay over too, if you like," I said. "I have a guest bed."

"Thanks, but if she's stable, I should probably get home." He grinned. "Need to feed my cat."

"You have a *familiar*?" Healer warlocks, gay warlocks—that I could handle. But...

He laughed. "She's just a cat, nothing more. And she's probably pretty hungry by now."

Elnor, at my feet, took the opportunity to remind me that she, too, had been denied her dinner, and was on the verge of certain, dire, imminent starvation.

Sebastian pronounced Logan the same as before, and took his leave, promising to return in the morning.

Now Jeremy sat quietly by Logan. In answer to my offer of tea, or brandy, or dessert, or even a more comfortable chair, he said, "I'm fine. You rest."

"Soon," I said.

I went through the double doorway to the front parlor and stood staring down at Raymond. It had been several hours since I'd spelled him to sleep. Were there still vestiges of the spell in him, or was he just sleeping normally now? I tried to search his essence, but it's harder to tell with humans. Many of them have latent, vestigial magical pathways in their bodies, a holdover from the days when we were all one species. Yet they were far too atrophied to read easily.

"Wake up," I whispered to Raymond, directing a magical line of energy at him to reinforce my words and unmake my sleep-spell. "Wake up."

He murmured and shifted on the couch. I could still smell the alcohol heavy on his breath—not just beer, but something stronger underneath.

"Wake up."

After another minute, he blinked, then blearily focused on me. "Callie?"

"How are you feeling?" I asked him.

"Um." He closed his eyes, then opened them again. "Hung over? Did I...?" He sat up a little and looked around. "Did I pass out on your couch?"

"Sort of." I gave him a gentle smile. "Do you feel okay enough to get yourself home?"

"Home?" His face fell as his awareness sharpened. "I can't stay here?"

"Honey," I said, "we do need to talk, but right now, I need you to go home." I could almost feel Jeremy carefully ignoring our conversation, in the next room.

Raymond sat up further, putting his feet on the floor, wobbling a little. Then he glanced through the open double doors, noticing Jeremy...and Logan. "Who...?"

Don't make me fog you again, I thought. "These are friends of mine, and one of them is very sick." A brilliant thought struck me. "Probably highly contagious—we're not sure, but we think it might be hemorrhagic fever. It would be a lot safer for you to not be here."

"Oh. Um. Right!" Raymond slowly got to his feet, still blinking. Shaking away the fog, the spelled sleep, the alcohol, or some combination of all three. "Yeah." He looked around. "Did I have a jacket?"

"You're wearing it." I gave him another gentle smile, then herded him into the front hall. Good, it seemed like he didn't remember anything. "I'll call you...in a few days."

"Yeah. Um." At the front door, he stopped and turned to me, confusion written all over his adorable face. "I'm...sorry?"

"Oh, Raymond." I pulled him into a strong hug, holding him for a while. Then I drew back and kissed him. "You have nothing to be sorry for. But go on, now, while you're still safe."

"Yeah." He kissed me, then turned to leave.

I locked the door behind him and sighed, then went into the second parlor.

"Hemorrhagic fever?" Jeremy asked with a minuscule smile.

"Oh, Blessed Mother." I sank down into a second chair. "That was awkward all the way around."

Now Jeremy gave a small snort of laughter. "Awkward! Yes, that would be one way to put it."

I looked down at Logan. She was so very, very still. "No change?"

"I don't think so." Jeremy looked up at me. "I gave her some of my essence, but I cannot tell if she's holding it or not."

"Let me try." Witch essence would be better suited for her than warlock essence, though in a pinch, they would both work. It's not quite as fussy as blood type—his essence wouldn't harm her—but mine would be a better match.

I put my hands on her chest and concentrated, sending her a measure of my own essence—my strength, my power, the ineffable energies that made me a witch. I felt it flow into her, find its way into her system. After a minute, I closed the channel and removed my hands.

"There. We'll see how that does her." She did seem to be breathing a little easier, though she hadn't stirred.

"You should get some sleep," Jeremy said.

"I don't need to, I slept last night," I said.

"It feels graceless to say this, but I disagree. It seems to me that you are in desperate need of sleep—and you were even before you donated so much essence. Of course I will wake you at once should anything change."

His words seemed a bit pompous, but the tone—and the kind intention clear in his face—were anything but. He was trying to take care of both of us, in the best way he knew how. And, to tell the truth, I was completely exhausted. The dinner party—and every-thing leading up to it. Raymond. Logan. The transfusion. Now that I thought about it, *had* I actually slept last night?

I smiled at him. Elnor rubbed against my ankles, somehow unders-tanding that bed was under discussion, now that dinner had been taken care of. "All right. I'll be up on the second floor. Let me know if *anything* changes."

"I shall."

I got up briefly at five a.m. and went to check on Logan. Nothing had changed. Jeremy sent me back to bed.

The next time I woke, I was already weeping.

Jeremy was sitting on my bed, holding me by the shoulders, and trembling; no, he was shaking me. "Callie, please wake up!"

Strong sunlight was pouring through my bedroom windows; my pillow was moist with drool as well as tears. My dream had been of Raymond—his warm strong body, his cool soft hair, interwoven with a strong sense of loss—but the sorrow I felt was more immediate.

"I'm so sorry," Jeremy said, when he saw I was awake. "I don't know what happened, she slipped away, between one moment and the next..."

I jerked away from him as understanding dawned. Beside me, Elnor gave a low hiss, the fur rising on her back. Jeremy let go of me and stood up. "What?" I asked as I scrambled for some clothes; I'd been sleeping in a T-shirt and underwear. "She...what? What are you *saying* to me?" I struggled to keep my voice from rising to a panicked scream.

"I just—just come." He averted his eyes as I pulled on a pair of jeans. I followed him down to the second parlor.

Logan lay on the daybed, perfectly still. It was obvious that her essence was completely gone. Her eyes were closed, almost sunken. Though she was pale, there was a faint rosy tinge in her cheeks: a cruel mockery of life. Willson was standing on her chest, wailing in bewildered misery. Elnor, by my feet, joined in his cries.

I fell to my knees by the daybed, leaning over my best friend, touching her forehead, her hands, her hair. She was cool, and dry, and empty. This vessel no longer contained her. "Oh, Logan," I said, my voice cracking. I turned back to face Jeremy. "What in the Blessed Mother's seven names *happened*?" I reached up to pet Willson, trying to calm him down, but I probably only made things worse. Elnor jumped up beside him, nudging him with her forehead even as she cried with him.

Jeremy stood in the middle of the room, looking lost. "I was watching her sleep. She appeared peaceful, resting. Then, she did not draw in a breath, and she was gone. It was quiet as that...between one breath and the next, she left us. I tried to give her essence, but she wasn't there to take it."

"No!" I shook my head violently. "That's not how it works. That's not what happened."

"Callie." Jeremy's voice was very gentle, very sad. "I am sorry."

"She can't be gone. Get Manka here—call to her!"

"She is already on her way."

"You didn't see Logan shift or move or...*anything*?" Did I think I could talk him into a different answer? Somehow change what I could see so clearly before me?

"Nothing," Jeremy said. His face held heavy grief, and bewilderment.

Manka was there in minutes, rushing to Logan's side. She quieted both cats, and even got Willson to move off his mistress and down to the floor. "What happened?"

Jeremy told her what he'd told me.

Frowning, Manka touched Logan's body once again, in all the same places she had examined last night. "Had she eaten or drunk anything further?" she asked Jeremy.

"Nothing at all," he answered. "We both gave her some essence, but that was all." He looked pale and drawn. Frightened. "What could it have been?"

"I just don't know." She shook her head. "I know no natural illness that moves this way."

"*Natural* illness?" I asked.

Manka said, "I'd like to get Nora here."

I nodded. Nora was not as experienced a healer as Manka, but her area of focus was different. More modern, more proactive.

But how do you heal complete departure?

Nora arrived not long thereafter, requesting admission straight from the ley line rather than bothering with the front door. *Enter*, I sent, and there she was, peering down at the body.

"Logandina made no decision to journey Beyond?" she asked, pushing her short auburn hair behind her ears. A lock escaped at once; she ignored it.

"No!" I cried, my voice catching. "She didn't want to move on! This is too crazy!"

Willson growled at my tone. I petted him again as Nora gave me a look. "I am truly sorry for your loss," she said calmly. "Do you wish to relax in another room while I scry?"

It was gently put, but pointed: my confusion and denial and despair would disrupt the energy in here dramatically. I took a deep breath. "That might be a good idea."

Manka patted my shoulder, sending me calming energy. Blinking back tears and swallowing against the giant lump in my throat, I walked back to the kitchen, managing to hold it together until I closed the door behind me. Then I collapsed, sobbing and shaking, sitting on the floor. My hair ran wild around me, twining and tangling, roping around my neck.

After a while, I gathered myself, pulled my hair back into a ponytail, and returned to the second parlor. "All right if I come in?" I asked, trying for a brave smile.

Nora nodded. I stepped in and stood by Jeremy, averting my eyes from Logan—the sight of her dear face was liable to send me back into sobbing. I held my energy as still as possible as the warlock and I watched the healer work.

A scrying mirror and a number of small pots of oils and powders sat on the side table. Nora was clearly in the middle of a complicated ritual, occasionally asking Manka to hand her things. I didn't recognize the magic. Which wasn't surprising, as it was about as far from laboratory magic as possible. It involved a low, quiet song, and oils that smelled like mushrooms, and long moments of gazing into her mirror.

"Is she finding out what happened?" I whispered to Manka, after a while.

"Not now. She's searching the Beyond for Logandina herself."

And clearly finding nothing, if the look on her face was any indication. I sat quietly, trying not to interfere, even with my silent emotions. Jeremy put a gentle hand on my shoulder, then took it away a minute later.

"I am sorry," Nora said at last, returning her attention to the room. "I had hoped to contact her spirit, but it is not in any of the realms I have access to."

"What does that mean?" I asked. "Are there other places besides the Beyond?"

"Yes and no," Manka said with a sad smile. "There are levels of Beyond, and layers and folds within those levels that we do know."

I nodded impatiently. "And you can't access them all?"

"No one can," Nora said. "Just as you cannot travel past wards that are designed to block you, and Manka cannot hold someone here if she's decided to move on, and your cat cannot speak to you in human language. There are limitations in everything and everyone."

"But it is not unheard of that a spirit's transition to the realms that we do have access to should take a little while," Manka put in. "The journey is not always instantaneous. We should be able to contact her soon, and that will help us untangle what has transpired."

"Okay." I dropped my head, closing my eyes as they filled with tears, trying not to let myself feel the pang of hope. Once a spirit departed, it often came back to communicate with us here, though without returning to its former body. "I just...it can't..."

Jeremy touched my shoulder again, softly. "I will help you in any way I can."

"Thank you." It was kind of him. He was grieving too. They had barely started their romance, but he must be feeling her loss keenly.

Nora began repacking her bag, then paused a moment, clearly engaged in ætheric communication. "The Elders would like to send a few channelers to look around, if you will permit it, Calendula," she said.

"Channelers?"

Jeremy looked up. "That's a good idea."

Manka nodded as Nora said, "Yes, they may pick up on any invasive energies that Manka and I might miss."

"Um...sure," I agreed. I was so swamped with helpless emotion, I was starting to feel almost numb. "Whatever—anything that might help..."

— CHAPTER NINE —

I sort of lost it for a while. That thing they say, about the stages of grief? They're actually not tidy. They don't come in order, one finishing up politely before the next begins. They come all at once, in a horrible jumble—pain, denial, shock, sadness, anger, exhaustion, more pain, then more denial, such hard denial. And clever, clever bargaining—that was awful. My stupid brain would think, *Oh wait, I know!* and offer up some worthless thought, one I'd had a hundred times already. One that changed nothing.

The channelers—two middle-aged warlocks I knew only slightly—went through the house very thoroughly, poking and prodding at every corner. They, like Elnor, paid particular attention to the under-stair closet.

Leonora came to my house while they were there, bringing Niad and Honor with her. "We will take Logandina's body to the coven house; there is much to prepare before the ceremony marking her journey to the Beyond," my coven mother announced. "The healers can continue their searches no matter where her body lies."

"All right," I said, relieved, and helpless, and confused, and frustrated. I didn't have any experience with our transitions. Leonora, alas, did.

Jeremy and I stood back while my coven mother and sisters attended to the body. Niad was quiet, for once, as they gently smoothed out Logan's crumpled party dress and wrapped her in a long white sheet, leaving only her face free. She still looked like she was sleeping. How long would it take before any of this would seem real?

Marston, one of the channelers, came up to me as soon as Leonora and my sisters had left. "We would like to leave a monitor stone in this closet."

"What did you find?"

He frowned. "There is a thinness to the back wall that is not entirely of this plane."

"What does that mean?" I walked over and peered inside. "My cat is always interested in what's in there, but I don't sense anything."

"We are not sure. This is a relatively old house, so it might not be anything of importance—residue from human inhabitants, perhaps even a previous departure from the house. But in the event that anything shifts, the stone will pick up on it."

A previous departure. Because now, of course, there had been another. I shivered. "All right."

He opened his satchel and pulled out a grey rock with a lot of sparkle in it. "Muscovite," he said, to my questioning look. Then he stepped into the closet and placed the stone in the very center of the floor space, adjusting its position a few times until he was satisfied. "I would like to leave a few smaller ones in several of the rooms as well," he added.

"Of course."

The channelers placed their stones and left.

After such a bustle of activity, the quietness of the house was weird. I sat on the couch, huddled in a corner, Logan's blanket wrapped around me, Elnor at my feet. Jeremy sat at the other end, watching me without being too obvious about it.

"Where's Willson?" I asked.

Jeremy looked around. "I don't know. Did he go with…the rest of them?"

With Logan's body. He would want to be with his mistress even now. "He must have."

Jeremy shifted on the couch. "I know this is unfortunate timing, but I need to leave for a few hours. There are some things I must attend to, and they will not wait. Will you be all right here alone, or shall I escort you to your coven house?"

I shook my head. "No, I'd rather be here. Don't worry about me."

He gazed at me, his eyes kind and warm. Did I see pain in them? "I'll be back as soon as possible."

"You don't have to do that," I said. "You've done so much already."

He leaned over and patted me gently on the knee. It felt soothing. "I have done no more than any friend would do," he said. "I like you, Callie, and I liked Logan. I sorely wish I could have gotten to know her better. I've never met anyone quite like her."

"She liked you too." I gave him a rueful smile. "She liked you a *lot*."

He smiled back. "I had hoped that was true."

I looked at him, trying to figure out what he was feeling. Their romance had barely gotten started. Was he bereft, heartbroken? Not like I was, of course, but surely he must be hurting too. And yet he seemed so...calm. Like a diplomat.

After a moment, he got up. "I will return this evening."

"All right, but seriously—"

"I know I don't need to. It's just—well, if you want to know the truth, it will help me too, to not be alone."

"Oh. Right. Yes."

He stood up and put his hand on my shoulder, then caressed my cheek, nudging my hair out of my face. It felt good—almost too good, though he was clearly not being romantic. He cared, and he was hurting; he was looking for mutual comfort. I leaned into his touch and smiled up at him.

"I'll bring dinner when I return."

"There's..." I started to say "last night's leftovers", which brought another round of sudden tears to my eyes. Logan's last dinner. She would never cook for me again.

Had it ended her? "Oh, Blessed Mother..."

Jeremy stood still, waiting for me to regain my composure.

"Thank you," I said at last. "Yes, bringing some food would be good."

"I will see you later. Call if you need anything. Are you sure you don't want to have one of your sisters come over?"

I shook my head again, and gave him a small smile. "No. Go."

After he left, I wandered aimlessly around my house in befuddlement. When that didn't bring my best friend back, I gathered up Elnor and took her to the top floor. Ignoring the dusty lab bench, we sat in the center of my pentagram. I cleared my mind, dropped into a light trance, and waited for the energy to stabilize around me.

So maybe she wasn't in the Beyond yet, or at least in the areas we knew; she had to be *somewhere*. I knew Nora had tried this, but Logan was *my* friend.

"Logan?" I called out, after a few minutes. "Logan, can you hear me?"

No response. I felt the familiar, cool brush of the channel to the Beyond move into reach, but thinly. I also felt the resonant energy of the monitor stones noticing my efforts. Would the channelers know what I was doing?

It is hard to contact the Beyond alone; much easier with the coven's full strength of thirteen. And with one's own strength in solid working order. "Logan? It's me, Callie. Are you there?"

I waited. Her spirit would be confused, especially since she hadn't decided to take this journey. It might take her some time to answer.

Elnor settled more heavily on my lap, weaving her feline energy through mine in the circle. I called out several more times. Logan did not respond.

A loud ringing jarred me out of my trance. I dropped the energy of the circle; it let go with a snap that made me shiver. *What the…?*

It was my cell phone, in my jeans pocket. Raymond.

Crap. I let it go to voicemail. I just. Could. Not.

After a minute, it beeped. He'd left a message. Brushing away tears, I took a deep breath, then pushed the button to listen to it.

"Hey, babe, I just wanted to…you know, check in on you. I'm kinda hung over, and—babe, I dunno, I don't even know what happened but I'm sorry, whatever it was, I'm so sorry. Let me know what I can do? I want us to be okay again, I know we're not okay, and I don't… Um. Call me? Love ya. Bye."

I set the phone down and closed my eyes. What could he do? *Come and hold me. Don't ask me to explain anything. Give me some space. Understand me. Know me. Let me stop hiding. Bring Logan back.*

No, there was nothing he could do.

Over the course of the afternoon, a number of people sent ætheric inquiries, checking on me: my mother, several of my coven sisters, my young student Gracie, even Dr. Fallon—Sebastian. *It's shocking*, he said. *It makes me question everything.*

I know, I said. *Me too.*

It's like some sort of medieval, Old Country story. I could almost hear him shudder across the æther.

What do you mean?

Some sudden, unheard-of fatal disease out of nowhere—sounds more like a plague than a modern illness.

Now I shivered too. *I know.*

I understand the healers are still scrying.

Yeah. I supposed they wouldn't be telling him anything. *I'll let you know if I hear anything about what they find.*

I'd be interested to hear.

Channelers were here too, I told him. *It feels like my house is still full of presences, even though I'm alone here.*

Ugh, he commiserated. *I am so very sorry about your friend. She seemed like a lovely young witch. Have her parents been informed?*

I sighed. He had obviously not heard the conversation at our end of the table. *She...had lost touch with her parents.* I did not want to go into it. They were obviously not dead; no one had been able to contact them in the Beyond either. Perhaps, from the next plane, she would at last be able to find out what happened to them? I tried to take some small comfort in that thought, without much success.

Oh, I am sorry to hear that.

Yes. There was a tiny awkward pause. *Well, thank you for calling,* I told him.

My pleasure. Let me know if you need anything.

I will.

I was resting on the couch when Jeremy came back at dinnertime, as promised. He brought takeout pesto linguine, green salad, and white wine. I'm sure it was delicious and perfectly prepared and all that, but I might as well have been eating cardboard.

"I don't think you should sleep here alone tonight," he said, after we were finished.

I looked up at him. "What?"

Jeremy frowned. "We don't know where the illness came from—a miasma in your house, something in this neighborhood—we are still at a complete loss. I don't like to see you alone."

"I'm fine," I said, automatically. "The monitor stones..."

"I would offer to stay again," he said, ignoring my objection, "but I cannot. I would like to take you back to the coven house. Leonora and your sisters will see to you."

I shook my head. "I don't want to go there. This is my home." I liked this warlock, he wasn't pompous like the rest of them, but if he kept on like this...

"Callie, listen to me. Even if there were no danger, you're confused, you're distraught. Grief is a complicated thing. You should not be alone with it."

"I'm not alone. I have Elnor," I scritched her ears, "and Petrana."

He looked confused. After a moment, he said, "Your *golem*?"

"Well. I have Elnor, anyway."

Jeremy sighed. "Please, Callie. A familiar and a constructed creature are not the same as people. Your coven will understand, they will care for you. And I must go."

"My coven..." I started, then said, "I don't know."

He gave me a quizzical look. How much did he know about my sort-of estrangement from the coven? He wasn't stupid. And he'd been at my dinner party.

I thought about it. Was I being stubborn? I hardly knew how to think.

Was it dangerous here? I could put up wards, but they didn't screen out disease, or *miasma*, in Old Country terms. But, I had to admit, the place didn't feel all that cozy to me at the moment. The traces of everyone's spells. The low but intrusive energy of the monitor stones. The air Logan had breathed last.

He was right, I had to admit: the coven house was full of witches who cared about me, whatever our current differences, and however bossy they could be about it. I let out a breath. "Okay. That will make Leonora happy, anyway."

"Good." He looked relieved. "You can take your companions with you."

"Not Petrana," I said. "I doubt Leonora will let her in the house again."

"Oh? What did she do?"

"Exist."

Jeremy raised an eyebrow. "I see."

When dinner had been cleaned up, I let him guide my familiar and me along the ley line. He seemed to want to be chivalrous. Old Country manners and all that. Maybe it made him feel better. Like he was doing something. Maybe he wanted the company. He hadn't said where he had to rush off to. Probably his father.

Jeremy brought me to the edge of the garden fence, before the first of the house wards, and promised to contact me tomorrow. "Thank you," I said.

"It is my pleasure. We'll talk soon."

When he had seen me safely pass the house's first wall of wards, he smiled and vanished.

I set Elnor down and we walked through the garden slowly, letting the house and grounds recognize us and welcome us in. Once we got inside, Leonora sort of fussed over me. It was only a few minutes before I found myself in bed, tea and cookies beside me on the nightstand. Sweet, and weird.

My coven house bed was too small. How had I slept at all here, and for so many decades? Elnor fidgeted all night long, the room was too hot, and I felt the stifling presences of too many witches around me.

On the plus side, breakfast was ready when I got up, laid out buffet-style on the island and stove for the sisters to take as it suited their schedules. Huge stained glass windows sent dappled light across the kitchen, highlighting the eight-burner Maglin stove—a great cast-iron monstrosity weighing down the western end of the kitchen. It, like the rest of the house, was powered almost entirely by magic, though Leonora insisted on tapping into the city's gas and water lines, and even using them periodically. "A house this large with no utility bills attracts unwanted attention," she had said, so we sometimes cooked the human way.

The room was empty—it was nearly ten-thirty in the morning—and the stove was polished so clean it practically glowed, though the food in covered pans on three of its burners remained hot and fresh. I served myself some toast and scrambled eggs, ignoring the quail hash and red wine gravy—too much, too rich. I conjured myself a cup of pennyroyal tea, found a can of tuna for Elnor, and sat on the window seat, looking out through one of the few clear panes. The view from here was spectacular: a wide swath of downtown and the bay beyond it.

It was a nice house, I had to admit. It took being away for a while to let me actually see it again. Three stories high plus a half-basement built into the slope, it perched atop a hill on the south end of the Castro on a quarter acre of land. Unthinkable in San Francisco, but there it was. Of course, this San Francisco hadn't existed when it was built, over a century and a half ago. Leonora had acquired it in the chaos following the 1906 earthquake and fire, and had spent the last hundred or so years making it comfortable, useful, and intensely magical. To humans, it just looked like a fancy house on a big lot with a view. Nothing special. But it bristled with wards and defenses, laid deep into the earth and soaring to the sky.

I ate half my eggs and a few bites of toast before setting the plate on the windowsill. As I sipped my tea, I heard tentative footsteps entering the kitchen. "Hello, Gracie," I said, without turning around.

"I'm sorry about your friend." My fifteen-year-old student came and sat by me on the window seat, her heart-shaped face filled with concern.

"Thank you."

"Leonora says we should all stay indoors till they figure out what caused it."

"That's probably a good idea," I said to her. Whether I agreed or not, I wouldn't undermine Leonora's authority here.

Gracie looked a little disappointed, but she nodded. "Do you think it's contagious?"

"I have no idea. But the healers and the Elders are working on it, and I'm sure they'll figure it out very soon."

She looked at me, brown eyes serious under dark hair. I could see she wasn't entirely buying it.

"I know they're doing all they can," I added.

Niad walked into the room. "Oh, good, I thought I sensed you in here."

"Good morning, Niad," I said.

"She has not let go, you know."

I gave her a blank stare. "What?"

"Your friend. Her body is not going to the soil."

"What are you talking about?"

Niad sighed. "She's not *decaying*. It's as though she left a moment ago."

"What?" A bright strand of hope stabbed through me. "Do they think that—" Had she just stepped out of her body—if we found her spirit, could she rejoin it—come back?

Niad shook her head, clearly following my line of thought. "No. The body itself is quite dead; she has left it. And yet it won't break down."

"Oh." I set my teacup down, dismayed and confused. There had been that odd spark of color in Logan's cheeks. "Several of us have tried to contact her spirit."

"Leonora has as well. She tried all night, in fact, but never found her. Not even Nementhe could help." Niad gave me a probing look. "What was she up to, anyway?"

"Nothing! What do you mean?"

Niad shrugged. "Drained essence, body not spoiling, spirit missing, all from some mysterious 'disease' no one has ever heard of...sounds to me like she may have been involved in some pretty dark stuff."

"She was not!"

"You sure she wasn't trying to get hold of demons?"

"No! Are you crazy? She read tarot cards for tourists on Pier 39."

"Wasn't she always poking around the Old Country, looking for her parents?"

"She's never been to the Old Country. All she did was divinations, from here."

"I see. Well—"

"Niadine, that is enough," Leonora interrupted. I hadn't even noticed her come in. "I shall speak to Calendula alone, if you please."

"Come along, Gracie," Niad said.

"Shall we go into my study?" My coven mother nodded at the door of the converted sun-porch off the kitchen, her worn face gentle and caring. Calmness exuded from her, bathing me in comfort and warmth. It was at times like this that I remembered why I had joined her house.

I hadn't counted on Logan's body also being in Leonora's study, but it made sense. Here was where Leonora performed her more private works and divinations. The seat of her power, as it were.

Still, it was unsettling. The fur on Elnor's back rose, and she glanced up at me. I petted her as I looked at the body.

Niad was right. Logan looked like she had departed moments before—or as if she were sleeping. I almost expected to see her take a breath.

"Please, have a seat," Leonora said, her voice still gentle. She arranged herself, and her familiar, into her large easy chair. A huge stained-glass window depicting a regally gowned queen shone at Leonora's back. All the windows on this floor depicted some form of female power and strength; upstairs, smaller windows held images related to magic—the moon, various botanicals, cats.

I chose the left-most chair and turned it slightly, so that Logan's body was out of my line of vision. Elnor jumped into my lap and took a moment to settle. Only then did I realize what was missing. "Is Willson here?"

"Her familiar? No. Isn't he at your house?"

I shook my head, blinking away tears as I looked away for a moment. "No," I managed.

"Hm. Perhaps he returned to her apartment." Leonora leaned forward slightly and caught my gaze, scanning my essence. "How did you sleep?"

"Not well," I admitted.

She nodded. "You must take care, especially now, for the next few weeks. Your emotions are fragile, and the moon is waning: do not do any strenuous work or make any major decisions during this period."

"I hadn't planned anything major..."

She gave me a pointed look. "As Logandina was your particular friend, and the incident was in your house, I would like you to refrain from participating in the search for any cause."

"What?" I leaned forward in my chair. "Are you kidding?"

"I most certainly am not. It would be dangerous for you on several levels. I would also like you to stay away from your laboratory work, until the new moon at the very soonest."

"But...what does that have to do with anything?"

"It is a drain on your resources, and of no actual urgency. And I want you to stay here at the house until further notice."

The look on her face was deceptively mild. I wanted to protest, but I was too exhausted and distraught to say more than, "Yes, Mother."

Leonora shifted her weight in her chair. "Logandina was a peculiar witch. I confess I have always been surprised at your close friendship."

"She was sweet, and gentle, and kind." I struggled to keep my voice calm.

"She was weak, obsessed with her parents' disappearance, and would have been entirely friendless if not for you."

I leaned forward again. "What are you saying? That she deserved to be yanked off this plane without warning and thrown—*somewhere*? Just because she wasn't like the rest of us?"

"Of course not." She scratched at Grieka's ears. "I do not mean to upset you, Calendula. I am merely observing that, of all of our city's daughters who have been educated here, she is one of those I understand the least. And that is problematic, in any search for what has taken her."

"So why keep me *out* of the search? Shouldn't I be involved?"

"If and when I become assured that you are not also a target, I will consider involving you." She got to her feet, ushering me up as well. "But until then: I want you to stay safe, here, and get plenty of rest."

"A target? What do you mean?"

"I mean that the incident took place in *your* house. A place where none of our kind has lived before. Such a change may not have escaped notice."

I gaped at her. "Notice by *who*? Do you think some...intelligence is behind this?"

"At the moment, when nothing is clear, anything is possible. I wish to take no chances."

"My house is safe, I know it is."

She looked at me pointedly. "How do you know this?"

"I work powerful magic there. It feels like home to me, it welcomes me in. And all the investigators found nothing amiss." *Well, nothing much.*

"Even so. I myself am not yet convinced. I wish you to rest and recover from your distress, Calendula."

It was pointless to argue with her, and, well, she wasn't wrong about my state of mind. "Yes, Mother."

The study door closed behind me. I walked through the kitchen, then took the back stairs to the second floor, avoiding everyone.

I hadn't thought I ever wanted to see that stupid tiny bed again, but now I welcomed it. My pillow could barely contain all my tears.

— CHAPTER TEN —

I managed to stay a week or more at the coven house, almost without thinking about it. That's another thing about grief: it distorts time. I lost countless hours, sometimes a whole day, existing in a sort of shocked daze. I slept a lot—almost as much as humans do. I picked at my food, when I remembered to eat at all. I looked through the æther at my house only once. It appeared unchanged, uninhabited except for Petrana standing idly in the kitchen.

It had been silly of me to designate a bedroom for her, hadn't it? She wasn't a person. She would just stand forever where I'd left her, and think nothing of it. What was she going to do with a bedroom—sleep? Change clothes? Read a book?

Maybe Niad was right, to mock me for naming her. But...I had created her.

But...it wasn't as though she was a daughter. Or even really alive.

Leonora and my sisters kept me out of whatever they were doing to assist the investigations into Logan's departure—not that I tried all that hard to participate. I got calls through the æther from my birth mother, from Sebastian Fallon, and from Jeremy Andromedus. All very sweet, and all without any answers.

I ignored Raymond's increasingly anxious voicemails, until my cell phone's battery died.

It was like waking up from a particularly bad dream, when I came back to myself. Except it hadn't been a dream...Logan was still gone. But I was here.

I washed my face, pulled on some clothes, and went downstairs in search of a cup of tea. I thought I'd make it by hand. Use some physical resources, keep up our disguise.

Leonora was in the kitchen. "Calendula, I was about to call to you," she said.

"Yes, Mother?" I rummaged through the cupboard, finding the pennyroyal.

"Dr. Andromedus has contacted me. The Elders have scoured the city and its environs, and there is no evidence of any infectious agent, nor of any being or creature with evil intent. We still do not know the cause of the departure of Logandina's spirit. But they have lifted the advisory that we should all stay indoors, behind wards."

"Oh." I filled a kettle with water and put it on the stove, lighting the flame with a flick of my fingers. "So…nothing?"

She shook her head. "Nothing that anyone has been able to detect. And as no one else has become affected, they feel it is safe to resume our normal activities."

"That's…" I didn't finish the sentence; I didn't know *what* it was. Unsatisfying. Stupid. Impossible. Confusing. Wrong.

"I still would prefer that you take care of yourself," she went on, in a more gentle tone. "Of course."

"Of course." The kettle whistled. I poured hot water over the tea leaves and stirred absently. The leaves collected at the bottom of the cup. "I, um, should maybe go check on my house?" I asked, cringing at my own tentative tone. Would I ever be my old self again? Clearly I wasn't fully back.

"You may do so," she said. "Although the Elders have investigated the house quite thoroughly, I would appreciate your letting me know if you notice anything unusual."

"Yes, Mother." She was right: as it was my house, increasingly bound to my energetic signature, I might well perceive things that were invisible to anyone else.

I pointed at the cup; the leaves vanished, leaving only brewed tea. Leonora went into her office. I drank my tea. I sort of tasted it.

When I was done, I rinsed the cup, picked up Elnor, and slipped onto a ley line.

Instead of going straight to my house, I went to a small café near it, one I'd been to a few times as I was getting to know the neighborhood. It was a human spot, so I had to cast a tiny zone of inattention around Elnor. Fortunately, she was as happy to get out as I was, and didn't meow and screw it up.

From this safe distance, I scanned the energetic surroundings of my home, probing as much as I could. But I detected nothing amiss—beyond the fact that it had been full of strangers over the last week. The channelers had been back through, checking their stones, replacing several of them. Had I given them permission to? I must have.

It did, at least, seem to be safe there now.

I sighed, sipping an overpriced cup of watery human-strength tea I didn't even want, thinking about...everything. It made no sense. And my brain was still going in circles. I was never going to figure anything out all alone. I just didn't know enough.

Opening a channel to the æther, I sent a message to Jeremy: *Leonora told me that the Elders have declared the city safe.*

He responded at once: *Well, they have said we need no longer shelter indoors, behind wards. Not exactly the same thing.*

What does your father say? I could have asked my mentor directly, but it was Jeremy who had been keeping in touch with me over the last week. We were connected by our loss, however unequal their magnitudes.

He is still looking into the matter. But he agrees that the danger appears minimal at best.

They still have no leads at all?

A pause this time. *You are not with your coven, are you?*

Hmm. *No, I'm at a café near my house.*

May I join you?

Please do.

Within minutes, he sat facing me across the tiny table, stirring an excessive amount of sugar into an Americano. "How are you doing?" he asked.

I sighed, shaking my head. "I've never lost anyone before."

"You are young."

It could have sounded condescending. He wasn't all that much older than me. Yet, as with things he'd said before, his tone and expression were full of empathy. And, this time, a sad understanding as well, hinting at knowledge born of painful experience.

This felt like more than just his loss of a promising new romance.

I looked down at my tea, feeling vulnerable and exposed, all my nerves rubbed raw and left in the sun. After a minute, I cleared my throat. "I've been forbidden to participate in the search for the cause, but...I really need to...to know. To do something."

He gazed at me a moment before looking away with a gentle nod. "I have been helping my father investigate, but as you know, we've found nothing." He took a sip, staring off across the street.

"So why do they think it's okay to go out now?"

"There is no evidence of any disease in the air or food or water, and no one else has fallen ill, or even sensed unusual toxic energies. It may have been something wrong with her system—a congenital problem, as yet undetected. It may even have been a curse set inside her in the past, triggered for a particular time, or set of circumstances."

"A curse?" I asked. "Who would do such a thing? And why?"

The warlock looked back at me, his green eyes deadly serious. "Her parents traveled to the Old Country at the request of someone involved in the troubles, then disappeared. Their spirits are not in the Beyond. It is quite the coincidence that their daughter has now suffered a similar fate."

I felt myself coloring with embarrassment. Yes, I was definitely not my normal self. "Oh. Of course."

Jeremy nodded. "Yet since we find no clear threat in the here-and-now—beyond, of course, what happened to her—we are forced to consider other options."

I didn't want to ask, but knew I had to. "If they keep finding nothing...how long before everyone decides we're at a dead end and goes on with their lives?"

Sadness etched tiny lines around his eyes. "Of course the question will never be dropped entirely. But with every avenue explored, and explored again..." He gave me a helpless look. "You must see how impossible this is. At a certain point..."

"Yeah." I gave a frustrated sigh, trying to stifle sudden anger. "Just some unaffiliated witch who got herself tangled up in the Old Country's troubles, nothing that affects us here—why waste everybody's time on it?" I hated how bitter I sounded, but there it was.

He leaned forward, his gaze intense. "It's not that at all, Callie, and you know it. The Old Country's issues *do* reach us here, though I am learning that most local folk don't like to be reminded of that." He gave a wry smile. "We just don't know where to start. Everywhere anyone has looked has reached a dead end. If you have other suggestions, do please make them."

"I know, I know," I said. "There's a lot of grains of sand on the beach. Not even witch-folk have the time to examine every one." *Especially if they are searching out of duty, not love*, I added silently.

"Like I said, no one's giving up entirely. Not while I'm still here."

Sympathy and guilt suddenly poured through me, quashing my anger as fast as it had arisen. Here I was, practically accusing him of not caring—the only warlock who had ever shown interest in Logan, romantic or otherwise. "How are *you* doing?" I asked, trying to search behind his eyes. "This can't be easy for you either."

"No, it has not been." He looked back at me. "I understand what you mean about wanting to *do* something, to help. I have probably been a terrible bother to my father and his associates."

"Oh, I'm sure you haven't," I said automatically.

Now he gave me a rueful smile. "I am not a biologist. Or a research historian, or a crime investigator, or an occult worker, or even a healer. Yet I do wish to help, all the same."

"Yeah." We sipped our drinks in silence for a minute. Elnor shifted under the table. She was being very, very good, not reacting at all to the close proximity of a warlock. "Well, it's nice of you to spend so much time on this," I added.

"What do you mean? What else am I supposed to do?"

"Well—" Now I felt stupid. Again. "I'm sure you didn't come to San Francisco just to get caught up in local drama. Don't you have a—?" A job? "Things to do?" Why *was* he here? How much diplomacy did San Francisco need? I struggled to remember what he'd told us the night we'd met him.

Jeremy shook his head. "Callie. I came here precisely to *join* this community, to get involved in it—and the departure of Logandina Fleur is most certainly not 'drama'. I cared about her, and I care about you. Beyond that, this is my father's chosen home, and I want to be part of it. *This* is what I am here to do."

I smiled at him. "Even so, it's generous of you."

"I'd say the generosity is all on your part. You've invited me in, made me feel welcome, and shared so much with me—a complete stranger."

I studied him across the table. "You...don't feel like all that much of a stranger, honestly. A lot has happened since we met." I thought a moment. "And I've known your dad all my life."

He smiled, flashing those gorgeous white teeth. Wait, what? I shouldn't be noticing how attractive this warlock was. Logan's almost-boyfriend. What a jumbled mess my mind and heart were. Reaching for comfort anywhere. "I am so glad to be getting to know you," Jeremy said. "It does help."

"I'm glad. And I'm glad to know you, as well."

Having thoroughly embarrassed one another, we concentrated on our beverages for a while.

Jeremy cleared his throat a few minutes later. "Did Logan's familiar ever show up?"

"No. He didn't go back to my place, or to her apartment, or even to the cattery coven—Leonora sent one of my sisters to look for him several times." I frowned, reaching absently down to pet Elnor, now calmly snuggled between my feet. "I'll go look at her place myself, soon. It's really strange. He should at least be staying with her body, until…"

Jeremy frowned as well. "There is too much that is peculiar about this."

"You're telling me." I set my empty cup on the table.

"What are your plans now?" he asked.

"I don't know. I didn't really have much of a plan. I just…couldn't be in the coven house anymore. Leonora let me come out to check on my home, but I stopped here to scope it out from a distance. Anyway, I should probably be getting over there."

He looked up at the sky, then back at me. "Let's walk."

"What?" I blinked.

Jeremy laughed. "Walking clears the mind and helps the soul. And San Francisco is a very good walking city."

"That's true, but…"

"We can stop by your house first, if you like; but I will point out that the sun is shining right now. No promises about later."

I thought a moment. "Okay, sure."

We headed west, walking up and down hills, then turned north before we reached Ocean Beach. Elnor darted around us like an unstable electron, rushing ahead and then lagging behind. Being January, the sun didn't hold, but the mist and fog were lovely, especially as we delved into Golden Gate Park.

It was a brilliant distraction. I was able to keep my mind off of Logan for whole minutes at a time. Jeremy asked me about my life, my research, my goals and dreams. I found myself increasingly comfortable with him—laughing together at some small thing, touching his arm to make a point when we stopped to rest.

Though we almost pointedly didn't talk about it, he knew what I was going through, and was sharing at least a degree of it. We had been together when the awful thing had happened; he understood. I didn't have to *explain* anything to him. It was really, really nice.

At the end of the day, I steered us closer to my neighborhood. Elnor must have tired; I was somehow now carrying her, though I hadn't remembered picking her up. "I still need to stop by my house. Do you want to come along?"

"I would be honored to."

I sent a message to Leonora: *I'll be staying out a little while longer.* I thought a moment, then added, *I'm with Jeremy Andromedus, and I'm taking care of myself. He's being very kind.*

She answered a minute later: *All right, Calendula.*

I paused on the sidewalk in front of my house, admiring it. It really was a handsome building. Though when I painted the next time, I ought to opt for a little more color. This was San Francisco, after all.

We walked up the stairs, and Jeremy waited beside me as I unlocked and opened the front door. He shivered as we stepped across the threshold, though it was warmer in here than outside.

"You okay?" I asked.

He gave me a sheepish grin. "Oh, I am sorry. I just cannot get used to this unwarded space. I automatically prepare to be granted entry to your home—and then there's nothing! Like reaching for that extra step at the top of a staircase, and it isn't there."

I smiled again at his Old Country ways. "I like it, actually. It feels clean to me."

We stepped into the front parlor. Elnor stretched and jumped down from my arms, beginning her sniffing ritual. "It feels dangerous to me," Jeremy said. "Particularly...now."

"It must be so odd, to live that way. But I guess you must get used to it." I wondered if I would. If our world was now dangerous like that.

"If it is all you know, it does not seem peculiar at all. Like putting on one's clothes before going outside."

I gave a soft laugh, shaking my head as I glanced around the room. Then I walked into the second parlor, and from there out into the hallway and around to the dining room. Nothing seemed out of place—beyond bits of medical detritus and evidence of the searches done here. I noticed scrying marks in the corners of each room, lightly traced in chalk. Someone had dropped a handkerchief. I picked it up and set it on the sideboard, then walked into the kitchen. Petrana stood by the back wall. "Greetings, Mistress," she said.

"Hello, Petrana. Is all well here?"

"There is nothing to report that you do not already know."

I gazed back at her a moment. She knew what I knew? Just how connected were we? "Thank you," I said, at last.

After I glanced into the backyard, I returned to Jeremy. "It seems all right in here."

"Did you want to check upstairs?"

"I do, yes. Be right back."

The rest of the house seemed safe as well: only the lingering traces of energy from the Elders' channelers who had been through here. And their stones. Dust was growing thicker on my lab bench. I walked back downstairs. Jeremy was standing by the front window, looking out at the street; he turned and smiled at me as I entered. "It's all fine," I told him.

"Good."

I motioned at the chair next to him. "Have a seat. Do you want something to drink?"

"No, thank you—I have monopolized far too much of your time already today." Before I could protest, he added, "I should be getting back to see my father; he had some errands for me to run. May I escort you back to your coven house?"

"Actually, I think I'm going to stay here a bit longer, but thanks."

"Are you certain?"

I gave him a very patient smile. I liked this warlock, I truly did, but sometimes his Old Country courtesies left "charming" and edged a little too close to "patronizing." "Quite certain, really. I was there an entire week, Leonora is not expecting me at the moment, and the Elders are not telling us to keep indoors any longer. I'll make my way back later."

He gave a polite nod. "Very well, then. I thank you for a lovely day."

"Thank *you*," I said, as I walked him to the front door. Feeling a bit bad about my stridency, I added, "Let's do it again—soon."

There might have been a touch of surprise in his eyes as he glanced up at me. Or relief? "I would enjoy that tremendously." He bowed over my hand, gave it a quick brush of a kiss, and took his leave.

After I locked the door behind him, I shook my head again, smiling. Yes, it had been a nice day, and I did like the guy. Formal and weird though he might be.

I certainly could use a friend. Particularly right now.

Stopping myself before I could spiral down into grief once more, I began tidying the house—straightening, dusting—working by hand as I let myself reinhabit the place. Petrana offered to help, but I told her no, for now. Though I did intend to spend a few more nights at the coven house, I lived here, and I didn't want the house to forget me, or my magic.

After a few hours, the energy began to feel more settled around me. I sat in the kitchen, sipping a cold glass of water. Now I let myself feel the sorrow of being here, in this room, where Logan had cooked her last meal. Where she had calmed me down when my dinner party looked like it was going south. Where, just a few weeks before that, she had read my tarot cards.

A reading which had predicted catastrophic change for me. My getting hurt.

"Understatement of the century," I said aloud. In her corner, Petrana didn't react, but Elnor walked over and rubbed against my legs. "It's too bad we didn't do *her* reading. Maybe we would have had some better warning. Or any warning at all."

If we had, would we have been able to do anything about it?

Not that I really believed in tarot anyway. Not in any literal sense. I knew Logan had valued its insights, and our reading had been…well, uncomfortably on point even at the time. It was truly tragic now. So how could I still say there was nothing to this?

I finished my water, then sat a long time at the table staring at nothing. The evening stretched.

Eventually, I made my way back to the coven house, arriving too late for the communal dinner. Not an accident.

The next day, I again went to my house, spending a few hours this time up in the lab room. I didn't run any experiments, but I thoroughly cleaned the bench area and reorganized all the supplies and equipment. This was only partially procrastination. Mostly, it was the next part of the process of reintroducing myself to my life. My new life, whatever shape it would take.

Besides, it would be a waste of time to attempt finely pinpointed magical insight when my emotions were so scattered and distressed.

While I was cleaning, I also finally charged up my cell phone, which had died sometime in the last week or so. Once it came back to life, I saw that Raymond had called twice more, leaving one brief voicemail.

I had to talk to him…but oh. What to say? I held the phone, staring at it without really seeing it. At last, I pulled up its keyboard and composed a text: *Raymond, sorry to have missed your calls, but I've been dealing with an emergency. It has nothing to do with you, but it's taking all my focus right now. I'll call you soon.*

I hesitated a moment, rereading the message, then added *Love, Callie* and pushed "send" before I could rethink.

I did love him. Right? I knew I did. He made me feel all squishy and happy inside. I missed him.

But what was love, anyway? Logan had been right, of course: I couldn't even tell Raymond what was going on. I'd had to control him with magic when he showed up here drunk, and then hide the fact from him. And now I was still hiding from him. How could this be anything resembling a real relationship?

So what to do? Just break it off? I didn't want to do that. We had too much that was good. I'd never felt this way with any warlock I'd dated—easy, comfortable, relaxed. Ironically, with Raymond I felt like I *could* be me: the me that was just a person, not entangled in this huge structure of witchkind rules and expectations and secrecy and traditions.

And grief.

But I *was* a witch. I couldn't just pretend that part of me away—recent events had made this all too painfully clear. This wasn't *Bewitched*. The person-part of me might want a different life, but wanting something and being able to have it were very different things.

My phone beeped: a return text. *Oh babe, I'm so sorry—can I help with anything? I could be there in half an hour. Love R.*

I smiled through gathering tears. Yes, he was a good man. I couldn't just dump him. I didn't *want* to just dump him.

But no, alas. There was still nothing, really literally nothing, he could help with. No human could. No matter how much I loved him.

Thank you, but you can't. I'll explain later, but for now, I just need to keep dealing with this.

OK. Luv U.

I love you too.

I sighed, slipped the phone into my jeans pocket, and went back to tidying.

A few hours later, I felt the telltale energetic shiver of an ætheric query. Someone was requesting to speak with me, rather than just dropping words into my mind.

I only knew one person who was that formal. *Jeremy?*

Calendula, how are you doing?

I'm all right, I sent back. *Just doing a few things around my house. How are you?*

I am well, considering.

Remembering how we'd left things yesterday, I said, *I was just thinking about a walk. Are you busy?*

I would be honored to take another walk with you, Calendula.

Twenty minutes later, we were setting off from my house. "I thought you were on board with calling me Callie."

He gave a soft laugh. "My apologies. Calendula is such a lovely name; I enjoy the sound of it in my head, and the feel of it on my tongue." I glanced sharply over at him—was he *flirting* with me? "But I will try harder to honor your request. Callie."

"Thanks," I said, still watching him as we walked. No suggestive grin; no sign that any double entendre had been intended. Okay then. "How is it going, with the investigation? Has your father found anything?"

"Nothing more."

I wasn't surprised. Leonora had indicated much the same thing, when I'd asked her this morning. Indeed, she'd chided me for my impatience. "These things take time, daughter."

At least Jeremy was more polite than that. "I will be certain to let you know if and when there is anything to tell," he said.

"Thanks."

We walked in comfortable silence for a few blocks. I had felt like I'd wanted company, but now I had nothing much to say. Jeremy seemed to sense that; he walked beside me, looking around at the sights. I fell into my own thoughts, enjoying his gentle presence.

After a while, I looked up, startled to realize where I had unconsciously steered us. I stopped, pointing. "That building there," I said, "that's where Logan lived."

"Oh!" Jeremy looked nonplussed. He paused, then walked closer to the building, looking at it carefully. "I did not realize that. Is that why...?"

I shrugged. "Not intentionally. I was just wandering. But I wonder if my undermind was trying to tell me something."

"We did go to lunch, but we met at the restaurant," he mused, still looking at the building. Sadness carved lines into his handsome face. "It's a nice building."

"She was happy here." I stood next to him, casting my senses about. After another minute, I sighed. "I still don't sense Willson anywhere about."

"Her familiar?" I nodded, and Jeremy echoed my sigh. "I must confess, I do not know much about feline companions, but this does seem peculiar. I hope he hasn't met an unhappy end."

"Me too. He was a good cat." No animal shelter could contain a witch's cat. Perhaps he was just grief-stricken, confused, emotionally lost. I could certainly relate to that.

"Do you want to go inside?" Jeremy asked. "Look more closely?"

I thought a moment, then shook my head. "I don't see that it would help. And I'm not..." I trailed off.

He patted my arm. "I understand."

We stood there sadly another minute, and walked on.

— CHAPTER ELEVEN —

I t became a nice daily ritual, an afternoon walk with Jeremy. After the first few days, I began sleeping at my house again, though I still spent a lot of time at the coven house. No breakthroughs were made in whatever investigations were still ongoing. Life was going to go on, despite my having lost my best friend to a mystery.

I began inviting Jeremy in for a drink after our walks. He would stay an hour or so before taking his leave. We talked of many things, large and small. I do not remember most of our conversations; their details were less important than the fact of our building a new friendship, atop the ruins of our loss.

One day, a week or so later, the sun had been shining, and we had walked farther than usual. Relaxing after the journey felt marvelous; we were joking about how old and out-of-shape we both were. Jeremy sat next to me on my couch, a little closer than was technically necessary.

Our walk had been strenuous enough that I'd sweated going up and down those hills. And the scent I caught from him told me he'd worked hard too.

I'd never smelled any exertion quite so alluring.

Startled, I scooted back against the arm of the couch, facing Jeremy even as I drew farther away.

"What's the matter?" he asked, looking around with some alarm.

"Nothing—nothing here. Just...I don't want to..." But that wasn't true. Because I *did* want to, at least part of me. I just didn't think it was a good idea.

And why was that?

Because it was far too soon. I was too much of an emotional mess. And Jeremy had been at least halfway in love with Logan. And I was not single, even if I hadn't yet resolved anything with Raymond. I had put him off with texts a few more times, but that was no answer. I had to face him soon. I had just not yet mustered the resolve. "I'm not in a good place to...you know, start anything," I finally managed.

Jeremy smiled and leaned back against the couch arm on his side. His scent retreated further as he did. "I understand, of course, Calendula Isadora." His use of my formal name sent a confused thrill through me—he'd been so good about calling me Callie since I'd mentioned it. "But, if I may, I would like to say a few things. With your permission, of course." His green eyes shone with earnest, careful energy.

I swallowed. "Yes, please, you can say anything. If we're going to be friends, we have be able to be honest with each other."

He took a sip of his Bulgarian frog brandy, then set the snifter down on the coffee table. "You may know that my father was interested in us becoming acquainted...and perhaps far more than that."

I nodded. That had been clear enough, when I'd visited Gregorio in his lab. Though it felt like a thousand years ago, now.

"I felt much the same way as I imagine you did," Jeremy went on. "In this modern world, arranged unions are quite out of fashion." I had to smile at this. And I *had* to visit the Old Country some day—did everyone there talk this way? "But I admire and respect my father, and saw no reason to refuse his quite reasonable request: to simply get to know you. I want to know everyone here, after all; no reason not to start with his dear friend's daughter."

"It's funny that Gregorio didn't say anything to me about it," I said. "Or my father, for that matter. I never even knew you existed."

"No, not so funny, when you think about it from their perspective. Remember how old our fathers are, mine particularly. When they came of age, courtship was entirely the responsibility of the warlock. Witches were presented to society when they were eligible, but all they were expected to do was look lovely and develop their powers."

"That's not exactly true," I said. "Maybe it looked like that, but witches have always been in charge of matchmaking. That's what coven mothers do: they assemble their own covens, and arrange strategic unions for witches who want them. Or who are willing, anyway."

Jeremy shrugged. "Perhaps it could be seen that way. Or perhaps your own training, at the hands of a very powerful coven mother, emphasized the importance of covens." I started to protest, but he went on. "I did not mean to start an argument! All I meant to say was that my father would not naturally think to consult you, at least not in the preliminary stages of any potential arrangement. Leonora, perhaps, but not you." He grinned at me. "Frankly, I'm lucky he even mentioned it to me."

I smiled back at him. "I don't want to fight either. But these issues are...touchy, to say the least."

"Oh, I understand. And thank you for hearing me out. As you said, we must be able to speak honestly to one another." He had such a nice smile. "What I wanted to say was that...whatever my father's agenda may be, and whatever has transpired since then, I have become interested in your company for entirely my own reasons."

"I like you too," I said. "I've enjoyed spending time with you. These walks have become the part of my day I most look forward to. They've helped..." I waved my hand. He understood.

"They have helped me too," he said. "A great deal. I do not know whether you are interested in a union—now or ever. I myself was not, until I met Logan. I...found myself quite taken with her. And quite unexpectedly." He paused, gazing into the distance a moment. "She... awoke feelings in me that I imagined had been long dead." Now he turned toward me. "My apologies, this must be a very awkward surprise for you."

"I...um..." I didn't know exactly where he was going with this, but I was beginning to have a pretty good idea.

"I do understand that, given your loss of such a dear friend, entering into any sort of romantic entanglement is likely not a priority."

"Well, um..."

"And now I am putting words in your mouth, Calendula. Please correct me if I am misperceiving anything." A tentative flash of grin.

"No, you've pretty much got it right." I noticed he didn't even mention Raymond. No doubt he shared witchkind's notions about such things: dabbling with a human was barely worth noticing. I reached over and patted Jeremy's knee. In a sisterly sort of way. "I do feel like...yeah, romance is sort of not where my heart is right now. It's nothing about you at all, though. I like you a lot."

He put his hand on mine and gave it a gentle squeeze, pressing it to his warm knee. That sisterly contact suddenly became...a whole lot more. He held my gaze with those green eyes. "I am glad to hear it. Because the final thing I wanted to say is, despite how we met, and despite what has transpired for both of us since then, I find you *very* attractive and desirable, and I do hope that circumstances might change in the future. I would be honored and thrilled to explore a romantic venture with you. Even one of short duration, though not ruling out a longer term."

"Um." I stared back at him. He released my hand; I slowly took it back. My heart was thumping, my cheeks were on fire, and words fled my brain. "I. Um. Thank you?"

Jeremy gave me a wry smile. "I am getting the strong impression that this is not how such things are done in this country."

I giggled, the tension slipping away. "No, not really. Warlocks here are more...well, nobody's direct, you know? You're always guessing: what did that mean? What should I do?"

"How tedious," he said, still smiling. "I prefer directness."

"I...can see that that would save a lot of miscommunication," I said. "So what do Old Country warlocks do for amusement, if they are not playing romantic guessing games with witches?"

Jeremy laughed. "Ah, Callie, your sense of humor is delightful." He finished his drink and set the empty glass on the table. "Well. At the risk of declaring myself, only to flee, perhaps I ought to let you alone with your thoughts. I imagine you are wanting to get back to your coven house soon?"

"I don't know," I said.

"Didn't you say earlier you planned to dine there tonight?"

I shrugged. "I'm thinking I might make dinner here instead."

He nodded again, ignoring my subtle invitation as he stood. *So much for speaking directly*, I thought, chagrined at myself. "Thank you for a lovely day," he said.

"No, thank *you*."

We grinned stupidly at each other for a minute. Then he said, "Shall we walk again tomorrow?"

"Absolutely."

I saw him to the door, and then I was alone in my house. Well, alone with Elnor. I sat back on the couch and called her onto my lap.

We sat there as I replayed the conversation in my mind. It was fascinating, the frank but pressure-free way he—what, propositioned me?—no, not quite that, or not entirely. He had expressed his interest, as well as his understanding of the situation.

How rare. How charming.

I scratched Elnor behind the ears, enjoying her purr. Had I wanted him to stay? Yes, definitely, part of me. Well, I could have asked him to, couldn't I? Yes.

But he'd made it quite clear the door was open for the future. That he was giving me time to think, in fact. He hadn't even expected an answer, at least not yet. I hadn't ruined anything by not being ready.

Was I developing feelings for him? I seemed to be. I liked him. He was kind, and interesting, and humble. He was sexy, and sensitive. He came from a good family—the very best, in fact. But he wasn't an arrogant ass about it. About anything.

He was a warlock. I was a witch.

If I had been looking to date any warlock, he would be the top candidate, no question.

But I wasn't. I'd been happy in my relationship with Raymond... until recently, anyway.

I didn't know how to even talk to Raymond now. When the biggest thing happening in my life was wrapped in so many secrets, I couldn't figure out how to tell him about it.

But I couldn't see him and *not* tell him.

So I kept avoiding the issue, hoping I'd figure out what to do...later.

I got up and set Elnor on the floor, then went down the hall to the kitchen. Petrana still stood in the back corner.

She watched me, impassively, as I walked in. Waiting for orders, undoubtedly, with no impatience whatsoever, though it was hard not to project emotion onto her. I knew, intellectually at least, that she didn't care that I just left her standing here for weeks on end, or that both healers and the Elders' investigators had subjected her to some rather unpleasant-looking probes, to determine if she had been in any way responsible for Logan's demise—even tangentially.

"Petrana," I said. "Would you please give the stove a good cleaning? I will be cooking here this evening."

"Yes, Mistress Callie." She ambled over to the stove and got to work.

"I could have asked him to stay," I said to Petrana, fully aware that I was actually talking to myself. "I could even call him now and invite him back."

"Yes, Mistress Callie," she said.

"I mean, I can totally talk to him tomorrow. I will, in fact. We're walking again."

"Yes, Mistress Callie." She scrubbed methodically, from the back of the stove to the front, removing nothing more than dust. She finished by drawing a clean cloth over the surfaces, then turned back to face me.

"Thank you, Petrana," I said. "That's all for now."

"Yes, Mistress Callie."

I sent a message to Leonora, asking her to convey my regrets to the other sisters, and to the students, particularly Gracie. My coven mother wished me a pleasant evening and reminded me to stay vigilant.

Yes, Mother, I assured her.

I made myself a light dinner, then puttered around, contemplating going up to the lab, perhaps even to start an experiment. Eventually, though, I just went to bed, read a few pages, and turned off the light. I had nearly drifted off to sleep when I felt a pressure at the foot of the mattress. I bolted upright, my heart pounding.

Niad sat there, gazing at me, arms folded across her chest.

"Good god!" I gasped. "Where did you come from?"

"The ley line."

"I didn't sense you." *And I didn't invite you in.* I drew the covers up; I wasn't going to sit here naked in front of her.

"Clearly." She smiled, quick and catlike, as her eyes danced around the room. Looking for someone? "Sorry if I startled you. Leonora was wondering how you were doing."

"We talked earlier this evening, she knows I'm fine." I peered at her. "She did *not* send you."

"I did not say she did." Niad put a carefully constructed look of concern on her lovely face. "We're all worried about you, Calendula."

"I'm fine, as you can plainly see." Her words might be more convincing if she'd ever given me any indication that she actually liked me. "I'm trying to sleep. Why are you here, *really*?"

She frowned. "You are not yourself; you are still heavy with grief. It makes you vulnerable. Frankly, I am surprised at finding you alone."

"What are you talking about?"

Now she sniffed. "You spend an awful lot of time with Jeremiah Andromedus these days. Don't think it's gone unnoticed."

I clutched the sheet to my chest. "Oh, I see. Jealous much?"

"Of course not. Just worried about you." She gave me a patently fake smile. "You really should be spending more time at home."

"This is my home. It's perfectly safe, and I have every right to be here." Now I sounded petulant. I calmed my voice and said, "Go *away*."

Her taut poise cracked; I felt a flash of power in her, barely restrained. "None of this would have happened if you hadn't messed with magic that's bigger than you—than any of us. If you had stayed where you *belonged*. Everything would be in control, we'd all be safe.

And *whole*." Her lips were a thin white line, her eyes blazed with anger.

I leaned forward, my fingers white around the sheet. "What in the Blessed Mother's name are you talking about? I didn't cause any of this!"

"So who did?" She was almost shouting. "You can't just...do what you *want* all the time! There are rules for a reason! How far are you going to push this?"

Fury overtook me. "Are you insinuating that something *I* did sent my *best friend's* spirit out of her body? And *why*? So I could steal her *boyfriend*?"

Niad tossed her head, sending blond waves cascading back over her shoulder only to twine back up into the air around her. I could feel her working to get control of herself, even as she pushed me over the edge. "No, you likely did not smite her *directly*, Callie," she said, biting the words out coldly. "But there are systems at work in the world, so many of which we know nothing about. Particularly if one is muddled as to one's own motives. Pluck one strand of the spider's web, and the reverberations are felt throughout."

I shook my head, trying to calm myself as well. "Who do you think you are, to lecture me? Get *out. Now.*"

"I am your coven sister. I care about you."

"You care about the coven, I'll grant you that." I glared at her. "So go back there. Get out of *my house*."

"This is not demarcated space." She vanished onto the ley line before I could respond.

I sank back against my pillows, heart pounding, and sent a message through the æther to Jeremy before I'd even had time to think. *You're so right, I do need wards here.*

He replied promptly. *I would be happy to assist you.*

I laughed, but then thought about it. If I made them myself, my sisters could still have easy access, unless I blocked anyone specifically—say, a certain blonde vixen. So much of our magic was shared, even if we did each have our individual strengths. But if I added warlock magic to the mix? That would be different, and powerful.

Then I felt ashamed, and a little frightened. I was blood-sworn to this coven, for life. Was I seriously considering building such a blatant wall against my chosen family?

But if it could keep Niad out...if I was just seeking to preserve some privacy in my own home... Everyone else politely asked permission to enter. Why did she have to be such a jerk?

I don't know, I answered Jeremy. *It's tempting, but…not exactly friendly, you know?*

As you like.

Had I offended him? It was hard to tell with æthereal communication. There were no visual cues; even the words themselves did not take on the normal spoken tones. I wished we could talk about it in person.

Boy, did I feel lonely.

Are you busy right now? I asked, after a minute.

I am not.

Another pause. *Would you like to come over?*

I would be delighted to.

Ten minutes later, we stood together in my kitchen. Elnor lurked in the corner, watching while affecting not to. Petrana…stood there.

"I feel weird about this," I told Jeremy. "It's like I'm rejecting the coven, when I just want some privacy."

"Did it not already feel like a rejection when you moved into this house?" he asked.

"Well, yeah, but…it was a rejection that went both ways, to be perfectly honest."

"And you, and your coven, have dealt with that, have you not?"

"More or less." I'd told him about Niad's "friendly" little visit. "We've been doing better, lately; I spent so much time there after Logan departed, and they were very nice taking care of me. I worry that doing something like this will just make it all worse again."

He thought a moment, frowning. "Actually, I beg to differ. Niadine, whatever her motives and however clumsily she may have expressed them, was actually conveying a legitimate concern: we have safeguards for very valid reasons. Building wards would demonstrate to your coven, as well as to the entire community, that you are taking our traditions seriously, by putting in place measures to protect yourself."

"Huh." That did make some sense.

Jeremy went on, "I think you may be projecting too much meaning onto the symbolism of wards. It will be easy for you to invite your sisters—or anyone—inside any time you like; this will merely save you from unannounced interruptions, such as you experienced this evening. Not to mention any actual danger." He glanced toward the window. "We have learned to protect ourselves over the centuries with good reason, you know."

"I do know that." I sighed. "And I know you're right, but it still feels weird."

"I notice you lock the front door. A good set of wards is no different than that."

It was true. I'd been foolish, not thinking it through. "Yeah."

"If you don't like them, we can take them down at any time."

"Okay." I nodded. "Let's do this thing."

"Good!" He smiled at me. "If we build both of our essences into it, it will be that much stronger—not just doubled, but multiplied, and in unexpected directions."

"Yes, I know that," I said. Warlocks did love to explain things to witches, didn't they?

He caught my tone and smiled. "Though of course, you know far more about this than I do, being both a coven witch and a working scientist."

I shrugged. "I bet there's a thing or two about the world you could teach me. But wards are something I do understand."

Jeremy laughed. "Good! Then let us build some."

We cooked up a small potion of firewort and sage, more for my benefit than for his, and each swallowed three drams. Then we climbed the stairs to the third floor and sat cross-legged over my pentacle. "Elnor," I called; this was work I'd need my familiar for. She followed and settled in my lap, facing Jeremy across the design on the floor.

"Ready?" he asked.

I nodded, reaching out to take his hands. They were warm and comforting; a gentle thrill ran through me, blending nicely with the potion.

I led the chant, drawing on both of our energies as I sent strong protective magic around the space of my house and surrounding yard—a 360-degree sphere, not neglecting the ground beneath. After I established the rhythm, Jeremy joined in, echoing my words, changing a few of them, reinforcing them by lacing his in the opposite direction. Wards built thusly would withstand many different kinds of assault. And he was right: together we could take them apart easily, if ever I changed my mind.

Within minutes, the spell peaked, and the wards snapped into place. I took a deep breath as the magical feel of the air around me shifted, then re-formed in its new pattern. "Wow, that actually feels great," I said, confused and unable to stop grinning. My sleepiness had vanished entirely. I felt like I could climb every hill in the city again.

"Have you ever had wards built specifically for you before?"

I thought a moment. "No. I've always lived in places secured by others."

"Well, I believe that makes my point. See? I did not expect that you would mind this."

"No!" I laughed, setting Elnor onto the floor as I got to my feet. "Wow." I stretched and wiggled my toes. "It's so…I don't know, juicy or something. Thank you!"

Jeremy got up and stood before me. "You are welcome. It was my pleasure." He grinned too. "I enjoy them as well. I feel much more comfortable inside their bounds."

This close to him, his scent was hard to ignore. And we were both smiling and feeling proud of ourselves, and it was the dead of the night, and the privacy and security around us was quite compelling. Even so, I didn't have to kiss him.

But I wanted to.

I leaned in. He was ready for it, watching me closely as he took me into his arms. My hair twitched against my back, trying to touch him. His kiss was warm and enthusiastic, yet still left room for me to pull away if I came to my senses.

But I didn't.

Or maybe I was responding to a different set of senses. Maybe I was answering that deep, sad, alone part of my heart, the part that had found a listening ear in him. Maybe I was seeking some comfort and solace, from someone who truly understood me, in a way that Raymond—or any human—would never be able to. Maybe I was looking for the ultimate life-affirming act, in the face of grief. Or maybe I was even looking to seal our joint magic in one of the oldest and most traditional ways of our kind.

In any event, the last rational thing I did that night was to lead him down one fight of stairs to my bedroom. I was far too old for sex on a hardwood floor.

— CHAPTER TWELVE —

The sun shone brilliantly through my bedroom window the next morning. Illuminating the warlock sleeping next to me.

Well, this is complicated, I thought. I shifted slightly in the bed, nudging his warm body with my thigh. He sighed in his sleep, nestling a little closer, bringing me his scent—delicious.

I have to talk to Raymond. No more texts. My heart gave a thump as I pushed the thought away. *Later. Today, I will call him. Later.*

This was not like me. It wasn't that I had anything against one-night stands. I'd gone to bed with Raymond the night I'd met him, after all. But I'd been single then, and had been for a long time.

I'll just talk to Logan before—

It was a momentary brain melt: A crazy thing happened, I must tell my best friend all about it! But I couldn't. Just another of the long list of things that would never happen, ready to ambush me at any time. I closed my eyes as a wave of silent grief rolled through me.

When I opened them, Jeremy was gazing at me across the pillow. He clearly waited for me to regain my equilibrium before saying, "Good morning, my dear."

I gave him a small smile. "Hi."

He propped himself up a little. "May I get you some tea, perhaps a pastry? I hear breakfast in bed is a powerful medicine for melancholy."

"Can you read minds?"

It was not entirely a joke, and he knew it. "No, but my perception of emotional emanations is unusually acute. A byproduct of my diplomatic training," he added with a wry smile, as he reached down and brushed a lock of hair out of my eyes. "In another few hundred years, if I keep studying, I may be able to perceive unshielded thoughts. But not yet." His hand lingered on my cheek, caressing it lightly. It felt good. "It is more like heightened empathy at this point. I don't mean to pry."

"That's okay. I just wondered. You do seem to know what I'm thinking."

"I don't, not in its particulars. You just looked so sad." He smiled at me. "Don't ever play poker."

I smiled back. "Ha. If I played cards, I'd probably cheat anyway."

"Somehow, I doubt that."

Why did he always know the right thing to say?

He'd been a very courteous bed partner, too. I mean about sleeping. He hadn't snored, or stolen the covers, or fidgeted. A perfect gentleman. Did they teach bed manners in the Old Country too?

And then the breakfast he brought was delicious.

"Are you trying to spoil me?" I asked, dropping croissant crumbs on my sheets.

"I desire nothing more than to spoil you, Calendula my dear."

"I can't believe you can say stuff like that and sound like you mean it." I sipped my tea, then set the mug on the nightstand.

He raised an eyebrow as he took a swallow of coffee. "I am perfectly sincere."

"I know. I can tell. That's what's hard to believe," I said with a grin.

But what did it all mean? Nothing, of course. It was just a momentary fling, giving in to lust, loneliness, comfort. Completely casual.

Well, but I did like him.

I reached for my tea again, more as a way to avoid meeting his eyes than because I wanted it. Once more, Jeremy did the not-exactly-mind-reading thing and said, "Another croissant?"

"Sure."

And he understood just how long to stay—and when to give me space. When I finished eating, he took his leave, promising to check in with me later.

I sat alone, still in bed, questions rolling through my mind. Fling, or something more? He did want to date me, or whatever they called it in the Old Country. He'd made that clear.

Or did he? His proposition—or whatever it was—had, for all its directness, been rather nonspecific. Maybe he'd just wanted a tumble in bed.

It had been an awfully good tumble.

Did I feel differently about him after sleeping with him?

Well, of course I did. I just didn't know what it *meant*. One night of sex—however great—didn't necessarily mean love, or commitment, or anything. All of witchkind understood that.

But it doesn't have to mean anything, I argued back to myself. I was just in an emotionally vulnerable place, searching for some larger significance in a night of good sex. In any event, Leonora was right: this was not a time for me to be making big decisions.

However, it was definitely time to call Raymond.

So I did. I waited, of course, until he could reasonably be expected to be awake; then I waited a little longer, because he was a musician and might be sleeping late.

And then I waited a little longer than that, because I was cowardly that way.

But then I did call him. He picked up on the first ring. "Hey, babe." The words were casual enough, but I detected a strong note of caution.

"Hey," I said. "I'm sorry I haven't called in so long, but…"

"That's all right."

Then we enjoyed an awkward pause, before both speaking at once.

"What are you doing today?" I asked, as he said, "What's going on?"

I laughed. "Sorry. Are you free?"

"At work till four," he said. "Free after that."

"Come over?"

Only the slightest hesitation; then, "Sure, I'd like that." Another pause. "Can I bring anything?"

"No, I'll cook."

"You'll *cook*?" Now he sounded more like himself.

I laughed. "Oh, I'll probably get takeout. But don't worry, it's on me. You just bring yourself."

After we hung up, I sent a message to Jeremy. *Can I take a raincheck on our walk today? I have a…thing I need to take care of.*

Of course, Callie, came the response. *Is everything all right?*

Yes, it is, and it's nothing about you, or…last night, I quickly sent. *I just need a little process time.* A bit disingenuous, perhaps, but not exactly untrue.

I understand. We will talk later, I hope?

Yes, absolutely.

I did decide to cook. A way of honoring Logan's memory? I don't know. I just felt sort of…domestic. In the same spirit, I shopped for the groceries in person, rather than pulling things through the æther. Walking out, alone this time, would give me a chance to think.

To prepare for Raymond's visit.

What *was* I going to say to him?

I came home with the fixings for burgers and a green salad. Things I knew I could do. And I stashed Petrana upstairs at least an hour before Raymond could be expected to arrive.

He showed up a little before five o'clock, six-pack of beer under one arm. "It smells...interesting in here," he said, glancing around the entryway as if in pursuit of an elusive memory. "That's not Chinese food."

"I cooked! And beer will go perfect with it."

"You really did?" He grinned and handed me the beer, rather than leaning in for a kiss or embrace. Playing it safe.

"I did. Come on, it's almost ready."

I'd set the table in the kitchen; I couldn't face the formal dining room, not yet.

"Open us a couple beers?" I asked, as I toasted the hamburger buns. "You want a glass?"

"Nah."

I brought the platter of burgers to the table and set it down with a flourish. "Voilà!"

"This is awesome," he said after the first bite, wiping his mouth before taking another.

"Thanks." He was right. These were damn good burgers. I smiled as I watched him eat, as he took a generous swig of beer to wash down a bite. Yes, he was a good man. I didn't want to let him go. If I never again got to touch that body? The thought filled me with a keen physical ache. (Despite how I'd spent last night.) I thought of Raymond smiling at me over a carton of Chinese takeout. Of how much I enjoyed watching him play his bass on stage, the marvelous times we'd had in bed... But not just our physical relationship. I missed all the conversations we'd had, his gentle humor, just his intense, well, *goodness*.

How could I make this work? Could I tell him just enough to make him stop trying to get to the parts I couldn't share?

And if I could, would that even work for me?

(And where did Jeremy fit into any of this?)

"Babe? You okay?"

"Huh?" I shook my head, realizing I'd been staring at him like I could magically will everything to solve itself. "Sorry. Woolgathering."

He looked at me. "Yeah. You'd mentioned...things going on."

"Yeah," I said. "I just...I'm sorry." *Open your mouth, witch*, I told myself. *Talk to him. You invited him here to talk to him.* But I still didn't know where to start. I gave him a helpless smile.

He sighed, and took another swig of beer before setting the empty bottle on the table, obviously coming to some decision. "So. Things aren't...right. You know, between us."

"I know," I said, my voice gentle.

"And I...babe, I don't want to break up, but I feel like...you know, I need more, okay? I need at least *something*." He grabbed his bottle and started picking at the label. A little strip tore off, which he rolled absently between his fingers as he went on. "I know you've got... other stuff in your life. Your—community, whatever. And that's all cool with me! That's the deal. I get to see other people too, and that's just fine!"

"Yes," I said. "It is." Though I knew he hadn't, in the year we'd been together.

Neither had I, until last night.

"But, well, we never really talked about it, so...I've kinda been reading up on polyamory, and, well, the important thing there is *no secrets*. It's okay to have separate lives and...all that...but everyone *tells* each other stuff. The primary partners do, at least." He looked up at me, his eyes pleading. "And that's the thing—I don't even know if we *are* primary partners! I mean, you're mine, but I don't know a damn thing about the rest of your life. The people you...used to live with. Aren't they supposed to meet me? Or your family, even?" Again, that vague, searching look on his face, there and gone in a moment. How much did he retain through the fog I'd put on him the night of the dinner party? Anything?

"You're right," I said. "We haven't worked any of this out. And it's long past time that we did."

His face softened. "Oh, babe. Thank you." He reached across the table and took my hand. I squeezed it.

"The first thing you need to know..." I paused. But no, it couldn't wait. "You need to know that my friend who was here, the one who was very sick? She...died. A few weeks ago." Tears filled my eyes as I uttered the half-truth. Well, it wasn't like he could understand what had really happened. And she might as well be dead. She was certainly gone.

"Oh my god! Why didn't you tell me!" He got up, still clutching my hand, and pulled me up into his arms. "I'm so, so sorry!" He stroked my hair, rocking me gently. We fit so well together. He kissed my forehead, then bent a little lower and kissed away some tears.

I kissed him back, snuggling closer as I sniffled. He was so warm, so solid. Familiar. Loving.

"I'm…still processing it," I said, into his chest. "That's why I've been out of touch, what I've been dealing with. I'm sorry, I should have—"

"Oh, jeez, no, of course!" His hand moved from my hair to my shoulders, rubbing me as he held me. "We don't have to talk about… any of this other stuff."

"We do, though. I just…" Now my throat was filling with that lump. The one that says the good cry is imminent. Inevitable.

And there it came. I sobbed in Raymond's arms, soaking his chest. Vaguely, I felt Elnor sniffing around my ankles, but she understood that the crazy foreign human male-thing was giving me comfort, so she backed off.

I cried a long time, clinging to him until the tears finally abated. His caresses continued, making their way to my lower back. And then, as I didn't pull away, the top of my butt.

I shifted closer, not raising my face to his, still holding him tight. My braid nudged his hand; I turned my head a bit so he wouldn't be startled.

His hands roamed down, cupping my ass, then up again, this time finding their way underneath my T-shirt. Oh god, his warm hands on my skin, moving forward, upward…I sighed and leaned into him, shifting my hips. Heat overtook me as I let myself fall into our familiar dance. It felt so *right*. Not just a distraction, or our familiarity, or the like—I mean, it was all those things, plus something more. In that moment, I knew exactly what I wanted, exactly how to communicate with him, how to find comfort, how to express our connection. In all its wordless complexity.

It felt as though I was receiving wisdom from somewhere else. I listened to it, helpless to resist.

Not wanting to resist.

"This…okay?" Raymond asked, in a rough half-whisper.

"Oh yes."

Through kisses, I led him to the couch. Despite my unaccustomed burst of domesticity earlier, I had not managed to change the sheets on my bed.

Sadly, even the most delightful distractions only distract for so long.

"Mmm," I murmured, nestled in Raymond's arms. "Thank you."

"It was my pleasure." He nibbled my ear.

I sighed and sat up, extracting myself from his warm embrace. It felt almost physically painful to pull away from him. "So."

"So." He gazed at me from his end of the couch. No, he did not look like a scared puppy; that was just me projecting.

I took a deep breath. "So."

"You said that." He gave me a tentative grin.

"Yeah." I smiled back. "You're right: there are a lot of things in my life I haven't shared with you. And for very good reasons—which I also can't share." He started to answer; I held up a hand. "No, please, I'm going to tell you as much as I can, so let me just say it all out. Then you can ask questions if you want."

He nodded. "Okay."

"I told you when we met that I lived in an intentional community. And that's true, but it's not what you think. I let you believe it was some sort of free-love commune, because I knew that would make more sense to you. And it would stop you asking too many questions." I gave him a sheepish smile. "But...it's a religious community, actually. One with a very, very long history of deep privacy. Which looks like secrecy from the outside, I know."

I don't read minds either, but I could almost see the words going through his brain: *She's in some sort of* cult?

"I'm still a full-fledged member of that community, even though I moved out of the...main house," I went on. "I still participate in the practices and rituals and important communal meals. I still teach younger members of the order. But they agreed to my moving out for a little while; perhaps a few years. We all agreed I needed a little more space of my own.

"My birth family also belongs to this community, though by joining this other household when I came of age, that sort of...reconfigured the significance of the people in my life. This is how it's done with us. I'm still very fond of my birth parents, but my house members are my true family." I smiled again. "Complete with sibling rivalry. Which is part of the reason I'm trying to develop more of an outside social life. I really like your friends, and I love you. But, well, there's a limit on how much I'm going to be able to share—with you or anyone on the outside. There are always going to be secrets. I don't really have any say in the matter."

Raymond just kept watching me. He looked very unhappy, and rather confused.

"You can ask questions now," I said.

"You can't even tell me the name of the...religion?"

"It's, ah, a form of paganism. You won't have heard of it."

"Oh." He thought a moment. "And you're not...I mean, you could leave it if you wanted to? You don't need...help?"

A surprised chuckle escaped me. "Oh, um, it's not like that. It is intrinsic to my very nature that I practice this religion, and I am quite happy doing so. Nobody's keeping me captive, don't worry." I gave him what I hoped was a reassuring smile.

"Okay." He paused, thinking again. "But you are poly?"

I snorted. I might have known he'd return there. "Technically, yes, though we don't call it that. And not everyone acts on it, not like hu—I mean, the rest of the world. Think of it as a different culture. One without an underlying assumption of lifelong monogamy. Just... different rules."

Sudden understanding dawned on his face. "Ohhhh. You're not supposed to be dating outside the community, are you? *I'm* the secret."

I started to correct him, then realized what a gift he'd just handed me. "You're right—sort of. I mean, I'm an adult, I'm allowed a certain amount of freedom in my personal life, but—yeah, we would never be allowed to marry or anything. I could never bring you home to meet my family. Any of my family. So, it's just been better that I've kept you separate." I reached over and took his hand. "I'm sorry if this is painful. I never meant to hurt you. It's...been harder than I realized, keeping such important parts of my life entirely apart from each other."

He leaned forward and took me into his arms. "Callie, hon, I understand. It's all right."

"No, it's not all right," I said, into his chest. "It's not fair to you, and I'm sorry I didn't figure out how to explain it better than this before. It's just...we worked so well, when we were seeing each other once or twice a week when I lived at the...house. I thought it would be easier when I moved here, not harder."

He laughed, softly. "Yeah. I knew I wasn't gonna move in with you, but I did sorta think you'd maybe give me a key."

I tensed in his arms. "I..."

"No, babe, stop," he said. "I'm cool. I know you need time, that it must be a big adjustment for you." He squeezed me gently. "I'm cool, really. There's no rush."

"Thank you." I tilted my face up for a kiss.

And then another kiss.

And then I got a message through the æther. *Callie, I hope all is going well with you? I have been thinking about you all day...very fondly, and in lavish detail.*

Jeremy! Oh, Blessed Mother. How long had it been since I'd told him I'd talk to him soon? Had I missed an earlier ping? What time *was* it now?

I froze mid-kiss. Raymond drew away and looked into my eyes. "Hon?"

"I'm all right." I flashed him a quick, uncomfortable smile as I sent *Hang on* to Jeremy. "But I think I need a little time to be alone right now." At least the warlock was being polite and not just peering into my house. Or showing up! There were those Old Country manners again. Thank goodness.

"Okay..." Raymond dropped his hands and took a step back. "I'll see you soon?"

I am at your disposal flashed into my head.

"Yes. I'll call you."

"Sure." A sad look crossed his face, though I could see him trying to hide it. "You know you can talk to me about anything...I mean, anything you *can* talk about. You know."

"I know." I drew him into another strong hug.

After I released him, Raymond gathered his things. I tried to give him a decent kiss at the door, but my thoughts were elsewhere. And we both knew it.

I closed the door behind him. *Well, that didn't really solve anything.* I went into the front parlor and flopped into a chair with a sigh.

Elnor came and snuggled on my lap. I scritched her for a minute, then sent a message to Jeremy. *Hello, and sorry about that.*

Not a problem. Of course you have a life.

He didn't know how right he was.

Well, at least I could stop digging myself deeper into secrecy and half-truths. *Raymond was over here when you sent your message*, I told him.

A pause. *Oh?*

Boy, was it hard to read someone's tone in æther-communication. Was he miffed, jealous, annoyed? Or just waiting for more information? *Yes, I needed to explain some things to him, after sending him away the night of the dinner party.*

An even longer pause. *Is everything cleared up now?*

More or less. I sighed again. *Maybe, I don't know. For the moment, anyway. Humans are complicated.*

Are they? I haven't found them so, but I confess I haven't had much in the way of relations with them.

No, I supposed he hadn't. *Well, it's cleared up enough,* I said, suddenly not wanting to talk to Jeremy about this. Not remotely. And not now. *So! Have you had a good day?*

He sent a chuckle across the æther. *I have told you before that I will respect your privacy, Calendula, and I meant it. As for my day…yes, and no.*

What do you mean?

Though my day has been filled with thoughts of our night, he said, *other things have happened as well. Two more witches have taken ill.*

What? My heart started pounding; I sat bolt-upright, startling Elnor. *What's going on?*

May I come see you?

Absolutely.

A few minutes later we sat in my front parlor, beside one another on the couch. "It's an unaffiliated witch named Lucinda and a young witch from Gloria's coven named Dreanor. My father is setting up an emergency clinic near where the healers live."

"Drained essences?" I asked.

Jeremy nodded. "Yes, though not as fast nor as badly as with Logan. My father thinks they might pull through." He glanced down at the floor, then back at me. "Assuming, of course, that they don't worsen. But for now, their spirits are holding fast."

"And there is still no sign of the cause? I suppose we'll all be sent back indoors once more," I added. It was odd, in fact, that I hadn't heard from Leonora yet. Surely she knew.

"No. These instances aren't quite the same as Logan's; they were slower to build, with no moment of sudden onset. Both witches reported feeling poorly for some weeks. Lucinda tried all manner of herbs and nostrums before she contacted Hesta."

"But it has to be the same thing." I frowned. "Essence doesn't just leak away for no reason. This had to come from somewhere…or someone. Right?"

"There have been no unknown practitioners in our community since the Elders last searched, and there are no strangers here now," Jeremy said. "In fact...the last stranger to enter the community was me."

I looked up at him sharply. "Surely they don't think—"

He laughed, but without humor. "I am not stealing essence from witches. Or from anyone." He reached out his hand; I took it and gave it a gentle squeeze. "I did insist that they examine me thoroughly, just to put everyone's minds at rest. My father was mortified, I am sure, but he did not object. They found no sign of ill intent in me, no harmful spells cast."

Still holding his hand, I opened my senses to him, seeking... anything. I felt good intentions, fear, confusion, and a strong burst of warm tenderness. Aimed at me. He had clearly opened himself to my scrutiny, knowing I would want to take the measure of him. I smiled at him. "Thanks."

He pulled my hand to his lips and gave it a gentle kiss. "Of course, Calendula. Privacy is one thing; secrecy is quite another. You may look into my heart whenever you like."

It was a very sweet sentiment, even if it was only sort of true. No one was an open book, not even to uber-powerful practitioners who could read actual thoughts. Even so. I appreciated what he meant.

So much so that I invited him to spend a second night.

"No breakfast in bed this morning, I am sorry," Jeremy said. "Father expects me at the new clinic. He has a lot for me to do."

"I'll come with you," I told him, getting up and looking for a clean pair of jeans. "I can help."

"Hmm." He looked slightly pained. "Let me check with my father first. Between all his research assistants and the healers, we've got more doctors than patients at the moment. We don't even really know what we're looking for."

"I'm happy to ask him myself," I said, tactfully not pointing out that I likely knew his father better than he did. As the clinic was to be for both research and treatment, I wouldn't be getting in any doctors' ways by looking at the research side of things.

"Please, Callie. Let me ask."

I waited, expecting that he would send an ætheric message.

He looked back at me. "I would rather ask him in person, when I'm there. I will send you a message if he wants your help."

I started to argue, but stopped myself and said, "All right." Jeremy looked relieved. No doubt his very unfamiliarity with Gregorio explained his being extra careful in trying to please him. Now that I thought about it, Gregorio seemed rather formal with his son as well. They needed time to become more comfortable with one another. It would happen. They were both good warlocks.

After he left, I went to the coven house and knocked on Leonora's office door.

"Come in, Calendula," came her voice from the other side.

I went in and took a seat. Logan's body seemed unchanged. I gazed at it a long moment before looking away.

Leonora closed a large ledger book, set her quill pen down, and looked up at me. She started to say something, then paused, scrutinizing me. "Are you feeling all right, Calendula?"

"What? Yes, I'm fine…considering. Why?"

She shook her head. "It's nothing, I'm sure. I just thought I saw something amiss."

Grief, probably, I thought. "I heard from Jeremiah Andromedus that more witches are sick."

"Yes, quite mysteriously. It is most disturbing."

"Yes—to say the least. Have you seen them?"

"Not yet," she said. "I am visiting Dr. Andromedus's new clinic in an hour. He has asked all the coven mothers to come and give their assessments."

"May I come along?"

"No. This is a meeting for coven mothers and medical practitioners only."

I struggled to stay calm. To feel capable in the face of my coven mother's withering gaze. All the while remembering Logan's words from our tarot reading: *Leonora has infantilized you over the years.* "I am a biological researcher. The first witch fell ill in my house—and departed there. And she was my closest friend. I might be able to help."

"Your biology work is at the microscopic level—you are not a healer. And being Logan's friend, your judgment is clouded by emotion. You are not yourself; I can see it in your face, in your energy." Before I could argue again, she went on, more gently. "The other coven mothers and I will visit first. If we find ourselves in need of additional opinions, I will consider your request." Then she reached for her quill pen again.

"Yes, Mother," I murmured, and left her.

Back at my house, I made a cup of tea and flopped down into a kitchen chair, seething with frustration. Leonora did treat us all as children. I'd moved out, yet I still had to answer to her, just as everyone else in the house did. Every witch was expected to show deference to any coven mother, particularly our own. Yes, I was still young, as witchkind counted things—the youngest in our coven—but I'd lived nearly half a century. Would I, and my work, ever be taken seriously?

I sipped my tea, which tasted stale, as I calmed down slowly, thinking it all over. We were supposed to be a community, a family, even if Leonora was our leader. Was Logan right, that my coven was more hierarchical than most? More unhealthy? Niad was ninety-three, witchkind's equivalent of her mid-thirties. A human woman in her thirties would most likely have been independent for ten or fifteen years—living alone, or with friends or a partner, or married— yet Leonora didn't go any easier on Niad than she did me. My older sister was smart and powerful and gorgeous, and she let herself get bossed around by a woman three hundred and fifty years older than her and showing no signs of slowing down. Was that why Niad was such a cranky bully all the time?

It didn't mean she had to take it out on me, though. I was frustrated myself, yet I still tried to be nice to people. It wasn't like I picked on the students or tortured humans or something.

Well, Jeremy and Leonora might be able to keep me away from the clinic—for now, at least—but there were other parts of this mystery I could look into. Logan's apartment, for example. No one had seen Willson yet, and that was truly odd.

Elnor accompanied me along an unfamiliar ley line to its branching point. We switched to the more familiar line leading to Logan's building; I hadn't lived in my house long enough to have a habitual way over there. Another pang at my heartstrings…now I never would make such a path.

I stood on the sidewalk where Jeremy and I had paused on our walk the other day; Elnor kept close to my ankles. Logan's building was old and majestic, two stories of apartments above shops on the street level, on the cusp between the Castro and Church Street neighbo-rhoods. Mostly humans lived here, though I knew that one other unaffiliated witch had recently moved in—a transplant from New

Orleans. Logan had talked about befriending her, even joking that they should establish a sort of Outcasts Club, but I didn't know if they had actually ever spoken.

I sent my senses into the building. The other witch wasn't home, though I felt her lingering energy, and that of her familiar. Elnor's nose twitched as she detected it too. I glanced around; no humans were watching, so I spelled the lock on the street door and we went inside.

Logan's apartment was at the far end of the top floor. I spelled that door too, opening it a crack. I waited, peering in but not crossing the threshold yet, taking the measure of the place.

Energetically, it was eerily like Logan's body: it seemed as though someone had left it just a moment ago. But it was entirely still, lifeless. Suspended. Was her spirit lingering here, somehow, some way? "Hello?" I called out softly, not wanting to attract the attention of any neighbors.

Nobody answered.

I pushed the door open and we stepped into the tiny entryway. Her wards hadn't been set, yet their presence hovered in the air. Ready to be triggered. Did she not ward her place when she left it? Had she been so distracted by our dinner party?

I walked into the living room. The air was not stale or dusty, like an abandoned apartment should have been. Perhaps Willson had come back here after all. Although he would not have swept up or opened windows. Elnor prowled the corners of the rooms, sniffing as usual.

Logan's favorite corner of the sofa, where she had liked to curl up with a cup of tea and a book, still bore her impression. I ran my hands along the cushions and half-closed my eyes, searching for anything—a trace of essence, a scent, any sort of clue. I found nothing but memories.

I sat down on the couch and closed my eyes the rest of the way, letting my inner senses seek without any confusing visual input. Again, just a sense of stillness. Almost peace. It was the same feeling she had imbued the place with when she was here: gentle, kind, quiet. After a minute, my cat joined me on my lap.

"I don't understand," I whispered to Elnor. After another few minutes, I got up to look through the rest of the apartment.

Logan's kitchen was tidy; one plate with stale toast crumbs sat in the sink. Her bathroom was spotless.

In her bedroom, I found the bed unmade, and some clothes draped over the footboard. On the dresser was something I hadn't seen before: a fetchingly arranged little display of pink and white and red candles, dried red tea roses, cones of lavender incense, a few curls of red ribbon, and a tarot card, but not one from her working deck.

I picked up the card. It was The Lovers, from the Romance deck—all frills and lace and Valentine's hearts. Practically a toy deck, but very pretty.

"My goodness," I whispered. It was a love-shrine. To Jeremy? He had liked her without any trickery; anyone could see it.

Anyone, that was, besides her.

It made me want to laugh and cry all at once. "Oh, Logan," I said, sitting down on her rumpled bed. "I'm so sorry." I felt a surge of guilt, as if I'd lured Jeremy away from her, as if she hadn't left us all...

I felt a tingle in my belly, a moment of warmth. Was it her spirit, trying to communicate with me? Reassuring me? I put my hand there, sensing it. No, there was nothing. Maybe I was just hungry. It had been a while since breakfast.

After I collected myself, I got up and continued searching the bedroom, opening all my senses to any spirits that might have come through here in the last weeks. There was no evidence of Willson, not since the night of the dinner party. Had he been hit by a car? Had some well-meaning human family adopted him? Would he even let that happen? It was very unusual for a familiar to abandon his witch, but he might have been confused, or frightened. He was a fairly young cat, after all.

And not all familiars were created equal. I scritched Elnor's ears, feeling grateful for her.

I looked through Logan's closet, and the drawers of her dresser. Nothing unusual. Returning to the kitchen, I made a thorough search of her food and dishes, paying particular attention to her herbs and other potion ingredients. Again, I only found the usual items a working witch would have. She must have visited the communal magical garden fairly recently: there was a good supply of hellebore.

Ultimately, I went back to the living room and sat on the couch again, stymied. I didn't know what I'd expected to find, but it seemed that there should have been *something*.

On the coffee table, next to a dry teacup, was her tarot deck. I picked it up, a little surprised that she'd left it here the night of the dinner party—she usually kept the cards in her purse. Opening the box, I took the cards out. For a minute I just held them in my hands; then I shuffled, as she'd always had me do before our readings.

As I moved the cards between my hands, I thought about our last reading. Of course, it had been about me, not her—but even so, shouldn't it have at least hinted at a great loss in my near future?

Well, there had been that Tower card at the very end. That had seemed to frighten her. But she'd insisted that it meant good things... ultimately. There was nothing good about my best friend's spirit being wrenched from her body—not now, not ever.

I folded the deck back together and was putting it in its box when I heard a noise at the window—a sharp scratching, as of claws. Startled, I looked up, dropping a card to the floor. "Elnor?" But she was sitting on the couch beside me; she stared at the window as well.

"Willson?" I got up and rushed to open the window, but there was nothing on the ledge. I leaned over and looked out, along the fire escape, then down to the alley below. Nothing there. I sent my magical senses out. Amid the same random jumble of human and animal energies as before, I did sense her cat's essence.

"Willson!" I shouted. "Come back!" Elnor joined me at the window, meowing at her lost friend.

Willson's essence faded fast, as if he was darting away. Was he afraid? Why come here, only to flee before seeing me? He knew me, and liked me. He loved Elnor.

"Willson! Here, kitty kitty!"

Nothing.

After a few minutes, I went back to the couch and started to close the box, then saw the card on the floor. It was The Devil. With a shiver, I tucked him into the box too.

When I left, I took the cards with me. I told myself it was because I wanted something to remember her by.

— CHAPTER THIRTEEN —

Other than that first week or so when I had been so undone by grief that I would have been useless, I'd continued my teaching. The distraction was comforting. The witchlets were curious and energetic, full of hope for the future, full of drama and despair about the present. I loved being surrounded by them, helping shape their creative minds. It brought out the maternal in me, leaving a pleasant ache in my heart.

After I left Logan's apartment, I felt almost too tired and frustrated to go teach my biology class, but I did it anyway. And, as usual, I found it encouraging, uplifting.

Gracie hung back after class, pretending she didn't have anything special on her mind. I gave her a minute to screw up her nerve before I said, "Hey. How's it going?"

"Oh fine," she said, implying just the opposite. Then she seemed to catch herself. "How are *you* doing?"

I stood behind the desk in the small second-floor classroom, packing my satchel. "I'm all right. Still sad, but I suppose I'm getting used to it."

"It must be awful, to lose a friend."

"It is. We were very close."

"There is still no sign of her spirit?"

"None." Neither of us had to say how baffling this was.

"I'm so sorry." She shuffled her feet.

"Thank you." I gave her another moment. "Mina scored 100 percent on her taxonomy quiz. You've been tutoring her, haven't you?"

Gracie shrugged and mumbled something I couldn't hear.

"What was that?"

Now she looked up at me. "*Someone* had to."

I sighed and pulled up a classroom chair. "You're miserable. Spill it."

"You said you'd be here all the time, and you're not! Even when you were, you never left your room hardly. We never see you. And I feel like I can't even say anything, because...Logan. And now I'm just being a big jerk."

"Gracie, you're not a jerk. It's entirely fine to miss me, to have your own feelings of loss. It's not a competition. And you're not wrong. I... miss me too. I hardly know who I am at the moment, or what's going to happen."

I took a breath and stopped. I had moved out to try to take more control over my life—yet it felt as though events were just tumbling me down a hillside.

Gracie kicked at an invisible spot on the floor. Not looking up, she said, "I heard you're dating a human."

My heart gave a frightened jump. Had I really just slept with two different men in the last two days? "Yes, Gracie, it's true. Did Leonora tell you?"

"Niad." She looked up at me, her pretty face guarded, and glanced away again.

Ah, of course. "Is that what you're afraid of, that I've fallen in love with a human and I'm giving up being a witch, or something? Like *Bewitched*?"

She shook her head, though I could see the truth in her eyes. "Well, I don't know..."

"Even if that were possible, it's not happening. It's perfectly acceptable for a witch to spend time with humans. Sometimes even romantic time. I know you have human friends—many of us do. It's not much different than that." *Should I tell her I'm seeing a warlock too? Am I seeing a warlock?* It was too soon, too new, too uncertain. Nothing to gossip with a student about, however much I liked her. "Anyway, it's not serious."

"It's not?" She looked up, hopeful.

"No. He's a very nice man, but we're fundamentally pretty different." I smiled at her, as if I had it all worked out and everything was great.

"Hm."

We both turned at a sound at the door. It was Sirianna. "Oh, sorry, Callie! I was just... Potions is next, and..."

"We're just clearing out, Siri," I said, getting up and grabbing my satchel. "Come on, Gracie. I'll see you at dinner Tuesday."

"You're not coming back till *Tuesday*?" The witchlet followed me out of the room; Sirianna and several other girls filed in, closing the door behind them.

"I don't know my schedule for the next few days," I started, before I had a better idea. "I can come take you out for lunch on Saturday. Would you like that?"

"Yes!" she said, adding politely, "I mean, if it's not too much trouble."

I pulled her in for a hug. "It is not the tiniest bit of trouble."

She hugged me back, then pulled away, awkward but happy. "Or I could see your house?"

Oh, Blessed Mother, I'd promised the girls to show them my place ages ago…before events had overtaken me. "Of course! Lunch at my house it is."

"Yay! Thanks!" Smiling, she turned and headed toward the stairs.

I watched her go. Fifteen was such a tough age. Though at the moment, I wasn't finding forty-five a whole lot easier.

"May I help you with that, Mistress Callie?"

"What?" I yelped and nearly dropped the groceries, I was so startled. I shouldn't have been; I'd been trying to teach Petrana to take initiative. But she surprised the wits out of me, practically pouncing on me in the entryway.

I'd been woolgathering. Thinking about my life. Days had passed, and everything felt stuck in amber. There was nothing new about Logan, or the newly sick witches. Jeremy had spent one more night, and it was good, but…my heart was still unsettled. My research had stalled. I didn't know what to do about anything.

I sighed, looking back at Petrana. "Yes, thank you." I shifted my hip so she could take the heavy bag of groceries. She reached out her large, awkward hand, managing to grab both the shopping bag and the strap of my purse, nearly pulling it from my shoulder. "Whoah! Hold up there, big girl," I said.

"I am sorry," she said, emotionlessly, freezing in place.

I replaced the strap. "Okay, go ahead." She took the bag and then stood in the entryway, staring at me. "You can put them away in the kitchen," I added. "But leave out the bread and the turkey."

"Yes, Mistress Callie." She turned and shuffled off.

Was this just a stupid waste of time? I still didn't really know what she was for.

But I didn't want to unmake her.

I sighed. Just another unresolved thing in my life. And Gracie would be here in less than an hour. Maybe I should teach Petrana to make sandwiches? Surely they wouldn't taste like mud.

Can I come in?

"What?" I said aloud as I followed Petrana toward the kitchen, then *Gracie, you're early.*

I know! I want to show you something!

Sure. I started back for the front door, but Gracie popped into the hallway in front of me. "Wow!" I said. "You're getting really smooth with your ley line travel. That's great."

"I know!" She grinned, practically shimmering with pride; her dark curls bounced. "I've been practicing."

"Well, come on, you can help me with lunch." I turned back to the kitchen.

"No! I want to *show you* something!"

"I thought you just did."

She tossed her head and gave a dramatic teenage snort. "Callie! Not that! *This*!" She reached into her jeans pocket and pulled out a smartphone, swiping open the screen as she said, "Which one should I choose?"

I led her to the kitchen table and took the smartphone from her. It showed a picture of a calico kitten.

"Here," she said, reaching over my arm to swipe to the next picture, a longhaired tuxedo kitten, much like a young Elnor. Gracie's phone was sure fancier than mine; I had no idea how it worked. Did mine even hold pictures? Then she brought up an adorable tabby.

"These are cats?" I asked, displaying a stunning grasp of the obvious.

"Sapphire's coven has three litters ready to adopt, and Leonora said I could choose my familiar now. How about this one?" She held up the phone, showing a shorthaired marmalade with yellow eyes.

"Sweetheart, you don't choose the familiar—the familiar chooses you." At my feet, Elnor purred and rubbed against me, though she couldn't have understood my words, exactly. "These kittens are all adorable, but you will want to meet them in person."

"Can we?" Gracie looked up at me eagerly. "Can we go right now?"

I laughed. "I thought you wanted to see my house. And have lunch."

"I do! Can we do everything, right now?"

"Whatever you like, but not all at once. Which do we do first?"

Gracie glanced around the kitchen, obviously noticing it for the first time. She was practically quivering with excitement. "Cat first! Then back here for lunch."

"All right."

We took a ley line to Sapphire's coven; I followed Gracie, noticing again how deftly she managed the ley space. I took the opportunity to send a quick inquiry to Leonora, making sure she actually had given the witchlet explicit permission. *Yes, Calendula, and thank you for your help with this,* she sent back a moment later. *Young Graciela's birth mother has been just too busy,* she added, with a note of disapproval.

The cat-breeding coven was a big home out near the ocean, not far from the Cliff House. The cattery, like our own coven house, occupied a double lot and looked ordinary, if large, from the street. Once inside its perimeter gate, however, the differences were plain. The yard was crammed with cat toys, cat trees, cat food bowls, cat exercise ramps—and cats. Dozens and dozens of cats, of every shape and size and age. "Ooh!" Gracie exclaimed, crouching down to pet a tortoiseshell. The cat mewed and rubbed its cheeks against her fingers. "This one's chosen me, Callie!"

I patted Gracie's shoulder and tried not to laugh aloud. "No, sweetie, she just wants a scritching. Come on inside, you'll see."

She reluctantly left the tortie and followed me to the front porch, where we paused while I sent ahead the formal request to be admitted. As we were standing there, my phone chimed with a text. Since it could only be one person, I reached into my pocket to silence it. I'd talk to Raymond later.

The door opened; Sapphire herself stood there, smiling at both of us. A faint smell of cat dander wafted out on the breeze.

"Do come in," Sapphire said, stepping aside for us. "Hello, Callie; and you must be Graciela."

"It's a pleasure to meet you, Miss Sapphire," Gracie said.

"Come this way."

Once inside, the cat smell was quite a bit stronger. We followed Sapphire into a small parlor set up as a low-key interview room, where she offered us comfy chairs and tea. A minute later, cups of pennyroyal beside us, we were settled. The older witch studied the witchlet as I sipped my tea. It tasted sort of off; I set the cup down. Must be too much cat in the air.

I was glad my coven was for teaching. Who could live in a cattery? Maybe you stopped noticing after a while.

Gracie sat politely and sipped her tea as well, though anyone could see she was bursting to look at the kittens. Sapphire continued to watch her as she made small talk with me, taking the measure of the young witch, sensing her essence and personality.

Finally, the coven mother set her own empty teacup down and said, "Well, Graciela, are you ready to meet the candidates?"

"Yes, please!" Gracie grinned back at her.

"Come with me." She rose to her feet.

"Shall I stay back?" I asked.

Sapphire glanced at me. "No, they'll sense Elnor's essence and won't bother looking for a bond with you."

I followed them down a long hallway past many small rooms, then up a flight of stairs. The house was even larger than it looked from the front, and even more full of cats and their equipment and toys and dishes. It was also badly overfurnished, though most of the plush chairs were claw-damaged and fur-covered. Even so, it was a comfortable place, if chaotic. All the cats seemed sleek and well-adjusted.

A large back room on the second floor was the nursery. Mama cats filled the place, snugged in their dresser-drawer beds placed all around the room. There were probably two dozen litters, of every age, from newborn to spunky electrons ready to be weaned. As Gracie had said, three litters were at prime adoption age. Kittens bounded around the room, tumbling and playing.

"So many!" Gracie exclaimed. "Are there this many witches needing familiars?"

"Not at all," Sapphire said. "Most cats, even of our breeding stock, do not possess the capacity to become true familiars—the long life span or the magical potential." She leaned over to pet a pure white mama cat in her drawer bed, snugged in among a jumble of towels. "We must breed a lot of cats to get even a handful of the right ones."

"How can I tell?" Gracie asked from the floor, where she was already being leapt upon by kittens.

"You don't need to. Your cat will choose you." Sapphire smiled at me. "It shouldn't take very long."

"It can take all day as far as I'm concerned," Gracie said happily, tickling the fuzzy belly of a black cat as a little calico nibbled at her fingers.

"Have a seat," Sapphire offered me, pointing at a low sofa by the door, which was so matted in fur I could hardly tell what color it had once been.

I sat anyway. Maybe I could teach Petrana how to use a clothing roller.

Sapphire sat next to me. "How are you doing, Callie?" she asked in a low voice.

"All right. Adjusting. Thank you for asking."

"Of course. And how is dear Elnor?"

"She's great—strong and healthy."

Sapphire beamed. "I'm so glad. If you change your mind about letting us try for a litter out of her, do let me know."

"I will. I think she'd let me know if she wanted that, don't you? I mean, in some way?"

"It's possible. She may not know herself. How are her heats?"

"Mild. So far, at least."

The coven mother nodded. "Well, she is young yet."

"She was close to Willson," I said. "He still hasn't shown up here, has he?" He was only a few years old—even younger than Elnor. He might feel a pull to his birthplace.

"I am sorry, no, he has not. We will keep watching for him, though."

"Thanks."

Within a few minutes, I felt the energy in the room solidify and focus. Sapphire nodded at me and we both watched the witchlet as she played with the kittens, giggling and teasing them as they darted around her. But one kitten in particular stood out: a tawny Himalayan mix. It couldn't be a purebred—there were no Himalayan mamas in the room, and most witch cats were mongrels at least to some degree—but it sure looked like one, with its long fluffy hair; dark brown face, ears, and paws; and stunning blue eyes. This kitten attacked Gracie with all the ferocity it could muster, returning again and again to the fray; then it abruptly gave a tiny hiss, batted at its siblings and playmates to chase them away, and plunked itself into Gracie's lap.

The witchlet looked up at us. Sapphire nodded. "I think she has chosen you," she said.

"What's her name?" Gracie asked, petting the fuzzy creature. I could hear the rumble of her purr from across the room.

"We do not name them until they have either chosen witches or aged out," Sapphire said, walking over to a large filing cabinet on the far wall. She opened a drawer, looked through a few file folders, and pulled one out. "She is called M2T9-4317 for now. You will name her." The coven mother made a notation on a sheet of paper from the file and brought it over to Gracie, who now stood with the kitten in her arms, beaming. "We have a few forms for you to sign, and then she is yours."

"Wait to name her," I advised. "She won't literally tell you her name, but once you live with her a few days, it should become obvious."

"I love her *so much*!" Gracie exclaimed, burying her nose in the tiny creature's soft fur. "She's the most adorable thing ever!"

"She's gorgeous," I agreed. "But you should probably put her down for a moment so you can sign the cattery's forms."

"I only need one hand to sign!"

Back at my house, lunch was further delayed while we both played with the new kitten until it was tired out enough to crash into the cutest little nap ever, face down on the ottoman in the front parlor. Elnor, who had tolerated the new arrival with stoic forbearance, relaxed considerably once the energetic creature zonked out.

I had Gracie help me prepare chicken salad sandwiches—with a few morsels for Elnor along the way, as reward or apology—and we ate them in the formal dining room. It was my first meal there since the dinner party; I couldn't keep avoiding the room forever. Gracie's cheerful presence helped reset the tone of the room.

At least, that's what I kept telling myself.

After lunch, we left Petrana to the cleanup while I gave Gracie a tour of the rest of the house. "Should I wake the kitten?" she asked. "Won't she want to inspect the space?"

"Let her sleep; you'll have plenty of opportunity later. She'll be your cat for at least twenty-five years, most likely. Perhaps a lot more."

Gracie grinned, and her hair twitched in its ponytail.

She dutifully oohed and ahed at my house as I showed her around, but it was clear that the kitten had eclipsed any excitement that the witchlet once had about architecture, furniture, or rugs. Until we got to the third floor lab, anyway: then she stood in the center of the room, looking around with wide eyes. "Oh, Callie, this is great," she gushed. "You are so lucky to have all this space to do whatever you want in!"

I chuckled. "Unfortunately, I'm not taking advantage of it like I should." There was dust forming on my lab bench again already.

"You will," she said, seriously. "Just give it time. You've been through a lot."

Sometimes, she could be so mature.

"It's true," I told her. "It's also true that my research feels kind of pointless at the moment—in the face of what's going on. Across town, all our eminent biologists are working on what's attacking witchkind, and I'm supposed to stay over here fiddling with little reproduction creatures?"

"They won't let you help?"

I sighed. "No, Dr. Andromedus and his team have pretty much taken charge. Along with the healers, of course."

Gracie rolled her eyes. "Warlocks."

"Yeah." I laughed. "Tell me about it."

"You should just volunteer."

"I have," I said, not trying to hide my annoyance any more. "Many times. But Leonora and Dr. Andromedus—and his son—keep having such very good reasons why I should stay away. 'Later,' they tell me. And later never comes."

"So just *go there*—show up. What can they do?"

"Not let me in." Now I gave her a helpless smile. "Sorry, Gracie; I shouldn't burden you with this. I'm sure they have very good reasons, and they'll let me help when it makes sense for me to."

She looked back at me, her expression dubious. "I still think you should just waltz in and take charge. You're the smartest witch around. Have any of *them* built a golem?"

I reached out and gave her a hug. "Gracie, you're so sweet. But I do need to respect our elders."

"Not if they're being stupid!"

"Come on," I said, leading her to the door. "Let's go see if your kitten is still asleep."

"Kitten!" she said, almost jumping up and down again. "I forgot about my kitten!"

I chuckled. "She won't let you forget her for long."

Yet Gracie's words, however adolescently framed, continued to nag at me. By the following afternoon, I was in a near-teenage tizzy myself. "She's right," I said to Elnor, who twitched her tail as she gazed back at me. "I *will* just go there. Let them turn me away in person."

I knew where the clinic was, more or less; even though it was screened, it's impossible to disguise entirely such a quantity of magical focus in one place.

After a small internal debate, I left Elnor at home. I could call for her if I needed to.

I emerged from the ley line a few doors down from an old warehouse South of Market, only to find Sebastian standing there on the sidewalk. Bingo.

"Callie, how are you *doing*?" he asked, taking my arm and gently but firmly steering me away from the building.

Digging in my heels, albeit equally gently, I said, "About how you'd expect, and why aren't you letting me in there?"

"Come have coffee with me." He gave me a significant look and whispered, "Callie, I'm your friend. *Trust* me."

Sighing, I let him lead me down the block to a noisy café and buy me a cup of tea. "Okay, seriously, what?" I asked, once we were seated at a small table by the front window.

"You know the coven mothers have decided not to let anyone but the Elders and the healers see the sick witches. It might be contagious."

I rolled my eyes. "Yes, Leonora told me. But you don't really know that, and I can take the same precautions as you guys. And I might be able to help."

He glanced around, as if afraid of being overheard. "Three more witches have sickened. We still have no idea what's behind this."

"Wait, what? When?"

"Just in the last few days. We're keeping it quiet. We don't want a general panic."

"Oh, Blessed Mother." My stomach sank with worry. "What about the first two?"

"They have actually shown some slight signs of improvement." He looked at my face. "No one else has…departed."

"I'm glad. But—" I paused as Sebastian's dark eyes went vague; he was clearly talking with someone through the æther.

When he returned his attention to me, he said, "Flavius is on his way."

Flavius? It took me a moment to remember who he was—Dr. Winterheart, who'd been in Gregorio's lab the day I'd brought my samples by. The one who didn't come to my dinner party at the last minute. "He's not a healer, or an Elder," I protested.

"No, but he is on the Elder path," Sebastian said. "He's smart, but also a nice guy. And it doesn't hurt that he's Dr. Andromedus's current favorite."

"I don't really know him," I said. "He seemed kind of tightly wound, the last time I saw him."

"Oh, he's fine. Probably he was feeling the effects of working under such scrutiny all day." Sebastian gave me a wry smile. "You know."

"I suppose I do." Gregorio was my mentor as well, though I hadn't worked with him on a day-to-day basis for years now.

The young researcher slipped into the café and took a seat at our table. "Hi." He shrugged off his jacket—just as rumpled as his hair—and hung it on the back of his chair. "Sebastian told me you want to help, Calendula Isadora. I was—"

"Callie," I said, automatically. "And yes: I've been doing biomedical research for over twenty years now." I peered at the young warlock. Probably not even much past fifty. Where did Gregorio find all these guys?

"Um." He stopped, flustered, and pushed the mop of hair out of his eyes. "Callie. Right."

"I've told her what the coven mothers have said," Sebastian put in. "But don't you think we could speak with Dr. Andromedus on her behalf? I mean, it seems like we could use all the help we can get at this point." He gave Dr. Winterheart a shy smile; and was that a glimmer in his eye? *Sebastian, really?* I thought, as I turned back to look at Flavius. Yeah, I supposed he was cute enough. But was he really Sebastian's type?

Not that I knew anything about Sebastian's tastes. Except, I liked him; but did that mean we should be in agreement about everything? *Callie, really?* I chided myself. *Focus.*

Flavius frowned, clearly thinking. "I don't know," he said, giving Sebastian a helpless look. "Dr. Andromedus was pretty clear that we were to keep this all in-house at the moment."

"You could, I don't know, bring me material to look over in my home lab," I offered. "Quiet-like."

Flavius glanced at Sebastian again before looking back at me. "He's asked me to try my Melanian Assay on the newest patients. He didn't actually specify where I should do the work, though."

"Melanian Assay?" I asked. "What is that?"

The young researcher sat a little taller in his chair. "It's a new design of mine—a method of measuring the levels of certain endocrine hormones by filtering them through ætheric rhythms."

"That sounds just like a basic kel assay," I said, confused. "What's the difference?"

He looked a little embarrassed, though still with an eager light in his eyes. "Well, it is similar, though I did tweak a few of the parameters, and I don't use the traditional hormones."

"Oh, really? Which endocrine hormones do you use?"

"It's a little complicated to explain in a café—it'd be a lot easier to show you in the lab."

"You have a lab in the clinic?" I asked, now leaning forward myself.

"Well, er, sort of," he hedged.

"Callie, we *will* get you in there," Sebastian broke in, "but please understand, we can't just yet."

"I can try to get you some tissue samples," Flavius said. "I'll tell Dr. Andromedus I need to work on it at the lab in Berkeley, that it's too emotional here." Sebastian nodded agreement. "That's part of why they want to keep everyone out—it's just crazy. What with the coven mothers and the relatives of the sick witches, there's not a moment's peace, and that's with keeping the general community out."

"Right, good idea," Sebastian said. "You need a quiet, clean place to work. Awesome." He patted Flavius's arm, lingering a moment before withdrawing his hand and tucking it into his lap.

"And I should get back—I told him I was just grabbing a coffee." Flavius stood up and pulled his jacket back on. "Callie, I'll be in touch soon about those samples."

"Thanks."

After he left, I leaned back in my chair and studied Sebastian. "So?" I asked.

"So what?" He was trying not to grin.

"He's all right, I suppose," I said.

Sebastian tossed his head and affected a look of utter disinterest. "I have *no idea* what you're talking about."

In my pocket, my cell phone rang. Crap. I hadn't answered Raymond's text. I'd meant to. I'd even been keeping my phone charged up.

"Do you need to get that?" Sebastian asked.

"No, I...it can keep." I pulled it out and tried to refuse the call, but fumbled with it, accidentally answering it and then immediately hanging it up. "Oh crap," I swore. "That was smooth."

"Was that...the human?"

I rolled my eyes. "Why the dramatic pause? You're as bad as everyone else. Plenty of witches and warlocks date humans."

Sebastian gave me a cheerful grin. "No, Callie, plenty of witches and warlocks *sleep with* humans. Don't you remember our wise elders explaining that to us at your dinner party?"

"I would hate you, if I didn't like you so much," I grumbled.

As I waited for the samples from Flavius Winterheart, I tried to work on the rest of my research. But a few days went by, and then a few more, and nothing. *Any progress?* I sent him through the æther. *Working on it,* he responded. *Hang tight.*

And everything just seemed to get harder and harder. I continued to not call Raymond back, like the cowardly coward that I was; after another unanswered text, he fell silent.

I kept the phone charged, though. I would call him back. Soon.

I told myself I was busy. But I wasn't. I would think about climbing the stairs to the third floor, only to find something else more pressing to do. Even if that was reading a book on the sofa. I should have been building my microscopic research assistants, sending them through their paces, winnowing out the unsuccessful ones, breeding more of the stronger ones. The few times I had used it, I'd found that the pneumative Gregorio had given me was indeed much more effective than the old stuff. That was promising! So why couldn't I focus? I just felt so dang *tired*.

Finally, I forced myself up there, made myself set up a batch of potion and seeds to run. After mixing a solution of neutral wash and bathing them, I set the beaker on my lab bench, wiped my forehead, and pulled up my stool. "Whew," I said aloud as I sat. You'd think I'd just run a marathon.

Elnor looked up from her station guarding the top of the stairs, watched me a long moment, and went back to her divination. Or nap. They looked much the same.

Why was I so tired? Yes, it was a little warm up here, on the top floor. But this was San Francisco. It was probably fifty-five degrees outside.

Oh Blessed Mother, was I the next victim of this mysterious illness? Heart pounding, I put a hand on my chest and one on my belly, taking a quick scan of my own essence, and then a deeper probe. A minute later, I breathed out in relief. Both scans showed that my essence was as strong as ever—perhaps even stronger than usual, coursing bright and firm through my system. And it wasn't just the sudden fear-spiked adrenaline. I was healthy.

But I still just wanted to take a nap. It was barely noon. Was the emotional overload finally getting to me? The loss of Logan, the mysterious illness rampant in our community, the sudden complexity of my romantic life, on top of my ongoing tensions with the coven... Yes, perhaps I should go a bit easier on myself.

It wasn't too early for lunch. I nudged Elnor awake on my way to the stairs. "Come on, kitten, let's go find something tasty."

Once in the kitchen, though, I suffered a bout of indecision. I conjured up a cup of pennyroyal tea without much thinking about it, but then didn't even want to take a sip: it smelled wrong. Weird, kind of off. I dumped it in the sink and drank a glass of water instead. I looked through the fridge, but I didn't want any of my Chinese leftovers, or an apple, or a piece of cheese. Finally, I found some stale crackers in the cabinet. They didn't taste very good, but at least they didn't make me feel ill.

"If I didn't know any better, I'd say I was pregnant," I said to Elnor.

Then I stopped, standing in the middle of the kitchen, hand on my belly.

"No."

I sent my magical senses through my fingers once more, probing. It was confusing; life energy is complex, and the many threads just doubled back on one another. It is very hard to diagnose oneself. Determining whether essence was strong or weak was simple, as easy as feeling a pulse. Discerning particular energies within that essence, trying to untangle them from the dozens, even hundreds of others in the same thread? Far more complicated.

I couldn't be pregnant! Though my own line conceived more easily than most witchkind, I still would have had to consciously, deliberately try—and with a viable warlock, of course; witchkind is sterile with humans. Even with a viable warlock, I would have had to actively open my system's energetic channels, release an egg, invite and welcome the new spirit to reside in me. I had done no such thing with Jeremy. My mother had told me that she and Father tried for nearly five years before conceiving me.

And yet the odd feeling persisted.

I went into the living room and sat on the couch, my hand still on my belly. The warm sensation I'd noticed a week or so ago, at Logan's apartment...it was still (or again) there, though more subtle than before. And now that I thought about it, my breasts were sensitive. Had been so for several days.

No! Not possible.

"Elnor!" I called. My familiar came to sit in my lap. I scritched her ears and waited for her to settle. I should probably have done this in my circle upstairs, but I could do a simple scan here. Maybe I just had a touch of the flu.

A breast-hurting flu?

No!

Once Elnor was open to our working, I started the process of clearing my mental decks, noticing and letting go of irrelevancies and distractions before focusing on what I was looking for. I led my consciousness downward, releasing my surroundings, dropping into a light trance. I focused my awareness inward, settling into my own skin, my muscles, blood, and bones. I envisioned myself as one of my own tiny homunculi, coursing through my veins, taking note of everything I saw—down to my toes, to the back of my right shoulder, to the ends of my hair. Elnor's feline-huntress energy joined mine as we traveled.

Releasing the extremities, I ventured further inward, continuing the process of centering. To the middle of my body. Noticing and setting aside its normal functions. The crackers I just ate, breaking down in my stomach. The water I drank, absorbing into my tissues, hydrating me. Enzymes and hormones doing their work.

Hormones...

I focused, focused, focused. My ovaries, with their lifetime supply of eggs, ready to be deployed. My Fallopian tubes, an open channel, leading to...my uterus.

My womb felt full, rich with blood, active and warm. Was I about to have a period? I was at least as regular as most witches—which is to say, not tremendously so. Four or five times a year, maybe.

Was that what my uterus was busy with? That would explain sore breasts.

I waited, focusing. Listening. Was there a second spirit there, a second set of energies?

Don't lead the witness, I told myself, with an internal laugh. It's so easy to project, when you think you know the answer. So hard to wait, and listen, and not decide.

I heard a second heartbeat.

I gave a sharp gasp—not surprised, exactly, since this was just what I'd been listening for, but astonished. Because this was so, so impossible.

And now there was too much noise in my mind to hear anything. I tried calming myself once more, but gave up after another minute. Elnor had started fidgeting as well, reflecting my own emotional turmoil.

I had to get a second opinion. Actually, I had to get a qualified *first* opinion. And with the healers busy...

Mother? I sent to Leonora. *Are you busy at the moment?*

I am always occupied, but you may come.

Five minutes later, I was at the door of her office in the coven house.

"Let us find a quieter place," she said, after a glance at me. I don't know how much she was reading off my face and body language versus what she was detecting magically, but she clearly understood this wasn't a casual visit.

We climbed the back stairs and went into a seldom-used parlor on the second floor, beyond the classrooms. Formerly a bedroom, this room was small and oddly shaped, stretching around the southeastern corner of the building and furnished with mismatched chairs, an ugly sideboard, and a coffee table stained decades ago by a spilled potion.

This room, far from the rest of the house's common areas, was our place for private talks. If this door was closed, everyone understood why.

The air smelled musty, unbreathed for some time. I wished I'd brought Elnor, but she'd been too unsettled, so I'd left her home.

Leonora sat in a straight-backed wooden chair; I chose a flowered overstuffed chair with a small tear on the right arm. I tucked my legs up under me and looked at her.

"Can you tell if I'm pregnant?"

My coven mother gazed at me. "Very likely. Do you have reason to believe you are?"

"Yeah...I kind of do. I think."

"I thought I noticed a disruption in your energy. I was unaware, however, that you were attempting such a thing."

"I wasn't. It was a complete accident."

"Witches do not get pregnant accidentally."

I shifted in the chair. "I know! But...I can sense something, there. And my breasts are sore, and most food is unappealing."

She studied me another long moment, then raised both hands. "Sit very still, but also relaxed. Is that position comfortable?"

"Yes."

Tendrils of her magic surrounded me, then searched within. It was not unpleasant—it could be, if I resisted, but of course, I'd asked for this. I wanted to know.

I waited, feeling her intention following the paths I'd followed at home. I felt her come to the same conclusion.

She lowered her arms and sat back in her chair. "Well. I do believe you are with child, Calendula Isadora."

I sighed, my hand going automatically to my belly. "Wow."

"By Gregorio's son, I take it?"

"Um, yeah."

"Does he know?"

"No—I came to you first. And, like I said, I wasn't trying! I had no idea this was possible."

She frowned. "It shouldn't be. But your line is more prolific than most."

"I've only had sex with him a few times! And I was never even *thinking* about a daughter."

"Perhaps not consciously..." She trailed off. "Well, be that as it may, the solution is simple enough."

I felt unaccountably relieved. *This* was why we joined covens. The wisdom and experience of our elders.

She nodded, still with a small frown on her face. "And it were probably best done quickly," she went on. "I see no reason to inform the warlock, or his father."

"Wait. What?"

"Yes," she said, more decisively. "I believe we have all the required herbs here in the house. We can begin at once."

"The herbs?" My stomach clutched in fear.

Leonora looked at me gently. "For the miscarriage. You can, of course, terminate the pregnancy by your own power, but I believe that is needlessly taxing, and could cause damage that would come to haunt you later."

"No." I got to my feet and started backing toward the door, without even realizing I had done so. "No, no miscarriage! What are you talking about?"

She got up as well and took a step toward me, arms raised in supplication. "Calendula, please, sit down."

"But—but this is crazy!"

"The whole thing is crazy. You are not even in a union with the warlock; there has been no provision for children. And, more importantly, you are blood-sworn to this coven. These things are planned years in advance, not leapt into willy-nilly. I do not even know if any members of the Artemis Guild are available to step in to take your place." She put a gentle hand on my arm and drew me back to my chair. "Calendula, you know that *all* major decisions must come through me—daughters *particularly*. If it even *is* a daughter—if you had no conscious control over the conception, it could very well be a son!"

I trembled, but took my seat again. "It feels...female to me."

She sat back down too. "I believe so as well." Then she leaned forward, holding my gaze. "Did I not warn you about undertaking anything of importance during this period of mourning?"

I nodded.

"And during the waning moon, at that!" she went on. "I am sorry, but this daughter really should not be allowed to enter our world. We have no idea what her nature might be; such a spirit could have come from anywhere. She could have some very malevolent designs. Something is very, very wrong here. Calendula Isadora, think about it."

"That's just the problem! I haven't had a chance to think about it. I... suspected I was pregnant, and I came straight here to ask you about it—and you just want to kill her!" My hand strayed to my belly once more. I'm sure it was my imagination—impossible, for just a tiny bundle of cells—but I thought I felt an answering tremble under my fingertips. "She can't be bad—I would feel it. You can't make me kill her."

"As a matter of fact, I can." Her voice softened. "But I will not. Take some time, then; clearly this is very overwhelming, particularly with everything else that's happened to you recently. I am sure that, once you think it through, you will see the truth of my words. We can speak about this again in a few days. That will be soon enough."

"Thank you, Mother," I said, quietly. "I appreciate the time."

"I will advise you, however, not to speak to the warlock about it," she said. "That will only muddy the waters, and create confusion. If you do decide you want to establish a union—with him, or any other warlock—you are welcome to do so. You will have plenty of opportunities to have a daughter; perhaps even more than one, if you so choose. But this is no way to go about it. I knew I should never have let you move to that house."

I bit my lip. "I'm sorry, Mother. But I do think I ought to tell him."

"Why?"

"Just...it seems fair? She's his daughter too."

"He's not likely to be even as understanding as I am," she said with a wry smile. "He will feel deceived, ill-used."

Would he? Or would he understand that it had been a bizarre accident? I wished Logan were still here to talk to. Now that she was gone, Jeremy was the only person who seemed to understand me. Well, maybe Sebastian too; but this was hardly his business. Wouldn't Jeremy want us to solve this problem together?

"You're not going to make me move back here, are you?" I asked.

She paused a moment, considering. "No, I will not have you moping around our congenial home like a prisoner. You clearly need additional time to explore your independence, and I will grant you that."

Even though it was what I wanted, the way she put it, well, it sort of soured it. The familiar Greek chorus of Logan's words echoed in my mind yet again: Leonora did treat us all as children.

"Thank you, Mother."

"So go and do your thinking, and we shall talk again in a few days. We will need to take action soon, before it quickens."

I swallowed a lump in my throat. *It.*

Not that I was going to argue the point with Leonora. "Yes, Mother," I said. "Thank you for seeing me."

She gave a genuinely warm smile. "Of course, daughter. I know this must be a terribly hard passage. Do not think me unsympathetic." She got to her feet, her heavy robes rustling at her ankles. "I am glad you came to me first."

Am I? I wondered.

— CHAPTER FOURTEEN —

I opened the front door and let Jeremy in. "I am so sorry, my dear," he said at once. "I know how this must seem, but truly, it's been absolute chaos and I haven't had a moment to get away. I understand that you came by the clinic the other day, and I know how much you want to help, but you must know—"

"It's not that," I said. "Come in. Sit down, I have something to tell you."

He followed me to the couch, looking bemused, as well he might, after my no doubt irrational-sounding demand to see him as soon as possible.

"Well?" he prompted, after a silence that had dragged on a minute or so.

"Yeah. I, um."

He reached over and caressed my knee. "Whatever it is, I am certain it will be all right."

"Oh, I hope you're right." I took a deep breath and blurted, "I'm pregnant."

He blinked at me, staring blankly, as though I'd uttered a string of gibberish. He opened his mouth. "Er." Then he seemed to almost willfully recover, leaning forward to pull me into his arms. "Calendula! That is marvelous news!" He kissed me firmly on the forehead, then drew back to look into my eyes. "Just...newly?"

Okay, it was a fair question. Sort of. He knew I hadn't been seeing any other warlocks. Didn't he? "Yes."

He nodded. "I knew there was a powerful energy between us. It's..." He trailed off, as if searching for words. "I confess I am rather... baffled, though. This is a large and, frankly, stunning decision. I might have thought you would—"

"It wasn't a decision. I wasn't trying."

He looked back at me again, even more blankly than before.

"It just happened," I went on. "I don't know how."

"I…did not know that was possible."

"Neither did I."

More blankness. "You're quite sure?"

"One hundred percent." I patted my belly.

"Hmm." After another long moment, he gave his head a little shake, and then brightened. "Well! All right then. I shall get my father's advisors working at once on the terms of the contract. Not to worry."

"I…" Contract?

"Should we be working with Leonora's representatives, or with those of your birth parents? I confess, the more time I spend here, the less I feel I understand the local customs."

I found my voice at last. "I'm flattered, Jeremy, but really, there's no need—I'm sworn to my coven, you know, and…" I watched his face, flustered. He looked very confused.

"You do not wish a contract with me? You…will be terminating the child?" He glanced down at my belly, as though there was something to see there. Besides my hand.

"No! I don't know, but not that. It's all happened so fast. I don't know what I want."

He frowned. "Well…you may be sworn to your coven, but as far as I understand, coven witches do not bear children. Even here. Children happen in unions. That's what the Artemis Guild is for—when witches take leaves of absence."

That doesn't make it a biological imperative! I thought. And there he was, warlocksplaining again. But, well, he wasn't wrong. About the custom, that was. "I do want you in my life, and in *her* life. But I don't even know if I *can* sign a contract right now."

His face softened, and with it his tone. "Anything is possible, if you want it."

"I…don't know what I want."

He smiled tenderly. "Callie, given the circumstances, I feel that I must say this: I hold you in very high regard, and no one can deny the energy between us. Though our courtship has been unusually abbreviated, I believe it is clear that we are quite compatible, in bed and out of it." He put a gentle hand on my belly, next to my own hand, as his smile grew. "I also recognize that you are young, and do not understand everything about how things are done, but you must know that no witch honors a warlock thusly without feeling quite serious about him."

I looked back at him, my emotions in a tangle. He wanted a union with me? (Or was he just bending to custom?) He wasn't angry, at least. That was good. But he clearly didn't believe me, that it was unintended. And did he have to be such a patronizing jerk about—well, everything? I wasn't *that* young! "I really, truly didn't plan this," I said. "I'm still not quite sure how it happened. I'm not making that up."

His smile started to look a little frozen, as his puzzlement warred with it.

"I mean, I do care about you too, of course," I went on. "I care about you a lot; we *are* good together. I let myself get swept away, and I must have lost control, without realizing it." I mingled my fingers with his over my belly. "And she's amazing, I can already tell. She's something you and I did together. I've never met anyone like you. But, it's kind of all too fast for my brain and my emotions to catch up with. You know? With everything that's happened in my life lately…" I waved a hand vaguely; he nodded. "Does that make sense?"

"Of course it does, my dear. I should not have pressed. But I was, as I said, quite surprised." He leaned forward once more and pulled me into his strong arms. "I am sure, once the shock has worn off for both of us, our path will be clear and simple."

I relaxed into his embrace, letting him distract me with passion once more. He was awfully good at it.

But later, much later, as I lay alone in my bed (he had offered to stay, but I'd pleaded exhaustion, and a need to think things over), I thought about…her.

About my daughter, growing within me.

She was mine…no, she was herself—her own self. Even if I had no idea what her personality was, what her strengths might be, what color her eyes and hair would be—anything about her—those things were already there, becoming *her*.

And yet to the rest of the world, she wasn't a person. She was a complication, a message, an opportunity, a scheduling problem, a breach of protocol. The tangible result of an alliance between two strong families…an asset. A challenge to the integrity of a powerful coven.

Even, perhaps, a threat.

How screwed up was it that the first two people I'd brought my news to had assumed *they* were in charge of it? That they owned—well, her. And, by extension, me.

Leonora could, if she chose, reach into my womb with powerful magic and crush the growing life there. I didn't think she would actually do that, she had said she wouldn't...but I didn't know that for sure, did I?

Could Jeremy—or Gregorio—force me into a union against my will?

Did I *not* want a union just because Jeremy had blithely assumed that I would? I was, in fact, quite taken with him. And unions didn't have to be monogamous—that was just another detail to put in the contract, or not.

But it was way too soon! Blessed Mother, I'd known the warlock, what, two months? And for much of that time, he'd been courting my best friend, with me cheering along on the sidelines. I'd only been intimate with him a few weeks—this was all just completely absurd. You don't make even a twenty-year commitment after such a whirlwind romance; more typical durations were thirty or forty years.

Besides, none of this meant that my heart was resolved about Raymond. I hadn't stopped loving him, just because I was seeing, more clearly all the time, why we were not a viable couple. How much I could not tell him.

I was forty-five years old. It seemed high time that I be able to make my own decisions about my life...and my body.

And yet, I had *not* decided to conceive. I knew that. Even as I was more certain every minute that I wanted to keep this baby, I could not ignore the fact that I had no idea how she had come to be.

If such things were possible, just how much agency could any witch ever have?

Apparently, pennyroyal is dangerous for a growing child. Yet another thing I didn't know about pregnancy, despite my being a biologist. Chamomile is highly recommended.

Chamomile tastes like stale lawn clippings that have blown through a paddock, then been swept up with a dirty broom and brewed in the horse's drinking water, before being left outside for a few days.

I hate chamomile tea. Just in case that wasn't clear.

I sat in the solarium of my parents' elegant Pacific Heights home—a house that put my own wonderful home to shame. Mom had settled me on the couch and produced a cup of the nasty stuff. She had taken my news thoughtfully, quietly.

(Except for her absurd, heartless insistence on chamomile.)

"Do you love this warlock?" she asked, after we'd gone through the *No, I don't want to miscarry the child* and *No, I don't want to rush into a union* conversations.

"No, of course not, it's too soon." I stopped and thought a moment. "I don't know, maybe I could in time. I've never met anyone quite like him."

"That's not the same as love."

"I know." We sat silently for a minute, sipping our tea. Elnor curled near my feet, snoozing. "He seems fond of me. I do like him a lot, and we get along very well. But it's way too soon."

She nodded.

"He's really something," I went on. "Powerful, and gorgeous. And there's no arguing with the family he comes from!" Was I trying to talk myself into him?

"Indeed." She gazed out the window, a ghost of sadness on her face. The sun, hiding behind its veil of fog, was making its way higher in the sky; it would soon leave us in even deeper shadows, taking a lot of the charm of this room with it. "A good warlock to make a daughter with."

"The best I've ever met."

"What about the human? Have you told him?"

"Um...I actually haven't seen Raymond in a while. We're..." I trailed off.

"You're not seeing him anymore?"

"I don't know. Nothing's been said precisely, but...I think it's over. And I think we both know it." Well, if Raymond hadn't known it before, he was clearly figuring it out now.

She nodded again, sympathetically. "You know, Callie—"

"I know," I said, before she could go on. "It could never be serious, we're too unalike, this was bound to happen sooner or later so it's better that it was now, I know, I know." I softened my outburst with a smile. "So how are *you* doing? You look..." I had been about to say *good*, but in fact, she looked tired, and a little pale. I'd been so caught up in my own problems, I hadn't really looked at her. "Is everything okay? How's your essence?"

"Oh, I'm fine, it's strong as ever," she said with a smile. I shifted my vision to check; yes, she was right, pretty much. "Lucas has had a number of late nights this week, helping with Gregorio's new clinic, some of the setup and research. I've taken on more of the work around here. I must have grown quite lazy to be finding just the general maintenance of wards and housekeeping spells a bit of a drain." She gave a self-deprecating laugh.

"You ever think about getting another cat?" I asked. "With Dad so busy?"

Mom shrugged. "His allergies..."

"Yes, I know. I've told you I can help with that. And the cattery has a bunch of cute kittens ready to adopt."

"Not just yet."

Well, she would be ready when she was ready. "I can't believe they're letting Dad help at the clinic."

She gave me a puzzled look. "Why not? He's a brilliant researcher, and one of Gregorio's closest colleagues."

"They're not letting *me* even walk through the door," I said, chagrined at how churlish I sounded, but unable to help myself.

"Callie, I'm sure it's not wise to expose the baby—"

"But that's just it," I interrupted. "Nobody knows I'm pregnant."

"You just told me you've talked to Jeremiah Andromedus about it," she said, softening her words with a gentle smile. "And Leonora."

I snorted, frustrated. "Sure, yesterday, and the day before. But they haven't let me near the place since it opened, weeks ago."

"Oh, Callie," Mom said, "I'm sure they have very good reasons for doing so."

"Well, I'm sure they think they do," I muttered, sipping my tea. It was even worse as it cooled. Did I have any sugar in my bag? I poked at it with one hand as Mom rather pointedly changed the subject and started telling me about some work she was doing in her herb garden. Since I wasn't looking, of course I knocked my purse over. Everything toppled out, lipsticks and tissues and amulets everywhere. Logan's box of tarot cards tumbled to the floor with a thud, waking Elnor, who shot to her feet with a squawk, then stood glaring at the pile of clutter.

"Are *you* working with *tarot* cards?" my mother interrupted herself to ask, a surprised smile on her face.

"Gosh, no, these are Logan's. I...looked through her apartment, and found them. I didn't want to leave them there."

"May I see them?"

"Sure." I retrieved them and handed them over.

Mom opened the box and held the deck loosely in both hands. Then she shuffled them a few times, cut, reshuffled, then turned the deck face-up and spread it on the coffee table.

She sat staring at the fanned-out cards for a minute. "This is a good deck. How long had Logan used it?"

"I don't know."

"It's not very old. The cards are a little stiff; the colors are bright and unworn. I would say, if she used them much, that she acquired this deck less than a year before she departed."

"She made her living telling fortunes for humans. She used them a lot."

"Then she may have had these only a few months." Mom ran her hands over the cards, spreading them out the length of the coffee table. "The energy is still fresh, too, very strong." Her hand hesitated briefly over the Devil.

I chuckled. "That Devil guy, he's something."

Mother smiled. "He frightens you?"

"No, no," I said. "It's just—his eyes follow you across the room. He's cleverly drawn."

"No, he frightens you," my mother concluded, after gazing at me. "Which only goes to show how little you understand the tarot—no matter how much I tried to teach you, and Logandina after me. The Devil doesn't represent any outside evil. He's an aspect of yourself, the negativity and hubris that holds you back. Look at the chained figures beneath him. They could step right out of their bonds, but they don't. They believe they're captive, therefore they are."

"So evil is just our imagination?"

"No, there is indeed evil in the world, but it's not embodied in the cards. If you will have the patience and open-mindedness to honor them, they can tell you a lot."

"Logan always said the same thing. But I'm a scientist, Mom. Wild magic—that's not my thing."

"I think it's finally time for you to really learn the tarot," she said brightly, gathering the cards together.

"Gosh, no. No need for that." I reached out to take the deck from her, but she did not hand it over.

"Callie, what are you afraid of?" Mother began shuffling the deck again.

"Nothing."

"No, of course not," she teased, then glanced at the grandfather clock at the end of the room. "Lunch is set to be ready in forty-five minutes, which gives us plenty of time for a quick lesson."

I sighed and settled back. "I'm not hungry," I grumbled.

"Of course you are. Now, the cards are organized into four suits, plus the major arcana..."

My resistance soon fell away: Mother was a good teacher, and I did enjoy spending time with her. She first gave me a review of the use of the cards and the meanings of each suit—things I'd already learned from being forced to sit in on her regular tarot circles with her friends when I was growing up, not to mention Logan's occasional readings for me since then, but Mom insisted on going over it all again.

"Each suit has a theme. The cards numbered ten represent the logical conclusion of these themes," she said, laying down the Ten of Swords.

"That one is just horrifying," I said. It was a picture of a thoroughly dead man, lying face-down in the dirt, ten tall swords stuck in his back.

"Yes, and the usual meaning is some catastrophic event, arising out of an excess of negative, destructive power. But it can also be a card of hope. See here, in the background?" She pointed. "The sky is growing lighter, in anticipation of sunrise. That signifies that the worst of the blackness has ended, and a new dawn is beginning. It's an opportunity to learn from one's mistakes and go forth anew, keeping the hard lesson in mind. Seen from this perspective, it's a card of action, despite the ostensibly dead imagery. It can mean a fresh start."

For everyone except that poor dude with the swords in his back. "So, the theme of Swords is action?" I asked, trying to remember past lessons.

"Yes, and rationality. It's a very mental suit. Cups, on the other hand, has to do with the emotions."

"And relationships," I said.

"Of course. Relationships have everything to do with emotions, do they not?" She pulled out the Ten of Cups and set it beside the first card.

"That's pretty positive." A happy couple, arm in arm, their children frolicking nearby, and a rainbow of golden cups across the sky.

"If it comes up reversed, however, it can mean the opposite—a broken home, an end of love."

"What's reversed?"

"Upside down."

"Logan did readings for me," I said. "But I don't remember cards ever coming up reversed."

"Some practitioners shuffle their decks in only one direction, to prevent that," she said. "Especially for, ah, less experienced querents." She smiled.

"Querents?"

"The querent is the subject of the reading. That would be you."

"That isn't cheating?"

"Not at all; just a different way of asking questions."

"Okay."

"And much in tarot is down to the skill of the interpreter, in any case. The cards do contain many layers."

As we continued to go through the deck, it seemed like most of the cards we examined had at least two meanings, even without being reversed. An end of something meant the beginning of something else; too much of anything, even a positive trait, turned it negative. Nothing was clear-cut; all depended on the situation in which each card appeared, and the intuition of the reader.

"See," I said after a while, "this is my whole problem with the cards. If they can be interpreted however best fits in the moment, then what are they good for?"

"What do you mean?" Mom drew the cards together and shuffled them again.

"Well, if all these 'negative' cards can mean a horrible ending but also the hope of new life, and all the 'positive' ones are full of cautions and warnings—well, which is it? How is this any different from real life, from just deciding what you want to do on your own? What are we even learning here?"

Mother smiled. "You're being deliberately obtuse."

"I'm not meaning to be," I said. "When I run a Genara Goldbane assay, the results come out purple if it's negative and bright gold if it's positive. When I culture a new strain of bacteria in LB and agar, it either lives or it dies—and if it does live, I can measure exactly how long, and quantify the amount that grew. But this? This just seems"—I waved my hands—"made-up."

"Callie, you're focusing on only part of the story. Yes, your biological science is measurable and precise and tidy like that. Is life that way—real life?"

"No."

"So is *life* made-up? Meaningless?"

"Of course not."

"Or creating your golem. How much of that was a scientific recipe and how much was your intuitive sense?"

"I followed a very precise formula for her," I said. "I studied a long time to figure out how."

"And yet no one else has managed to create one, not for centuries. You know many have tried. Did they just not study hard enough, or did you bring something extra to the mix?"

I gave her a helpless shrug.

"You know as well as any witch the power of the unseen energy that surrounds us all, and the individual differences within each of us," she went on. "Despite your scientific recipes and formulas, real life does not offer such clear sign posts: we are possessed of free will, and we must respect nuance, interpretation, and intuition. We must consider all the ramifications of any decision, if we wish to act wisely. The tarot aids us in tapping into the unseen, and helps guide our thinking. It is a tool, and a very powerful one in capable hands." She smiled again. "Wild magic is real magic too—at least as much as scientific magic."

"Well, I suppose," I allowed. She was right: I did not understand everything in my science. Yet the presumption of understanding was always there, in research. That which you did not know was discoverable. You just needed to find the right tools, ask the right questions.

"Do you not meditate?" Mom asked. "Or seek messages from dreams?"

"Not really."

She smiled. "And to think you're my daughter... Though, of course, you're even more your father's daughter."

I didn't respond, just smiled back at her. It was undeniable.

"What about at your coven?" she went on. "How do you contact your ancestresses in the Beyond?"

I looked at her, puzzled. Surely she knew how this was done? "In a Circle, all thirteen of us, every Tuesday night—"

"Yes, yes," she said, waving her hand dismissively. "I mean the magic itself. Does it always work precisely the same way? Does it always take the exact same amount of time? Are the results always identical?"

"Of course not. But that's usually due to something different on our end—someone's energy is lower or higher, someone is in a bad mood, the cats might be squabbling. Although Nementhe might also be more or less responsive depending on what she's doing over there." I thought a moment. "The same with science, for that matter. What I said earlier, about the tests and stuff—it only works that way if I've controlled the variables. If my flasks are dirty or my herbs are stale, I'll get different results." *Or if I've been using off-brand pneumative,* I thought.

"Tarot isn't really much different from that," she said. "You just need to open your mind a little, think about it all differently. Let go of your preconceptions." She pushed the deck toward me. "Here—just draw a couple cards, we'll work with them."

"Mom, we don't have time to do a reading." I pushed a strand of hair behind my ear. It had started to fidget; I'd have to bind it if it was going to keep this up.

"It's not a reading. We're just practicing. Go on—two cards, and you will interpret them."

I wanted to resist further, but knew that would only make it take longer: when Mom dug in her heels, she couldn't be budged. I plucked the first card off the top of the stack and turned it over on the table: the Queen of Wands. The Queen sat comfortably on her throne, holding a sunflower and, of course, a wand. Images of lions and more sunflowers decorated her throne. A black cat perched at her feet.

"What do you see?" Mom said.

"It's a good card, I think," I started, then went on before she could tell me that each card was intrinsically neither good nor bad. "I see… um, strong female energy?" She nodded encouragingly. "And, creativity maybe, and some spirit. Is she a witch?" I looked at the black cat as I absently scritched Elnor's ears—my familiar having moved to the sofa next to me sometime during the course of the lesson.

"Perhaps, perhaps not. Creativity for sure, though: she does represent fertility." Mom gave me a significant look. "The Queen is also a natural leader, independent and charismatic. It's interesting to me that this card chose you."

"I just picked it up off the top of the pile," I said. "The pile that you shuffled."

"So pick another."

I reached into the middle of the deck, trying not to guide my awareness at all. My fingers chose a card; I pulled it out and turned it over. The Tower. On a dark and stormy night, a lightning bolt hits a tall tower, knocking a golden crown from its top and sending the inhabitants plummeting to jagged rocks below, amid flames and smoke.

The same card that had come up in the final position in Logan's last reading for me.

"Oh, Blessed Mother," I whispered.

Mother looked grave as well, but only said, "What do you see?"

"Um, very dark. Chaos and destruction, the sudden falling apart of everything." I looked up at her. "Which pretty much describes my life these days."

"Now, don't say that," my mother chided. "Yes, certainly one aspect of your life—but that is only if you focus on the negative."

"Losing my best friend is pretty negative!" My hair fluttered again, picking up on my emotional disturbance.

"Remember that when things break, it's the chance for new beginnings," Mom said gently, and nodded at my belly.

"You think Logan had to move on for me to get preg—wait, you think this could be *Logan's* spirit in here?" I gasped.

Mom shook her head. "That is vanishingly unlikely; you have not sensed her at all, have you?"

I shook my head. "But everything about this has been vanishingly unlikely."

"Even so. Spirits have been known to return for another cycle on this plane, but they always do so from the Beyond. And with the express permission of the witch who is to bear the child."

"Assuming the witch in question even intended to get pregnant," I grumbled.

"Yes, I know. But I do not think that is her spirit in there. I think you would feel it, that she would find some way to speak to you. I believe the cards are expressing themselves more metaphorically."

"And saying what?"

"That you are facing challenges, to be sure. But these two cards together, I see them as a sign that you will have the strength to navigate this hardship, and will emerge far more powerful for it." She gave me a sympathetic smile. "Have faith, my dear. Look at this Queen: try to see her maturity, her power, her control."

"I do see that," I admitted. "I just…"

"Yes. I know." She gazed at me. "And now I can see that it is time to feed you lunch."

It had been sitting for a few hours, but the spell Mom had used in its making had kept the meal perfectly fresh. We ate in the formal dining room, on the south side of the house. The sun had just broken through the fog, so we opened the large casement windows and enjoyed the rare San Francisco late-spring warmth as we ate cracked Dungeness crab and sourdough bread, a huge salad, and a tarragon-cream soup that was to die for. I fed morsels of crab to Elnor under the table; Mom pretended not to notice. Lemon meringue pie was our dessert, followed by coffee and little chocolates.

I really need to visit Mom more often, I told myself, pushing back from the table, rubbing my belly, and apologizing to the tiny bundle of cells who now had no room whatsoever. Good thing she was so small.

"Well, that was amazing," I said. "Thank you."

"It was my pleasure—the meal and the lesson both." Mom smiled back at me, then gazed at the cluttered table. "I think I'll save the cleanup for later, though. Our tarot work must have been more draining than I realized. Or maybe I'm still absorbing your news."

I looked carefully at her, then shifted my sight to take the measure of her essence again. "Mom, you *are* tired. Are you sure you're not sick?"

"No, I'm just overextended, I told you. I'll take a little nap and be right as rain later this afternoon."

"I shouldn't have made you do all this! I could have at least made lunch." I got up and went to her, putting a hand on her forehead so I could get a deeper reading. "I think we should get a healer in here."

She reached up and pulled my hand down, shaking her head. "Don't be absurd. There's no call for that." Before I could protest further, she added in a softer tone, "But I appreciate your worry for me. If you like, we can drop by Gregorio's clinic."

"I'm not allowed there, remember?"

She smiled. "The healers would let you accompany me, I think. I'd like to see Lucas about something anyway. There are always at least two healers present; one of them can take a look at me, if it will make you feel better."

"It would, yes." I studied her a moment longer. "And we're going in a taxi, not on the ley lines."

"Oh, Callie," she said, but she didn't argue as I sent my cat home on a ley line and pulled out my cell phone.

— CHAPTER FIFTEEN —

T he taxi let us off on a familiar dilapidated street South of Market, not far from the Potrero Hill house that the healers Nora and Manka shared. This time, there was no Sebastian on the sidewalk whisking me immediately away, which gave me a chance to actually study the new clinic. It had apparently taken over an abandoned warehouse; no one seemed to have given any attention to the exterior of the hulking dark brown building. There were broken windows on the higher floors, and one whole corner had caved in and then been boarded up haphazardly. The walls that remained were covered with spray-painted graffiti.

"Well, isn't this confidence-inspiring," I said, stepping over a broken construction brick with a little piece of rebar sticking out of it.

"Look closer," Mom murmured, leaning on my arm a little.

I did, and then even more closely, as I finally saw what lay underneath the disguise. In fact the building was modern and new, just wearing a skin of decrepit illusion—merely the image of the warehouse that used to be there. The illusion was unusually powerful. The graffiti were real enough, though not made by any human hand. They were potent protection and healing spells, inter-: laced with the more usual wards. "Oh, that is clever," I said. Because they had been physically painted onto the building, they had an extra degree of solidity and force.

"Lucas helped with the design," she said, a note of pride in her voice. "Come, the door is here."

Even though I'd adjusted my sight to see the reality underneath, the illusion was still strong enough to be disorienting. We stopped at the front door, where Mother put her hand on a small panel in the center.

"Aren't they expecting us?" I'd called Father through the æther after I'd summoned the taxi. He had agreed that we should come in right away.

"It's just another layer of security," she said. "You next." She guided my hand to the nearly invisible panel.

I felt the building's spells brushing over me inquiringly, then relenting. The steel door swung open, and we stepped in.

The entryway continued the theme of abandonment and neglect. "Just in case anyone does manage to get in?" I asked Mom, looking around the cavernous space, empty except for the beer bottles and piles of trash. And was that a rat in the corner, watching us with bead-bright eyes?

"The reception room is further on. They haven't built out this space yet."

"I see."

A door off to the right stood partway open, golden light emanating from it. I followed Mom. We walked down a long hallway, eventually arriving in a small room that at least had fresh paint on its walls, if not much else. "This is the reception area?" I asked. "Would it kill them to find some plastic chairs? A fake fern? Maybe a few back issues of *Pot and Kettle*?"

Mother gave a soft laugh. "The important part is in the back."

Which, of course, I knew. I was just chattering, covering my nerves.

Mom closed her eyes briefly and wiped at her forehead, which I could see was damp. She looked completely exhausted.

I stepped over to the second door, the one which presumably led to the back. "Hello? Anyone here?"

I heard Manka's voice. "Calendula, Belladonna, is that you? I'll be right there."

A minute later, the healer herself stepped in. "Greetings," she said, wiping her hands on a small white towel. "Lucas mentioned you might be dropping by."

"We're not *dropping by*," I said, struggling with my growing unease. "Mom's not well. It's her essence—same as everyone else. Manka, what *is* this?"

"Callie, I told you—" Mom started, but Manka was already scrutinizing her. The healer took my mother's hand, frowning as she continued her examination.

"We have plenty of beds," Manka said after a minute. "Belladonna, if you will come with me?"

"Let me talk to Lucas," Mom protested weakly as she complied.

"He will come to you," the healer said. "I want you to lie down."

I followed them into the main part of the clinic, down another hallway with closed doors on either side. Manka opened one of them. "In here."

A strong scent of lavender tinged with a hint of ground mace filled the darkened room. The carpeting was thick and lush underfoot. I heard the burble of a creek, though I saw no water. Actually, I saw not much of anything, because the lighting wasn't merely dim, it was so low as to be almost nonexistent. I thought I could make out a large, comfortable bed in the center of the room. A low table next to it held a teacup, a basket of what might be cookies and scones, and a pitcher of water. The whole effect made me want to crawl into the bed and fall asleep at once.

Beside me, my mother sighed, as if she was thinking much the same thing.

"All right, Belladonna, here we go," Manka said in a soothing voice.

I yawned. "Nice room. It's not what I expected."

Manka smiled as she helped my mother climb in and get snuggled under a poofy, sage-colored down comforter. "No one ever got well in a sterile white hospital room, did they?"

"I don't know," I said. "I've never been in one." I yawned again.

"You might want to wait in the hall, Calendula," Manka said. "The healing spells can be a bit overwhelming if you're not used to them."

"Right…" I said, trying to stifle a third yawn.

"Do not open any other doors."

"I won't." I stepped back out into the hallway and took a few deep breaths, trying to clear the cobwebs from my brain. She was right. Powerful stuff.

Manka joined me in the hall a minute later. "Your mother is sleeping."

"I'd be astonished if she wasn't." I looked up and down the hall, only seeing more closed doors. "Where's my father?"

"I'll take you to the warlocks."

I followed her down that corridor and another one beyond. I could sense the presences of other witches behind some of the doors, though faintly. Low Essence Fever was clearly becoming epidemic.

My father, Gregorio, and—I was happy to see—Drs. Sebastian Fallon and Flavius Winterheart were gathered in a makeshift laboratory room set up in what must have been the back corner of the giant building. "Calendula!" my father said, coming to give me a light kiss on the cheek. "Where is Belladonna?"

"We've put her into room seventeen, and she's sleeping," Manka said behind me.

"I'd like to see her now."

"Of course," Manka said. Dr. Andromedus nodded as well, and my father hurried out.

Sebastian set a vial down on the lab bench and came over to me. "Callie? Are you all right?"

"I'm fine," I said, my hand automatically going to my stomach. I had never understood pregnant women doing that, but now I did. It was a powerful reflex. "I...I'm just worried about my mom, you know."

"Yes, of course," he said with a sympathetic frown, as Flavius chimed in: "We'll take super good care of her, Callie."

"Indeed," Gregorio said. "You did the right thing, bringing Belladonna here."

I smiled at him. "I know, Dr. Andromedus. Thank you for doing this."

Gregorio gave me a kindly look. "Nothing is more important than putting everything we have into solving this worrisome mystery."

I nodded, looking at the crowded lab bench. Piles of spell books on every subject reached nearly ten feet into the air, surrounded by dozens of cauldrons and flasks kept warm by Eternal Flame. At last I'd gotten in here, but it was still unclear to me where their inquiry might be focused. If there was any focus here at all. "What have you found out? What can I help with?"

Gregorio started to answer, then stopped, looking at me...at my hand on my belly. I sensed his second, more probing glance. The subsequent confusion on his face was plain even without magical vision.

"Yes," I said, before he could figure out a polite way to ask. "I'm pregnant."

"Why...that is...remarkable, Calendula."

"Wow!" said Sebastian. He bumbled over and gave me a strong hug, pushing past Flavius and nearly knocking a flask to the floor in the process. "Congratulations! That's awesome!"

"Thank you." I smiled at the baffled Dr. Andromedus over Sebastian's shoulder. "And yes, Jeremy is the father," I said, once my friend had released me. Because of course that would have been the next awkward, impolitic question.

On to the third. "It wasn't planned," I went on, "but I'm very, very happy about it. And I've talked to Jeremy and he's happy as well."

"Not...planned?" Gregorio stared at me, shaking his head. It was taking him a long time to find his conversational footing. "But that is quite impossible."

I shrugged. "I thought so too."

"My son is...very fond of you, I know. But still, I had not imagined..."

"I know! It's crazy, isn't it?" I kept smiling at him. Perhaps, if I headed this off at the pass, he wouldn't immediately dive into acting like the situation belonged to him...maybe we could even get back to the real reason we were all here...

"Of course, I expect Jeremiah has already talked to you about the matter of the contract, then," said Gregorio. "Frankly, I am surprised he did not mention anything to me when I saw him earlier today. Our representatives—"

Oh well.

My smile grew even bigger. "Oh, Dr. Andromedus, there's no need for representatives! Jeremy and I have agreed to just let everything be for now. Since it was so very sudden and all. I'll keep living in my house, we'll keep dating, and we'll talk about any contracts somewhere down the line." *If at all.*

Gregorio grew very still. Behind him, I could see that both Sebastian and Flavius were watching with avid interest. Manka had made herself scarce; I hadn't even seen her leave the room, but she wasn't here now.

Finally, Dr. Andromedus forced a cordial smile. "But this is...not how we do things. Contracts are for the protection of the child! And the parents." His smile grew a little more genuine as he found his way once more. "You will want her to have the bare minimum social advantage of legitimacy, as well as the financial resources that an alliance with our house would bring, will you not?"

My smile was growing more stale by the moment. *Legitimacy.* Of course he wasn't going to let me brazen this out. But why in the Blessed Mother's name was this entity in my belly any less *legitimate* than any other living thing on the planet, just because some papers hadn't been signed? "I have plenty of resources of my own," I said, trying hard not to grit my teeth. "As does my family, and my coven."

I had surprised the eminent Gregorio Andromedus for the third time in as many minutes, for he blanched once more. "You are not proposing to raise a daughter in a *coven*, are you?"

The whole blessed thing was so ridiculous, I realized, standing there in that makeshift lab room, facing my eight-hundred-year-old mentor, two young warlocks gaping at us. The whole damn system, everything I'd swallowed, my whole life. Who had made all these rules anyway? Why *couldn't* a witchlet be raised in a teaching coven? Or by a single mother? Humans raised babies any old way all the time. Why were we locked into one way and one way only?

When I'd moved out of the coven house, I had thought I'd wanted more freedom, more independence and agency—the mental and physical space to do complex independent research, and easier access to my human boyfriend. But I suddenly saw that it was so much bigger than that, that this was far greater than me or my daughter. These rules and strictures and "how it's done"s were a straightjacket on all of us—all the way up to Gregorio. Eight hundred years old, and he couldn't receive the news of a granddaughter on the way without rushing to swaddle her in legal papers?

"I don't plan to raise her in the coven, no," I finally said. "I've hardly had time to plan anything, to be perfectly honest. I'm just going to sit with the news for a little while and see what makes sense." Sebastian nodded, behind Gregorio. I felt a sudden pinprick of annoyance at that—*come on out here and nod where he can see you!*—but I pushed it aside. He had his own battles. "As I said, we might consider a contract. I just can't know yet, and we've got months to work this out. *Today,* however, my mother is sick, and I'm very concerned about her. And I want to hear more about the clinic in general. How many witches are here now?"

"Fourteen," Sebastian blurted, as Gregorio opened his mouth. The elder warlock turned to glare at the young intern. "Counting your mother," my friend went on.

My father chose that moment to rejoin us. "Belladonna rests well," he announced. "Her essence is low, but not nearly so low as some of the others' we've seen. It's good you brought her in, Calendula." Now he glanced around the room, clearly just noticing the tension. "Did I miss something?"

"Your *daughter* has just announced her *pregnancy,*" Dr. Andromedus said. "Lucas, were you aware of this?"

"What?" My father turned to me, shock on his face. "Callie—"

I put a hand up. "Father, I just found out. I told Mother this morning; I would have told you, had you been there. I'm delighted about it, it was unplanned, I have no idea how that happened, and I am *not* interested in discussing it further at the moment." I stared back at him. He looked stunned, and sad. My voice softened as I went on. "I'm sorry you had to find out like this. We can talk about it more—later. Because what I'm really concerned about right now is hearing about

Mother's illness, and what the rest of the witches are sick with, and what is being done about it!"

"Calendula, there is no need to become overwrought," Gregorio put in. "I am sure you can understand how startled everyone is by this—at, as you point out, a time when we are already experiencing a great deal of turmoil."

I nodded.

He frowned slightly as he went on. "In fact, I cannot help but wonder if the two phenomena might not be so unrelated as they seem."

"What do you mean?" My dad and the research assistants looked confused as well.

"It seems to me that we have two sudden, inexplicable medical situations, in a species that has been quite stable for—so far as we know—millennia. Certainly witchkind has been stable for the many centuries I have been here, and those of my mentors before me. Magical essence does not just drain away on its own, without cause. And as a biologist, Calendula, working on this very issue, you know better than almost anyone that an 'accidental' pregnancy has always been impossible." He gazed at me appraisingly. "If you are quite certain you did not set this in motion intentionally, it is worrisome indeed."

"Believe me, I was *not* intending to get pregnant."

Gregorio shook his head. "What is happening to witchkind? What will be the next fact we have been certain of to come tumbling apart in our faces?"

My father pulled up a lab stool and sat on it, frowning just as Gregorio was. "The illness, at least, behaves like an infectious agent. Though we have been unable to pinpoint the cause."

I took another stool. "It's only witches getting sick, right? Not warlocks?"

"Thus far," Gregorio said. "Though of course, witches make up a great deal more of our population. If whatever this is affects only, say, one or two percent of us, it may be some time before a warlock sickens."

I nodded.

"We're hoping to find the cause—and eliminate it—before that happens," Sebastian said. Then he blushed, seeming to hear his own implication. "I mean, before any more witches get sick too—before anyone else gets sick!"

"What could cause both drained essence and increased fertility?" I asked, still baffled. "And a vanishing spirit?"

Gregorio looked at me soberly. "At this point, the only commonality we have found in the affected witches is a greater than usual degree of interaction with humans."

My face fell. Raymond...Logan and her tarot work for humans... "But wait, Mom never has anything to do with them, and she's sick now."

"It is only a correlation, and not entirely across the board," Gregorio said. "Sadly, epidemiology is only fully useful with a large enough sample population."

I leaned back, putting my hand on my belly again. It was just too mysterious, foggy and ill-formed. "Have you found anything in the patients' blood? What tests are you doing?" Flavius had mentioned his Melanian assay, but that wasn't going to show much. I glanced at the lab table behind us, with its clutter of books and flasks and beakers and equipment.

Gregorio sighed, looking at me carefully. He wasn't going to kick me out now, was he? I'd been in the building for half an hour, in both a patient room and back here in the lab. The argument about "it might be contagious" just wasn't going to hold water.

Perhaps he came to the same conclusion, because he walked to a big Magitech Fluoro-Blot machine that sat on the far end of the bench. "We are only just getting started," he said. "But I can show you the results from tests we have performed on the first three ailing witches."

"Dr. Andromedus," Flavius said, "I had been hoping to let her look at some of my samples—and results—as well."

I shot him a quick look; he shrugged and glanced at Sebastian.

Gregorio, of course, did not miss the exchange. He smiled indulgently at all three of us. "Ah, sneaking around behind the old man's back as usual, I see. Well, that is fine, Dr. Winterheart; you may show Calendula the work you have done as well. She has a keen eye and an even keener intellect. She is likely to see things you have missed."

I blinked, startled. I shouldn't be surprised at the compliment—I knew that Dr. Andromedus respected my work—but I was still smarting from his reaction to my pregnancy.

He's ancient, I reminded myself. *When he came of age, there were no witch biologists. Heck, there was hardly biology.*

———⊂●⊃———

When I left the clinic an hour later, my purse bulging with blood samples that had been run through both Gregorio's tests and those Flavius had done, I was not much wiser than I'd been before, though at least I now had something to work with. The sick witches—now Mom among them—were being treated with the same kinds of essence transfusions that Jeremy and I had tried with Logan, from the healers and the warlocks. As with blood donation, essence naturally rebuilt itself in time, in a healthy witch or warlock. Gregorio had told me that a call to the community at large would be going out soon, but he'd refused to take any from me. "Not from a pregnant witch."

"You need everything for that baby," my father had added.

I felt as though I could spare plenty, but I did not argue with them.

When I returned to my house, an anxious Elnor met me at the door. "Sorry, kitten. She's going to be okay. Of course she is." I scratched her ears, then picked her up and carried her to the kitchen, where Petrana stood, idle as usual, in the back corner, like some discarded broom.

Of course I wasn't afraid of her. A golem is made to carry out the intention of its maker, after all. Any golem's mud body is imbued with echoes of the traits and talents of its creator; the same song at a lower volume. A rabbi's golem would have a spiritual element, or a thirst for learning. A human man who desired power and control could perhaps create a brutish creature, one with the capacity to harm others.

When a powerful witch made a golem, it should contain echoes of her potential for magic. Manka had practically said as much, the night of Logan's illness. And I knew that. It was why I had made her. But, having done so, I seemed to have lost my nerve.

In my defense, life had been rather distracting of late.

Elnor squirmed in my arms. I put her down, still looking at Petrana. My golem gazed back at me without expression. Of course. I could stare at her all day and she would never feel uncomfortable, never wonder what I was doing. Yet she was alive, after a fashion; she was not a machine. I had given her that life.

Could this thing really be an echo of me?

By now my cat had wandered over to the cabinets. She glanced up, then at me, then up, pointedly. "Yes, yes," I said, getting out a can of tuna and a dish.

While Elnor ate, I thought further about Petrana, and about my 'tiny helpers' upstairs in the lab, and the samples in my purse, and about donating essence to sick witches.

And about my inexplicable pregnancy. As a scientist, I was very suspicious of coincidence. Yet I could not see how my pregnancy could have anything to do with mysterious essence-draining. I would need to talk further to Gregorio about this. Perhaps I would gain more insight as the pregnancy progressed.

For now, I focused on what I could do today, with the resources at hand. In my research, I had always imagined my homunculi as the end product. I had poured everything into their ingredients, methods, and spells, but once they appeared, I had considered them immutable. But was that really the whole story? Could I modify existent homunculi? Could they learn and grow, as Petrana did?

"Petrana, come with me."

"Yes, Mistress Callie."

Upstairs in the lab, I laid my golem out on a long table in the center of the room and ordered her to remain inert, nonreactive. "I'm going to be doing things to your bodily systems," I told her. "Please ignore anything I do until I say, 'Petrana, wake up.'"

"Yes, Mistress Callie," she said.

I focused on her a minute, then added, "And please close your eyes."

"Yes, Mistress Callie."

Putting my hands on her forehead, I began by taking the measure of her, as I would do to a flesh-and-blood entity. Familiar essence and energy ran through her—mine—though modified to animate the mud and sticks of her body. And, as I'd known, at a lesser volume... for the most part. The spark that had brought her to life could still be seen within her head: a bright, almost ultraviolet orb, quietly pulsing with contained power. A network of tiny tendrils emanated from it, leading from her head down throughout her body, much as our muscles and veins and meridian lines do.

I withdrew my hands and studied her. To augment her capacity for magic, should I add to the orb in her head, or try to plump up some of the energetic lines? Or should I try to implant a separate center—in her chest, perhaps—that would contain and control magical abilities?

I put my hands on her chest, closed my eyes, and "looked" inside her torso. More mud and small sticks, of course, but I also saw a stone there, about the size of a hen's egg, sitting just a little below where the heart would be, if she had had one. I nudged the stone with my mind, looking at it from all sides, seeking its story. It was pinkish—rose quartz?—no, it was mostly morganite, with a little dull sandstone clinging to it. Interesting. Morganite opened channels to connection and communication. Though I hadn't intentionally placed it there, it could hardly be an accident that such a thing had found its way into my golem. She had certainly picked up speech with ease.

The dirt of Petrana's making had come from the coven house's backyard, of course—an area which had grown a century's worth of magical plants, seen countless rituals and workings, and even contained the buried bodies of Nementhe and the two sisters who had gone Beyond before her. Any stone from that soil would hardly be a normal, mundane rock any longer.

Could I wake it up?

Elnor had followed us up to the laboratory once she'd finished her repast. She sat in the corner grooming herself, waiting for me to need her, or just wanting not to be left out if something interesting happened. Like more tuna. "Come here, kitty," I called now.

I picked her up and set her on the table next to my inert golem. "Watch my energy depletion," I told her. "I'm going to put some essence into Petrana. Meow if you sense anything amiss."

Elnor blinked her yellow eyes at me, purring. She might not have understood my words exactly, but she knew it was time to be a familiar, not just a cat.

I closed my eyes again, laying both hands on Petrana's still chest. I brought the stone into my inner vision once more, and held it awhile, making sure there was no latent spellwork in it, held over from years or decades ago. Then I drew my attention back into my own body, exploring my own essence. It still beat strong and supple throughout me, embracing the baby even as it supported my own well-being.

"Okay," I whispered. "Here goes."

I channeled a bit of my essence down into the stone in Petrana's chest, just as if I were donating essence to a sick witch. The stone glowed slightly to my inner sight as it absorbed the magical infusion. Elnor purred and rubbed her head against my arm, encouraging me.

After a few minutes, I closed the flow, leaving my hands in place a moment longer to make sure everything settled, and to keep taking the measure of Petrana and her stone. It still glowed, now pulsing a little bit like the brain orb did. And, yes! It was sending magical power—just a small bit, but measurable—through Petrana's system.

I took my hands away and grinned, cracking my knuckles and shrugging the tension out of my shoulders. "Petrana, wake up," I said.

She opened her eyes. "Yes, Mistress Callie."

"Petrana, please say something to me without speaking aloud. Send me a thought. Do you understand what I mean?"

She opened her mouth and closed it again, still gazing at me. I could almost read puzzlement on her face, though I'm sure I was projecting it. Damn, had I given her a paradox? She wanted to speak to answer me, and I had told her not to speak…

After a long moment, I heard, very faintly in my head, *Like this, Mistress Callie?*

"Yes!" I squealed with delight. How easy was that! "I did it, I did it!" I picked up Elnor and danced around the room with her. She put up with it very nearly graciously.

"Whew." I collapsed into a chair, letting the cat down as I did. Oh, that was draining work. Or was it the pregnancy tapping me out? Either way, I was suddenly as exhausted and starving as if I'd done a major working.

Which, now that I thought about it, I had. Not as large as creating Petrana in the first place, but certainly not small.

Can you hear thoughts I send you? I asked Petrana.

Yes, Mistress Callie.

Her words were stronger this time, though I felt a twinge in my chest as I heard them. As though she was using my own energy to send them. Hadn't I closed the channel? I sought inside myself, looking at where I tapped my power. Yes, it was closed, but it also seemed…permeable?

Say something else, I commanded.

What would you like me to say?

Again, the twinge. Damn. Would she always have to use my power in order to do anything? But I didn't get tired when she performed physical tasks—that was kind of the whole point of her, at least so far: to save me from having to do things. Why did she drain my magical power by doing magic?

Was it just a matter of degree? Perhaps the mechanism was different. Or maybe I just didn't notice when she took my physical energy. After all, people got tired all the time. Unless it was dramatic, I would likely think nothing of it.

I would have to do more experimentation. But not till I felt more energetic—I'd drained myself enough for now. "Okay," I said. "Don't do the thought-sending again until I ask you to. Go back to just saying words out loud."

"Yes, Mistress Callie."

I went downstairs and grabbed a big hunk of sharp cheddar cheese out of the fridge: instant protein energy. Then I walked more slowly back up to the lab, bringing my purse this time, and its collected samples.

I bound my hair back tightly before laying everything out on the lab bench to look over. Gregorio had packaged everything up together in a spellsack, but the differences were clear. Flavius's work was cruder, yet with a lot more raw vitality to it. I could see why he was on the Elder path. His magic had strong power and potency. His big challenge was going to be to learn how to temper his brute force, to introduce subtlety and insinuation to his work. If he could do that, he would be an amazing practitioner someday.

For now, at least, the force of his work made it easier to follow his pathways. I set Gregorio's samples aside and laid Flavius's three vials in an empty tray, unopened. I decanted a bottle of angelica root bath over the vials, to cleanse away any magical residues from the clinic or my journey on the ley line—or, heck, anything they might have picked up in my purse. I swished them around, making sure the bath covered the vials completely, and let them sit.

After a few minutes, I pulled the vials out and dried them off. They were labeled by date; I poured the earliest sample into a Petri dish. As it spread, I pulled out my Mabel's Glass and leaned in, just to get a sense of what I was looking at here.

I saw at once how his Melanian assay differed from the traditional kel one, though I wasn't sure it made much difference to the results. He'd used a shortcut through a curling ribbon of the essence pathway that controlled minor magical aspects such as tenor and resonance of power. Just as I'd already noted: crude, strong magic. It would save a lot of time to do it this way, leaving more resources for a more refined search down the line. So, okay, I could see the point to this; a way of quickly weeding out directions that were not fruitful.

I drew back and set the Glass down, feeling a little queasy. Yep, this was clearly a blood sample from a sick witch. As I looked so closely at it, trying to understand what I was seeing, my own magic automatically tried to reach out, to relate to them, to draw it into myself. My boundaries were more open than usual, after the work I'd done with Petrana earlier. This was the basis for how we communicated with one another, after all. I took a deep breath, willing my own essence to stay put, closing my internal borders. Whether this illness was due to an infectious agent or not, it was not healthy to be immersing myself so carelessly.

Elnor jumped up onto the counter and peered into the dish, her nose twitching. Then I heard the heavy step of Petrana as she approached the bench.

I turned around to look at my golem. "Petrana? What are you doing?"

"Did you wish my assistance, Mistress Callie?"

I had been teaching her to take more initiative...and I had just linked us much more closely together, magically... "I had not thought I had, Petrana, but I do need to take a step back, myself. So please feel free to let me know anything you perceive here."

She stood by the bench, staring expressionlessly down into the dish. Should I offer her the Mabel's Glass? I was beginning to feel a little weirded out. Was she an intelligent being or not? Had I actually asked this of her, without realizing? What was she thinking—*was* she thinking? What could she see?

I narrowed my eyes as I touched the channel between us. Yes, she was exercising magic. Yet it didn't give me a twinge, this time. Was it because she was drawing less power, or were we getting smoother with the transfer? Or was she generating her own magic?

"That is not a good thing, in there," she said at last.

"No, it's not," I said. "It's a blood sample from a very sick witch."

"Yes, Mistress Callie, I see that; but I also see something unnatural."

"What do you mean?"

She stared back at me. Boy, the next time I built a golem, I'd try to engineer some capacity for facial expression. "I do not know the technical words for it, but I see a device for stealing away power."

I gaped at her. "A device?"

"By the third and fourth red dish-like elements. Counting from the top left."

Red dish-like elements... "The erythrocytes?" I grabbed the Mabel's Glass again and focused on the red blood cells, following her directions. "I'll be damned..." I whispered, seeing a dark smudge there, which flickered in and out of view. I started to reach out with my own magic to nudge it, hold it still, maybe even magnify it, but reconsidered. "Petrana, can you make it easier for me to see?" Since I didn't know how she'd seen it in the first place, I didn't want to be any more specific—didn't want to trample on her process.

"I will try, Mistress Callie." She stared at the dish again. I saw nothing in her face, felt nothing in our bond. After a minute, she turned back to me. "Look now."

I did. And saw, very clearly, an alien element. It looked for all the world like a microscopic parasite, draining the red blood cell of its essence.

I stuffed myself with more cheese and a dark beer, and brought a box of crackers up to the lab with me. Then I examined, with Petrana's guidance, the rest of Flavius's samples, and then those from Gregorio.

Flavius's all showed the artifact. Gregorio's did not.

After that, I went and paced around downstairs for a while. Fed Elnor again. Contemplated a nap, but, though I was exhausted, I was also too wound up to rest.

Back to the lab. I looked through all the samples again, slowly and carefully. I reviewed my notes. I made Petrana rearrange the dishes behind my back so that I examined them all blindly.

There was something very wrong here.

But was it deliberate or accidental? Where was the essence going— were these parasites capable of independent action?

If this was something running unchecked through witchkind, why was it only in Dr. Winterheart's samples? Both he and Gregorio had run their tests on all the sick witches: I was looking at samples from the same witches. Furthermore, the direction was all wrong: these assays were run on blood *after* it had been drawn, of course. Even if Flavius was introducing something, how did it get back into the sick witches?

Or was it also in Gregorio's samples, but only Flavius's new, stronger method was capable of revealing it?

Why hadn't such powerful warlocks been able to see what my golem had?

We needed to run these same tests on blood from healthy witches. In fact, I couldn't believe that the warlocks hadn't done so already. Then again, they wouldn't have thought to double-check findings that had seemed so inconclusive to them; they were still trying for any results at all.

It was now past midnight. I had so many questions, but I needed to sleep on this.

On the way to my bedroom, I paused at the doorway of the adjacent room—the one I'd sort of given to Petrana. Though she didn't need a bedroom; she didn't sleep, or need privacy for changing, or anything.

I could stash her in any old closet when I needed to hide her. She stood in the kitchen otherwise.

My daughter, however...this would be her nursery.

She would sleep in here, when she was not in my bed. I'd get an adorable crib for her, a precious little dresser—precious little clothes! Books and toys, and a soft rug. I would find curtains for the window, cheery yellow ones, with lace trim. *She'll come bounding into my bedroom in the mornings, chattering happily...eventually I'll take her to get her first familiar...a few years later we'll choose her coven...*

My heart filled with a longing that felt both joyful and sad. I would raise my daughter here, love her and teach her everything I knew. And protect her. Whatever evil was running amok in our world, I would stamp it out, before she ever even had to know about it.

My lovely girl, I thought, smiling into the empty room. *I cannot wait to meet you.*

— CHAPTER SIXTEEN —

I n the morning, I went to the coven house, looking for Leonora. I found her at last in the side yard, pruning the jacaranda tree. Her gardening outfit was even more eccentric than her usual garb. Yards of crimson chenille hung to the ground, belted loosely with a four-hundred-year-old chain threaded with snake bones. The robe was lined with the skins of a hundred moles, and decorated with the preserved eyeballs of all the familiars she had ever shared her life with—except Grieka, of course. At least the excessive fall of fabric hid her shoes.

I stifled a smile and met her eyes. "Mother, when you have a moment, I'd like to talk to you."

"I am nearly done here, Calendula. You may await me in my study."

I paused in the kitchen for a cup of tea. Maybe peppermint would be more tolerable than chamomile. It could hardly be worse.

When I heard the front door open, I went and took my usual chair in her study, admiring the stained glass windows as I waited.

Leonora came in a minute later with a cup of tea of her own. Pennyroyal, I couldn't help but notice. Lucky witch. She took a seat behind her desk, arranging her robes. "You are looking a bit peaked, Calendula. Are you well?"

"Yes, but I'm worried about something." I explained to her briefly about the samples—she wasn't a biologist, but she did understand how our magical systems worked. "I know I need more information here, but I'm a little baffled that the warlocks and the healers haven't seen what I'm seeing."

She frowned, sipped at her tea, thinking. "Perhaps they have, but did not want to influence your observations?"

"Maybe. But they did say they found nothing. Gregorio even threw out some theory about human involvement..." I trailed off, not wanting to get into his further thoughts about my pregnancy. Completely ridiculous. "If he did know something, it would be more like him to tell me so directly, but not what it was, rather than to pretend he didn't."

"So why do you not bring this to him?"

I sighed. "I...wanted to run it by you first. It all feels weird, uncomfortable. I don't understand it, and I'm afraid it looks like I'm accusing Dr. Winterheart of something nefarious here."

"Are you?"

"I don't know! That's just the problem. It doesn't make any sense."

She took another sip of her tea. "I don't see the harm in taking the question to your mentor. Tell him just what you have told me: that you do not understand this; that though you do not necessarily suspect Dr. Winterheart, you do need more information. Running both tests on unafflicted witches is a clear next step. And are there other assays that could be run as well?" She smiled at me. "You have worked with Dr. Andromedus for many years, and he knows you very well. He will listen to you, without jumping to awkward conclusions."

"You're right. Thank you." I started to get up.

Leonora leaned forward. "We do have another matter to discuss, Calendula."

I sat back down, stifling the urge to put my hand on my belly. "Yes." Then I went on, blurting it out before I could lose my nerve. "About that. I have thought it through very carefully, and I have decided to keep this daughter."

Her gaze revealed nothing. "Are you quite certain that this is what you want?"

I opened my mouth and closed it again. Where was her anger? Her fierce command? "Yes. I am."

"Then you should do it." She picked up her teacup.

"I..." I gazed at her. "Why aren't you trying to talk me out of it?"

She gave a slight smile. "Because it is possible that I have done some thinking as well, once I recovered from my initial surprise. Because our children are rare enough that they should not be discarded without good reason. Because an alliance with the house of Gregorio Andromedus—official or not—can only aid and strengthen this coven. Because you would probably find a way to go ahead with it anyway. And because, despite what you may think of me, I am not a tyrant." She smiled more warmly. "I do care about you, daughter. It may look as though I am always saying no to you—to all my daughters—but I am only thinking of what is best for you, and for us all. I do want you to be happy."

I smiled back at her, as confused as I was relieved. "Um...thank you. But aren't you worried about her health, or power, or...?" *Why in the world am I suddenly taking the opposite side?* Was I simply a knee-jerk contrarian?

"I am still concerned about her waning-moon conception, yes. I will want to keep a very careful eye on you—and her—throughout. You will eat healthfully and get the proper amount of sleep. You will want to be sure and drink wine, particularly elderflower, at least three times per week."

"Yes, Mother."

"I will ask that you show the coven some consideration, as well. You have been spending very little time here, except for the moments of your fresh grief over Logandina, when you mostly kept to your room. I would like you to take far more dinners here. Your sisters, who love you, will be very interested in your health and well-being, just as I am. And they will be very pleased to have a new witchlet among us."

"Of course," I agreed hastily, thinking with an internal sigh of our stilted, formal dinners.

"Though you may leave the golem at your house."

"Right."

"We will still need to decide what is to be done with the child in her earliest years, if you do choose to forego a union with the warlock," she went on. "Although this is a teaching coven, we are not set up to accommodate witchlets younger than the age of seven or eight."

"I...imagine I would raise her in my house," I said.

Leonora waved a dismissive hand. "We have some time to work out the details. You may find you wish to apply for a leave of absence after all, to sign a contract with the warlock. I have already contacted the Artemis Guild and asked them to send me a list of available candidates." She frowned. "There is rather a shortage of Guild members these days, it seems, but I believe there are a few in New Orleans who might suit."

I could never be a coven mother, I thought. All her days, spent juggling so many details about so many other people's lives. Did she ever get to do anything for herself?

Or was this what she wanted for herself?

"I'm pretty sure I don't want to sign a contract with him," I told her. "I'm not seeing a lot of him these days."

"Oh?" She leaned forward, frowning.

"Yeah. He's been helping his father set up the clinic..." It sounded weak even to me. The clinic was fully up and running, and Jeremy was no healer—he wasn't even a scientist. "Other stuff too, I don't know what. And I've been busy, and…I've needed some space to think."

Leonora nodded. "Well, even if you do decide against a contract, ultimately, it is good to involve the father." *And his family*, she didn't have to add. "You do know about Niadine's upbringing, don't you?"

"What? No, I don't know anything." Niad was more than twice my age; she'd been an established member of the coven for decades before I even studied here. "She doesn't exactly confide in me."

My coven mother quirked a corner of her lips, acknowledging my understatement. "Well, much of her story is not mine to tell. But it is hardly a secret that her birth mother was both covenless and unionless. Niadine was raised with a great deal of uncertainty, in at times downright poverty. Which may account for some of her…more strident opinions about how things ought to be done."

"Oh." I sat back, very surprised. "I had no idea. She's so—well, yeah, strident. I thought she'd had a super-traditional upbringing."

"I am afraid not, though I see that she tries to convey that impression. In any event, that is an extreme example—of course you wouldn't be in anything like the same situation, with your family support and this coven. But it would be best to come to some sort of arrangement with the warlock—visitation, or shared parenting, or the like. And we should probably have a formal announcement, perhaps even a party…I should send word to Dr. Andromedus…" She was talking more to herself than to me at this point, I realized.

"Mother?" I interrupted gently. "Speaking of Dr. Andromedus…"

"Yes, of course." She smiled at me again. "Go consult with him. We will speak further of these other matters soon."

I slipped out of her office, closing the door quietly behind me, and nearly tripped over Gracie's kitten as the witchlet herself scrambled away from the door. "You're *pregnant*?"

"Blessed Mother, you scared me to death! Were you spying on the *coven mother*?"

Gracie hunched her shoulders in defense, then tried to cover it with a shrug. "I was just…walking by, I mean, Minky wanted a snack, and, well, but then I heard your voices, and—you're going to have a baby, Callie!"

"Yes, I know." I sighed. "And you didn't just accidentally hear our voices, not through that door. Doesn't Leonora usually set a privacy charm on her office?"

Gracie looked sullen. "I guess she forgot it this time."

I gave her a look. "Not likely. And even if she did, that would not excuse your behavior. Do you make a habit of such things?"

"No! I just...I knew something was up with you. In class the other day. You were, I dunno, weird. Distracted. You know?"

"I suppose I was," I said. "But that still doesn't make it right to eavesdrop. You could just ask me."

"Would you have told me?"

"Not until I talked to Leonora. I would have told you as soon as I was free to. It's always better to be direct about things, Gracie. Not sneaky."

"No it's not. No one ever tells me anything. It's always, *Wait till you get older.*"

"Gracie, that's—" I stopped myself before I could flat-out lie to her. "Yes, not everyone gets told everything. Leonora has plenty of secrets from me, and the rest of the sisters." *So why didn't Leonora set the privacy charm?* I wondered. That reflex should have been as natural as breathing for her. Or did she, and Gracie somehow broke through it? That was an even more disturbing thought. "We have this system, these rules, for a reason. It's for the protection of us all. You can't just go flouting them."

"You did!" she almost shouted. "You're *pregnant*, without a contract or anything!"

I glanced back at Leonora's closed door. Of course, if she wanted to, our coven mother could listen to any of us, anywhere. Even so, standing here in the kitchen felt a little too exposed. "Come on," I said, guiding Gracie toward the back stairs. "Let's go to my room."

She picked up her kitten.

"Minky?" I asked, as we climbed the stairs.

"Yeah! What do you think? She's so soft and fuzzy."

"I think it's an adorable name."

"I might spell it fancier—M-y-n-q-u-e-e, maybe."

I laughed. "Spell it however you like. She'll respond to the sound of it, not the letters."

In my room, we sat facing one another on the edge of the bed. Minky, or Mynquee, romped around the floor, exploring territory that had been off-limits to her before. "Gracie, I care about you a great deal, and I consider you a friend. But it is not appropriate to eavesdrop; and most of your elders would not take kindly to being challenged by a student."

She looked back at me sullenly. "I didn't challenge you."

"Yes, in fact, you did," I said, keeping my voice gentle. "And without all the information, even. If you had heard our entire conversation, you would know that the reason I am still pregnant is because Leonora is permitting it."

"What?"

"It's true. I may be going against custom, but I am doing so with explicit permission. So I am not, actually, breaking any rules."

"Well that's stupid, you shouldn't need her *permission!*" she fumed. "Just stupid! It's a free country, nobody should be able to tell anyone what to do. What does Leonora know, anyway?"

Was Gracie upset about my pregnancy or not? I imagined she didn't even know herself. "Leonora knows plenty," I told her. "She is ten times *my* age—she has lived through things neither you nor I could possibly imagine. And she's grown wiser and more powerful with each challenge, with every passing year. I honor and value that experience, and if you have the sense I know you do, you should too."

Gracie kicked her feet back and forth. Minky batted at her shoelaces.

I went on, more gently. "We've talked about this before. Witchkind traditions give our lives shape and structure. All Leonora's experience would mean nothing if she didn't share it with the rest of us. Our coven's collective magic is far stronger than any of us can manage alone. A life without those things isn't freedom—it's just…being lost."

"So why don't you live here anymore? Why did you have to leave?"

I gave her a small smile. "Gracie, honey, we've talked about *this* before too. I know it's hard to be at the bottom of the pecking order. What you are doing here is learning and growing. We all get to taste a little more freedom and independence eventually, if we want to."

"It's a stupid system," she muttered. "I'm supposed to just obey everyone, then join some stupid coven in a few years and hide indoors with a bunch of stupid old crones forever."

"If you let them, Leonora and the rest of the sisters can teach you so much that will be of value to you, even if your life ends up looking different from theirs—or mine. No one's going to lock you up forever."

"I've never seen Honor or Ruth or Elizabeth leave the house. Liza either."

"They could if they wanted to; nobody's stopping them. Many of the older sisters are just more comfortable with the old ways. Everyone's different. Times are changing. Nobody knows what the future holds. But we do know that we'll be better equipped if we face it together. Like with the essence-draining illness, and Dr. Andromedus's new clinic." Which I really did need to get to, soon. "You know we can't go to human hospitals for treatment."

"No." Gracie shivered, then shrugged again, looking contrite. "I'm sorry for eavesdropping, Callie. And for…"

"I forgive you," I said, tousling her hair. "Now we have to figure out how you're going to make it up to me. How do you feel about babysitting?"

I popped over to the clinic. Nobody stopped me on the street, so I went in, sending word to Gregorio through the æther as I went.

He met me in the hallway on the way to the clinic's lab. "Calendula, you have conclusions for us?"

"I have questions, at least."

"Let me hear them." He ushered me into a small but comfortable office outside the lab.

I laid out my findings. "I don't understand this, but I think we need to draw more blood from both the sick witches and some well ones—and warlocks too," I said.

He frowned, looking across his tented fingers at me. "I agree," he said, after a minute. "This is peculiar."

"We can take my blood, and there's bound to be at least a half a dozen witches at home in my coven," I said.

Gregorio shook his head. "Not yours; your pregnancy may needlessly complicate things. But I will ask your coven mother to ask for volunteers, rather than our usual donors; that is a good idea." He shifted his gaze, no doubt calling to Leonora. When he returned his attention to the room, he said, "Done: we will stop by your coven on our way out. And I have asked Dr. Fallon to collect fresh samples here for us as well."

"On our way out?"

"I would like to work at the laboratory in Berkeley," Gregorio said. "The emotional intensity is just too strong here, and the Zosimos cabinet I have there is far larger and better established. We need these samples to be as clean as possible."

"Right," I agreed.

Half an hour later, we were across the bay. I carried a large sack jingling with glass vials. Gregorio spelled open the door to his lab and we walked in.

It was messy as ever, but now it also had an air of abandonment. Dust motes caught the sunlight from the one uncovered window; no little creatures scurried about under our feet; no research fellows lurked at the back benches.

Gregorio noticed my look. "I have been working exclusively in the clinic and its laboratory since the crisis began, for reasons of expediency."

"Ah."

I unpacked the samples, after Gregorio cleared room on the bench closest to the Zosimos cabinet. "I would like you to perform all the assays, Calendula," he said. I noticed he hadn't touched any of the vials. "I shall keep as far from the process as possible."

"Good idea." I started opening vials and pipetting droplets of blood into the assay crucibles. "I just need you to walk me through the two procedures," I told him.

"Of course."

When the first round of assays—Gregorio's, Flavius's, and a third, older test, on both sick and healthy samples—was assembled, he told me how to adjust the shelves and wires in the Zosimos cabinet to accommodate them all. I loaded them in and shut the door. "Do you want me to set the cabinet going?" I asked.

"No, sadly, it only responds to my touch. Though I will take care to keep as much of myself as possible out of the process." The ancient warlock stepped forward and placed his hands on the door. Flashes of light showed, along with a high whine. When that all settled down, he stepped back. "Now we should leave the laboratory altogether while it works, and endeavor to think about other things."

We went out of the building and walked around the Berkeley campus, discussing its odd jumble of architectural styles and its colorful political history. As we passed through Sproul Plaza, we paused on the steps for a minute. "All the things that have happened here," I said, "just in my lifetime."

Gregorio smiled. "Yes, you have come of age in an interesting time."

For humans as well as us, I thought as we walked on.

After forty minutes or so had passed, I asked, "Do you think it's done now?"

"Almost assuredly," he said, and began to steer us back toward the library building. "But I wanted to give it an excess of time, to be completely certain."

Back in the lab, he had me open the now-silent Zosimos cabinet and draw out the assays. I laid them along the bench in random order, forcing myself not to think about which was which. When they were all out, I said, "Oh, I should have brought my Mabel's Glass."

"Use this," he said, reaching for a drawer before stopping himself. "Open that; you will find what you need in there."

"Ooh, fancy," I said, finding an elaborate version of my simple Glass, with small gems inlaid along the sides, and spirals of gold wire around each eye-hole. "Where is this from?"

Gregorio smiled. "I brought it from the Old Country. It was handmade for me several hundred years ago."

"Cool." I peered through it into the first crucible.

Gregorio added, "Do not tell me what you see until you have viewed them all. I will wait across the room."

"Sure." I stared into the crucible. After a long minute, I made a note and moved onto the next one.

At the end of the line, I set the Glass down and reviewed my notes. Then I walked over to where Gregorio sat, at the small table where we'd had tea a few months ago, and handed him the notebook. "It's in all the sick samples, and none of the healthy ones," I said, as he looked over my notes. "Could something in your assays have been quashing it?"

Gregorio sighed. "I was afraid of that, but I did not want to say anything until we had gone through all this."

"How do you think that happened?"

"I have been working so hard to understand this illness, and to effect a cure, it appears that my very will has affected my own scientific inquiry. This is most unfortunate."

"You mean, you've...cured the blood, after it was drawn?"

"It appears so." He continued to study my notes a minute longer before he set the notebook down on the table between us. "An excess of power can be as bad as insufficient power, without the means to channel and control it. All my life I have struggled against my own strength. Thus far, I have largely managed to keep it controlled— through internal discipline and external devices." He waved vaguely in the direction of the Zosimos cabinet. "If these measures are now failing..."

"But this is great," I said, leaning forward. "If you can cure the illness, now that we've figured out what it is, you can figure out how to focus and control it. You can cure all the sick witches!" *You can cure my mother.*

He smiled. "Yes, that aspect is encouraging, though we are a long way from determining whether my ability to chase the agent out of a few drops of blood can be translated to safely cleansing a witch's entire system. We will continue to pursue that path, do not worry," he added, seeing that I was about to interrupt. "But if I am not able to keep my unconscious interference out of my research, despite all the measures I have taken to do so, it not only bodes ill for my life's work going forward, but casts doubt on findings I have made up until now—perhaps for a great deal of time."

He looked so unhappy at this, I wanted to empathize, but all I could think about was that his mere presence, coupled with his desire to solve this problem, had banished the rogue element. How could this not be an amazing breakthrough?

"But I must confess," he went on, "that the most disturbing aspect of all of this is that it was entirely opaque to me. The presence of the infectious agent would have remained undetected if it were not for your insight and vision, Calendula. Not to mention your own considerable power. All witchkind owes you a debt of gratitude."

"I...well, thank you, Gregorio, but—actually, I didn't spot it. My golem did."

He gave me a quizzical look, the corners of his mouth almost turning up into a small smile. "Your golem?"

"Yes, Petrana—I didn't see anything until I had her examine the samples. She pointed it out, and even did something so that I could see it better. I'm not even sure what."

Now he did smile. It was a kindly one. "Calendula Isadora. Do you truly believe that your golem is some sort of independent creature?"

"What do you mean?"

"It is a *golem*. A golem is not only an expression of powerful magic: it is *your* creation, from start to finish. Your magic brought it to life; your magic runs through its system. Its every action is entirely a result of you—your knowledge, your power, your agency. Even the daughter growing in your very womb is, at best, a shared creation between you and my son; your golem is yours alone. So yes, Calendula, you made this discovery, even if you are not consciously aware of how, at the moment. And it will be you who will save us all."

"Um." While it felt good to hear my mentor's praise, it also felt... unwarranted. And a little over the top. "I...thank you, Gregorio, but I think she might actually be a little bit of an independent creature. I've been trying to teach her..." I trailed off as his kindly smile deepened. It was clear I wasn't going to change his mind, and what would be the point?

"Your modesty is becoming, but it is also acceptable to feel pride in your accomplishments. Have I taught you nothing over the years?"

I smiled back at him, still feeling super awkward. "All right. So. No matter whose amazing brilliance came up with this, we still haven't figured out what to do next. How do we translate this discovery into a cure?"

Gregorio laughed delightedly. "And that, Calendula, is why I have such complete confidence in you." Then he sobered. "You are correct: that is an important next step, but there is also a piece of the puzzle missing, and we will not get very far without it. We must determine where this infectious agent came from in the first place. If we do not understand its original cause, we will not be able to prevent its happening again."

I nodded. "Do you think it's a natural, random virus, or something else? Petrana called it unnatural, and a device. A device for stealing away essence."

"Again, your golem is merely reflecting your own insight. We need to look into it further, but I am inclined to agree."

"Where is the essence going, when it is stolen away? There has to be a way to trace that."

Gregorio pursed his lips, deep in thought. After a minute, he said, "I can think of a few possible paths to follow; nothing that will yield instant results, sadly. But you are correct: finding where the essence is going will lead us to our culprit. Assuming there is one."

I didn't want to ask the obvious question, but there was no avoiding it. "Do you think it could be Dr. Winterheart?"

Now Gregorio looked very, very solemn. "I hope he is not, but I fear…" He shook his head and looked away for a moment before turning back to me. "Let us not leap to any conclusions. Not only is it unfair to a brilliant young researcher, but it would taint our own investigation. We must keep entirely open minds so that we do not bring preconceptions to the table." He gazed at me more keenly. "In fact, Calendula, given what we have just learned, I am not going to do any of this work myself. I will show you the two tests I have in mind, and I want you to draw new blood samples yourself, and perform the tests in your home laboratory. I will stay as far out of the process as possible."

I nodded slowly. "That does make sense. Show me what you want me to do."

—◄●►—

It was late afternoon by the time I left Gregorio's Berkeley lab. Mindful of Leonora's request that I show up for dinner at the coven house a lot more often, I popped by my own place just long enough to drop off the herbs and sensor stones Gregorio had given me, and to pick up Elnor. I'd draw new blood samples tomorrow and start the tests.

I walked in the front door of the coven house to a delicious smell. Whatever I thought about the stilted formality, I had to admit, we did eat well here. My appetite had come soaring back in the last few days. Thank the Blessed Mother.

Leonora found me in the kitchen as I was peering into a covered pot: duck confit atop a bed of white beans and tiny sausages. "Calendula, a quick word?"

"Sure."

I turned to follow her into her office, but she shook her head and stayed put. Pans clanked behind us as Peony worked at the sink; the smell of roasted potatoes drifted out of the oven. "I trust you had a productive afternoon?"

"Yes. You were right—Gregorio was very interested in what I found, and we're going to—"

She put up a hand. "Tell me the details later. I am tardy for another appointment, and dinner is in half an hour." She lowered her voice. "Please do not make your pregnancy known to the house generally just yet. I shall speak to Gregorio Andromedus and come to an understanding about the particular arrangements before we begin a discussion here."

"Um, all right."

She turned to go before I could decide whether to tell her that Gracie, at least, already knew. If Leonora had been monitoring us, she'd be aware of that. If not, I might as well protect my student's privacy. I didn't know where Gracie was, so I sent her a message through the æther: *Have you told anyone my news?*

No, Callie, came her reply. *Is it going to be announced at dinner?*

No. Leonora wants me to wait.

Okee-doke. I could feel her smug glee at having a secret even through the æther.

The dinner was as yummy as it had smelled. And the company of my sisters and the students who boarded in the house was—well, not entirely onerous. Niad was even subdued, not needling me as usual. And I was doubly glad that Leonora had delayed my announcement. I was in no mood to deal with yet another flurry of shock, disapproval, and pointed questions. I sipped my elderflower wine as I looked down the long table: Honor, Ruth, Elizabeth, Liza, Organza, and Peony in a line to Leonora's left; the younger generation of Flora, Sirianna, Niad, Pearl, Maela, and then me to her right, with the students clustered at the foot of the table. Comfortable company, at least right now.

I took another sip of my wine and frowned, setting the glass down. I didn't like this brew; it was too heavy, too sweet. I had a fresher, lighter vintage at home. I'd have to remember to bring a bottle or two over.

Jeremy sent me a message through the æther about an hour after I'd returned to my house for the night. I was reading in bed, thinking about sleep.

May I see you this evening?

Sure, come on over, I told him. After thinking a minute, I got up and pulled some clothes on.

He materialized in the front parlor, coming straight off the ley line. Now that we had built wards together, he didn't have to apply for permission to enter. He did still ask, though, as any well-brought-up warlock should.

"Greetings, my dear," he said, taking me into his arms.

"Hi," I murmured into the hollow at the base of his throat. My, he smelled good, and felt even better. Being pregnant hadn't affected *this* appetite one bit.

He drew away, keeping hold of my hand. "I have just heard from my father that Leonora Scanza is in favor of...of our child."

"Yes. I was a bit surprised, but apparently she rethought her position."

He gave me a tentative smile and nodded at the couch. "Shall we?"

"Sure." We sat down together. He still clung to my hand.

"Furthermore, my father informed me that your coven mother is willing to consider the formation of a union between you and me. That she has already been in touch with the Artemis Guild." He looked earnestly into my eyes. "Callie, I know it was all very sudden, but I hope you will now consider a formal offer? The terms will be very generous, and you may add most any clause you like."

I sighed. "Jeremy, it was indeed very sudden. It still is. I know that this isn't the usual way things are done—but it's still too soon for me. Beyond keeping this daughter, I don't actually know *what* I want to do."

I could see the frustration on his face, and his struggle to control it. "It would be better arranged sooner than later; word will now get out to the community. None of us will benefit from unchecked gossip."

Now the fire of anger replaced my fast-cooling ardor. I took my hand back. "If you think I should sign a contract with you to save us all from *gossip*—"

"Callie, don't." He looked devastated. "I'm going about this all wrong, and I am sorry. I care *for* you, I want to take care *of* you—and our child. Can't you see that?"

"But can't *you* see that I don't *want* to be taken care of? That I get to make my own decisions about my life?" I put my hand on my belly. "No matter how she got here, this is a *person*, not some problem to be solved, *taken care of*. She's her own self first, and she's in my body second, and that's really all that should matter here. I know that goes against our customs, but you may have noticed I've been having a little trouble with our customs lately."

He gazed silently at me a moment, looking so sad. "I...do not know what to say to you, Callie. I do not understand this."

I put my hand on his arm. "It's not that I don't want you in my life," I added, my voice softening. "Or in *her* life. I'm not saying no, forever. I'm just saying not right now." He put his other hand on mine and gave it a gentle squeeze as I went on. "I expect that we will raise her together, in some way. Can't we just let things grow naturally between us, over time?" I turned my fingers over and took his hand. "This romance took me by surprise, you know. You and Logan were... and I already had a boyfriend."

He looked confused a moment, then nodded. "The human, yes, of course."

"And that's not really resolved yet either."

Now he looked up at me sharply. "It isn't? But I thought—"

"The particular issue of him dropping in unannounced is resolved. I haven't seen him in some time, but I don't know if we're...through." I did know, though. I just hadn't had the guts to do it. "Jeremy, my love life is a mess, and everyone knows it. Do you really think there wouldn't be just as much gossip if we rushed into a formal union when most people don't even know we're seeing each other?"

"Of course people will talk about anything. But I still think—"

"Yes, yes, I know. And I promise, I'm considering it. Can you please just let me do this at my own pace?"

"I shall, Calendula," he said, stiffly. I wondered how often people said no to this warlock. We sat in uncomfortable silence, looking at each other across the expanse of cushions. Then he gave a small sigh and reached out for my hand once more. "Callie. Again, I am sorry. I want to be with you, I want to protect you, to help you, to be your partner. I understand that you feel otherwise—" He gripped my hand harder, to stop my interruption. "No, I know that you care, and that there is something strong and real between us. I understand that it may take some time for us to come to an accord as to what to do about that. I will redouble my efforts to be patient. I will endeavor to understand you better. I am sorry if I have hurt or annoyed you. That has never been my intention." He smiled, humble and tentative. "Forgive me?"

"Oh, Jeremy." I squeezed his hand. With a sigh, I said, "Yes, I forgive you. But please, can we just table all this for now?"

"Of course." He shifted, looking ready to get up. "I will leave you in peace." Before I could respond, he nodded politely and vanished onto a ley line.

Which was kind of a show-offy thing to do. I don't know, maybe they did it all the time in the Old Country.

The next morning, well rested, my belly full of scrambled eggs, toast, and two cups of awful chamomile tea with lots of sugar, I set to work on the new assays.

I drew new blood samples from the sick witches in the clinic and the healthy volunteers. Sebastian offered to help with this part, but even if Gregorio hadn't also insisted on it, I did want to do all the work with my own hands, from start to finish.

It was nearly noon before I got back to my house with everything I needed. Working entirely alone, despite what Gregorio had said about Petrana's being a part of me, I laid out the batches of blood samples and herbs, then sang the incantations over them. Elnor, confused, sat outside the closed door of the lab.

I left the assays for two hours and went for a walk around the neighborhood. Upon my return, I sang the secondary incantation, very carefully did not inspect the contents of the dishes, and left again.

Six more times, I repeated this process. When it was late in the night, I again resisted the temptation to peer at any possible results, instead going to bed, where I did not sleep.

In the morning, I looked at the results—first alone, then with Elnor and Petrana. Then I looked at them again. Assay results can be ambiguous, sometimes very ambiguous, despite what I'd said to my mother during our tarot lesson.

When I was as certain as I could be, I sent a message through the æther to Gregorio.

I understand, he sent back, and then told me what we needed to do.

Are you certain? I asked. *Because if this much could be hidden...*

Now that we know what to look for, we can be prepared, he assured me. *Meet me at high noon at the clinic.*

I shivered, thinking of the ancient Chinese curse about living in interesting times.

— CHAPTER SEVENTEEN —

High noon was over three hours away. Checking the results yet again and then packing them up took fifteen minutes. Taking a shower and arranging my hair in a secure but non-hideous braid took another thirty.

I paced around my house, trying unsuccessfully to work out the nervous energy. When I'd tripped over Elnor for the second time, I hopped a ley line to Golden Gate Park, but it was of course full of human tourists. Their happy, relaxed energy rubbed me entirely the wrong way.

So I went back home. And took out my still-charged cell phone, and called Raymond.

"Callie?" He sounded very surprised. "Didn't expect to hear from you again."

"Yeah." I sighed. "Are you free for coffee?"

"Um. Sure. Okay."

A few minutes later, we met in a small bar near his apartment. I got a decaf Americano; he ordered a beer.

We found a table in the back, in a darkish corner. He took a long swig of his beer, set it down, and said, "So this is the breakup, huh."

"Raymond, there's just so much—"

He gave me a sad smile. "It's okay. I get it. I won't make trouble for you, hon." He glanced around the bar. "We didn't have to meet in a public place."

"It's not like that!" I protested, too quickly. Because I had sort of wanted neutral ground. Because the last time we'd been alone together... "I...just...things in my life are only getting more crazy, not less. I have no time, and no focus. I think...I need us to take a break."

"A break." He took another sip of his beer. "You mean, more than we've already been?"

I gave him a helpless look. "I'm sorry. I guess I just want to, I don't know, have it said, rather than just ghosting away like I did. I'm sorry I kept not calling back."

He thought about this a minute. "So what does a break mean, exactly?"

"It means…" Damn it, this had seemed more clear in my head, when he wasn't sitting in front of me, looking sad, and resigned, and gorgeous, and sweet. When I was just thinking about clearing the decks, getting ready for the challenges ahead. "It means I still love you, but this isn't working out right now, because of all sorts of stuff—stuff in *my* life—and, well, until that stuff is worked out, it's going to keep not working out." *Just how inarticulate can I be?* I thought with chagrin. "I don't want to say goodbye forever. But I can't give you what you need right now. I can't give you even a little bit of what you need."

"Yeah." He pushed his pint glass around on the table a little. "Yeah, okay."

I sipped my coffee. It was too bitter, but I didn't want to get up for more sugar. My taste buds were all off now. Couldn't imagine why.

Or was it just the air between us?

"So…can I call you in a month or two to check in?" I asked.

He drained his beer and set the glass down. "Callie, you can always call me." He cleared his throat. "I gotta jet." He got up, leaned over and pecked my cheek, and left.

I sat a long while over my bitter coffee. When I finally got up to leave, I found that he'd already paid for my drink.

I went to the clinic, carrying Elnor in one arm and a satchel in the other.

Gregorio met us in the empty front room, the part that still looked like an abandoned warehouse. I handed him the satchel; he took it without a word and, standing there in the dimly lit space, peered inside, first normally and then magically. Elnor sneezed several times, shaking off the last remnants of ley energy.

After a long minute, Gregorio nodded his head and looked up at me. "I see." He paused another moment. "Everything is in place."

We followed him down the long corridors, past my mother's room and those of all the other patients, toward the clinic's little lab in the back of the building. Gregorio stopped at his small office outside the lab door. "Go on in; I shall prepare these and follow you in a moment."

"Sure." I opened the strong metal door and eased it shut behind Elnor and me. Strange that there was no door spell, but I guessed there was no need for one; humans wouldn't be in the building in the first place.

Sebastian and Flavius were both in the lab, sitting across from one another at a small desk, poring over a printout. "Oh, hi, Callie," Sebastian said.

"Hey," I said, going to give him a peck on the cheek. Trying to stay casual.

"Hey, Callie," Flavius said, and I nodded at him as well. "What's up?"

"I'm here to see my mother," I said, "but also to let you guys know what I've found out so far."

"Oh?" Sebastian said. Both warlocks looked interested.

"Gregorio's looking at it now; he should be in any minute."

"But what can you tell us?" Flavius asked.

"It's actually kind of interesting," I hedged. Gregorio hadn't warned me I would need to stall them. "But...parts were unclear, so I asked him to go over it all. What's that you've got there?" I asked, pointing at their printout.

Sebastian gave a frustrated snort. "Nothing. I thought I'd found a correlation between the illness and a bad batch of botanical elixir from the east bay, but it's coming up blank."

"Ah."

Gregorio Andromedus finally walked in and set my satchel on the lab bench. "Calendula has some initial results she would like you two gentlemen to take a look at," he said.

Both warlocks jumped up and went to examine the unmarked vials that Gregorio unpacked. I stood behind, still trying to act casual. Elnor sniffed around the corners of the room. I wondered how often familiars came to this warlock-dominated space.

"I would like you each to look at half the vials, blind," Gregorio went on, "and then switch and each examine the other half. Calendula and I will leave the premises while you do so. Send me an ætheric message when you have reached a conclusion."

"Yes, Dr. Andromedus," Flavius said, as Sebastian nodded. I could almost see my friend forcing himself to resist sending me a private inquiry. Even if he wanted to be a healer, he was enough of a scientist to know they needed to examine the results without any external influence.

"Take all the time you need, gentlemen. Please be thorough."

"Of course, Dr. Andromedus," Sebastian said.

Gregorio turned to me. "Shall we?"

"I'm going to stop in and see my mom," I said. We left the lab together. Gregorio walked with me down the hallway, leaving Elnor and me at Mom's room with a promise to stay close at hand.

I tapped softly and opened the door a crack.

Mom was lying in the bed in the dimly lit, sleep-infused room. I couldn't tell whether she was awake or not. I took a deep breath of the unspelled air of the hallway and stepped inside, closing the door behind me. I hoped I wouldn't be in here long enough to be affected by the spells.

"Hey, Mom," I whispered, coming to sit in the comfy chair on the far side of the bed. Elnor jumped up and immediately curled at her feet.

"Hmm...Callie?" Mom murmured, blinking her soft brown eyes at me. Her hair lay quiet on the pillow. "Hi."

"How are you feeling?"

She shifted in bed, tugging the sage-green comforter up under her chin. "Marvelous, but so sleepy. They say they're going to let me go home soon."

"That's great!" As she'd turned and pulled the blanket, she'd left a little bit of her arm exposed, above the elbow. I reached down and patted her there, surreptitiously taking the measure of her essence. Indeed, it did seem stronger. The ends of her hair twitched a little. "I'm looking forward to another tarot lesson," I said.

She gave a gentle laugh. "Now I know I must have really frightened you."

"I'm just glad you're feeling better, is all."

I sat chatting with her for about twenty minutes, trying to stay awake. Elnor had given up at once; I could hear her soft snoring. How did the healers manage it? Maybe they had something they took to fend off the sleep spell. Or maybe they just built up immunity over time.

Or maybe being pregnant was making me more vulnerable.

I was relieved when the knock on the door sent a shot of adrenaline through me. "Come in," I called out, softly.

Flavius stepped into the room, holding a syringe.

"Callie, I'm glad you're still here," he said. His voice was calm, smooth. "Your results are astonishing—I've already called Dr. Andromedus back in, and he's whipped up a quick antidote. We'll put together something more subtle later, but he asked us to give this to all the patients at once—starting with Belladonna Isis."

"Gosh, that was fast," I said, as Mom looked up at him, still seeming muzzy and a little confused. As well she should be: I had told her nothing.

"So, Belladonna, if you'd let me see your right arm..."

The door opened again. My father stood there, looking stern and forbidding. "Dr. Winterheart," he said. "What exactly are you doing?"

"Oh, Dr. Grandion," Flavius said, taking a step away from Mom. "Dr. Andromedus has asked me to give this antidote to Belladonna Isis."

"That is only partially correct," Gregorio said, appearing behind Father. "Lucas, Calendula: get that syringe."

My father darted into the room, lightning-quick, and grabbed the stunned Flavius. I snatched the drug out of the young researcher's hand and took it to Gregorio, who flashed a spell of holding on Flavius, freezing him in position before taking the syringe. "I did ask you to administer an antidote to Belladonna Isis and the other sick witches," Gregorio said. "Perhaps you can explain to me, Dr. Winterheart, why you have brought *this* instead."

Flavius stared back at Gregorio, unable to move or speak. Could not even blink his eyes.

Gregorio waved a hand, releasing Flavius's head from the spell. "I—what do you mean?" the young warlock blurted in desperation. "That's what you gave me, Dr. Andromedus! I swear!"

"You have switched what I gave you with more of your foul poison. But you were careless—or arrogant."

"No! I came here straight from the lab! I didn't switch anything!"

"Then why do I have the *full* complement of the antidote here?" Gregorio reached into the large pockets of his lab coat, revealing a dozen loaded syringes. "You insult everyone's intelligence; you did not even try to hide the discarded syringes."

Sebastian stumbled into the room. His face was pale, and he held two more syringes in his hand. "Callie...Dr. Andromedus...what's going on?"

"My apologies for the subterfuge, Dr. Fallon," Gregorio said, his voice now more gentle, "but it was necessary in order to coax Dr. Winterheart into showing his hand."

"Showing...what?"

"Come, I will show you. You may put those down, they are nothing." He gestured at Sebastian's syringes; my friend set them on the counter in Mom's room. She looked up at all of us in growing confusion. At her feet, Elnor slept on, oblivious to it all.

Gregorio handed Flavius's syringe to Sebastian. "Have a look at that and tell me what you see."

Sebastian, his hands trembling, took it and opened his magical vision. His face grew even paler as he examined it, turning the glass this way and that. The violet-colored liquid inside shifted and shimmered. "I...don't believe it," he said at last.

"I did not want to either," Gregorio said grimly. "But I must face the truth—as must we all."

"I don't know what you're talking about!" Flavius sputtered. "This is crazy!"

"It is madness indeed, to think that you could deceive me, deceive us all. But your most desperate madness was your attempt to augment your own power by using the stolen essence of innocent members of our community." Gregorio waved his right arm with a dramatic flourish, and I felt the tug as we were all transported through the æther under his power—something I always hated. Blinking, I stumbled, regained my footing, and glanced around.

We hadn't left the building, but we were now all gathered in a large room. A conference room, perhaps, but one with space for dozens of people. There was a small wooden chair in the exact center of the room; Flavius was now confined there, tied by visible ropes of thick magic, shimmering golden about his ankles, wrists, and waist. A slender line encircled his neck.

Gregorio, Sebastian and I stood before Flavius in his chair. Beside me was my mother, still in her hospital bed. Father stood on the other side of the bed, his hand holding hers. Elnor blinked awake, looked for me, and hopped down to sit at my feet.

All around us were more people.

I swallowed a gasp as I understood. Gregorio had told me of his plans...but not that he had meant to implement them so immediately.

To our left, seated behind a long table, were four more Elders, and two empty chairs, for Father and Gregorio. To our right sat six coven mothers, including Leonora and Sapphire. I recognized Beatrice, who led a coven in San Jose focused on research and training in the healing arts, but I did not know the other three. Their cats were mostly at their feet, though Grieka sat on the table before Leonora.

I turned around; behind us there was a small audience. Jeremy was there, as were Niad, Peony, and Maela from my coven, along with a handful of other witches and a warlock.

Gregorio cleared his throat. "With six Elders and six coven mothers, this tribunal is at quorum. I call the proceedings to order."

In his chair, Flavius had been stunned silent for a moment. Now he erupted in protest. "Tribunal? What? Why?"

Gregorio wheeled on him. "You will speak when spoken to, Dr. Winterheart. Do not make me silence you."

Flavius shut his mouth.

Beside me, Sebastian took my hand; I gripped his, hard. Maybe it helped us both tremble a little less. Elnor curled against my ankles, purring nervously.

"Flavius Winterheart, in the presence of these witnesses," Gregorio indicated Sebastian and me, "and before the judgment of your betters," he indicated the Elders and coven mothers, "I charge you with a wicked conspiracy to steal essence from unsuspecting members of our community in order to boost your own power and position. I further charge you with disguising these intentions and misrepresenting yourself as an honest student of mine, in order to gain access to my knowledge and resources, and to spread your harm more widely. I finally charge you with so overstepping your own capabilities, as well as common witchkind decency, that you drained the unaffiliated witch Logandina Fleur beyond her body's capacity to contain her spirit. A spirit which is now missing entirely, lost somewhere between our plane and that of the Beyond. How do you answer these charges, Flavius Winterheart?"

I hadn't thought it was possible for Flavius to grow more pale, but he had done so, through Gregorio's recitation. Now he gulped, swallowed, and choked out, "I...I didn't do any of that, Dr. Andromedus. I've been trying to *help* the sick witches, not harm them. I don't have any extra essence anywhere in me! Can't you all see?"

"Of course you would not store any excess inside your person," Gregorio said, with a barely-voiced sneer. "You must tell us where the stolen essence is, so that we may restore it directly—whatever you have not already used up. The community has been most generous in supplying donations, which has been a drain on us all."

"I don't have it—I didn't do it! This is all crazy!"

Gregorio gave a sigh and slowly turned his head to the left and the right, taking in all the members of the tribunal before returning his gaze to Flavius. "My colleagues, the prisoner appears to deny all charges. What say you?"

"I move we look inside," Beatrice said. "I suggest beginning with a tanglefoot scry, and proceeding to a Foulian search if the scry does not suffice."

"I concur," Leonora said. One by one, the other coven mothers, then the Elders, gave their assent.

Gregorio turned back to Flavius, who trembled visibly in his chair. "I advise you to not resist these methods of questioning. We *will* find our answer. You have the choice of whether it shall go hard for you, or harder. You may still speak now and prevent this."

"I am telling the truth! I have nothing to hide!"

Gregorio shook his head slowly. He looked much closer to his eight hundred years than I had ever seen him. "Do not think this does not sadden me."

"Please!" Flavius wailed, but Gregorio reached out his right arm and pointed at the warlock.

I shivered, turning my eyes away, as though I could escape the feel of the ugly, invasive magic being wielded right beside me. Gregorio's spell, reinforced by the rest of the tribunal, entered Flavius's body and scoured through his energetic channels. I could almost feel the pain it caused him; I could not block my ears to his screams. Sebastian's grip on my hand grew tighter. I wanted to bury myself in his arms, but I didn't dare move, for fear of disrupting the wild dark energy flowing through the room. Elnor howled. I did not hear the other familiars, who were likely assisting in the spell. Poor cats.

It couldn't have lasted more than a minute, but it felt like hours. Gregorio at last dropped his arm, and the atmosphere in the room slowly returned to normal. I was not the only one gasping for breath.

Before us, Flavius wept and drooled in his chair. If he were human, he would probably have wet himself.

Gregorio turned formally once more to look at all the tribunal members. "His defenses are strong. He did not use the stolen essence lightly. I shall move to the Foulian search."

"No!" Flavius gasped. "Can't you see? *I'm not hiding anything!*"

Gregorio looked very, very sad as he raised his right arm once more.

This time I did close my eyes and fold myself into Sebastian's embrace. My friend held me tightly. We shivered together. I tried not to know it—any of it.

At last, it was done. I pulled out of Sebastian's arms and looked up, expecting to see an entirely broken warlock trapped in the chair before us.

Flavius did look shattered—a hollow relic of himself—but he opened his mouth to speak. In a cracked, hoarse voice, he said, "It is true. I thought I hid it well enough, but I was wrong."

A small intake of breath—not a gasp, but something below that—went through the audience behind us.

"It was not my idea," he went on, his tone wooden. His fight broken. "They came to me... They said I could have more power, and I would not need to harm anyone. That it would actually help, in the battle. I did overreach, though, at first, when I was learning. It felt good. And I regret that, I hate myself for that. I worked hard to soften the impact of my spell... It was not supposed to be so strong." He blinked, looking around at the tribunal members, at us, at the gathered audience. His eyes were wide, desperate. "Please...believe me. I did not mean to do harm. But I did. I tried to fix it, but...then I could not stop myself. It felt so good... I could not stop taking it."

"Who came to you?" Gregorio asked.

"Two men, warlocks, from the Old Country," Flavius went on dully. "They told me they were helping to fight the Iron Rose... I think now that they must have been lying."

Gregorio nodded his head curtly. "I am quite certain of it. Thank you, Flavius Winterheart. Your confession is sufficient; we shall not need the testimony of the witnesses."

Beside me, Sebastian sighed in dark relief. I took his hand again.

"Now we shall pass sentence," Gregorio went on. "What say you, tribunal members?"

"I say permanent ensorcelment," said Henrik, one of the Elders.

"I say banishment from this plane, and a petition to our ancestors for further punishment in the Beyond," said one of the coven mothers I did not know. Her face was grim and furious.

"I agree with Elder Henrik," my father said. "The crime was dire, but the criminal should remain on this plane, to witness the results of his actions. And to help us find and prosecute his confederates."

"The trouble with a permanent ensorcelment is that the word 'permanent' means no such thing," Gregorio pointed out. "We like to think we can control all variables, but I believe the folly of such notions should be clear by now. I had no idea that a warlock, working so closely with me on my own research, had deceived me so thoroughly."

"He would figure out a way to unsorcel his magic," the angry coven mother said. I wondered if one of her witches was lying ill in the clinic. "Look how crafty he is. I say send him Beyond, let them deal with him."

"I do not favor sloughing off our problems on our ancestors," my father put in. "The man committed his crimes here: he should atone for them here."

"Father, if I may?" Jeremy put in, from the audience.

All eyes turned to him. Gregorio raised an eyebrow. "Yes, my son?"

"In the Old Country, troubled times have, sadly, led to greater experience with grievous crimes. A way has been devised of effectively making an ensorcelment actually permanent."

"What does that mean?" Gregorio looked back at him, frowning.

"Well," Jeremy said, "it isn't an ensorcelment, exactly. It is a way of burning out magical power, leaving only...well, human bodily functions."

This time the room really did gasp. "Turn him into a human?" Sebastian blurted.

"Essentially, yes."

I shook my head. Awful...but then again, so was working with terrorists to steal essence. Stealing my best friend from me—and from herself, as Logan was not even enjoying the next phase of life in the Beyond. She'd been knocked out of existence altogether, for all that anyone could tell. I steeled my resolve and nodded. As though it were up to me.

Gregorio, however, noticed. He gave me a gentle glance before turning back to Jeremy. "You can perform this action?"

Jeremy looked very grim. "I can, Father. I have done so...twice."

My stomach hurt at the thought. I'd slept with that man, made a baby with him. And he'd... I couldn't think about it. I silently vowed *never* to travel to the Old Country. I did not want to know such ugliness any more closely.

Gregorio turned back to the tribunal. "What say you, colleagues?"

"If true, it sounds a meet and just sentence," my father said. One by one, the other members concurred.

"Then it shall be done." Gregorio looked at the prisoner. "Flavius Winterheart, after due consideration of your crimes, and the confession from your own lips, the Greater San Francisco Bay Area Elders and coven mothers hereby sentence you to a permanent removal of your magic."

"It's called cautery," Jeremy put in, softly.

Gregorio nodded. "Jeremiah Andromedus will perform this cautery at his earliest convenience."

In his chair, Flavius Winterheart wept.

— CHAPTER EIGHTEEN —

Gregorio asked to come visit me early in the morning a few days later. I received him in my front parlor. As we sat over cups of tea, he said, "I wanted to fill you in on what we have found out, and speak to you about something."

"All right," I said. "I'm still trying to figure out how he managed to drain the essence in the first place—how he got the agent to witches when he wasn't even near them."

"It functions something like a virus, as we suspected," Gregorio said. "Except that it can stay in the environment longer than actual viruses. I believe he was working on pinpointing his attacks, but he lost control of it once it left his hands, particularly in the earliest days." The ancient warlock paused. "I believe he used you as a carrier, to bring the affliction to Logandina Fleur."

I frowned, feeling sick and sad all over again. I had wondered. "You don't think he was targeting me? I have a lot more power than Logan…did."

"No; he says he was not, and he can no longer lie, after the Foulian. He was going for marginal witches at first, unaffiliated ones."

"But—my mother isn't at all marginal. Am I a carrier—still?"

"If you are, the potency of what you carry is nearly exhausted. But we will treat you, now that we know what we are looking for."

"Okay."

"I do not believe Belladonna contracted it from you, however. It had been loose in the community for some time by then. She very likely picked it up from someone in her tarot circle."

"Ah."

Gregorio took another sip of his tea. "A small portion of the missing essence has been found at Dr. Winterheart's home, though not nearly the amount stolen. I fear his Iron Rose confederates have absconded with the rest. We will continue our efforts in hunting them down, but meanwhile, the community here will have to continue its donation efforts for a while longer yet. Though I am also working on developing an essence-boosting supplement."

"I can—" I started, but Gregorio put up his hand.

"You are pregnant, Calendula. No donation from you."

"I was going to say I can help in that research," I said with a smile. "I'd like to participate in any way I can."

"Ah. Well, let me get started, and then I will see where I can bring you in."

"Thank you."

There was another pause as Gregorio finished his tea and set the cup down in its saucer. "I have learned more about cautery from Jeremiah. It must be performed by two practitioners, working in concert. Layering and reinforcing their magic."

"Oh," I said. This had a sickeningly familiar ring to it.

"Logandina Fleur had no living family, nor coven," Gregorio continued. "As her closest friend, you are the most aggrieved party. Additionally, you have already worked complex magic in collaboration with Jeremiah."

I glanced down at my belly and blushed.

The ancient warlock cleared his throat. "I meant your house wards, but, yes, that as well. In any event, the tribunal has decided that you and my son shall perform the cautery together."

I took a slow breath, trying to force down my thoughts: *No, don't make me do this, no!* "I…don't know how."

Gregorio looked grim. "You are not expected to. He will guide you. With your biological training, you will pick it up easily enough."

"All right." I blindly reached down to find Elnor, to take comfort in her feline presence, but she was back in the kitchen, keeping herself away from the warlock.

"My apologies for what lies ahead," Gregorio said. "I am told it is not pleasant."

"I would expect not."

His gaze softened. "Calendula Isadora, on behalf of witchkind and for myself personally, I would like to offer my sincere condolences on the loss of your friend Logandina Fleur, and to promise you that true punishment and atonement will be made, on this day."

It had the sound of ritual to it, though it was not one I had heard before.

Then again, I had never lost anyone before.

I felt a lump grow in my throat. "I thank you, Gregorio Andromedus."

He nodded and rose to his feet. "The cautery will take place at sundown today. If you like, I will return here and escort you there."

"I would like that. Thank you." I supposed it was the least he could do.

"Of course. Thank you for the tea."

It was a quiet day. I knew the whole community felt the grave weight of the deed we had sanctioned, though I envied them. They got to just let it happen, somewhere else.

I had to help do it.

Sending Flavius to the Beyond would have been larger, by one way of looking at it; but my father had been right. The Beyond was a wondrous place—though mysterious and wild, and of course only vaguely understood by those of us here. It was the next level in our progression to our ultimate joining with the Great Mother, and we all looked forward to moving there, even if a bit nervously, when our time on this plane was done. Sending him there could turn out to be a reward.

Turning him effectively into a human, forcing him to stay here among us all, could only be a punishment.

And what would happen when he eventually died? Or maybe not so eventually? Would the cautery remove his magic-given long life?

Was he destined to follow the humans to their afterlife—would he now be barred from the Beyond? Oh, surely not.

Probably.

I spent the day trying to distract myself by working with Petrana in the lab, reinforcing the energetic pathways we had built and strengthened between us. Preparing for the research work Gregorio would have for me later, I hoped. Preparing my golem to be a more useful adjunct for me.

In the late afternoon, Gregorio sent word that he was on his way over.

I am ready, I sent back.

I stood before the full-length mirror in my bedroom. What does one wear to execute a strange and terrible punishment? I had gone for something between "funeral" and "jury duty": narrow black pants, a long-sleeved maroon turtleneck, and a black jacket. My hair was tightly braided in a single tail down my back, and my boots were low-heeled and practical.

Gregorio gave a nod of approval when I let him in. He was dressed as if for an important business meeting, in a charcoal suit with a plum-colored tie. "Shall we?"

"Yes." I swallowed a lump in my throat and followed my mentor to an unfamiliar ley line leading southeast.

We emerged in a large grassy field somewhere near Pleasanton—many miles from San Francisco, and across the bay. This was clearly public land, and deserted of humans at this time of the year, unless they had been kept away deliberately. The sun lowered toward the horizon, peeking through oak trees at the edge of the clearing. The grass was still yellow from last summer; California was in drought, as usual.

Jeremy stood a few yards from us in the center of the field, looking down at a jumble of equipment and supplies at his feet. I took a step forward, curious despite my nerves, but Gregorio put a cautioning hand on my arm. Only then did I realize what I was seeing: Flavius Winterheart, strapped into an elaborate contraption. It was like a twisted version of the chair he'd been held in for the tribunal. Here, his arms and legs were all bound in painful-looking, awkward angles, and the line of power around his neck looked as though it were made of barbed wire.

Though he was clearly conscious, he lay limp, unstruggling.

Gregorio took his hand off my arm. "Jeremiah Andromedus and Calendula Isadora, the tribunal of Elders and coven mothers thanks you for the service you are about to perform. I wish you good speed and fortitude. Please let me know when it is completed."

"Wait—you're not staying?" I asked, turning to him.

He shook his head. "We've spoken before about the deleterious effects of stray magic, Calendula," he said softly. "You can do this. I have the utmost faith in both of you."

"Thank you, Father," Jeremy said. I was both relieved and alarmed to hear fear in his voice as well.

Gregorio nodded at both of us before vanishing onto the ley line.

I cleared my throat and looked at Jeremy, keeping my eyes away from the silent Flavius. Somehow, it was worse that he wasn't screaming or pleading for mercy. Just blinking up at us. Waiting to be cauterized. Broken.

Oh Blessed Mother I cannot do this.

"So," said Jeremy, reaching out to me. "Shall we?"

I took his hand and stepped forward. "What...do I do?"

Jeremy smiled at me, tension written all over his lovely face. "First we must gather ourselves, as with any large working. We have about twenty minutes until sundown."

"All right." I made myself look down, to face what we were doing. Only then did I see that Jeremy had already traced a Circle on the ground around us, next to where Flavius lay.

"I thought we'd draw the pentagram together," Jeremy said, handing me a small stick.

"No dagger or athame?" I asked.

He gave an embarrassed smile. "We...well, when this was worked out the first time, all that was at hand were natural ingredients. So that became the spell."

"Ah."

Jeremy took a second stick, and together we slowly walked the lines of the star, pushing our sticks into the dusty ground, tugging tall dry grass out of our way in places. His stick led on the first leg, mine the second, his the third, mine the fourth. At the fifth, without speaking, we positioned our sticks together and drew the line as one, pausing a brief moment before closing the pentagram.

As we touched the last point to the edge of the Circle, I felt the rush of magic as the working came together. It was strong, solid, true, and it calmed and strengthened me, as ever.

When I opened my eyes, I saw Jeremy watching me. "It is good," he said.

"Yes." We stood a moment in the demarcated space, letting it hold us. "Um..." I flicked my eyes to Flavius, who still looked as blank as my golem. "Were we supposed to bring him in?"

"No—the Circle would only protect him. He's bound to its outer edge, while we work from inside."

Now I saw the rest of it: the bizarre contraption wasn't just a torture device. Flavius was being held in such a way that each extremity, plus his head, touched our Circle. Maybe that was what was holding him frozen? I sort of didn't want to know.

The sun kissed the hills on the horizon, and I felt the liminality of twilight drawing nearer. Jeremy and I looked at one another. "I'm following your lead here," I said, though he knew that. Nervous chatter, I supposed.

"I know." He gave me his golden smile. "Join hands, so we can meld our energies."

I took his hands. We stood that way a long moment, as the sun sank further. The air grew just a little chillier. Flavius kept lying there, silent.

Jeremy began a chant, so low I almost did not hear it at first, just felt it through his hands. Once I caught its pattern, I followed along, harmonizing and weaving my power through his. It was indeed a dark mockery of our ward-building work—but I could not think that way, I had to pour everything I had into this. It did not matter that I hated it, that it frightened and sickened me to use magic to harm someone irreparably. Flavius Winterheart had committed a terrible crime, against my dearest friend; our community had together decided upon his punishment. Who was I to be so cowardly as to shunt this work off on someone else?

I redoubled my chant, feeding positive intention into it, seeking Jeremy's power. He met me halfway and more, sending his power wrapping around mine in return. In this way, back and forth, we built a huge mass of potency, swirling around us, enveloping and holding us.

When I felt it starting to peak, I began to ease off, in expectation of the next phase. But Jeremy shook his head without releasing my hands and fed yet more power in. I followed. It built, and built further. I started to tremble as my body struggled to contain even my share of it. Jeremy's hands gripped mine, and I clung hard to his. The build was everything. All we were was power.

"Amanū!" he shouted suddenly, dropping my hands as he raised his arms. I gasped for breath, then echoed his cry, my voice hoarse and croaking.

The power solidified around us, enveloping us in a hard shell, far beyond any warm magical embrace I'd ever felt before. I almost could not see out of our Circle...except for the twisted, bound figure of Flavius.

Blank no more, he stared in at us, eyes wide with terror. Panting, he whispered, "No...please...no..." He was so tightly confined that he could not move more than his lips.

"Follow carefully," Jeremy said to me, ignoring our victim. "It feels firm, but this is when it's the most fragile."

I nodded, only partially understanding.

Jeremy knelt at one of the points of our pentagram, close to Flavius's head, and put his hand up to the edge of the Circle. A midnight-blue light began to shine there. Flavius screamed, the sound of his voice oddly blunted by our shell of magic. Even muffled, it felt as though it was rending my soul in two.

"Now!" Jeremy's voice was harsh with effort.

I scrambled forward and went to my knees beside him, reaching my own hand to the Circle's edge. The blue light spread, encompassing both our hands, as I felt the force behind it. It was the pointed edge of the giant mass of power we'd built, and together, we were honing it sharper, sharper, sharper.

It was a dagger, then a scalpel, then a needle...and then Jeremy thrust it forward, into Flavius's head, at the point of his third eye.

His scream reverberated through our Circle. I gasped but held tight, my hand with Jeremy's, as we thrust that unimaginable point of power into our victim.

At once, I felt Flavius's magic flowing up through the point—whether in challenge or simply reaction, I could not say. It was as though we'd burst a sac of fluid that had been ready to overflow, and it was rushing back at us. "Hold fast!" Jeremy said, as I felt choked by the flood of it. The power was ugly—it was stolen, and crazily mixed—our assaultive power was ugly too—I could hardly tell what any piece of it was—it was going to kill me—

I drew in a deep, gulping breath and managed to find my grounding, just a bit. But it was enough. Jeremy and I were here; Flavius was there, still screaming; and the leading edge of our spell was inside him.

"There you go," Jeremy breathed out in a trembling sigh. "Just like that."

I just panted for a minute, holding it together. "Now what?" I asked, when I'd caught my breath.

"Now we begin our hunt."

Somewhere in the last minute or so, Flavius had stopped screaming. I noticed this with a corner of my attention. Jeremy and I both pushed forward, tentatively at first, then more aggressively, searching within Flavius. Energetic pathways...veins and meridians... "Here," Jeremy breathed.

It was a node, a tiny focal point near the top of Flavius's cerebellum, just below the pineal gland. "Okay...?" I said.

"Burn it out."

I started to ask how, but the answer became sickeningly clear a moment later as Jeremy sent heat through our needle, generated from his own power. I followed suit. Flavius moaned softly; he must be unconscious. I feverishly hoped so. As we burned it, the node shriveled, and there was a faint scent of sulfur in the air. Or in my veins or bones or energetic pathways, I didn't know—I could no longer separate my physical and magical senses of my body. Everything was the needle, and what we were doing with it.

"Good," Jeremy grunted. "Onward."

We moved downward, into Flavius's neck, pausing at the thoracic duct where we found a smaller node. We burned it out. We moved downward. We found and burned one next to a pulmonary lymph node, and then several in the tracheobronchial region. We moved downward. We burned more. Downward. More.

I lost myself in the work, the mundane, horrific repetition of it. Hunt. Burn. Hunt. Burn.

And then...there were no more. Stunned and exhausted, I sat back on my haunches and looked over at Jeremy. My hands—somehow both of them now—felt frozen to the energetic needle; I couldn't put it down if I'd tried.

"We need to doublecheck," he said. I just nodded, and we hunted through Flavius Winterheart's system once more, this time from the bottom up.

But we'd gotten them all. Every node that contained any bit of magical capacity.

"Let it go," Jeremy said. His voice sounded dead, empty. He dropped his hold.

It fell away from me as well, and the huge, hard shell of magic we'd built, and honed, and wielded, just...dissipated. Our Circle and pentagram were some lines scratched into the dirt. Mundane human Flavius Winterheart lay still before us, barely breathing.

"Oh, Blessed Mother," I sighed, and let myself fall backward on the dry grass, staring up. The sky was now completely black; it was close to midnight.

Jeremy sat down beside me, looking away. I couldn't make out his face; there was no moonlight. Flavius hadn't moved.

After a few minutes of silence, I asked, "He's still alive, isn't he?"

"He is," Jeremy said, his voice dull, but with a little more life than before. "He will sleep through the night, then wake and begin his life as a human."

"Will he remember...it all?"

Jeremy shrugged. "Enough."

Silence reigned again as I tried to muster the energy to find my way home on a ley line. I should be starving, after such an expenditure of resources, but I just felt ill.

"I will see you home if you like," Jeremy offered.

I shivered. "No, thank you. I'll find my own way."

I spent the following day sleeping, mostly. I forced myself to eat at least something, because I knew I needed it, though I didn't want it.

Near midnight, Jeremy sent me a quiet inquiry. *Are you awake?*

Yes. I was in my sitting room on the second floor, with a book and a cat on my lap, just trying to find my way back to myself.

May I come over?

Yes.

Five minutes later I received him in the front parlor downstairs. He accepted my offer of frog brandy and took a seat on the side chair. "How are you doing?" I asked, taking a sip of my own elderflower wine. It tasted off, strange, even though this was my preferred brew. I put my glass on the coffee table and looked up at the green-eyed warlock.

"As well as can be expected." He took a generous swig of his brandy. "You?"

"I'm all right. Recovering."

He nodded. "It takes a few days."

"Right."

After a pause, he said, "Well, I won't keep you long, but I wanted to let you know in person that I will be moving up my planned trip to the Old Country, following Dr. Winterheart's co-conspirators before their trail can grow even colder."

"When are you leaving?"

"Tonight. Directly from here, in fact."

"Oh." I reached for my wine again, for something to do, but stayed my hand.

"I also still need to do some research for my father, and I would like to visit some friends. If there is time."

"Okay."

After another uncomfortable silence, he added, "And I would still like to look into the matter of Logandina's parents. For my own peace of mind, if nothing else."

"I would like to know what happened to them too."

"Of course."

We sat in the awkwardness for another minute. "Well, thank you for letting me know," I finally said.

Now he raised his lovely eyes to mine. I could see the pain in them. Part of me yearned to comfort him, and to seek his comfort for myself, but to the rest of me...he seemed such a stranger. A warlock who could touch me so gently, and who gripped my hand as we snuffed the magic out of another living soul. I thought of his bringing me tea and croissants in bed, and of his blithe assumption that I would leap at the chance to sign a contract with him. His gentle evasions about how he spent his days; even the research that he was doing for Gregorio. I realized I did not know him at all.

He must have seen the conflict in my eyes. He finished his brandy and stood up. "I shall be off, then."

I got to my feet as well. "Jeremy, I am sorry about..." I lifted my arms and dropped them, helpless. "It all."

"I am sorry as well." Now he forced a brave smile. "I will be back, in a month or two." His gaze fell to my belly. Still flat, but we both knew what he was looking at. "Please feel free to send a message at any time, but know that the connections are spotty at best. I shall respond as I can."

"Right." It wasn't just the distance, though that was considerable; the Old Country was protected by so many shields and spells, most communication in or out was by handwritten letter.

"Right," he echoed me. "Well, do take care of yourself."

I opened my arms and pulled him into a hug. He embraced me back, stiffly, pulling away after a moment. Then he vanished.

"Goodbye," I whispered.

I took the glasses to the kitchen, poured my wine down the drain, and went to bed.

— CHAPTER NINETEEN —

The community grieved even as the sick witches healed. Flavius Winterheart moved out of his house, not telling anyone where he'd gone. It didn't matter; he was no longer any threat to us. It still made me shiver, thinking about how thoroughly he had deceived even our greatest, most powerful practitioners. Thinking about what Jeremy and I had done to him.

I did not hear from Jeremy, in the Old Country. I had not thought I had expected to, but then when weeks of silence went by, I found I had.

But I didn't call to him either.

On the night of the first full moon after Ostara—the spring equinox—I stood in formal evening wear on the sidewalk before the house of Gregorio Andromedus. My gown was black velvet, floor-length, sleeveless, and dramatically low-cut. I'd had to let out the bodice and the sides a bit, to accommodate my middle, just beginning to bulge with the baby. *This has to be one of the most cleverly disguised witchkind homes I've ever seen,* I thought. I had only been here a few times; he'd moved here several years ago, from a more ostentatious place in Nob Hill.

All I could see from the sidewalk was an iron gate with five doorbells. If one didn't know differently, one would think this was condos. Try as I might, peering through the trees, I couldn't see the building. And all magical inquiries were blocked by a set of wards so powerful, I could almost see them shimmering in the air.

The doorbells were neatly labeled with four ordinary human-sounding names, plus 'Ogdoad'—an ancient name referring to a pantheon of deities. I pushed that fifth button. Nothing happened for a few seconds as I felt myself being viewed by unseen eyes. Then the gate swung open, and the wards eased as Gregorio's voice surrounded me: "Calendula Isadora, welcome."

I passed through the gate and began climbing the stairs. They were long, and steep. I stopped about halfway up, breathless, leaning on the rail. *Lazy pregnant witches should find more time to exercise*, I thought. Through the trees, I could see the vague outlines of the house. Time to soldier on. I took a deep breath and climbed. By the time I finally got to the porch, I was thoroughly winded, wiping beads of sweat from my forehead. That stairway had to have been four or five times longer than it looked.

A massive front door stood open, revealing a huge hallway with rooms opening off to either side. Crammed bookshelves took up every bit of wall space I could see, in both hall and rooms, but it was still not enough. More books were stacked on the floors next to the shelves, and one of the side rooms appeared to contain just solid books, not even paths between them.

From the far end of the hall, I could hear the sounds of the party. I waited a moment, letting my breathing settle, wondering if I would find a roomful of folks sitting on piles of books, resting their cocktails on more books. Behind me, I could no longer see the street, or even the bottom of the staircase; the view receded into darkness as his wards closed back around the house. So peaceful, for the middle of a city. I drew one last steady breath and went on.

I followed the sounds of laughter and conversation to a large room filled with as many witches and warlocks as I had ever seen in one place—the entire witchkind population of San Francisco, it seemed, plus the East and South Bay contingents. I was relieved to see that there was normal furniture in here (with, of course, a few lovely antique bookcases scattered about). Bright, warm sunlight poured down through double rows of skylights. Which was really something, because it was after nine o'clock at night, and it hadn't even been a particularly sunny day in the first place. Gregorio did love his impressive illusions.

I stood in the doorway, scanning the crowd. I saw Nora and Manka and Sebastian actually chatting with each other, which warmed my heart. Maybe the healers were beginning to accept him at last. Leonora and several of my coven sisters had snagged a round table underneath a huge, ugly chandelier. I started in their direction, but then noticed Niad talking to the whole table, gesturing dramatically, ignoring any possible interruptions. I quickly veered off before they saw me.

Finally I spied Gregorio, far across the room in front of a pair of ornate French doors set with tiny panes of glittering glass, through which streamed more impossible sunlight. One of the doors was ajar, leading into what looked like a solarium. Even across the crowded room I could smell the lush, fragrant greenery within: lobelia, roses, gardenias, and several large mimosa trees.

Gregorio was deep in conversation with Henrik and two other Elders, all dressed in tuxedos. He noticed my entrance, though his attention didn't overtly leave the warlocks. I started making my way across the crowded room, keeping one eye on him so I wouldn't lose him in the thicket of bodies.

I was nearly there when Sirianna and Maela converged on me. "Callie!" Siri shouted, with a huge grin on her face. She stumbled into me; I caught her by the arms, which she turned into a smothering, sloppy hug. As her always-wild hair embraced and twined around mine, I stealthily sniffed the air. Uh-oh, Gregorio must be serving some pretty high-grade Witches' Mead. *I should warn her,* I thought, but as I extricated myself from her grasp, another look into her face told me it was probably too late.

So I just hugged her back. When she finally released me, I stood back to check out her floor-length shimmering silver gown. "Siri, you look great!"

"Thanks! I love parties! Why don't we do this every night?"

Maela stood next to me, also swaying slightly. She too had been into the Mead, though not nearly so heavily as Siri. She looked at Sirianna and gave me a crooked smile.

"I can see," I said to Maela.

"Miss?" said a small voice at my elbow. A pixie in a proper French maid's uniform hovered beside me. She wasn't real—Gregorio's servants were yet more illusions, complicated confections of light and magic—but what she was holding was: a single smoking glass of the brew on an ornate silver platter.

"Oh, no thank you, just water for me," I said sadly, nodding at my belly. Witches' Mead was *so* delicious…but if even elderflower wine wasn't going down well, I knew I ought to stay away from the hard stuff.

"On the contrary, Calendula, I have had it formulated to account for your pregnancy," Gregorio said, appearing at my side. "It is perfectly safe."

"Really?" I blinked at him. "How did you do that?"

Gregorio smiled and raised his own glass. "Now now, a good cook never shares his best recipes. Please, have a taste, see for yourself. And welcome to my home."

"All right. Thank you." I picked the glass up off the tray and took a tentative sip, swirling it on my tongue, taking its measure. It tasted great. I swallowed, feeling the powerful intoxicant/stimulant slip down my throat and into my bloodstream. Then I felt it move to avoid my womb, even as it strengthened my overall essence. "Wow. Seriously, how is this done?"

"Perhaps I will teach you some day," Gregorio said. "For now, it just seemed tragic that such an important contributor to our celebration tonight should have to abstain from the festivities."

I felt a moment of confusion as my witch-sense tried to figure out the spell, or recipe, or whatever he had done here. I couldn't find any edge to hold onto, though; it was very slippery. So I let go and smiled back at Gregorio. "Thank you for that; I do love Mead."

"My pleasure. It was enjoyable to do something so small after the recent...challenges."

"I imagine so." I turned to include my coven sisters in the conversation. Sirianna was busy gaping out at the sunny garden room; Maela, suddenly shy again, was just watching us talk.

"That's a neat trick too, by the way," I said to Gregorio, nodding at the sunlight all around us, trying to cover up Siri's drunken fascination.

He gave a small nod. "Complicated to set up, but once it is under way, it practically feeds itself."

Another handful of guests entered the room. "If you will excuse me," Gregorio added, putting his empty glass down on the tray of a passing server.

"Of course."

He left to greet them. "Is that *Marcus*?" Sirianna gushed, now staring into the center of the room at the little hipster warlock.

Maela's eyes lit up. "Marcus, really? Come on!" She grabbed Siri's hand and they disappeared into the crowd.

Oh, my poor sisters. They really needed to get out more often.

I was sipping my drink and looking around for Sebastian when a magical hush fell over the crowd. Gregorio stood in front of the bar, spelling conversations silent with a gentle touch and a warm smile.

Once he had everyone's attention, he began speaking in a normal tone of voice, carried on another spell to reach all our ears easily. "My dear friends, colleagues, and community. Thank you so very much for joining me this evening as we reaffirm our joy, our power, our very life, in the face of a pernicious challenge to our kind.

"Sadly, our celebration must be bittersweet: a traitor to our kind has been exiled permanently, his magic burnt to ashes; a threat we had believed distant has been revealed to have reached our lands; and, most tragically of all, a beloved member of our community has perished before we were even able to respond. Logandina Fleur was a true innocent, and she will be missed." He caught my eye briefly from across the room; I gave him a small, sad smile. "But we have now stopped the threat on our shores and are hunting it at its source. We are in the final stages of reversing any lingering ill effects it caused here. Our community is once more safe.

"And in the midst of our sorrow, new life blooms among us." A few people turned to glance at me, while others gazed back at him, confused. I felt my cheeks reddening, and took another sip of Mead to cover my awkwardness. This was surely *not* how he had wanted to handle this; it was very gracious of him to be, well, gracious about it. "I know you will all join me in welcoming the forthcoming daughter of Calendula Isadora and my son Jeremiah Andromedus."

A small murmur of surprise and happiness rippled across the crowd. People nodded, smiled, raised their glasses to me. I smiled back, wishing hard for a change of subject.

Gregorio obliged. "In addition to Calendula Isadora's heroic efforts on our behalf, many others assisted in the fight against Flavius Winterheart's attack on our community. The healers Nora and Manka put everything aside to help me build a clinic to care for the afflicted witches. My intern, Dr. Sebastian Fallon, has been by the patients' sides day and night, bringing them warm and capable care. My son, who regrettably cannot be here tonight, worked long hours on a veritable multitude of tasks for the clinic, and is indeed following up on the larger conspiracy in the Old Country as we speak. The coven mothers..."

My attention began to flag as he continued through a long litany of names and deeds. The Mead may have avoided my womb, but it looked to be taking up camp in my already-squeezed bladder. In force, and growing by the minute. I glanced around, looking for a bathroom. Ah—there was a door. I sidled over to it, whispering apologies to the witches and warlocks I brushed past on my way.

I reached the door at last and slipped through just as I felt a hard knock of Mead hit me. I stumbled, recovering clumsily. Okay, apparently it wasn't *all* in my bladder.

After I regained my equilibrium, I pulled the door shut behind me and looked around. I was in a small antechamber; closed doors led off in several directions. The walls and all the doors were painted a deep black. Dozens of black-painted shelves held candles and sacred objects, like a hundred tiny shrines—amulets, snippets of lace, dried fruit, and many symbols representing the tarot suit Wands. How peculiar. How un-warlock-ish.

Except for the ever-present stacks of books, of course.

The floorboards were rough pine planks; the ceiling was very high, and also painted the striking black of the walls. Was this the entry hall for whatever this house used to be, before all of Gregorio's additions and enhancements? The contrast with the party room, with all its heady illusion, was striking.

I stood there, looking at all the images of Wands, remembering my mother's lessons, and Logan's. This was the suit of fire, creativity, action, and movement.

Gregorio Andromedus, international man of action, I thought, making myself giggle.

Or maybe I was only giggling because I was staring at a picture of the Ace of Wands. A hand, gripping a thick stick, knobbed at the end.

Surely it wasn't the Witches' Mead that was making me this silly.

I shook my head, trying to clear it. Bathroom, bathroom, where was the blessed bathroom? I chose a door at random. It led into a small, untidy kitchen—and ah, yes! There was a tiny water closet just beyond it. I gathered up my skirts even as I was pulling the door shut behind me.

My business done, I stepped back into the kitchen. A very bright ceiling fixture illuminated every corner. Pots and pans crowded the stove; crucibles, not all of which had been cleaned out, littered the countertop. None of these containers held anything resembling food, and a strong scent of conjuration was in the air. Was this his home laboratory? It was such a different style than his Berkeley lab. Same degree of clutter, though.

I walked over to the sink and looked closely at one of the crucibles, fascinated. It had to be at least a thousand years old. Older than this house, this city, this country. Older even than Gregorio. I wondered if experiments would run differently with such ancient equipment. Did they bring their immense history with them, even in some tiny way? Setting down my glass of Mead, I picked up a tall clay container and looked it over. Probably the precursor to our modern beakers.

The spoons and stirrers were equally archaic: pewter, most of them, though some were solid gold. What a wealth of history here...

I took a sip of Mead as I kept looking through the room, opening drawers and poking into cabinets. After a minute, though, I started feeling like a trespasser. I was clearly not meant to be in this room—the water closet I'd found was obviously not a guest bathroom. *Well, there hadn't been anyone to ask,* I told myself. But it was time to get back to the party. Maybe the speechifying was done by now.

I grabbed my glass of Mead, which had become full and smoking again, though I was sure I had drunk more than half of it. *Okay, just this much more and that's all,* I told myself as I walked back through the black-painted entryway to the door I'd come through.

Blinking in the lush, realistic sunlight, I again had to steady myself. Everything seemed exactly as I had left it: the guests in just the same places, Gregorio still warmly congratulating everyone who had had anything to do with the clinic, the research, and for all I knew, the price of periwinkle.

I stood by the wall, trying to make sense of it. Yes, he was finishing the same sentence I had heard him start as I walked out. But time *could not* have stopped: that's physically impossible, even using magic. When people experience frozen time, they're really suffering magical manipulation of their memories and perceptions—not a lot different from what I had done to Raymond. Had I fallen afoul of someone's spell? I was out of the room for five minutes or more, subjectively.

I took another sip. It was soothing. The rush of the brew mingled with my own power. At least *some* time must have elapsed, because my bladder was happily empty. And here was my third glass of Witches' Mead, somehow replenished once more.

At last, Gregorio finished his speech. The crowd clapped politely. A few warlocks went up to have a word with him, while everyone else returned to the drinking, flirting, eating, and quiet negotiation that was the true business of any party.

Gregorio again caught my eye across the room. *A word, Calendula, if you please,* he sent to me, while still speaking to the warlocks.

Of course. He must have noticed where I'd gone.

He gestured toward the solarium doors. *We should be able to find a quiet table out there. I will join you in a moment.*

I nodded and made my way across the crowded room. Indeed, the solarium was much less populated; I easily found a small white table with matching chairs.

Gregorio showed up a minute later, smiling as he took a seat.

"I'm so sorry," I said. "I didn't mean to snoop, I was just looking for the bathroom. I would never—"

He waved my words away. "Goodness, Calendula, please do not apologize. It is not possible for anyone to enter parts of my house I do not wish entered." He smiled once more as he reached into a pocket of his suit and produced a simple gold ring. "Even someone who is, for all intents and purposes, a member of my family."

He held the ring out to me. It glittered in the dappled "sunlight". I took it; it felt good in my hand. It was thick and heavy, unadorned. I turned it over, looking for an inscription. There was a deep stamp inside, but too worn to make out. And I couldn't get a reading of the ring's age. Gold is quite inert, though it can also carry what is given to it.

"What…is this?" I asked, looking up at him.

"Please. Try it on."

I could feel that the ring wanted to be worn: it was a ring of power, to be sure. I slipped it onto the middle finger of my right hand, where it fit perfectly, seeming to snuggle into place, warm and comfortable, all rounded edges and solid, energetic gold.

A warmth started inside me, in the base of my belly below the baby, radiating up through her and into my chest, down my legs, out my arms to my fingertips, encircling the ring again, and bouncing gently back to the middle of my body. A smooth unbroken line of powerful, vibrant energy. "Wow. *That* feels good," I said.

"I am glad."

I took a sip of Mead. The warmth of the drink flowed down to meet the warmth from the ring. The two powers intertwined most agreeably, purring through my system. I felt alert, energetic, and lighter than I had for some time.

"So…this clearly means something, but I confess, I'm not quite understanding what," I said, as I tried to take the ring off. It wouldn't come. I pulled a little harder: my knuckle hurt; the ring wouldn't budge. It had slipped on easily, but now it was fixed, seemingly quite a bit smaller than it had been.

I looked up at Gregorio again. He was watching me closely. "Yes, it does mean something."

"Um, it won't come off," I said, feeling flushed with curiously impotent power. It was like racing downhill with my eyes closed. "Can you help?"

"I can, but I would rather not, just yet," Gregorio said with a gentle smile. "It is an old family heirloom. I had been planning to have Jeremiah give it to you to symbolize your union, except…"

"Oh, wow." I felt deeply awkward. "Thank you, but…it doesn't feel right. On me, I mean. It's very strong."

"It is powerful." He spoke gently, looking into my eyes. "I would be greatly honored if you would take it in gratitude for your efforts, at the very least. It will enhance your work in many ways."

I hesitated a moment. "This doesn't mean I implicitly agree to any sort of—"

"No strings attached," Gregorio said quickly. "You are carrying my granddaughter: that alone would be reason enough for a gift. Of course I do hope that you and Jeremiah will come to terms, but if you never do, I would still want you to have it." He smiled again. "Try it for a time? If you still do not like it, we can find a different symbol."

I took a breath. "All right."

His smile grew, and he seemed to relax. "Marvelous. Shall we rejoin the others?"

"Sure."

He took my arm and escorted me back into the main room, where I saw that Sirianna and Maela had found their way to Marcus. I saw Maela struggle to captivate him, and I felt for her. I could see the arrogant young warlock idly scanning the room over her head. Already looking for a better offer, and not even bothering to hide it. Ugh, warlocks. Who died and made them kings of the universe?

It could, I supposed, be argued that we witches had brought this on ourselves. Warlocks were far too rare; scarcity bred an entirely undeserved demand. We should probably have more sons, as troublesome as they could be.

(And, though it was uncharitable for me to even think it, nice guys like Sebastian weren't helping matters any, taking themselves out of an already sparse field.)

I sighed as I thought about the consequences of more warlocks among us. The out-of-control male energy. The arrogance, the entitlement. While I did know a few decent warlocks, most of them were no great shakes.

Maela continued to try, though even from here I could see her smile becoming strained. As unremarkable as Marcus was, everyone deserved a little flirtation at a party. *Pay attention to her, you jerk*, I thought.

A sudden spark lit up in Marcus's eye. All at once his body language changed. He turned directly to face Maela, tilting his head and gazing at her in apparent awe. He said something I could not hear; Maela blushed and laughed.

The gold ring glowed on my finger. *Did I do that?*

Maela laughed again, more deeply, and Marcus was ensnared. Everyone could see it, even Sirianna, from the depths of her Mead-head. Witches and warlocks parted around the two of them, stealing glances as they did.

I cupped my left hand over my right, covering the ring. I had to put my glass of Mead down to do it. Fortunately, an illusion-nymph appeared with an empty tray. She stood by my side, also watching the flirtation.

"Ah, to be young again," Gregorio murmured beside me.

"What's happening?" I asked, turning to him. The nymph with my Mead glass moved, ghostlike, so that my glass would remain close. To steady my nerves, and to honor her skill, I took the glass again and sipped.

The potion calmed me; the ring *did* feel right—energetically—even as it felt wrong emotionally. And still way too powerful, in a weird way. I didn't understand any of it, couldn't control it. Was I already into Mead-head? "I want to know what's happening with Maela," I said, speaking slowly and enunciating clearly.

Gregorio and I both looked across the room. Maela and Marcus were just talking and laughing...but the energy coming off them was striking. And clearly, everyone who saw them could feel it. "It appears that Maela is going to, as your generation would put it, get lucky tonight."

I gaped at him, then turned away and muttered, "Marcus is the lucky one." Maela was a smart, clever, level-headed witch—lovely, creative, and with a great sense of humor. She could see the future, and she made a mean guacamole. I didn't know if I'd ever seen her go on a date.

Gregorio chuckled and flagged down another passing pixie. "Have you tried the meatballs, Calendula? They are quite acceptable." He took two of them; the pixie smiled and offered the platter to me.

I was suddenly starving, though no less befuddled. "Thanks." He was wrong: "quite acceptable" didn't begin to describe them. They were *amazing*. The pixie offered a napkin as I felt the rich sauce dribble down my chin. She waited, so I snagged another meatball. "Yum."

"Ricardo!" Gregorio called out, then vanished into the crowd.

"Go on, shoo," I said to the pixie as I worked on the second meatball. "I'll eat them all."

"That would be fine, Mistress Calendula," the pixie answered.

"No, seriously, scat." I waved her away. She blanched and vanished even faster than Gregorio had.

"Oops," I said, looking down at the ring. It didn't feel right to threaten to smack even illusory creatures. I tested the ring again, but it still would not come off.

Even two meatballs threatened to fill my stomach to bursting, though the baby couldn't possibly be taking up that much room yet. The Witches' Mead was staying out of her bloodstream, even as it was coursing through mine, but I could feel that she was weary. Or maybe it was just me. I had to find a place to sit down. Much as I liked parties, this one was rather overwhelming.

I scanned for empty chairs; the place was really filling up. People shrieked with laughter and hollered greetings over one another's heads. The intoxication level of the room was almost visibly rising. I edged around the crowd, now recognizing nobody besides Maela and Sirianna. Maela was too busy, and Siri was too drunk.

"There you are," came Leonora's imperious voice. I had stumbled across the table my coven had claimed, after all. "What is that you're drinking? *Witches' Mead?*"

I sank into a chair. "It's specially formulated for my pregnancy."

She raised one steely eyebrow and studied me, then gave a short, harsh laugh. "What does that mean? What kind of spell? I did not detect anything."

I smiled unsteadily; I didn't know either. But I could feel it. It had to be true. "It's safe. Gregorio Andromedus told me so."

"Oh, if the great Elder says so..." Niad broke in, her face a smirking mask in the strange light.

"Hush, Niad," Leonora said. Niad made an even worse face and mimicked Leonora's shrill voice: "Hush, Niad." I cringed, waiting to see what punishment Leonora would bestow for this shocking rudeness, but she did nothing. Very odd.

I took another sip of the brew from my generously full glass. It was certainly delicious, and not really harmful. In fact, not harmful at all. Whatever spell Gregorio had put in it. On it. Whatever. I giggled to myself at the thought of his reassurance and my blithe trust in him. Spelled. Speld! Spellllllld. Hee hee. It was really a funny word, when you thought about it. Spell spell spill spull spelling bee blessed be... For all I knew, maybe the baby was half drunk already!

Leonora was still studying me, and now I saw that her eyes were bleary. "You are such a silly little witch," she finally drawled.

None of my other sisters had said anything. Peony was flirting with a ghastly old warlock at the next table, who had sidled his chair close. Niad was making faces at Leonora behind her back. Liza and Ruth listed glassy-eyed towards one another, their pale hair coming loose from their matching updos.

"Oh dear," I said, belatedly getting it. The whole party was drunk. And it wasn't just them. I was, too.

I don't remember a whole lot more after that. At one point, Niad and I were wandering around the room, suddenly the very best of friends, arms tight around each other…we were looking for my mother, I had to tell her something totally hilarious about the tarot and phallic symbols. We found Leonora, who had been with us all along, and I tried to tell Niad that *she* was my mother, but that wasn't exactly right, we all knew that wasn't right, but we didn't quite know why. Later I was standing on the table where some of my sisters were still sitting, or slumping, trying to get my hands on that ugly, ugly chandelier so that I could do Gregorio a huge favor by pulling it down from the ceiling and sealing it in an airtight magic spell at the bottom of the ocean for all of eternity. But I could not reach the chandelier, even though earlier I could have sworn it was hanging so low it was almost sitting on the table, and my sisters cajoled me down before I hurt myself and the baby, and that was lovely, because they had more of that delicious Witches' Mead waiting for me…

— CHAPTER TWENTY —

And then pain, nothing but pain. Elnor's piercing howl, shrill in the dark. "Oh, shit." Pain at the very thought of my words, pain at whispering them.

Elnor again, demanding food.

"Go 'way." Burying my face under the pillow, pushing her off the bed. "Go kill something."

Hours or days or centuries later, still the pain, and now a familiar presence, sniffing around me like another hungry cat. Holy...was it Sebastian?

"I'll kill you if you come any closer," I growled into the pillow. My pillow. Somehow, I was in my own bed. What was *he* doing in my house? Hadn't I set my wards?

I heard his cruel soft laughter; his essence was nauseating. How had I imagined I liked this guy?

Had I ever had a life before the pain?

Still later. Pain and nausea. At least Elnor had stopped shrieking, and Sebastian had receded somewhere, anywhere but here.

I will never eat again.

I will never drink again.

Saturday evening, I emerged from bed, stumbled into the bathroom, drank a glass of water, threw up, apologized to the baby, drank another glass more slowly, and went back to sit on the edge of the bed. Whew. I put one hand on my forehead and the other on my belly. Okay, maybe I wasn't going to die just yet. But that was close.

From somewhere down the hall, I heard Sebastian clear his throat. Obviously lurking somewhere, waiting for me to wake up.

"It's safe, I won't kill you," I called out.

I heard soft footsteps, and then he stood in my bedroom doorway. "Hey." Elnor poked her head around, peering through his legs as though she didn't mind his presence in the least. Little traitor, selling her soul for a dish of tuna.

The world wobbled again. I took a deep breath and stared at my feet until I was steady once more. "Why are you in my house?"

"Well, hello to you too." He was stifling a grin. He didn't honestly think this was funny, did he? "I brought you home last night. And I'm staying here until I'm sure you're all right."

I stifled a groan. "Yes, though that was quite a party. I'm fine."

His expression very eloquently conveyed how little he believed me. "I can see that you're alive, anyway, which is a relief."

"I'm totally fine."

"Can I get you anything?"

I put my hands beside me on the bed, tentatively exploring the concept of standing up again. "No, thank you. Really, I'm great. Just… humiliated. And a little dehydrated."

Sebastian gave a soft chuckle. "Let's get you something to drink, then."

"I'll get it myself." What part of "humiliated" did he not understand? I got to my feet and crept out into the bright hallway. Well, it sure seemed bright. The overhead light at the far end of the hall was on, as was the stairway light, and a soft lamp in the baby's room next to mine. Blinding.

I picked my way downstairs, Sebastian and Elnor following at a polite, or careful, distance. The front parlor was even more insanely bright: there was a reading lamp on by the sofa. "Ouch," I said, shielding my eyes and heading toward the kitchen. No way was I going to turn on the overhead light. I stood in the middle of the dark room, stifling a groan as I tried to decide what to brew.

Sebastian stood by the doorway and looked at my belly, a question in his eyes.

"Gregorio told me he'd brewed Witches' Mead specifically safe for pregnancy."

"Okay," he said, frowning. "How did he do that?"

"I have no idea. I could feel it work, though." I took a deep breath and closed my eyes as another wave of hangover meandered through me. "Sadly, whatever he did, it did nothing to reduce the Mead's potency."

"Do you want me to make you a pain potion?"

"It'll be better if I do it," I said. "You can help." I grabbed a pot down from the high shelf above the stove.

Unfortunately, the more potent the potion, the more noxious it is. Sebastian had plenty of ideas for increasing the brew's efficacy, to the point where I wondered if he was playing some sort of elaborate practical joke. "If this makes it worse—"

"I know, I know, you'll kill me. Don't worry, Callie. I'm studying healing, remember?"

Within fifteen minutes, six pots and my entire countertop were soiled, there was a purple splatter across the stove and halfway up the backsplash, and I held a steaming cup of yuck. I glared at it, steeling my nerves.

"Drink it fast, no breathing," Sebastian said.

"Yes, I know."

Then I stood there holding it a little longer, still wary of putting anything in my mouth. The last stuff I drank had caused such trouble. And it had been smoking, too.

Sebastian must have been biting the insides of his cheeks, he was suppressing laughter so hard. "I'm serious," I told him. "I built a freaking golem. I can make you hurt so bad—"

"*Callie.*"

I sighed. "Okay." I lifted the cup to my lips, catching a foul whiff before I remembered not to breathe, and drank it down. "Oh Unholy Father of All that is Beastly!" I gasped for breath, briefly blinded, the wind knocked out of me.

My vision returned slowly as I blinked away tears. It felt like the entire hangover had been condensed into an instant, and the pain had blown the top of my head off. I touched my forehead, as if my fingers would know any better than my brain. I turned my head slowly from side to side. The last of the pain was flowing away. My hand moved down to my stomach. It felt much better, too.

"Whew," I said.

Sebastian frowned at me, looking more concerned than ever. "Are you...okay?"

"Much better, yeah." I took another breath. "Huh. I actually feel pretty great."

"Good. 'Cause that looked kind of alarming."

"Didn't you know what it would do?"

He blushed. "Um. I'd hoped. I've never made a potion quite like that before. But I've also never seen a hangover quite like that before."

I gaped at him. "You told me to trust you!"

"And it worked! You feel all better, right?"

"That's not the point!" I put my hands on my hips. "Some healer you are, testing a random concoction on a pregnant witch."

"Callie, there was nothing toxic in any of that. Worst-case scenario would have been it just not helping."

"And then I would have killed you for raising my hopes."

"No, you wouldn't have. You were way too sick to be dangerous."

I laughed, shaking my head at him. "You jerk."

Sebastian gave a courtly bow. "I accept your unbounded gratitude, my friend."

"All right, thanks for the help. You jerk." I thought about the potion, trying to remember everything that had gone into it. Though I couldn't imagine ever needing such a thing again. Because I was never going to drink Witches' Mead again, no matter how delicious it was. Never. "How did you come up with using saltines?"

"Because I'm a genius." He grinned at me. "The baking soda reacts with the lemon balm, and strengthens it. Plus, they're easy on the stomach."

"Clever." I pulled out a chair at the kitchen table and sat down. "If I keep feeling this good, we may have to figure out what to do for dinner."

"Awesome. Drinks first, though. Want a glass of elderflower wine?"

"Ugh, no—just water."

He conjured up a beer for himself and water for me, and sat down, again gazing at my belly for a moment.

"Do you want to check the baby?" I asked him. "Or just stare at it?"

He looked flustered. "Well, if you wouldn't mind…"

"Go ahead, Mr. Genius Healer."

He leaned over and placed both palms on my belly. I could feel him sending the gentlest, most subtle inquiries first into my system, then into hers. "Huh."

"'Huh' what?" I asked, suddenly alarmed.

"What? Oh! No, she seems fine, but her internal processes…they're so different. Not just a miniature of ours, but like totally different pathways. It's intriguing."

I looked at him. "Have you never examined a pregnant witch before?"

He shrugged. "No. I mean, when would I have? We haven't had a baby in the community for six or seven years, at least."

"Huh." I thought about it. "And you've been studying how long?"

"Just over three years." He gave me a winning smile. "Callie, you have to let me examine her all the way along. I know you're going to the regular healers too, but as a favor—"

"Sure, of course."

"Thanks!"

"So you think she's fine?"

"Yep, totally healthy. I thought so, but the way you looked..."

"Yeah. I haven't gotten drunk like that since—oh gosh, my coven initiation, maybe. If even then."

Sebastian shook his head. "It was, as you say, quite a party."

"Gregorio pulled out all the stops. He's really relieved that we solved the mystery. I think it bothered him more than he wants to admit that he didn't suspect Flavius at all."

"He's usually pretty sharp," Sebastian agreed. "He must have let his guard down."

"I guess." I watched his expression as I added, "How are you doing with it all?"

"What do you mean?"

"Flavius. You were...?"

Sebastian shifted in his chair, staring at his beer. "I'm fine. We weren't—I mean, he was sort of an ass, actually. Kind of full of himself. I didn't see him as *evil*, but he wasn't really the nicest guy in the world."

"Okay." If he didn't want to tell me, that was his business.

"I'm glad they didn't decide to send him Beyond, though."

"Yeah. What we did should be punishment enough." I shivered again at the thought and took a sip of my water, the golden ring on my right hand clinking against the glass as I did.

"What's that?" Sebastian asked.

"Oh, this is hilarious," I said wryly. "Gregorio gave it to me, last night."

"Why?"

"He, um—I guess it was actually supposed to be from Jeremy. You know."

Sebastian gave a surprised laugh. "Seriously? The warlock gets his *father* to do his proposing?"

I shook my head. "Yeah, I know. But I can't take it off. It's kind of creeping me out."

"Let me see."

I held out my hand; Sebastian took it, gently pulling on the ring at first before sending a little magical intention to it. "Ouch," I said.

"I don't think I should mess with this," he said, dropping my hand. "It's got a lot of juice in it."

"Yeah, it's supposed to be increasing my power. And it does, but I don't like it."

"So just ask him to take it off."

"He said I should try it for a few days. I'll give it till tomorrow, I guess." I twisted the ring around on my finger, soothing the spark it had given me when Sebastian had tried to move it. The gold seemed to like to be touched; my fingers enjoyed the feel of it. What a strange thing. Though in theory anything could have spells added to it, magic rings were a little fairy tale-ish. And hobbit-ish.

Sebastian sipped his beer. "What d'ya want to do for dinner, then? Have you tried that new Italian place on Clay?"

"I have not." At my feet, Elnor glanced up. "You already ate," I told her. "Guard the house. I'll be back in a few hours."

Sebastian must have been convinced that I was indeed all right, because we went our separate ways after dinner. I was pretty tired; drunk sleep isn't nearly as restful as real sleep.

I awoke in the small hours of the morning, feeling better still. And more clear-headed than I had been in many days. I got up, made a cup of peppermint tea, and sat at my kitchen table, thinking.

How *had* Gregorio been so deceived by such a minor power as Flavius Winterheart? An eight-hundred-year-old warlock doesn't make careless mistakes like that.

Unless Gregorio was at last starting to lose his grip on his powers? Nobody could stay on this plane forever. Witches traditionally moved along at age four hundred (though, of course, not always); warlocks often hung around far longer, helping to balance out the genders somewhat, choosing to go Beyond when their magic began to fade.

But I had seen no other signs of decline in my mentor. The spells he'd unleashed on Flavius still made me shudder, all this time later.

What would it mean, though, if Gregorio was declining? He was the leader of the San Francisco Elders; my father was the next oldest and probably the next most powerful. He would inherit the mantle, if Gregorio decided to go Beyond. It would be a smooth enough transition of authority. Most witchkind would probably hardly notice.

I stood up and put my teacup in the sink. All this pondering was getting me nowhere: I needed to see him. I wanted this ring removed. And maybe I could ask him about the weird time-slip thing that happened at the party, and if he'd heard anything from Jeremy. Seemed like I should be kept in the loop, even if our romance was in a shambles.

Somewhere in all this, I could try and take the measure of Gregorio's power. If he was starting to lose it, and trying to cover it up, I'd have to talk to Dad about it. Not awkward at all, nope.

The sun was beginning to tinge the horizon a peachy-pink. I sent a message to Gregorio: *Thank you for the lovely party.*

It was my pleasure, came the response, a minute or so later.

I have something I'd like to speak with you about, I sent. *Do you have a few minutes any time today?*

I am free right now.

May I come over?

Please do. He sent an unusual energetic invitation: a personal portal of sorts, a tiny, private ley line leading directly into his house, bypassing his wards altogether. Very nice. And impressive. Not the sign of a warlock who was losing his mojo.

Following it, I materialized in a small, comfortably proportioned room I hadn't been in before. Several upholstered chairs were arranged around a low coffee table. A priceless Japanese urn taller than I was stood in a corner; the far wall was hung with a number of small sumi-e illustrations. The room was tidier than many of his I'd seen, though it still had several overfull bookcases. Large windows on the near wall looked out onto a lushly planted side yard—bougainvillea, phlox, hydrangea, and a wealth of ferns.

"Greetings," Gregorio said. "May I offer you anything?" He gestured to a sideboard well appointed with bottles, carafes and glasses. "I'm afraid I am out of Witches' Mead," he added, with a tiny smile.

"I believe I have satisfied my Mead requirements for the foreseeable future, thank you."

"Elderflower wine, then?"

"No, thanks—just water."

After a quick but measured glance, he said, "Of course," and stepped over to the sideboard. He poured a glass of water from a crystal decanter and waved a finger to chill it. He then poured himself something turquoise with small red bubbles in it, and brought both our drinks to the low table. "Please, have a seat."

I chose a chair and took the glass he handed me. "Thank you for seeing me on such short notice."

He nodded. "It is my pleasure, Calendula, as always. And I have something I wish to speak with you about as well."

"Oh?"

"Yes. But you first, please."

"Okay." I tried for a pleasant, relaxed smile, even as I tried to banish the thought of Sebastian joking that Gregorio had done his son's proposing for him. "So, I've spent a few days with this ring, like you asked, and I'm still not altogether comfortable with it. I'd like you to undo the spell so I can take it off."

He looked at me thoughtfully. "No, I am afraid I cannot do that," he said after a moment.

"But I thought—"

"Yes, that is what I indicated Friday night, but there has been a... complicating development."

"What do you mean?"

He leaned forward, steepling his fingers in front of his face. His drink sat ignored on the table before him. "Calendula Isadora. I have nothing but the highest regard and affection for you, and of course for your parents—the friendship between your father and me goes back hundreds of years. You are a bright and inquisitive witch, with unusually strong powers; I have long believed that you will grow to be a leader among us, perhaps even forming a coven of your own someday."

My hangover queasiness started to return. This had all the earmarks of leading to a colossal *But...*

"I find myself in something of an uncomfortable quandary," he went on. "We have a situation. Ordinarily, this kind of thing is easily dealt with, quietly, with no one any the wiser. Unfortunately, between your prominence, particularly recently; your relationship with my son; and the fact that the situation was allowed to progress to the extent of a very public announcement..." His grey eyes held mine. "It cannot be solved in the usual manner."

"What...what is the situation?"

"The child you are carrying was not sired by my son."

"What? Of course she was. I haven't...been...with any other warlocks. Not in several years."

"No, you have not." He gazed at me.

I stared back, dumbfounded.

He lifted an eyebrow. "There has been another lover, has there not?"

"You mean...*Raymond*? What does he have to do with anything?"

"Your human lover has sired your child."

I let out a surprised, relieved laugh. "Oh, Gregorio. You had me going there."

His expression did not change. "Calendula. This is not a joke."

"But...that's impossible!" My queasiness redoubled; my heart pounded. "We're sterile with humans. I know that better than most—so do you!"

"Have you ever done specific experiments using human DNA?" he asked, his voice maddeningly calm.

"Well, no. It would be a waste of time."

"That is close enough to being true that the rare exceptions, the occasional accidents, can be dispatched quickly. Unfortunately, the entire community now knows of your pregnancy. Your daughter is widely perceived to be of my line, and my son is quite besotted with you. Not only that, but we have just come through a dreadful trauma that has wounded and disheartened us all. If an 'accident' should befall you now, particularly given all the recent turmoil, it would raise questions. Questions that must remain unasked."

"I...but..." I stammered to a stop, at a complete loss. Had I stumbled into an alternate universe? Was Gregorio Andromedus actually talking about killing my baby? Or *me*?

Could Raymond *really* be the father?

And Gregorio *knew* this could happen?

"Dr. Andromedus, you and I are both geneticists," I finally managed. "Humans can't...I mean, Raymond and I...what makes you think it's not Jeremy's?"

He glanced at my right hand. "The ring, in addition to providing you with increased power, has enabled me to perform scans of greater subtlety and precision than I could otherwise have done. I had wondered at your refusal of a contract, and your sudden and peculiar aversion to elderflower wine. Now I understand."

"I—" I bit my lip and shook my head, thinking about it. Yes, humans were supposed to avoid alcohol during pregnancy...so in theory, my daughter could have that sensitivity as well as the witchly ability to convey that to me. But this was too impossible! "You're telling me that humans and witchkind can interbreed? And you've kept it a *secret*?"

"It is a fact that has long been known in the highest ranks of the Elders, and by some of the oldest coven mothers. It is a dangerous piece of knowledge, and you must guard it with your life."

"But...that's absurd! Gregorio, you and I are both working to increase the fertility of our kind—*because* we are too inbred. If we can add human genes to the mix—"

"Then in a generation, we will *cease to exist*."

I fell silent. *So I didn't "slip,"* I thought. Not with Jeremy, anyway. But how...?

Gregorio took a sip of his drink. "We have the powers that we do because we consciously selected for them. Thousands upon thousands of years ago, our human forebears mated the strongest men with the strongest women, generation after generation—anyone with a hint of magical power. They culled undesirable traits and reinforced desirable ones. And in so doing, they built witchkind. Only by keeping magically inert genes *out* of our mix do we maintain ourselves as a separate species. Yes, it is unfortunate that we seem to have culled out humankind's easy fertility. But if we allow that back in...we will be diluted into oblivion."

"So...these children get—what, aborted?"

"Hybrid pregnancy is quite rare, but yes, that is what generally happens. Occasionally one slips through the cracks, as your daughter has. The offspring is often weak, and does not reproduce."

Because she isn't capable of it, or isn't allowed to? But I didn't ask. Either way, it was not good.

"As you understand, this is not a common problem," he continued. "I know of only two other instances in the last hundred years. Warlocks who dabble with human women rarely linger long enough to find out what, if anything, has come of their dalliance. And since a witch needs to consciously release her ova—usually, anyway," he added with a pointed look, "those who choose human bed partners are at very low risk. Why would they waste the egg?"

"You're right," I said. "I didn't."

"So you say."

My anger rose. "Yes, I *do* say. Because it's *true*."

He shrugged. "Be that as it may, there is a half-breed in your womb."

I shivered at the term. It sounded so cruel, so diminishing of her. And so *impossible*. "What do you want me to do?"

"You will do *nothing*." He looked at me sharply. "And tell no one. Do you understand?"

"Then why tell me now?" I asked. "Why not just let me go on thinking she's Jeremy's?"

Now he gave a ghost of a smile. "It is as I was saying earlier, Calendula. You are bright, inquisitive, and powerful. And, even more importantly, trained in this very field. You would notice something unusual, perhaps not until after her birth; you would wonder about it. You would do some tests, and you would figure it out. And when you did, you would go running to Leonora, or Belladonna, or even Jeremiah. I cannot allow that to happen. No one must know."

I nodded, almost automatically. My head spun.

"Your daughter will likely have very minor powers at best," Gregorio went on. "This will disappoint Jeremiah terribly, I am afraid. But you can assure him that it is a rare fluke, that such things happen, and that you will be happy to try again. You can even pretend to do some genetic tinkering, if you like. A child *actually* conceived by the two of you should be remarkable. A force to be reckoned with. And we can find a comfortable, quiet existence for this one."

He has it all mapped out, hasn't he? It was bad enough when it was just me. It was worse when Gracie struggled against it. But now my daughter—barely a visible bump, and already relegated to a "comfortable, quiet existence"? My heart gave a painful echo at the phrase: I had used those very words about Logan. But with her, at least, it had been her own choice. My baby was being given no such choice. This was not right.

"I'll be sure to come up with some *pleasant fiction* for Jeremy, should the subject come up," I said, tersely.

Gregorio's face softened into a kindly, avuncular smile. "Calendula. I do apologize. This must be terribly shocking for you, and extremely confusing. Please, let us speak of it no further right now. I am sure you need some time to absorb the news." His mouth turned down in a sympathetic frown. "The first time I learned that the world was not as I had been told...I well remember how painful that was."

I bit my lip again, not trusting myself to speak.

"You will have more questions as time goes on, I imagine," he continued, rising to his feet. "Please, feel free to ask me at any time. You must speak of this to no one else, but you *can* talk to me." He smiled again, offering his arm.

I managed to find my way to my feet without assistance. "And what if I do tell someone else?"

His smile vanished, and his grey eyes grew cold and glittering. "Make no mistake, Calendula: I *will* contain this problem in any way I need to."

"I see," I said, and reached for the minor ley line he'd invited me to use. I stopped at the last moment, turning back to him to say, "Actually, I do have one more question: why can't you take this ring off me?"

"It enables me to monitor the situation. For the protection of the child…and of you."

Protection from whom *exactly?* It seemed our greatest threat was standing right before me. Without another word, I grabbed the ley line and vanished out of there.

I paced the first floor of my house, in turmoil. How could this be true? It was not just the physical impossibility of it—how it flew entirely in the face of all my training, my life's work. Worse: it was the incredible lie that we were all living under—all of witchkind. Who was in on it? Did my father know? He was a prominent Elder, and a biologist himself. Did Leonora know? How did everyone live with themselves?

My daughter would *not* live a "quiet, comfortable" life. I knew this all the way down to my bones. Her life would be interesting, rich, fulfilling. I would see to it myself. Nor was she doomed to be powerless, for that matter. I'd already shared my magic with a lump of animated mud, for the Blessed Mother's sake. What more could I not do for my daughter?

I raged about for a while, rattling the windows and alarming Elnor. Eventually, my rational brain regained a bit of control, and I went to my third floor lab. There, I drew a small vial of my own blood, sonicated it, added witch hazel and elemental protease, then examined the resultant DNA with my Mabel's Glass.

Gregorio wasn't lying. There among my own DNA were a number of clearly human strands. I opened my sight further, examining them more closely with witch vision, but I already knew. Non-magical DNA just *looks* different from ours, energetically. You can feel the energy coursing through it.

The baby had more witchly DNA than human, but…

My human boyfriend had fathered my daughter.

A pang went through me. Raymond and I hadn't talked since that awkward coffee "taking a break" meeting. How was he doing? Had he started moving on? I missed him still.

Even if I couldn't tell him about this, I would want to reestablish some sort of contact. He should be in our child's life, somehow.

Could I *never* tell him? Or her?

I unthinkingly started to reach for my cell phone, but of course it wasn't in my pocket. And wherever it was, it wouldn't be charged up. Besides, what would I say to him anyway?

Blessed Mother, what a situation.

As the night progressed, I realized more and more thoroughly what a trap Gregorio had put me in. And how truly alone I was.

Not only could I tell nobody about this—because he *would* punish me, I certainly believed him about that—but I couldn't even let anyone know there was a problem. I'd have to pretend that Gregorio was my kind, loving mentor and father-in-law. Well, father-out-law. I'd have to pretend to Jeremy that this child was his, and pretend to the whole world that she was a full witch.

Would nobody else see? How could this be sustained?

What did this mean about everything else I knew about the world? Was *any* of my biological training relevant any more? Was this why my research kept stalling out—was I starting from false first principles?

Were the "wild magic" practitioners actually on to something more than I realized?

I sat at the kitchen table, a cold cup of peppermint tea before me, toying with the be-damned golden ring on my right hand. Twisting it around and around on my finger. How much was this thing transmitting to Gregorio, anyway? Why had I ever put it on in the first place? I was too blessed polite for my own good.

Well, I'd had a bit of Mead at that point. But still.

I still couldn't quite get my brain around the fact that Gregorio Andromedus, my own mentor, my father's oldest friend, was…not a good man. That he knew such a vitally important thing, and that he was so clearly willing to harm my daughter, and me, to protect this knowledge.

I pointed a finger at my tea to reheat it. It went from cold to steaming to bubbling almost instantly. Yes, my power certainly was increased, with the ring. Yippee.

I sipped the tea as the questions continued to tumble forth, each one leading to the next. Was Flavius Winterheart really behind the departure of my best friend…or did Gregorio know more about this than he'd revealed as well? Had he set Flavius up to have someone to blame and punish? Had Jeremy and I cauterized an innocent warlock?

Had *Gregorio* stolen the essence?

He had said I could ask him anything, yet I so obviously could not trust him. No one sets up a fall guy just for the heck of it: Gregorio was hiding far more than a crucial fact about our reproductive biology. I would have to find the answers on my own.

I had never felt that I'd fit in terribly well. Long before I'd moved out of the coven house. But that had been minor compared to this. Oh, for the days when my biggest problem was a bitchy coven sister.

I was truly alone.

But I wasn't helpless.

"Petrana, come over here, please."

My golem shuffled over from the corner of the kitchen. "Yes, Mistress Callie?"

"We're going to get this ring off me." I held out my hand. She took it in her large one. I marveled, as ever, at the cool sensation of her skin, and the life so clearly in it—she was not a natural creature, but she wasn't an illusion like Gregorio's serving pixies either.

"What shall I do?"

I turned my hand in hers, positioning the ring between her thumb and forefinger. "Just hold it for now, as we balance our energies."

Elnor, sensing something, wandered in from the front hall. I patted the table with my free hand and she jumped up, butting my chin gently, purring.

We sat together like that for a few minutes, grounding and focusing. Then I stood up, keeping my left hand on Elnor, and said to Petrana, "Slowly, carefully, we will find the nature of the spell that holds the ring here, and unmake it. Do you understand?"

She stared at me a minute. "Yes, Mistress Callie."

"Okay. Starting now." I wondered if we shouldn't have gone upstairs to my pentacle, but we could always try that if this didn't work. "Stop if you get confused, or if something seems wrong."

"Yes, Mistress Callie."

I switched my vision to my witch sight, letting the mundane kitchen fall away around me. Elnor's honey-golden energy hummed under my left hand; Petrana's uncannier golem-force embraced mine as we focused in on the ring, and how it interacted with my finger.

For a long while, it was almost completely opaque to me, as if there were no spell there at all. Just a circle of gold that would not let go of me. I continued to send my vision around, around, around the ring, exploring, touching, probing. Petrana looked with me as we passed our power back and forth, sharing and building; Elnor added her help, supporting and monitoring us.

Eventually, on one pass around, I thought I noticed a tiny edge, no more than a nick of a few molecules. I sped past it before I could stop myself, but returned. I couldn't find it. I tried again, from the other direction, more slowly. And then again, further narrowing my vision.

"Oh, very crafty," I whispered, finding my way in at last. The spell was inseparable from the ring itself—the gold was inert, yes, but when the ring had been made, the metal had been spun into the smallest, thinnest "wire" imaginable, then wound around itself hundreds of times before being fused together with more magic than heat. In this way the ring could stretch or shrink to fit any hand, answering only to the magic of its maker. "Old family heirloom indeed," I muttered. Gregorio Andromedus had cast this ring himself.

Now that we'd found the tail of the wire, so to speak, we could begin to unravel it.

"All right, Petrana," I started, "just reach in here—"

The next thing I knew, I was on the floor, yelping from a blazing pain that shot all the way to my armpit, with smaller reverberations across my chest. The floor was shaking from a huge crash. Had that been me? Up on the table, Elnor wailed.

Petrana lay on the floor beside me. Or...well, most of her did.

"Petrana!" I scrabbled to my knees and crawled to her. My right hand stung horribly, and my whole arm throbbed, but I was in far better shape than my golem.

Most of her right arm was severed, crumbled into the dirt from which she had been made. The rest of her arm, and half her upper right torso, were heavily cracked. The damage continued down her right leg, though to a lesser degree. No blood or ichor or even water flowed from what would have been her veins. Just soil.

She stared up at me. "Yes, Mistress Callie."

"You're wounded!" I cried, displaying even more than usual of my subtle, penetrating insight.

"I am. I may not be of use to you any longer."

"Of course you are. You probably saved my life there."

"But my arm is ruined, and I cannot stand. My body is liable to fall apart completely." It was still jarring, how tonelessly she could say such a thing.

I leaned over her, putting my hands on her chest, sending diagnostic magic through her. I felt brokenness, but in an odd, detached sense.

"Does it hurt?" I asked.

"No, Mistress Callie. A golem does not feel pain."

"Small favors." I closed my eyes, deepening my exploration of her system. So much damage, all throughout: meridians leading nowhere, nearly every energetic connection ruptured or crushed. And nothing responded to anything I did—I tried to give her some of my essence, but it just drained right back out.

There were no healers for golems.

I was going to have to unmake her. Sudden tears stung my eyes. My stupid golem…it was going to break my heart to "kill" her.

Elnor jumped down from the table and came to us. She had stopped wailing, and was now purring more fiercely than ever. She butted her head against Petrana's chest.

I petted her. It was sweet of her to try to comfort the golem, but—or, wait. I put my hand on Petrana's chest where Elnor had nudged her.

The morganite stone, where so much of her power focused and which I had awakened, was still vibrant. It pulsed almost like a heartbeat.

Petrana may be damaged, and unable to function now…but could I rebuild her?

I got up and went out onto the back stoop, peering down to the tiny backyard below, dimly lit by the porch light. I had intended to start my own magical garden here, but what with one thing and another, I hadn't yet. The soil was no doubt magically inert, but if Petrana's essence remained within her, could it still work?

Only one way to find out.

There was a rusty short-handled shovel on the stoop, leaning against the house next to a bent pickaxe and (for some inscrutable reason) a push-mower. I picked up the shovel, went down the short flight of stairs, and tested the soil.

It dug easily enough. I could do this.

I went back in the house. "Petrana, can you get to the yard? Maybe if I help you?"

"I can try, Mistress Callie."

It was awkward, and my hand still throbbed a little, but together we got her out to the yard. More soil crumbled from her as we moved her, but the morganite stayed intact, and she remained conscious. I had her lie flat on her back, her remaining limbs stretched straight out, in the same position she'd been when I'd created her. Then I started digging.

The topsoil was loamier than the clay I found after a few inches. I squared my shoulders and dug on. If I was going to be this alone in the world, I needed all the resources I could bring to bear. A well-trained and magically fortified golem was nothing to discard lightly.

After a half-hour or so, I paused, wiping my forehead. As I was catching my breath, reflecting on how useful physical labor is for halting the brain-weasels—for distracting yourself, at least temporarily, from the terrible knowledge that the world is not as you thought, that the people you most trusted could betray you so thoroughly, that you are all alone in the world—a sudden thought struck me.

Am I really as alone as it seems?

In our last, awful conversation, Gregorio had told me that he knew about two other "instances" in the past century…two other terminated pregnancies, or two hybrids who yet lived? If so, who were they? And did they know—or did the *mothers* know? They would have to; how many other witches would have slept with a warlock and a human within a day of one another? They would know they'd only been with a human.

Had they been done away with? Or did they live still?

Before my sweat could cool in the night air, I began digging again. I had a good pile of dirt, but I'd need more for Petrana's thick, solid arm. I should probably rebuild it from the shoulder. In fact, could I make other modifications to her as I did this? Maybe I could make her a little less freakishly tall. Maybe I could even improve her face a bit, though I remained no artist.

I dug, still thinking. These mysterious witches: they would be my allies, if they lived. And their hybrid children. They would know things about the world that had been kept from the rest of us.

Could I find them?

After another hour, I had enough dirt, or at least enough to get started. I dropped the shovel and began shaping Petrana's new arm, careful not to rush with the fingers, and the elbow and wrist joints. She lay passively as I worked. It was a challenge to stay focused; my mind kept flitting back to the mysterious hybrids, and their mothers.

Now that I knew what I was looking at, I would recognize the traces in their DNA; the epigenetics would be more telling still. A number of vials of donated blood remained in my lab upstairs. Though it was probably too much to hope for that the witches I sought would be members of the San Francisco community, it would be a place to start. I could develop and test an assay working with the blood I had, while figuring out how to get my hands on more blood samples…perhaps propose a larger research program to the Elders, pretending that I was searching for a way to ensure that someone like Flavius Winterheart could never attack us again…Gregorio would be suspicious, of course, but I could put him off, tell him I was looking for ways to strengthen my hybrid daughter, to help carry out the deception…

I would find my allies. No matter how long it took.

Meanwhile, I had a golem to reanimate.

Elnor sat beside me as I laid my hands on Petrana's chest. The first rays of dawn touched the three of us as I began the incantation:

Merenoc gee'a folco Essūlå…

ACKNOWLEDGMENTS
AND OTHER MATTERS

In 2006—twelve years ago—I sat down to write a book.

I knew nothing.

In my happy ignorance, I cranked out a 250,000-word opus featuring a witch in San Francisco (where I then lived), and her human boyfriend, and a sexy warlock, and some bitchy coven sisters...and a whole lot of meandering plot lines, internal inconsistency about how magic (and everything else) works, excessive adverbs, and dreadful overwriting.

Then I gave it a little polish and marched out into the world with it, quite certain that a big New York publisher—oh, probably Farrar, Straus & Giroux, don't you think?—would offer me a major book deal before the month was up.

Reader, that did not happen.

So many other things did, though. Out there in the world, I met other writers. I learned that what I was writing was called "fantasy," not "a witch novel." I wrote, and published, dozens of short stories; and a different novel, *Eel River*; and several collaborative novels: *Our Lady of the Islands* (with Jay Lake), and the Chameleon Chronicles series (with Karen G. Berry). I wrote, and did not publish, four or five other novels.

But Callie and her story would never quite let me go. So I worked on this too. And, over the years, it got better. It was even slated to be published a time or two...but never made it all the way to the finish line.

Until now.

This novel has outlived a marriage, two crit groups, a serious relationship, and two small presses. It outlived my being represented by an agent (though as far as I know, the agent herself lives on). Sadly, it has also outlived much of my recollection of the many, many, *many* people who advised and helped in its creation, though I have done my best to reconstruct what I can. My deepest apologies to the folks I have inadvertently left out.

—◀●▶—

In something like chronological order, I would like to thank: My first crit group, the Critters (Todd Edwards, Kenne Morrison, and Mayuri Mandel), who read such early drafts, helping me see how much was wrong with the book while somehow not discouraging me; my second crit group, the Zombie Club (Scott Browne, Heather Liston, Lise Quintana, Keith White, Ian Dudley, Amory Sharpe, and Cliff Brooks—Cliff also drew a fantastic picture of Callie and her world). My mom, Donna Salonen, who reads so little, made it all the way through that first 250,000-word draft. Paul Cameron, who reads only serious nonfiction books about serious business things (or sometimes serious literary fiction), also read that first doorstop draft, and gave me so much generous encouragement to continue. Eric Murphy read an early draft and annotated it with marvelous suggestions.

Jak Koke and Karawynn Long, dear friends and the publishers of Per Aspera Press, took the book on and were planning to publish it, before Per Aspera closed its doors. Jak made several deep editing passes to the book, making it so much better each time. Karawynn stood in for Callie: that is her lovely image you see represented on the book's cover.

Jay Lake gave me so much helpful feedback, and introduced me to a whole community of genre folk—pretty much everyone I know in the field today traces back to Jay, in one way or another. I am so sorry Jay is no longer here to see this book finally emerge into the light of day. I know he would be so pleased.

My dear friend and Best Person Chaz Brenchley has edited this book mightily, and so generously provided a cover blurb. Any elegant bit of language you read probably has Chaz'z fingerprints on it.

My darling friend and collaborator Karen G. Berry read this book several times over, wrote copious notes, and has killed more than one bottle of wine with me as we brainstormed what *really* needed to happen in the story. This would not be the book it is without Karen.

My dear Barb Hendee, who read and loved the book, and tried so hard to help me get an agent. Barb also generously provided a blurb, and she feeds and houses Mark and me when we travel through Portland.

In the above-and-beyond department, several of the students in a weekend workshop Mark and I led for Cascade Writers volunteered to read and provide feedback: thank you to Kelley Frodel, Jill Webb, and Marit Hanson. Their insightful comments sent me back to the drawing board on a number of things, and the book is so very much better because of it.

Thank you to my "outlaw" Jay Ham for his encouraging, insightful comments. Thank you to David Levine for getting me out to the café to write on a regular basis, when I was ready to give up on my own writing altogether. Thank you to Lyla Payne for letting me steal the name "Graciela". Thank you to Alana Abbott from Ragnarok Publications for contracting to publish the series and being so excited to be its editor, even though that didn't come to pass either. Thank you to the entire team at Book View Café, and particularly Vonda McIntyre, for help and support in bringing this book out.

Thank you to the swimming pool at the LA Fitness in Portland for being such a crucible of creativity. Many important story elements appeared to me while I swam. Must be something in the water.

And, of course, thank you *so much* to my beloved husband and chief collaborator, Mark Ferrari. Mark not only read version after version of the book; he edited, brainstormed, and even role-played scenes with me. He conceived, drew, and designed the beautiful cover (and three more to come). He has challenged and encouraged me more than words can convey, from the moment I met him up to this very day—and beyond. He has my undying gratitude, for this and everything else.

Shannon Page
Eastsound, WA
April 2018

ABOUT THE AUTHOR

Shannon Page was born on Halloween night and spent her early years on a back-to-the-land commune in northern California. A childhood without television gave her a great love of the written word. At seven, she wrote her first book, an illustrated adventure starring her cat Cleo. Sadly, that story is out of print, but her work has appeared in *Clarkesworld, Interzone, Fantasy, Black Static,* Tor.com, the Proceedings of the 2002 International Oral History Association Congress, and many anthologies, including the Australian Shadows Award-winning *Grants Pass,* and *The Mammoth Book of Dieselpunk.*

Books include *Eel River;* the collection *Eastlick and Other Stories; Orcas Intrigue* and *Orcas Intruder,* the first two books in the cozy mystery series "The Chameleon Chronicles," in collaboration with Karen G. Berry under the pen name Laura Gayle; and *Our Lady of the Islands,* co-written with the late Jay Lake. *Our Lady* received starred reviews from *Publishers Weekly* and *Library Journal,* was named one of *Publishers Weekly's* Best Books of 2014, and was a finalist for the Endeavour Award. Forthcoming books include *A Sword in The Sun,* second book in The Nightcraft Quartet; a sequel to *Our Lady;* and more Orcas mysteries. Edited books include the anthology *Witches, Stitches & Bitches* and the essay collection *The Usual Path to Publication.*

Shannon is a longtime yoga practitioner, has no tattoos (but she did just get a television), and recently moved to lovely, remote Orcas Island, Washington, with her husband, author and illustrator Mark Ferrari. Visit her at www.shannonpage.net.